W9-CNN-290

COSMIC CADETS

CONTACT!

BEN CRANE   MIMI ALVES
PRISCILLA TRAMONTANO

COSMIC CADETS © 2023 BEN CRANE & MIMI ALVES

Published by Top Shelf Productions, an imprint of IDW Publishing, a division of Idea and Design Works, LLC. Offices: Top Shelf Productions, c/o Idea & Design Works, LLC, 2355 Northside Drive, Suite 140, San Diego, CA 92108. Top Shelf Productions®, the Top Shelf logo, Idea and Design Works®, and the IDW logo are registered trademarks of Idea and Design Works, LLC. All Rights Reserved. With the exception of small excerpts of artwork used for review purposes, none of the contents of this publication may be reprinted without the permission of IDW Publishing.

IDW Publishing does not read or accept unsolicited submissions of ideas, stories, or artwork.

Written by Ben Crane.
Illustrated by Mimi Alves.
Colors by Priscilla Tramontano.

Editor-in-Chief: Chris Staros

Design by Nathan Widick

ISBN: 978-1-60309-520-4   25 24 23 23   1 2 3 4

Visit our online catalog at topshelfcomix.com.

Printed in Korea.

CHAPTER 1

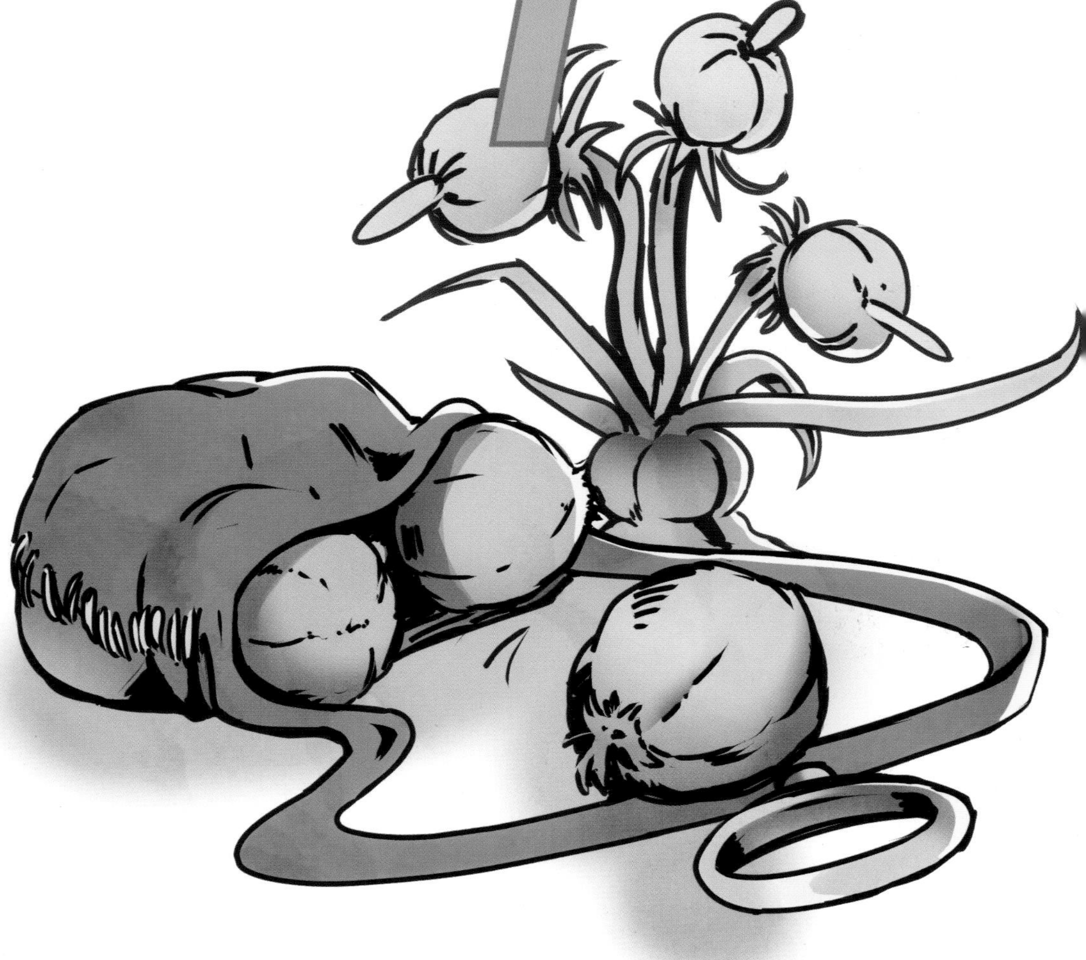

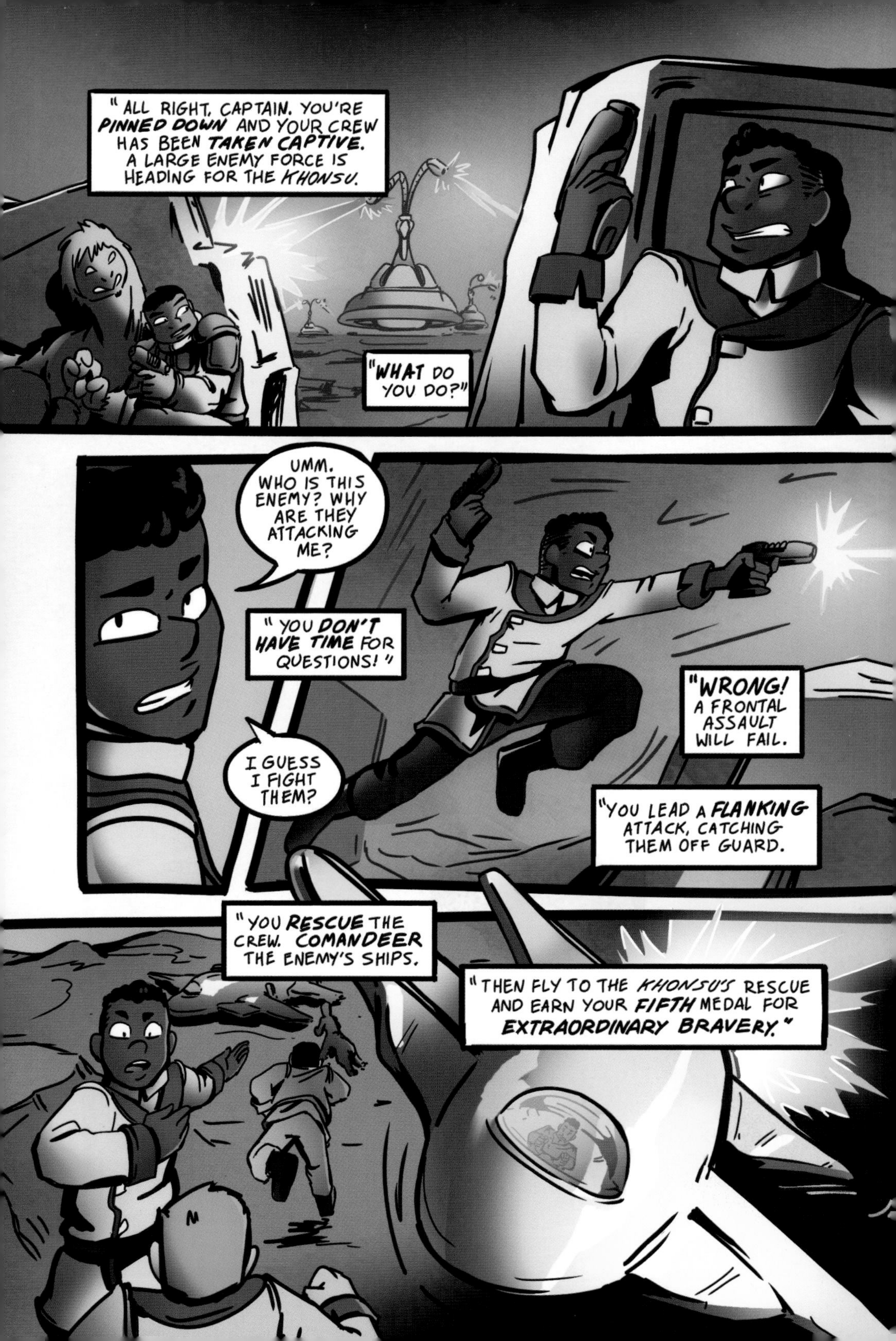
"ALL RIGHT, CAPTAIN. YOU'RE PINNED DOWN AND YOUR CREW HAS BEEN TAKEN CAPTIVE. A LARGE ENEMY FORCE IS HEADING FOR THE KHONSU.
"WHAT DO YOU DO?"
UMM. WHO IS THIS ENEMY? WHY ARE THEY ATTACKING ME?
"YOU DON'T HAVE TIME FOR QUESTIONS!"
I GUESS I FIGHT THEM?
"WRONG! A FRONTAL ASSAULT WILL FAIL.
"YOU LEAD A FLANKING ATTACK, CATCHING THEM OFF GUARD.
"YOU RESCUE THE CREW. COMANDEER THE ENEMY'S SHIPS.
"THEN FLY TO THE KHONSU'S RESCUE AND EARN YOUR FIFTH MEDAL FOR EXTRAORDINARY BRAVERY."

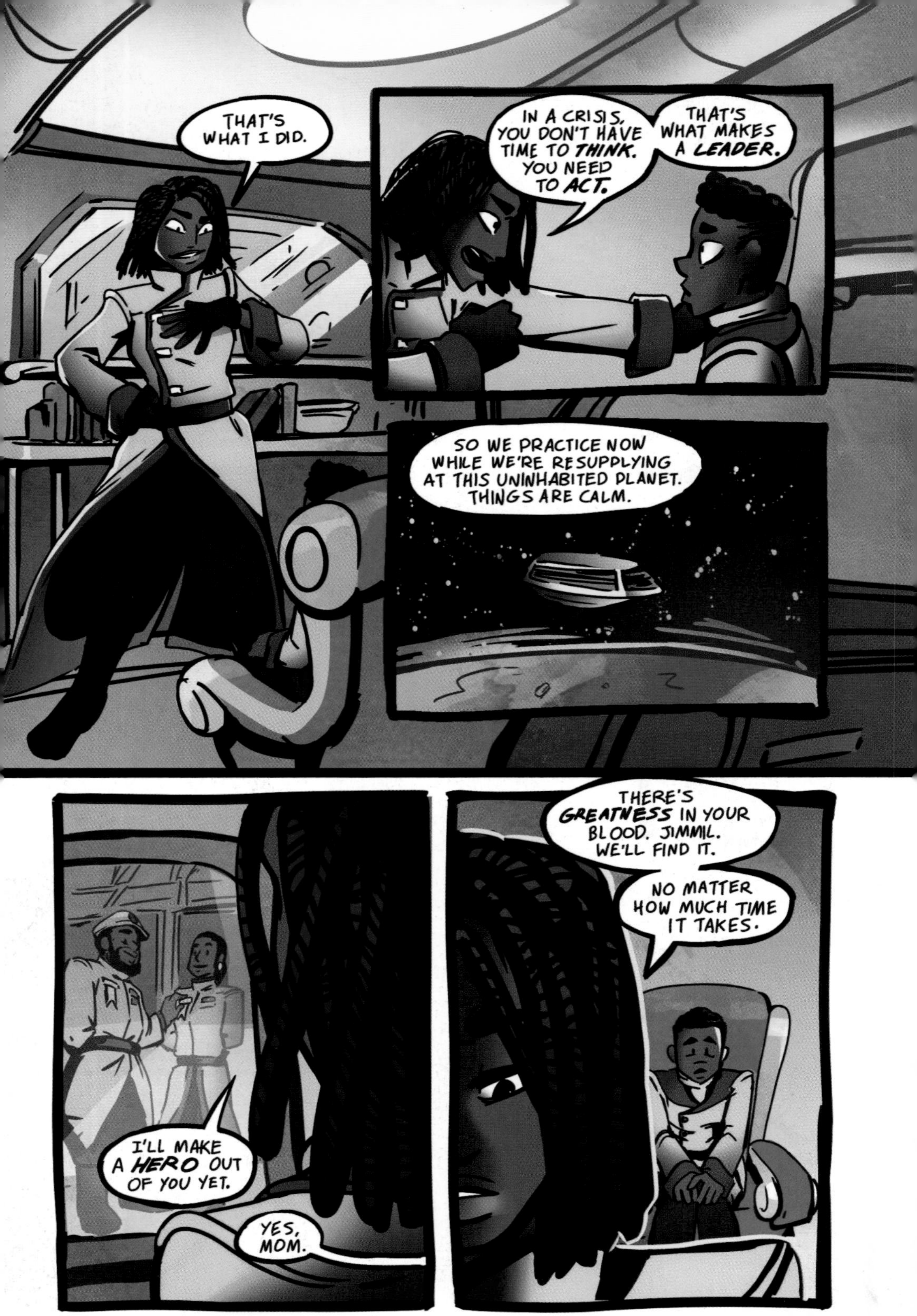
THAT'S WHAT I DID.
IN A CRISIS, YOU DON'T HAVE TIME TO THINK. YOU NEED TO ACT.
THAT'S WHAT MAKES A LEADER.
SO WE PRACTICE NOW WHILE WE'RE RESUPPLYING AT THIS UNINHABITED PLANET. THINGS ARE CALM.
I'LL MAKE A HERO OUT OF YOU YET.
YES, MOM.
THERE'S GREATNESS IN YOUR BLOOD, JIMMIL. WE'LL FIND IT.
NO MATTER HOW MUCH TIME IT TAKES.

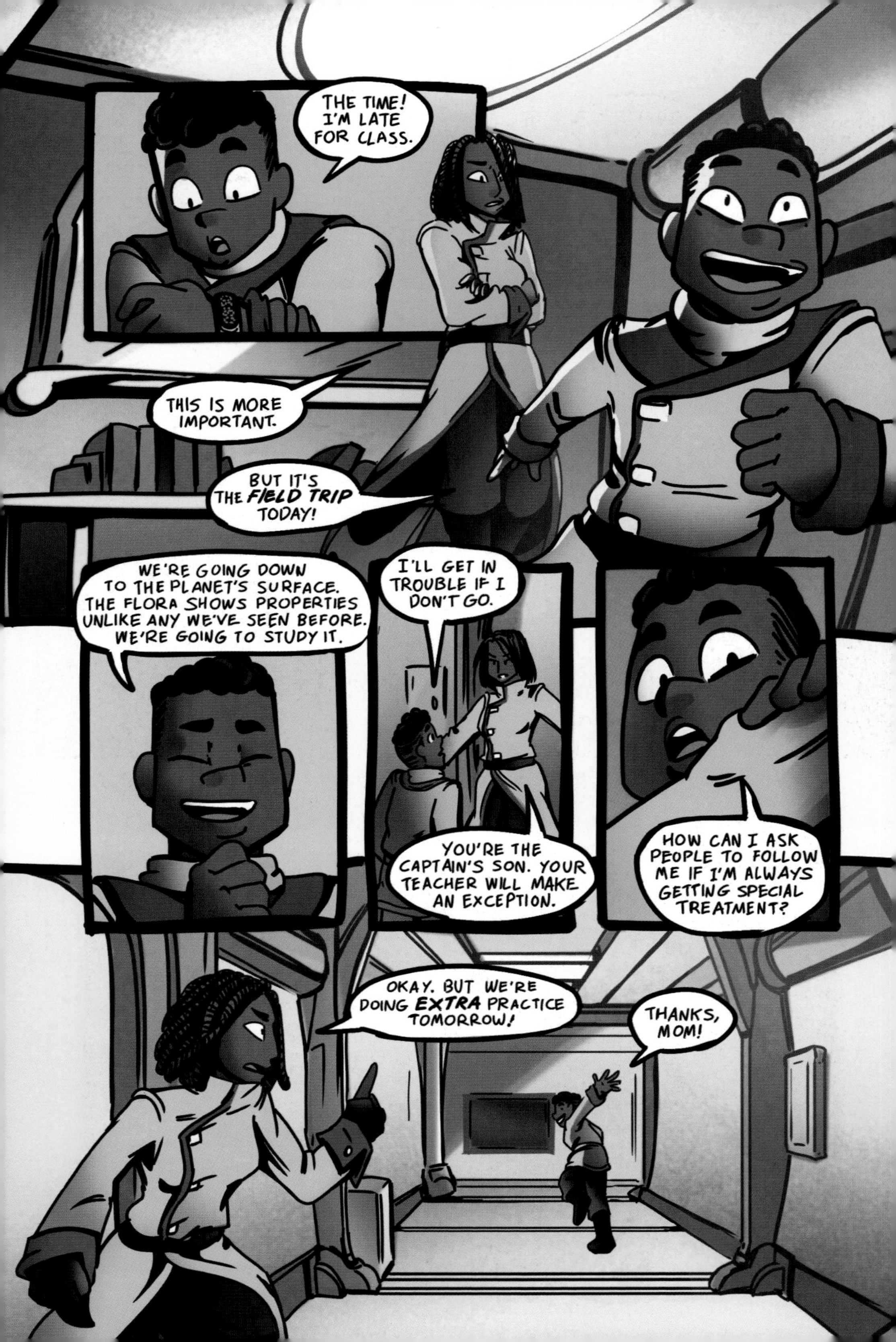
THE TIME! I'M LATE FOR CLASS.
THIS IS MORE IMPORTANT.
BUT IT'S THE *FIELD TRIP* TODAY!
WE'RE GOING DOWN TO THE PLANET'S SURFACE. THE FLORA SHOWS PROPERTIES UNLIKE ANY WE'VE SEEN BEFORE. WE'RE GOING TO STUDY IT.
I'LL GET IN TROUBLE IF I DON'T GO.
YOU'RE THE CAPTAIN'S SON. YOUR TEACHER WILL MAKE AN EXCEPTION.
HOW CAN I ASK PEOPLE TO FOLLOW ME IF I'M ALWAYS GETTING SPECIAL TREATMENT?
OKAY. BUT WE'RE DOING **EXTRA** PRACTICE TOMORROW!
THANKS, MOM!

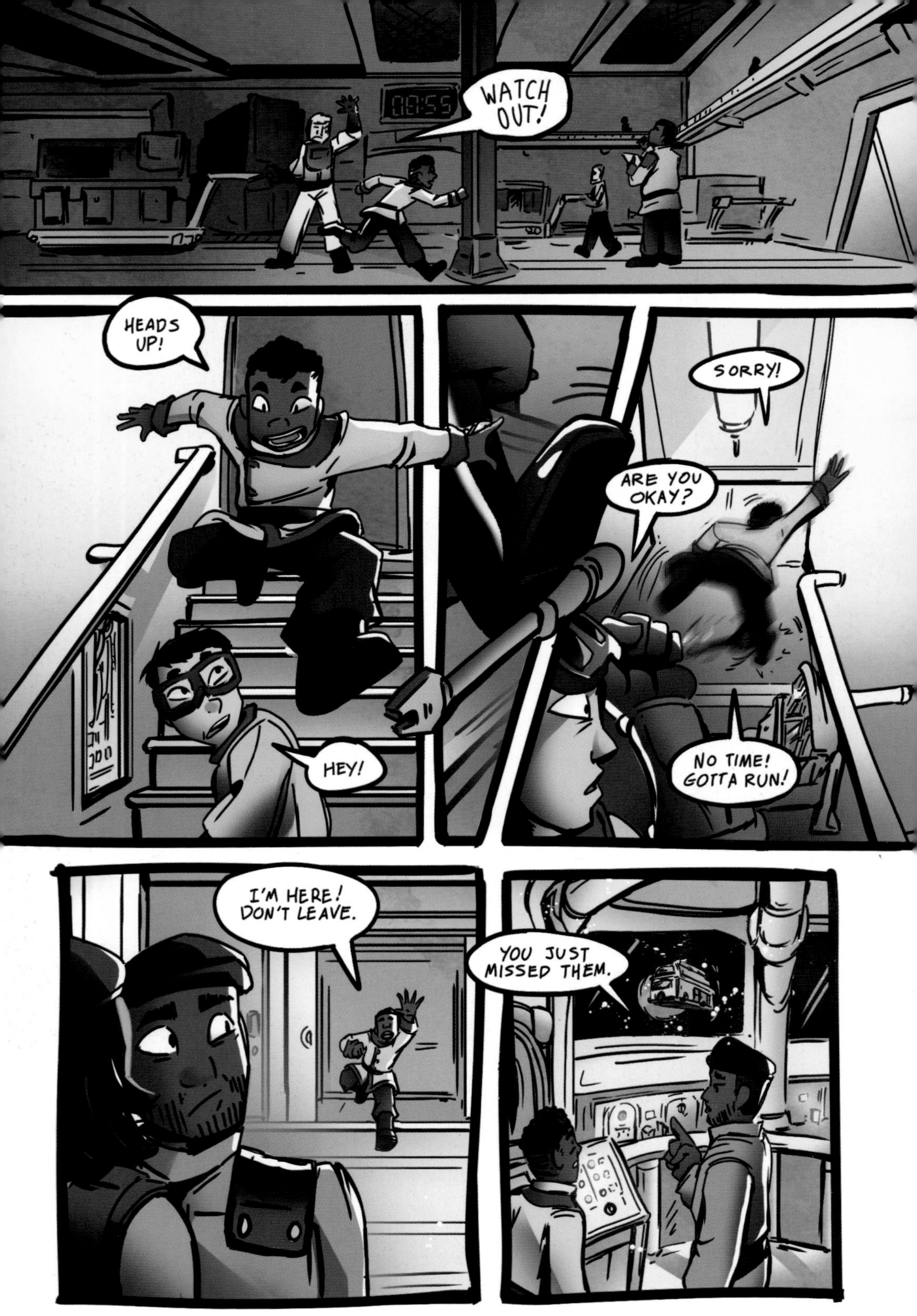
WATCH OUT!
HEADS UP!
HEY!
SORRY!
ARE YOU OKAY?
NO TIME! GOTTA RUN!
I'M HERE! DON'T LEAVE.
YOU JUST MISSED THEM.

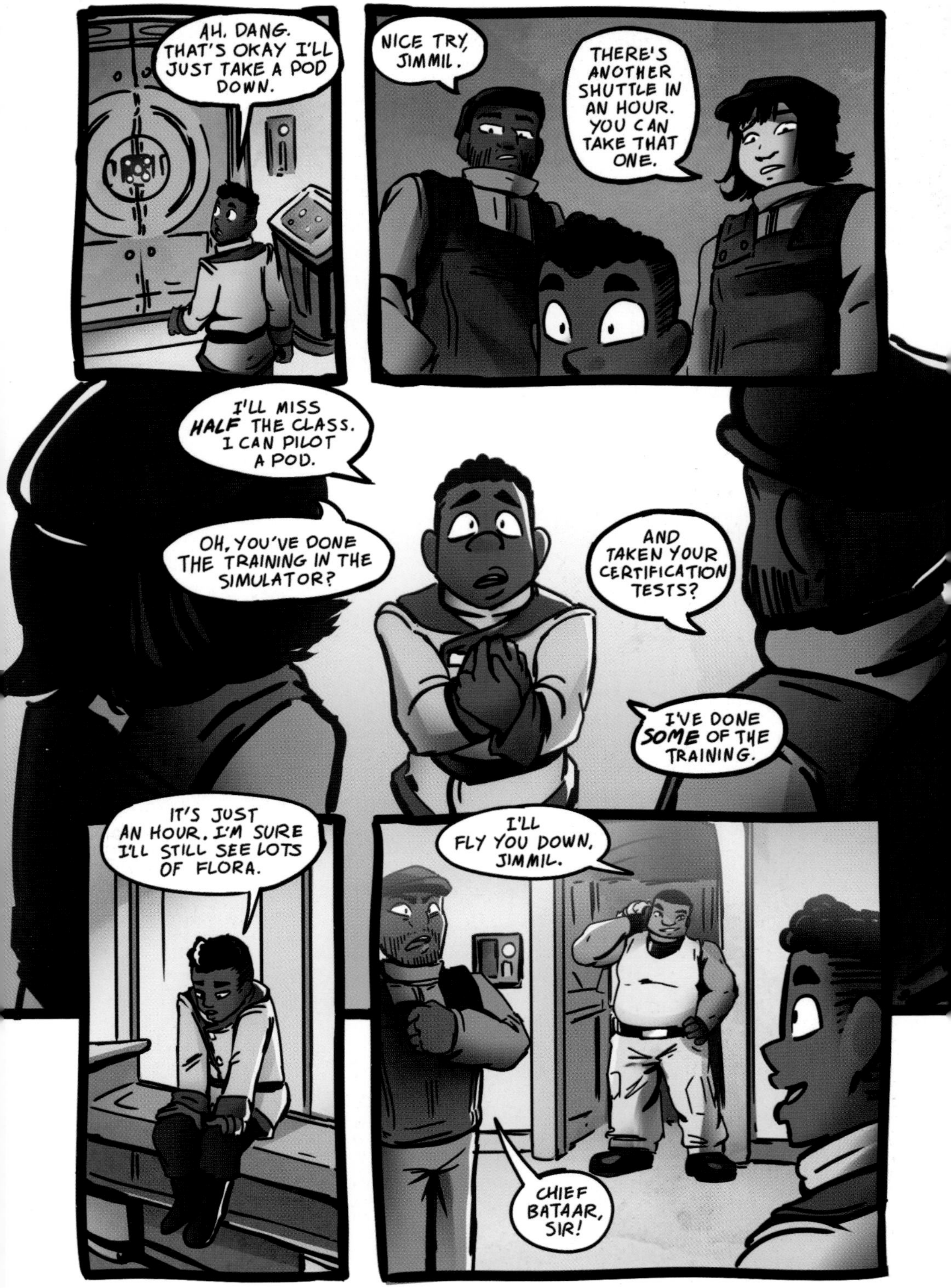
AH, DANG. THAT'S OKAY I'LL JUST TAKE A POD DOWN.
NICE TRY, JIMMIL.
THERE'S ANOTHER SHUTTLE IN AN HOUR. YOU CAN TAKE THAT ONE.
I'LL MISS HALF THE CLASS. I CAN PILOT A POD.
OH, YOU'VE DONE THE TRAINING IN THE SIMULATOR?
AND TAKEN YOUR CERTIFICATION TESTS?
I'VE DONE SOME OF THE TRAINING.
IT'S JUST AN HOUR. I'M SURE I'LL STILL SEE LOTS OF FLORA.
I'LL FLY YOU DOWN, JIMMIL.
CHIEF BATAAR, SIR!

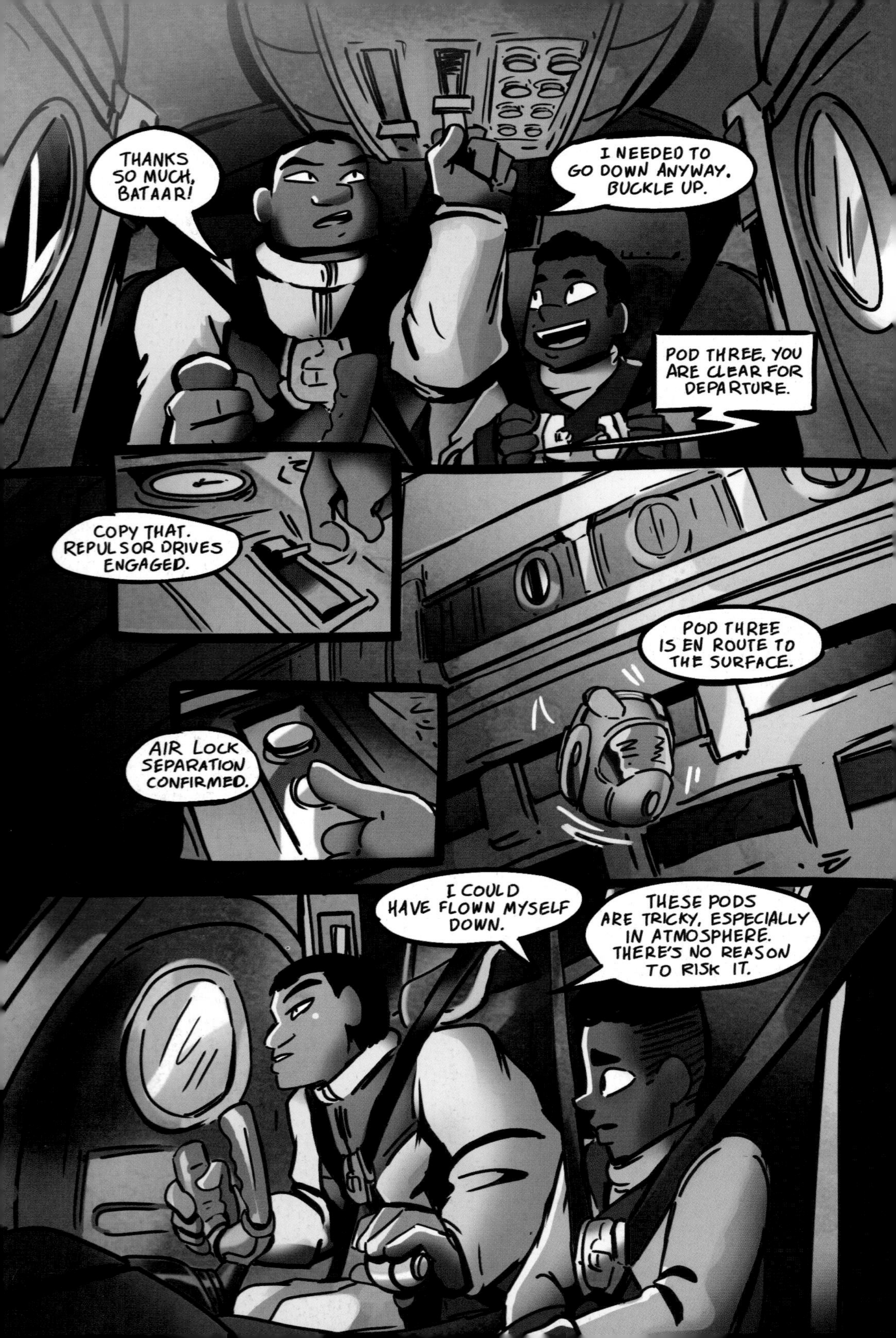
THANKS SO MUCH, BATAAR!
I NEEDED TO GO DOWN ANYWAY. BUCKLE UP.
POD THREE, YOU ARE CLEAR FOR DEPARTURE.
COPY THAT. REPULSOR DRIVES ENGAGED.
POD THREE IS EN ROUTE TO THE SURFACE.
AIR LOCK SEPARATION CONFIRMED.
I COULD HAVE FLOWN MYSELF DOWN.
THESE PODS ARE TRICKY, ESPECIALLY IN ATMOSPHERE. THERE'S NO REASON TO RISK IT.

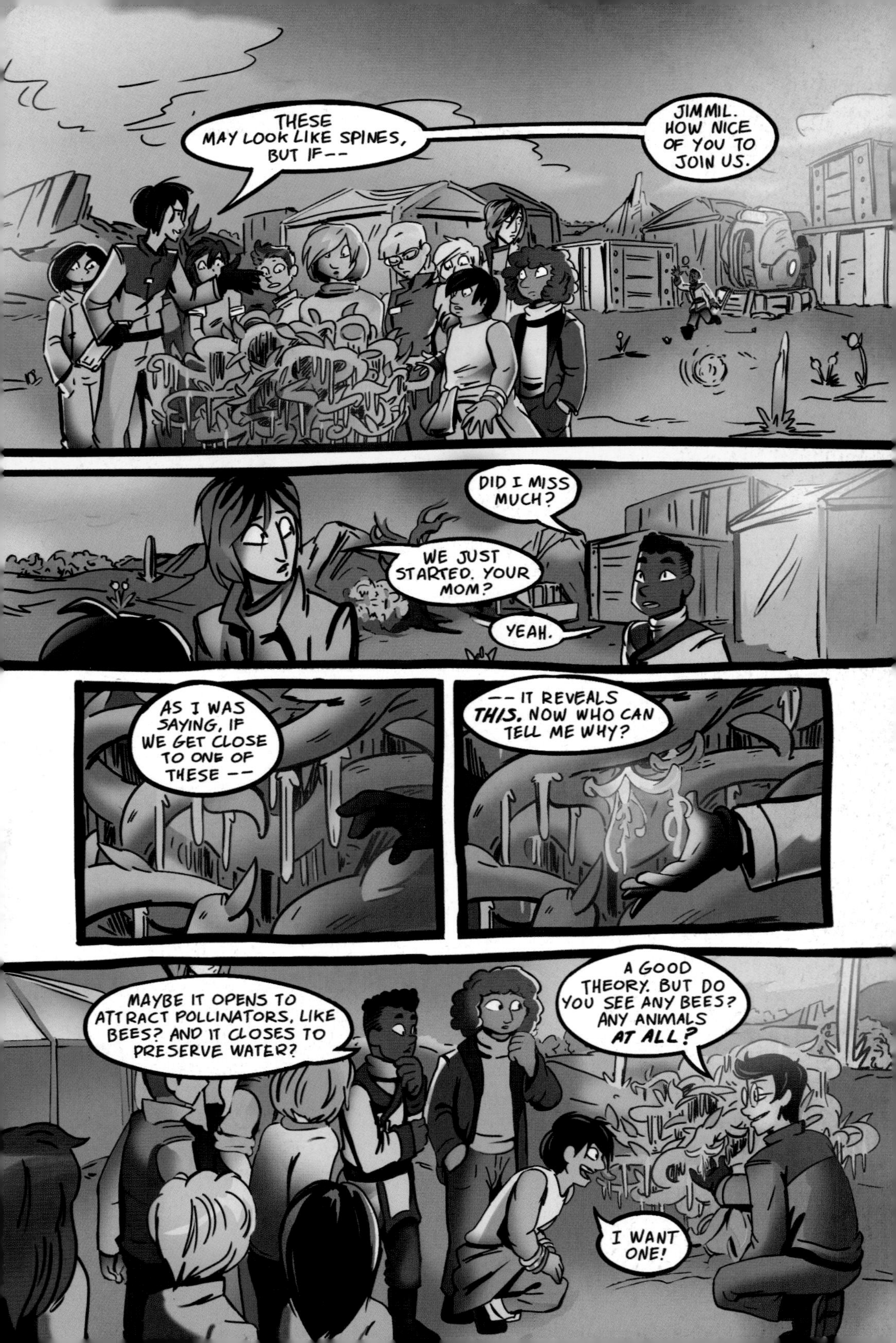
THESE MAY LOOK LIKE SPINES, BUT IF--
JIMMIL. HOW NICE OF YOU TO JOIN US.
DID I MISS MUCH?
WE JUST STARTED. YOUR MOM?
YEAH.
AS I WAS SAYING, IF WE GET CLOSE TO ONE OF THESE --
-- IT REVEALS THIS. NOW WHO CAN TELL ME WHY?
MAYBE IT OPENS TO ATTRACT POLLINATORS, LIKE BEES? AND IT CLOSES TO PRESERVE WATER?
A GOOD THEORY. BUT DO YOU SEE ANY BEES? ANY ANIMALS AT ALL?
I WANT ONE!

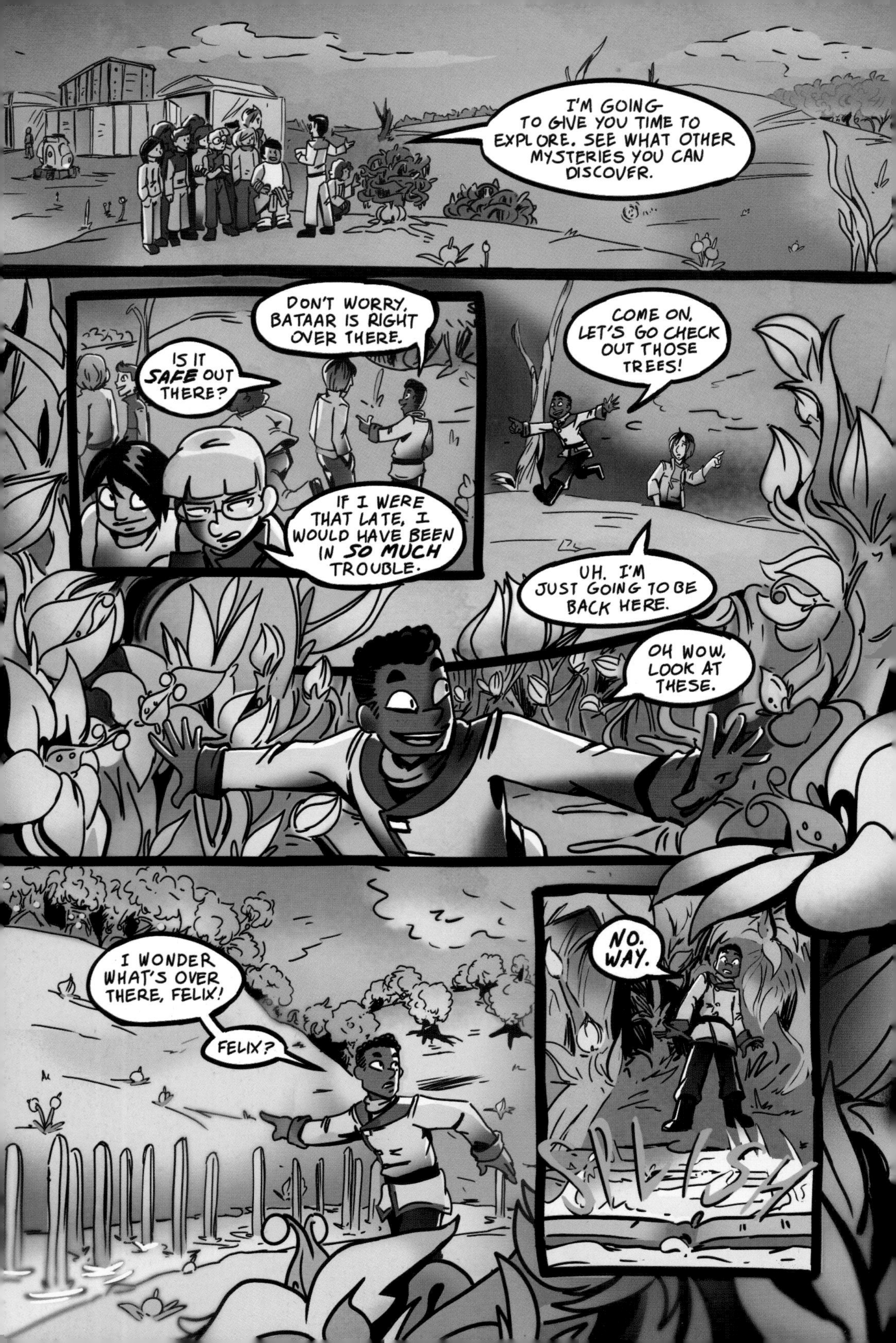
I'M GOING TO GIVE YOU TIME TO EXPLORE. SEE WHAT OTHER MYSTERIES YOU CAN DISCOVER.
DON'T WORRY, BATAAR IS RIGHT OVER THERE.
IS IT SAFE OUT THERE?
IF I WERE THAT LATE, I WOULD HAVE BEEN IN SO MUCH TROUBLE.
COME ON, LET'S GO CHECK OUT THOSE TREES!
UH. I'M JUST GOING TO BE BACK HERE.
OH WOW, LOOK AT THESE.
I WONDER WHAT'S OVER THERE, FELIX!
FELIX?
NO. WAY.
SWISH

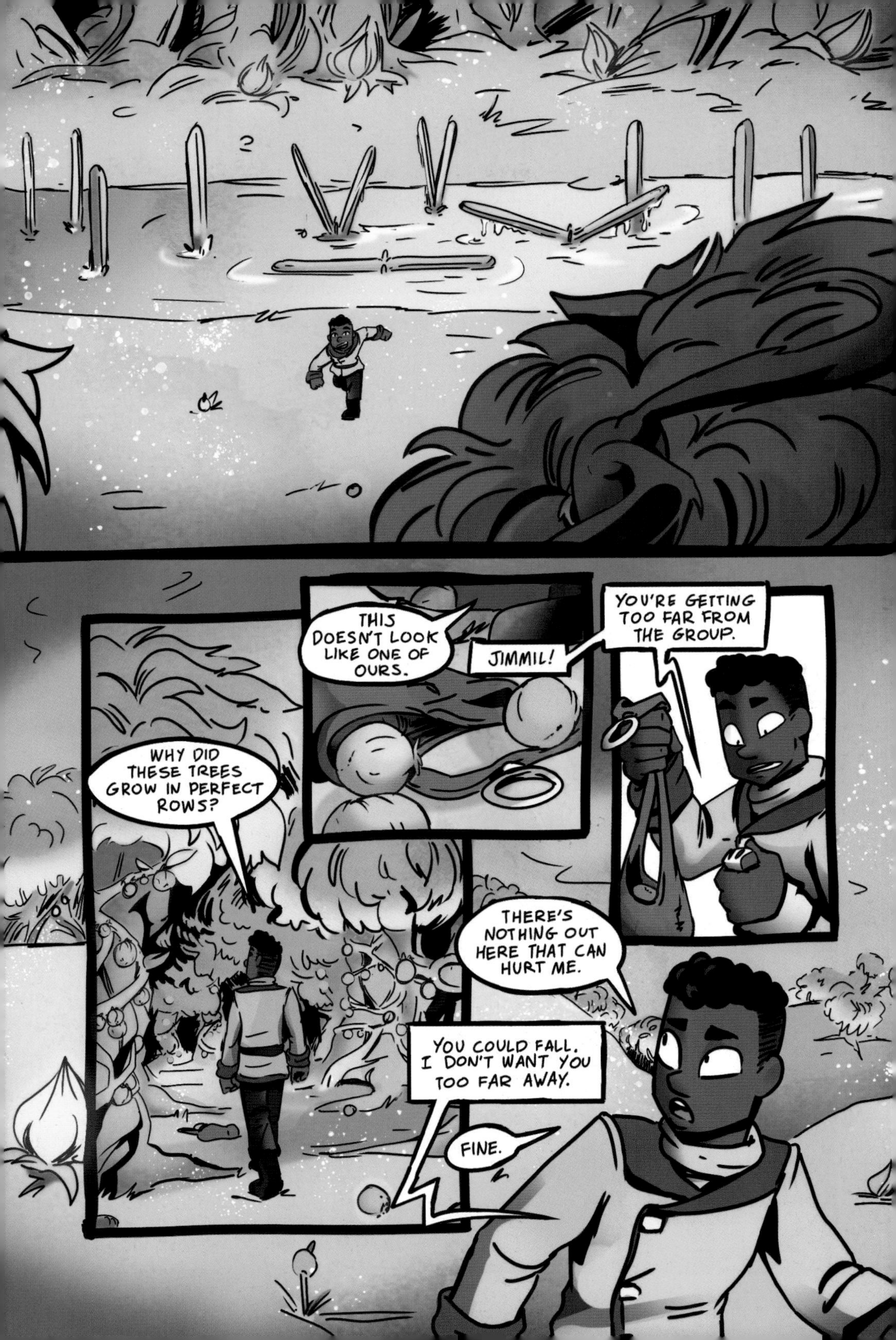
WHY DID THESE TREES GROW IN PERFECT ROWS?
THIS DOESN'T LOOK LIKE ONE OF OURS.
JIMMIL!
YOU'RE GETTING TOO FAR FROM THE GROUP.
THERE'S NOTHING OUT HERE THAT CAN HURT ME.
YOU COULD FALL. I DON'T WANT YOU TOO FAR AWAY.
FINE.

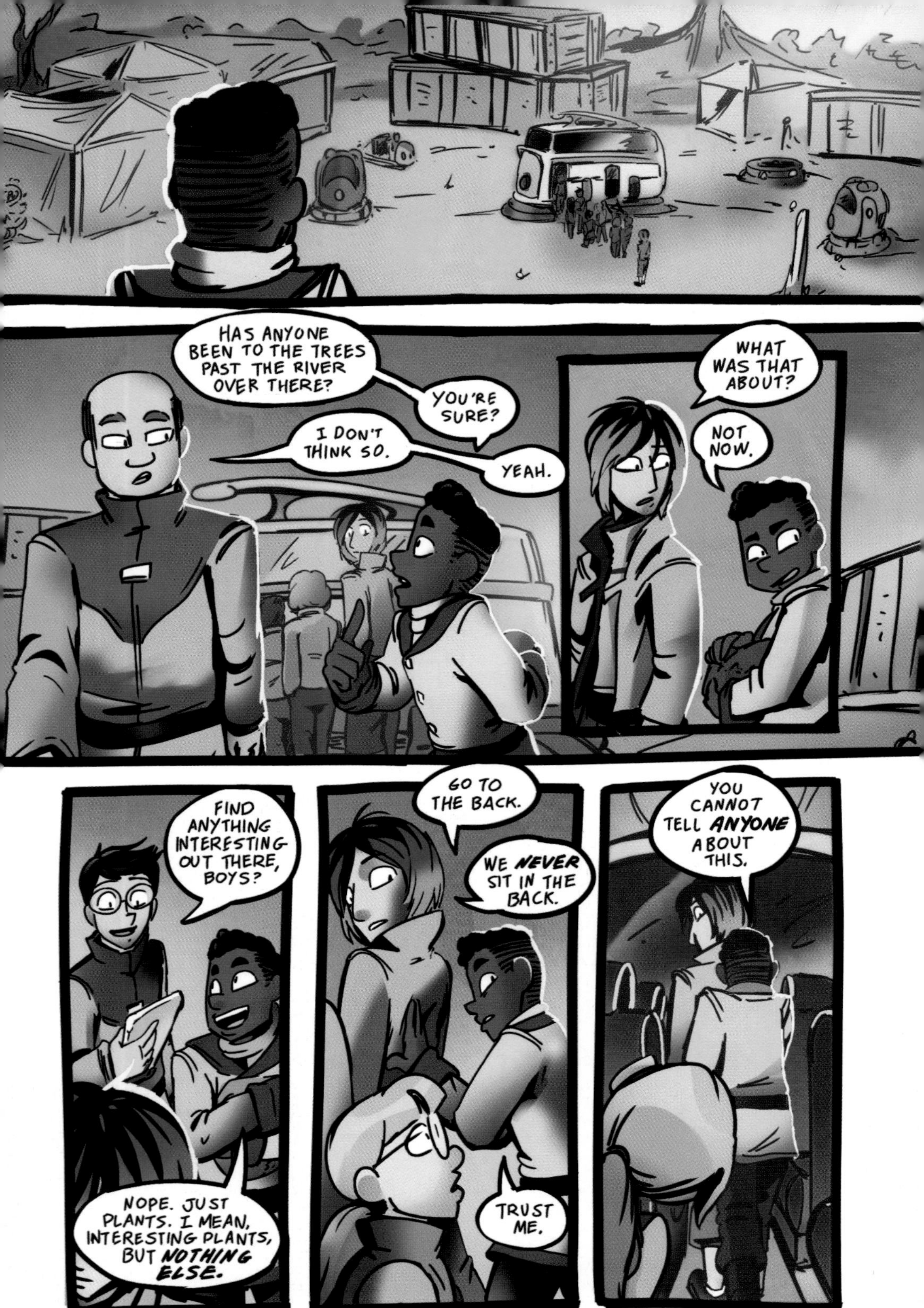

HAS ANYONE BEEN TO THE TREES PAST THE RIVER OVER THERE?
I DON'T THINK SO.
YOU'RE SURE?
YEAH.
WHAT WAS THAT ABOUT?
NOT NOW.
FIND ANYTHING INTERESTING OUT THERE, BOYS?
NOPE. JUST PLANTS. I MEAN, INTERESTING PLANTS, BUT NOTHING ELSE.
GO TO THE BACK.
WE NEVER SIT IN THE BACK.
TRUST ME.
YOU CANNOT TELL ANYONE ABOUT THIS.

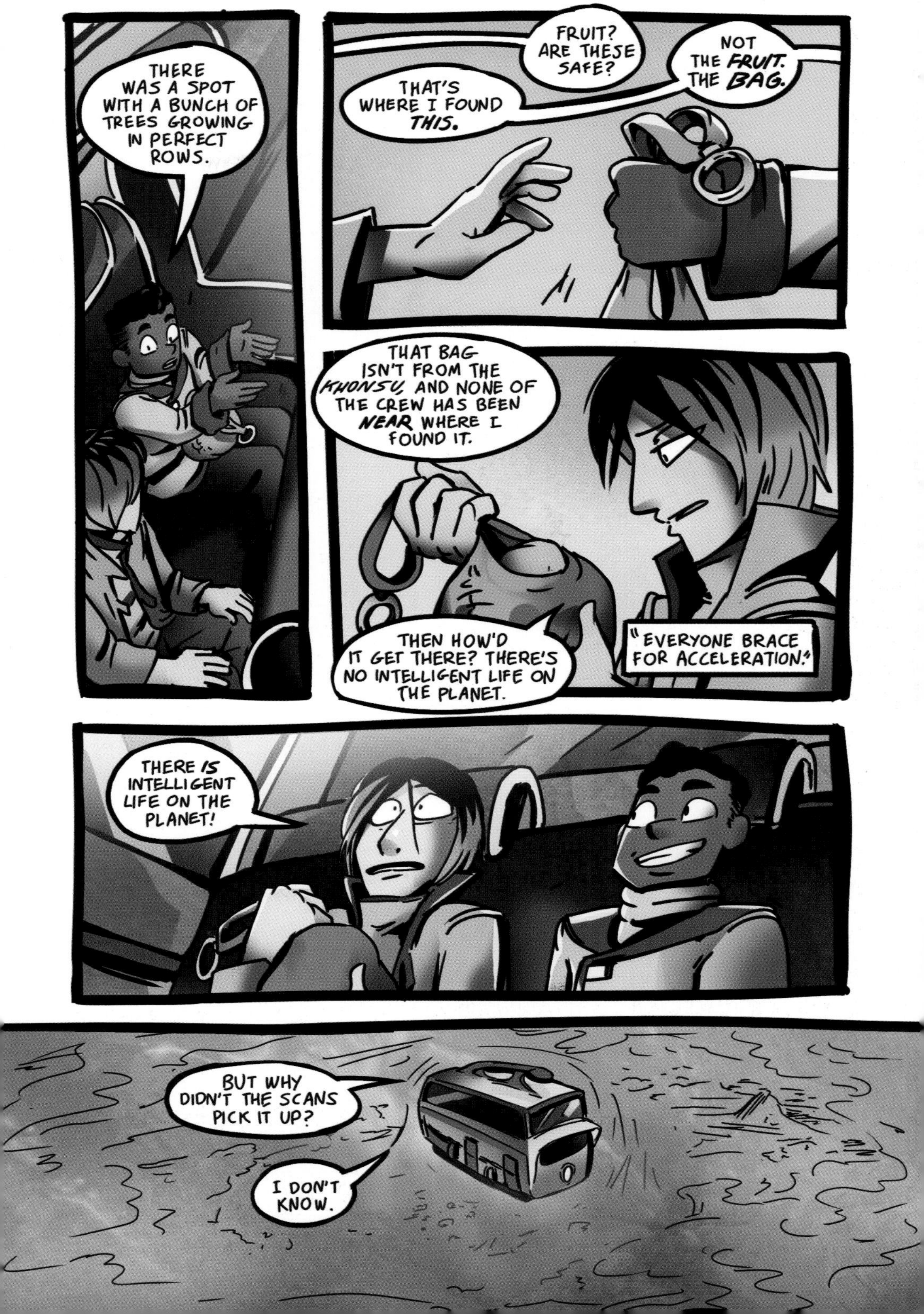
THERE WAS A SPOT WITH A BUNCH OF TREES GROWING IN PERFECT ROWS.
THAT'S WHERE I FOUND *THIS.*
FRUIT? ARE THESE SAFE?
NOT THE *FRUIT.* THE *BAG.*
THAT BAG ISN'T FROM THE *KHONSU,* AND NONE OF THE CREW HAS BEEN *NEAR* WHERE I FOUND IT.
THEN HOW'D IT GET THERE? THERE'S NO INTELLIGENT LIFE ON THE PLANET.
"EVERYONE BRACE FOR ACCELERATION."
THERE *IS* INTELLIGENT LIFE ON THE PLANET!
BUT WHY DIDN'T THE SCANS PICK IT UP?
I DON'T KNOW.

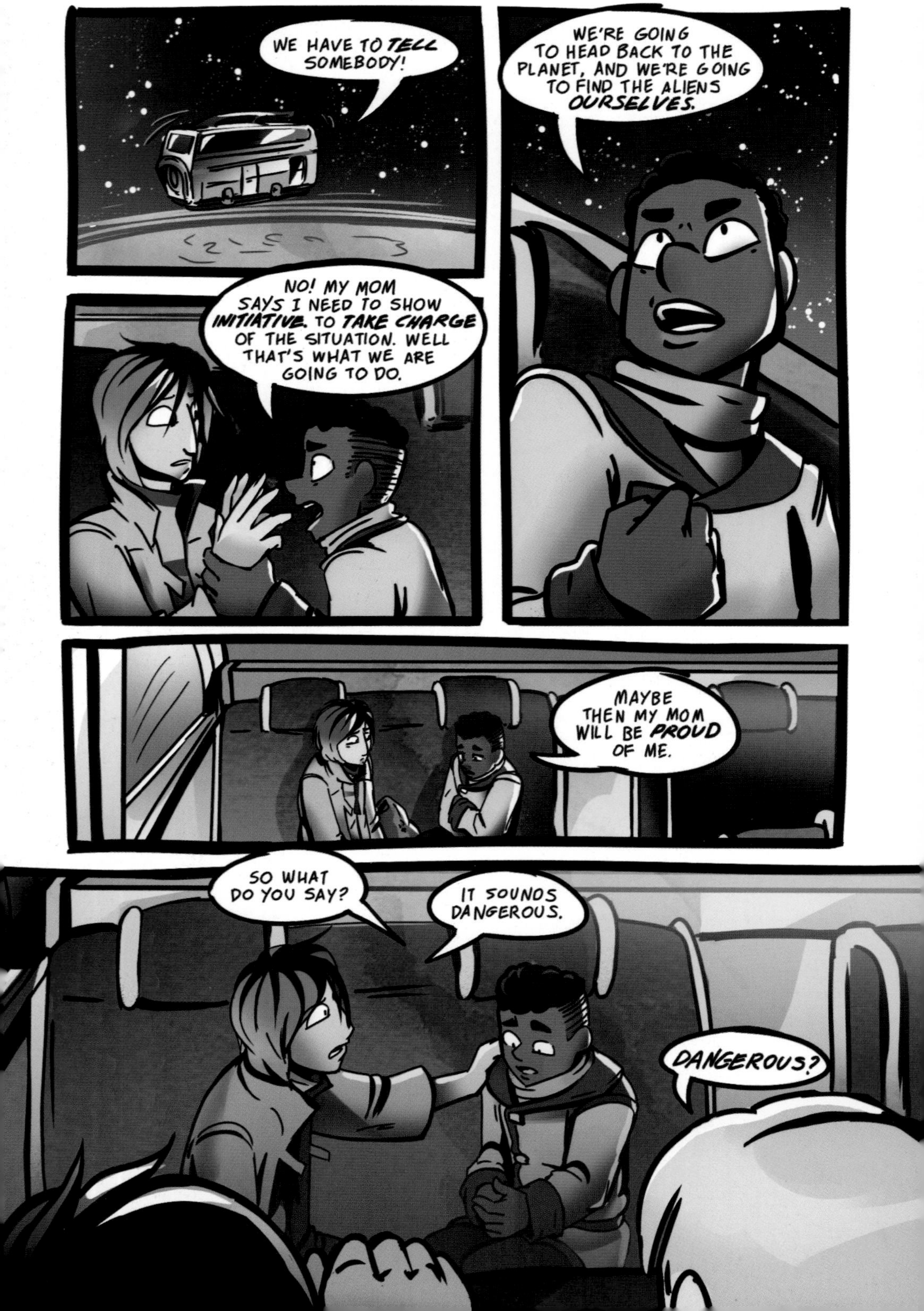
WE HAVE TO TELL SOMEBODY!
WE'RE GOING TO HEAD BACK TO THE PLANET, AND WE'RE GOING TO FIND THE ALIENS OURSELVES.
NO! MY MOM SAYS I NEED TO SHOW INITIATIVE. TO TAKE CHARGE OF THE SITUATION. WELL THAT'S WHAT WE ARE GOING TO DO.
MAYBE THEN MY MOM WILL BE PROUD OF ME.
SO WHAT DO YOU SAY?
IT SOUNDS DANGEROUS.
DANGEROUS?

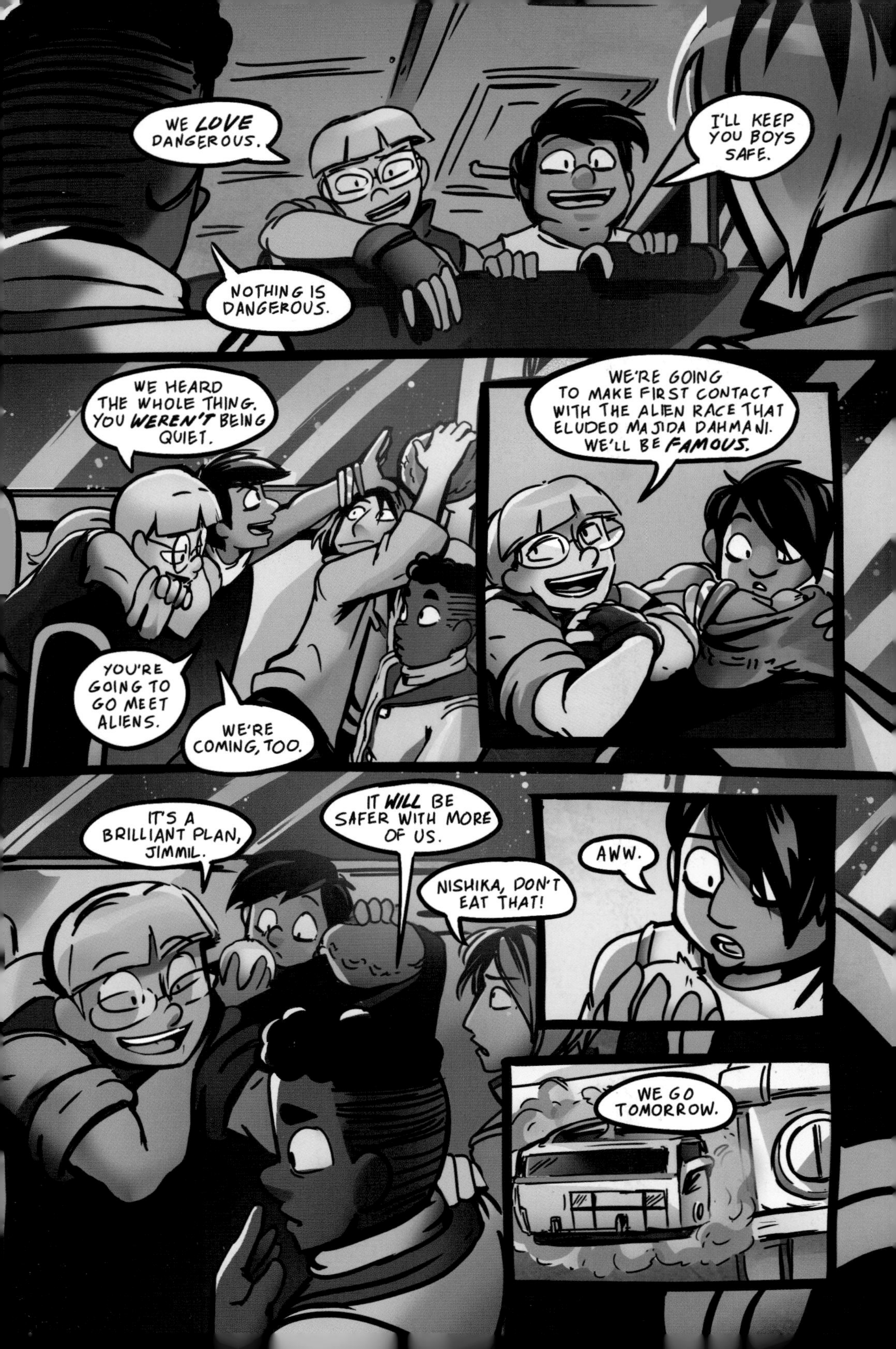
WE LOVE DANGEROUS.
I'LL KEEP YOU BOYS SAFE.
NOTHING IS DANGEROUS.
WE HEARD THE WHOLE THING. YOU WEREN'T BEING QUIET.
YOU'RE GOING TO GO MEET ALIENS.
WE'RE COMING, TOO.
WE'RE GOING TO MAKE FIRST CONTACT WITH THE ALIEN RACE THAT ELUDED MAJIDA DAHMANI. WE'LL BE FAMOUS.
IT'S A BRILLIANT PLAN, JIMMIL.
IT WILL BE SAFER WITH MORE OF US.
NISHIKA, DON'T EAT THAT!
AWW.
WE GO TOMORROW.

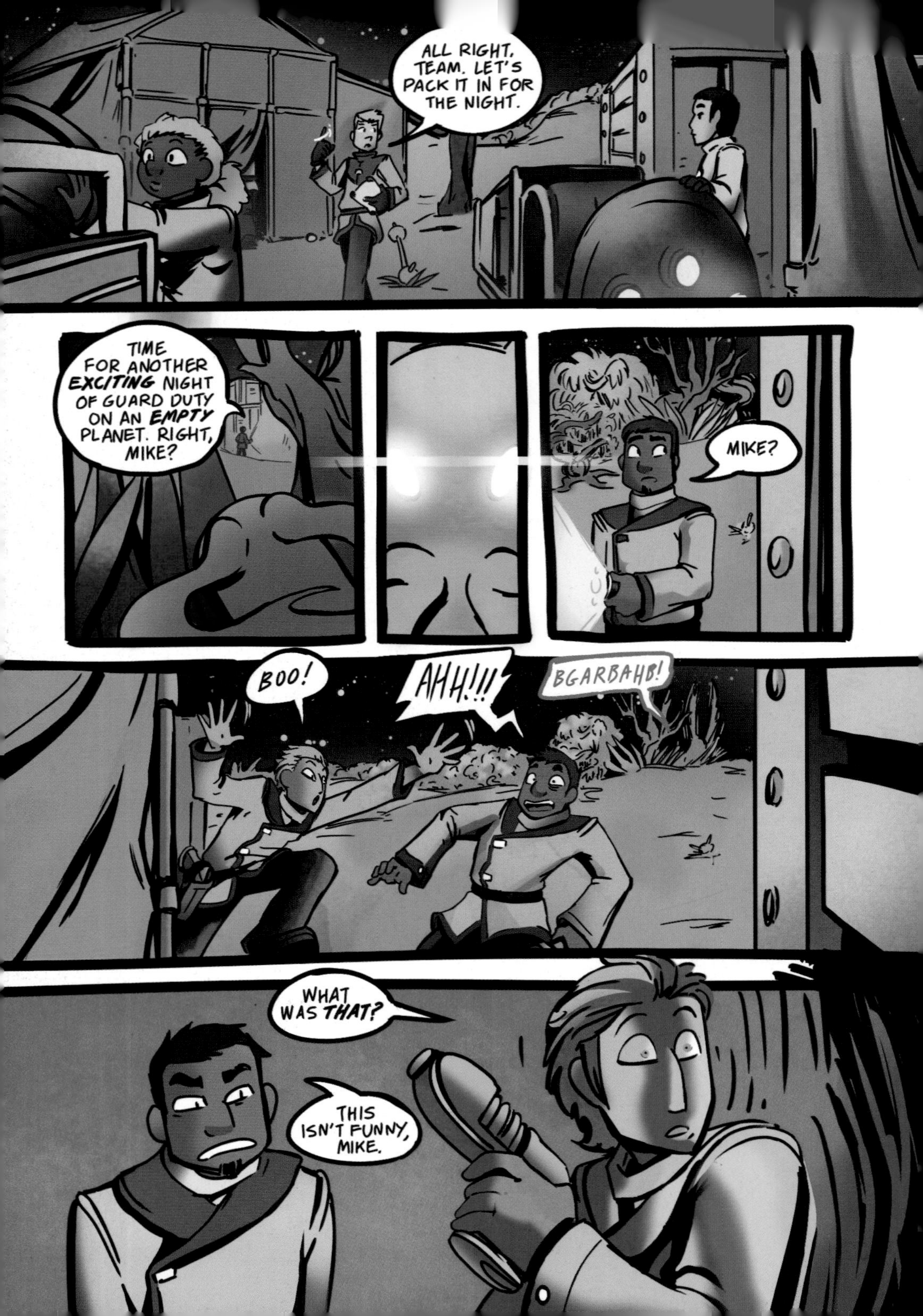
ALL RIGHT, TEAM. LET'S PACK IT IN FOR THE NIGHT.
TIME FOR ANOTHER *EXCITING* NIGHT OF GUARD DUTY ON AN *EMPTY* PLANET. RIGHT, MIKE?
MIKE?
BOO!
AHH!!!
BGARBAHB!
WHAT WAS *THAT*?
THIS ISN'T FUNNY, MIKE.

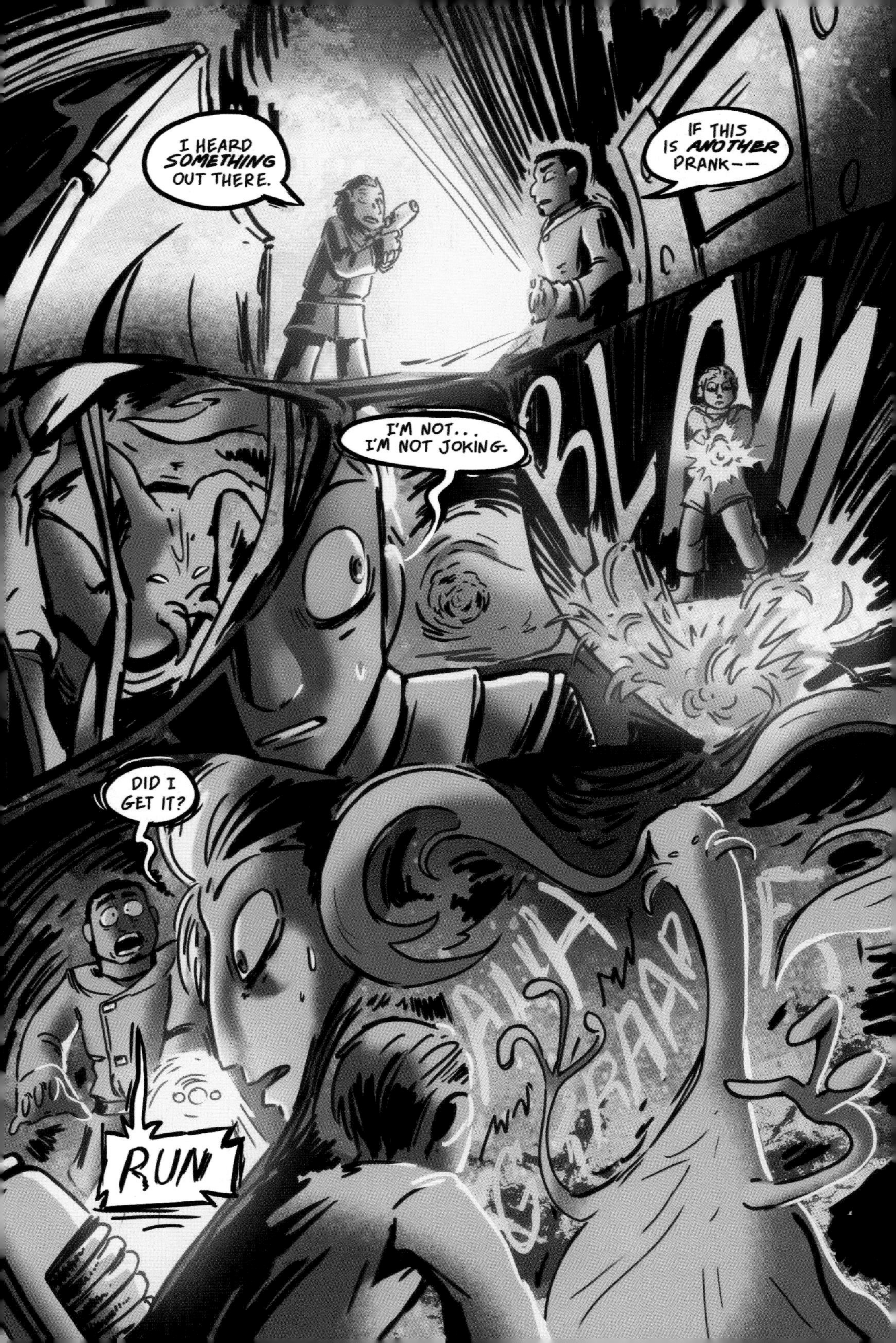
I HEARD SOMETHING OUT THERE.
IF THIS IS ANOTHER PRANK--
BLAM
I'M NOT... I'M NOT JOKING.
DID I GET IT?
RUN
AHH CRAP

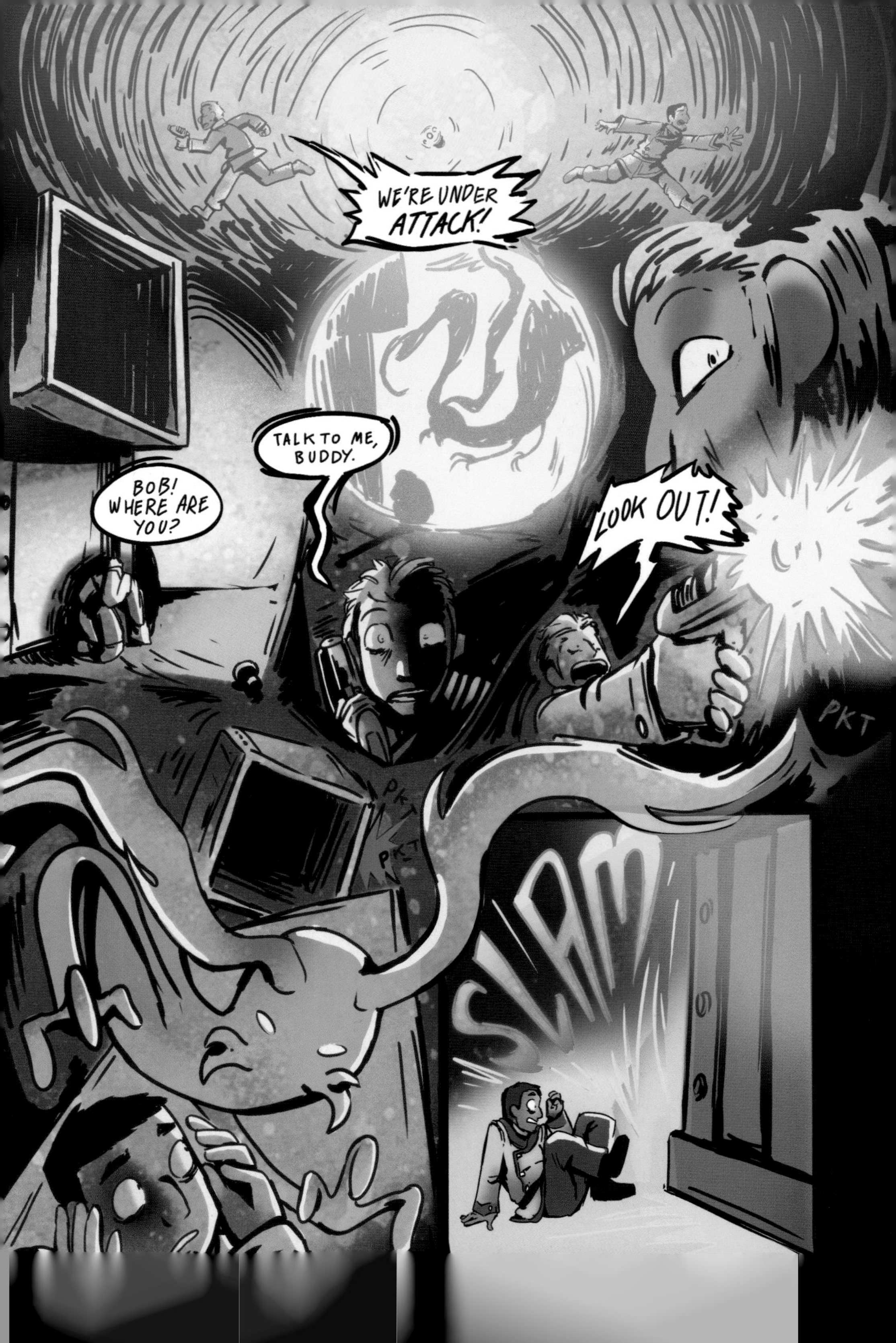
WE'RE UNDER ATTACK!
BOB! WHERE ARE YOU?
TALK TO ME, BUDDY.
LOOK OUT!
PKT
PKT
PKT
SLAM

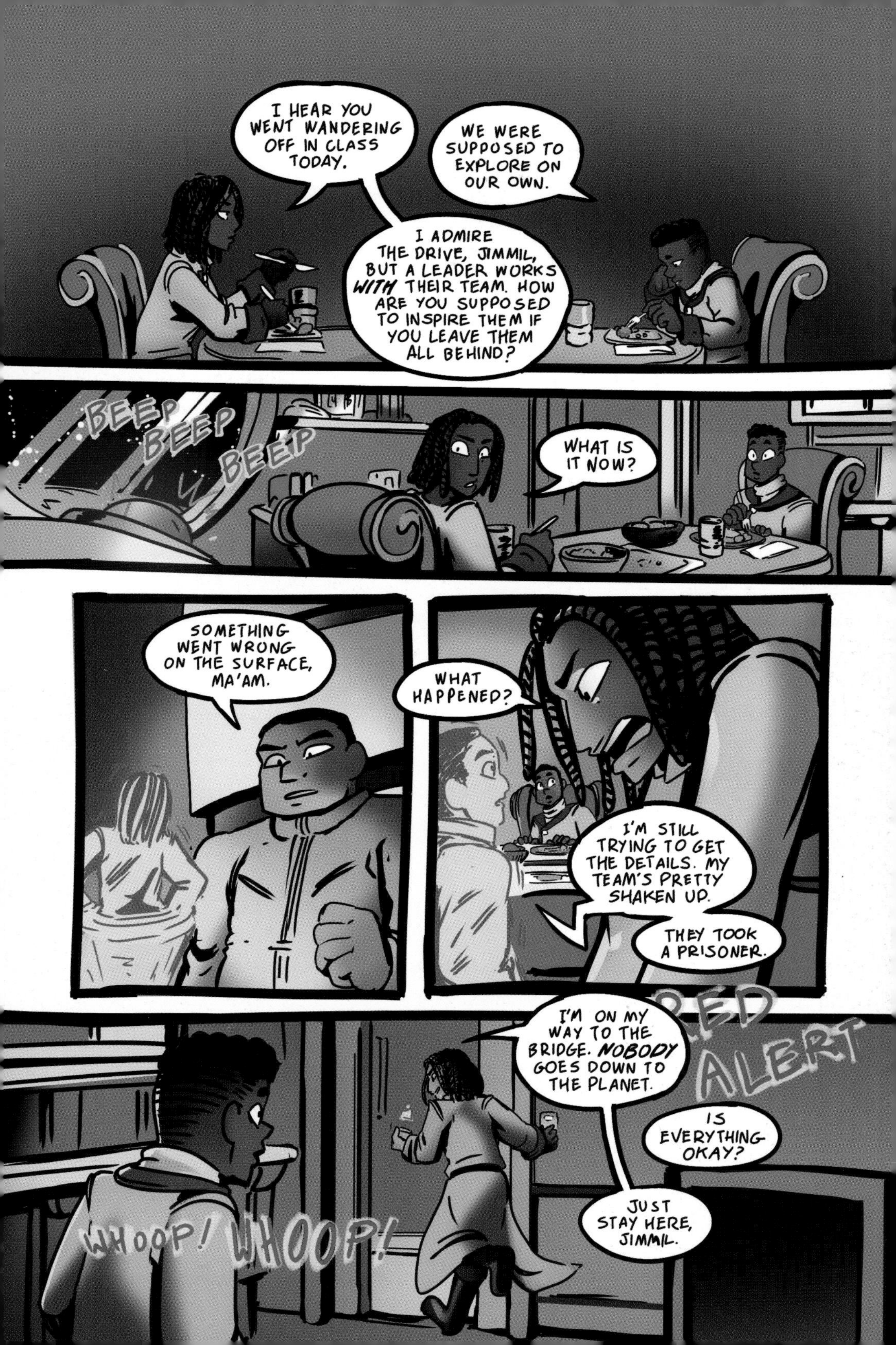
I HEAR YOU WENT WANDERING OFF IN CLASS TODAY.
WE WERE SUPPOSED TO EXPLORE ON OUR OWN.
I ADMIRE THE DRIVE, JIMMIL, BUT A LEADER WORKS *WITH* THEIR TEAM. HOW ARE YOU SUPPOSED TO INSPIRE THEM IF YOU LEAVE THEM ALL BEHIND?
BEEP BEEP BEEP
WHAT IS IT NOW?
SOMETHING WENT WRONG ON THE SURFACE, MA'AM.
WHAT HAPPENED?
I'M STILL TRYING TO GET THE DETAILS. MY TEAM'S PRETTY SHAKEN UP.
THEY TOOK A PRISONER.
RED ALERT
I'M ON MY WAY TO THE BRIDGE. *NOBODY* GOES DOWN TO THE PLANET.
IS EVERYTHING OKAY?
JUST STAY HERE, JIMMIL.
WHOOP! WHOOP!

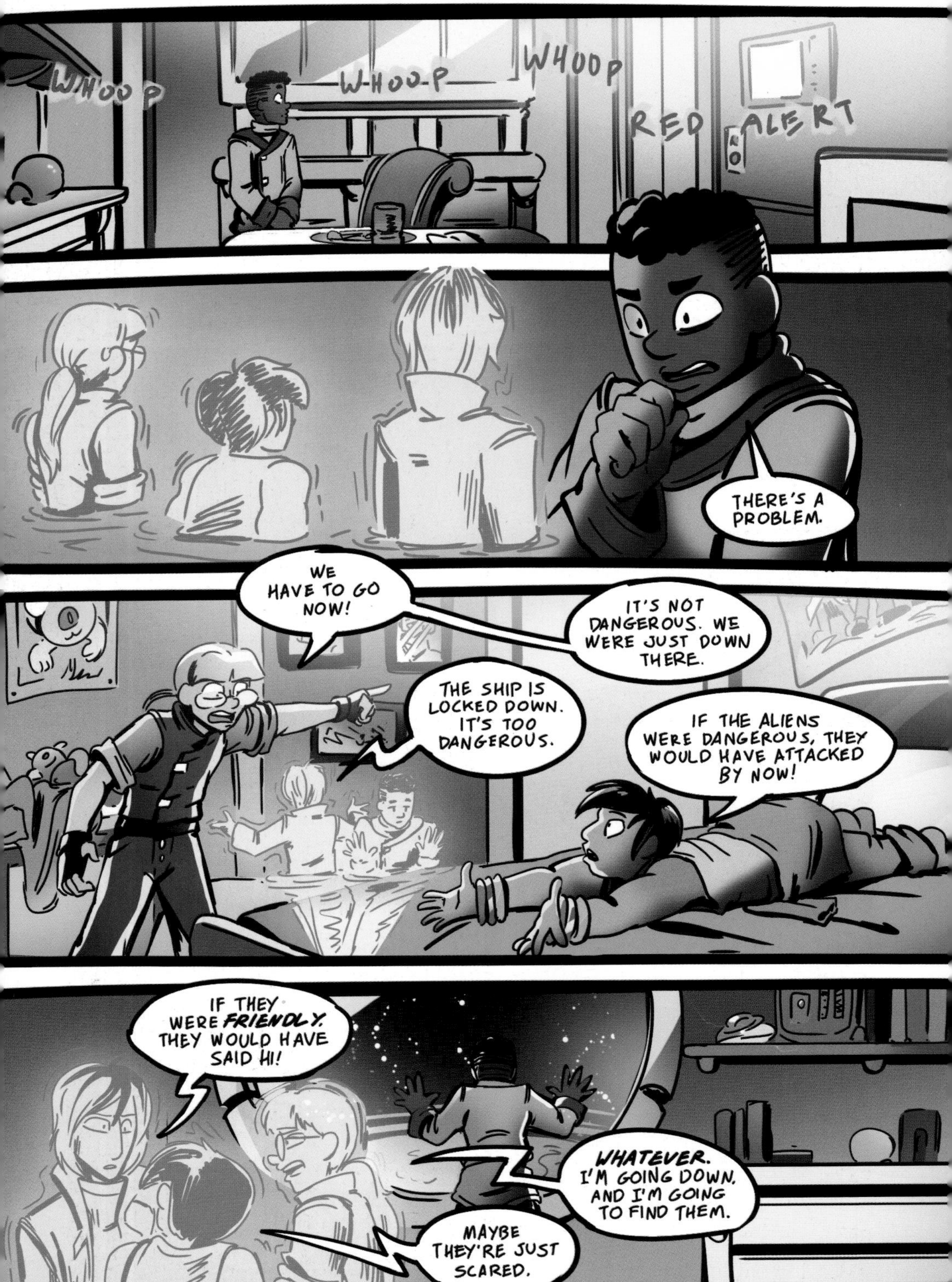
WHOOP
WHOOP
WHOOP
RED ALERT
THERE'S A PROBLEM.
WE HAVE TO GO NOW!
IT'S NOT DANGEROUS. WE WERE JUST DOWN THERE.
THE SHIP IS LOCKED DOWN. IT'S TOO DANGEROUS.
IF THE ALIENS WERE DANGEROUS, THEY WOULD HAVE ATTACKED BY NOW!
IF THEY WERE FRIENDLY, THEY WOULD HAVE SAID HI!
WHATEVER. I'M GOING DOWN, AND I'M GOING TO FIND THEM.
MAYBE THEY'RE JUST SCARED.

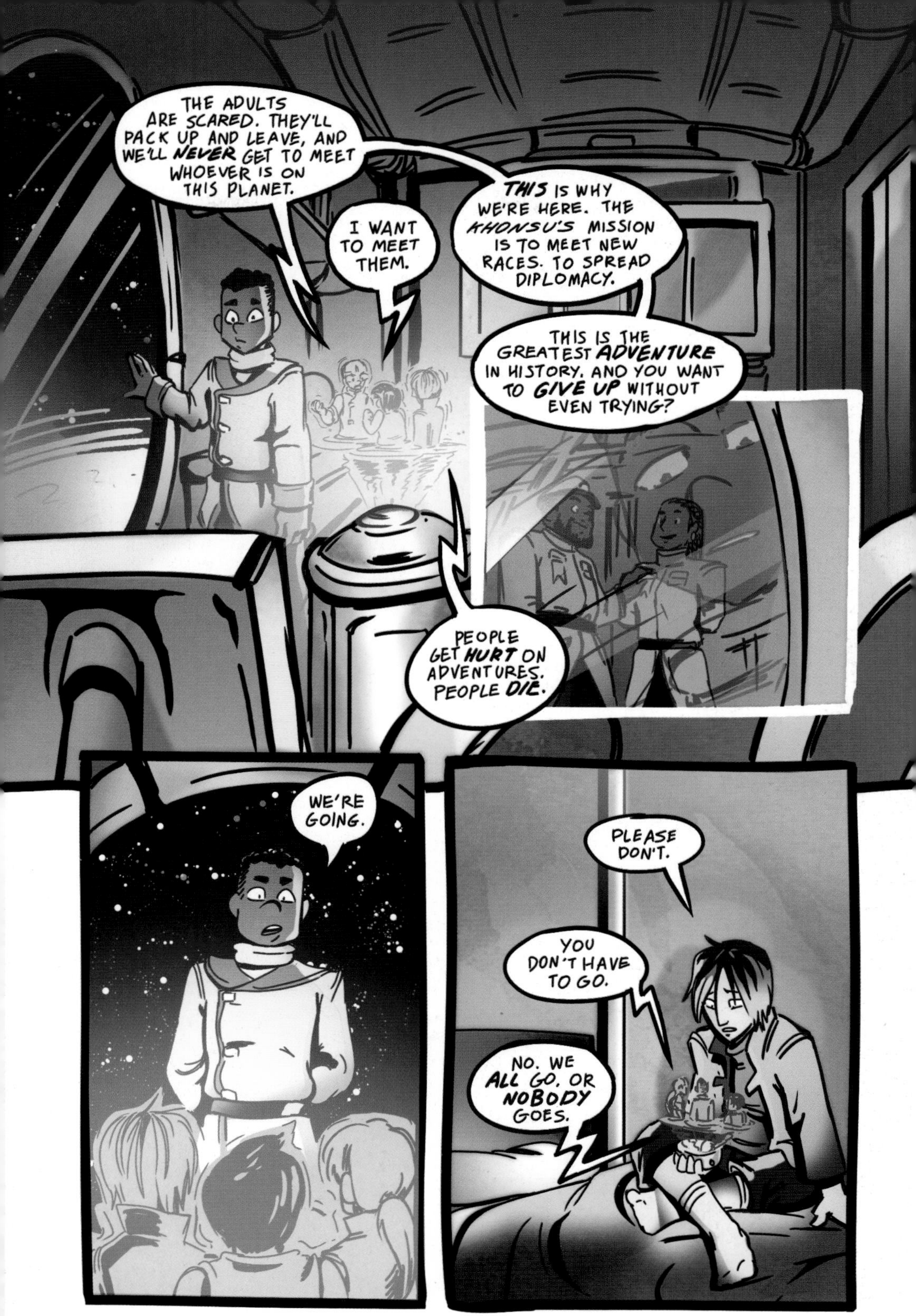
THE ADULTS ARE SCARED. THEY'LL PACK UP AND LEAVE, AND WE'LL NEVER GET TO MEET WHOEVER IS ON THIS PLANET.
I WANT TO MEET THEM.
THIS IS WHY WE'RE HERE. THE KHONSU'S MISSION IS TO MEET NEW RACES. TO SPREAD DIPLOMACY.
THIS IS THE GREATEST ADVENTURE IN HISTORY. AND YOU WANT TO GIVE UP WITHOUT EVEN TRYING?
PEOPLE GET HURT ON ADVENTURES. PEOPLE DIE.
WE'RE GOING.
PLEASE DON'T.
YOU DON'T HAVE TO GO.
NO. WE ALL GO. OR NOBODY GOES.

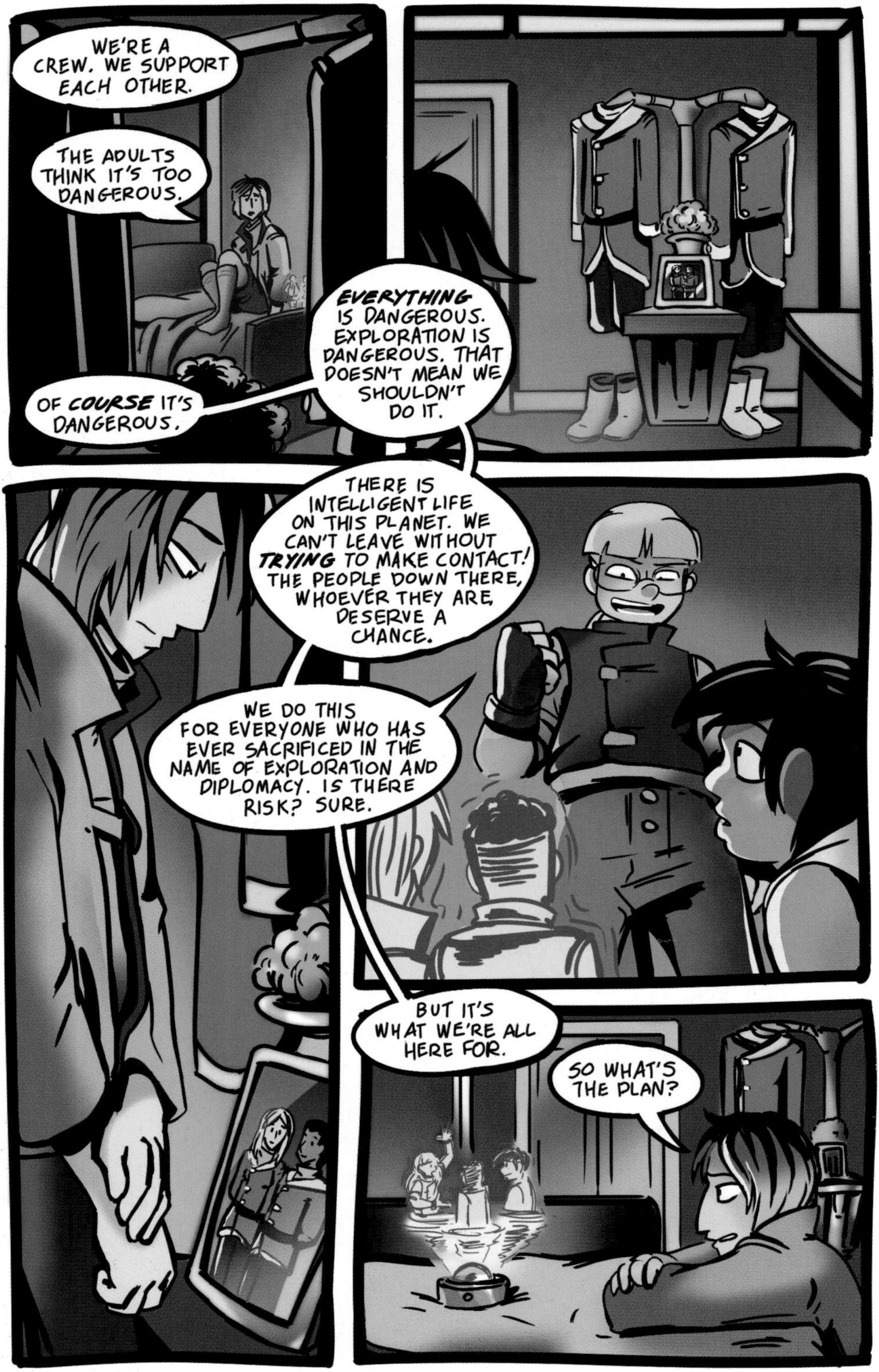
WE'RE A CREW. WE SUPPORT EACH OTHER.
THE ADULTS THINK IT'S TOO DANGEROUS.
OF COURSE IT'S DANGEROUS.
EVERYTHING IS DANGEROUS. EXPLORATION IS DANGEROUS. THAT DOESN'T MEAN WE SHOULDN'T DO IT.
THERE IS INTELLIGENT LIFE ON THIS PLANET. WE CAN'T LEAVE WITHOUT TRYING TO MAKE CONTACT! THE PEOPLE DOWN THERE, WHOEVER THEY ARE, DESERVE A CHANCE.
WE DO THIS FOR EVERYONE WHO HAS EVER SACRIFICED IN THE NAME OF EXPLORATION AND DIPLOMACY. IS THERE RISK? SURE.
BUT IT'S WHAT WE'RE ALL HERE FOR.
SO WHAT'S THE PLAN?

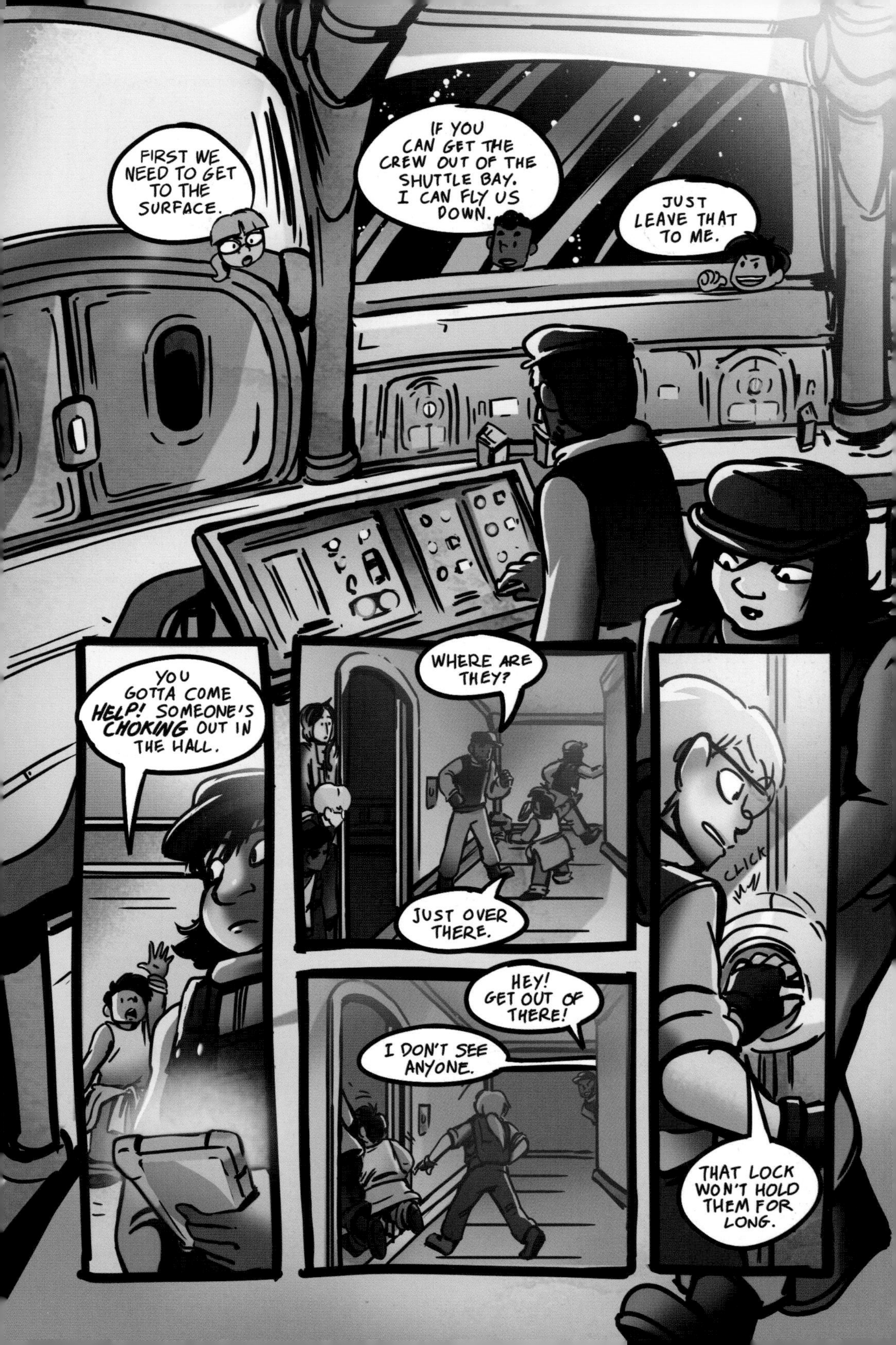
FIRST WE NEED TO GET TO THE SURFACE.
IF YOU CAN GET THE CREW OUT OF THE SHUTTLE BAY. I CAN FLY US DOWN.
JUST LEAVE THAT TO ME.
YOU GOTTA COME HELP! SOMEONE'S CHOKING OUT IN THE HALL.
WHERE ARE THEY?
JUST OVER THERE.
HEY! GET OUT OF THERE!
I DON'T SEE ANYONE.
CLICK
THAT LOCK WON'T HOLD THEM FOR LONG.

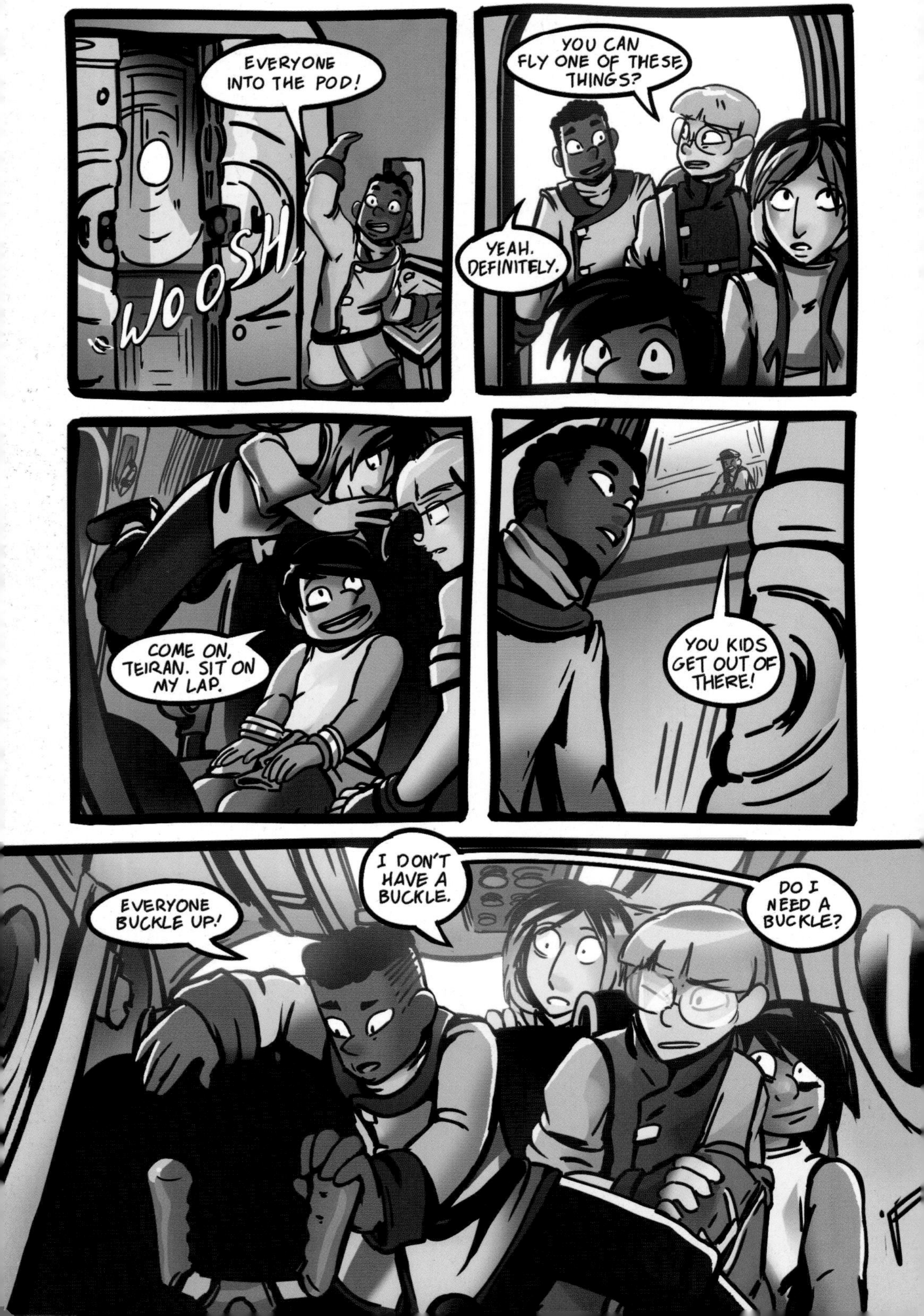
EVERYONE INTO THE POD!
WOOSH
YOU CAN FLY ONE OF THESE THINGS?
YEAH. DEFINITELY.
COME ON, TEIRAN. SIT ON MY LAP.
YOU KIDS GET OUT OF THERE!
EVERYONE BUCKLE UP!
I DON'T HAVE A BUCKLE.
DO I NEED A BUCKLE?

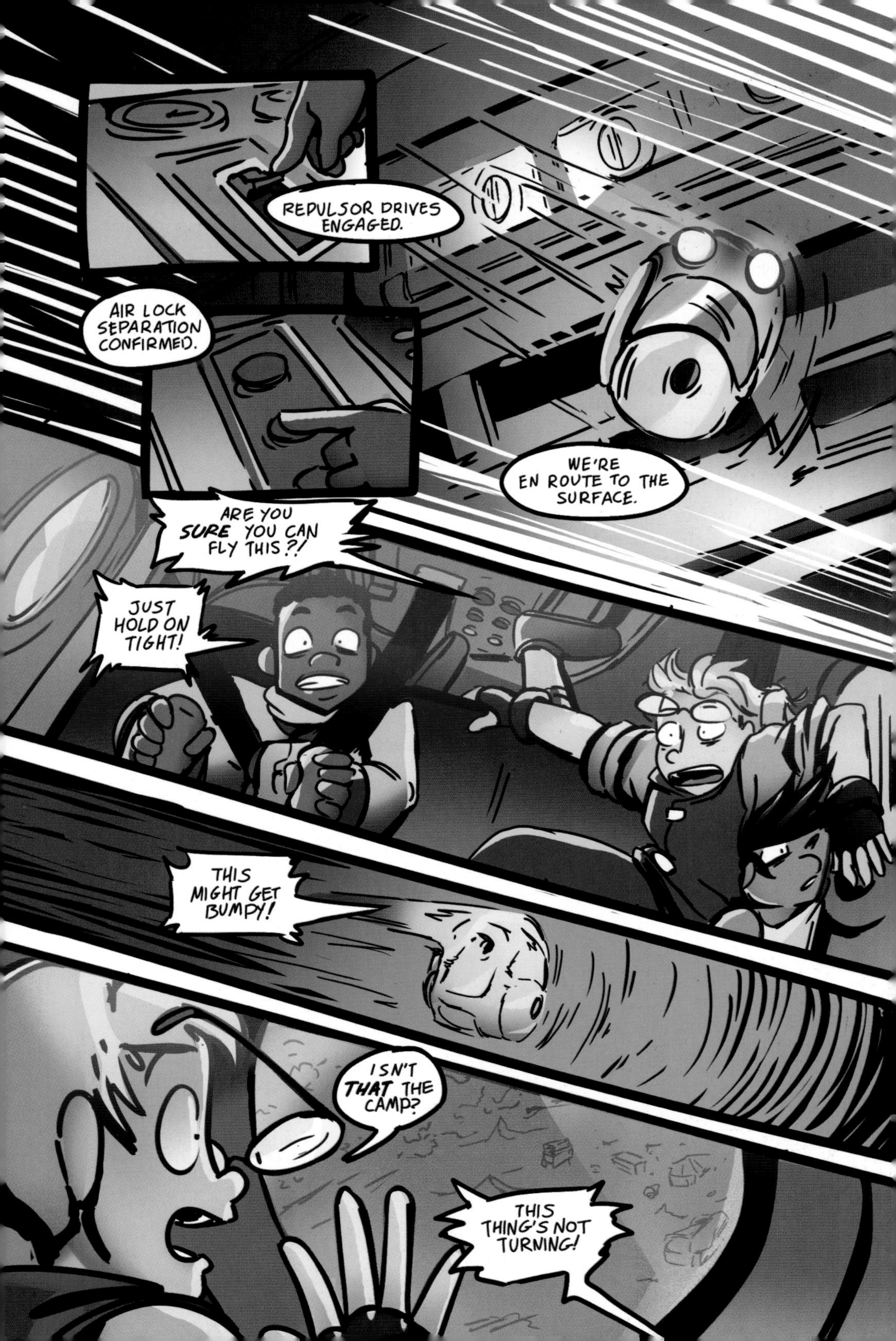
REPULSOR DRIVES ENGAGED.
AIR LOCK SEPARATION CONFIRMED.
WE'RE EN ROUTE TO THE SURFACE.
ARE YOU **SURE** YOU CAN FLY THIS?!
JUST HOLD ON TIGHT!
THIS MIGHT GET BUMPY!
ISN'T **THAT** THE CAMP?
THIS THING'S NOT TURNING!

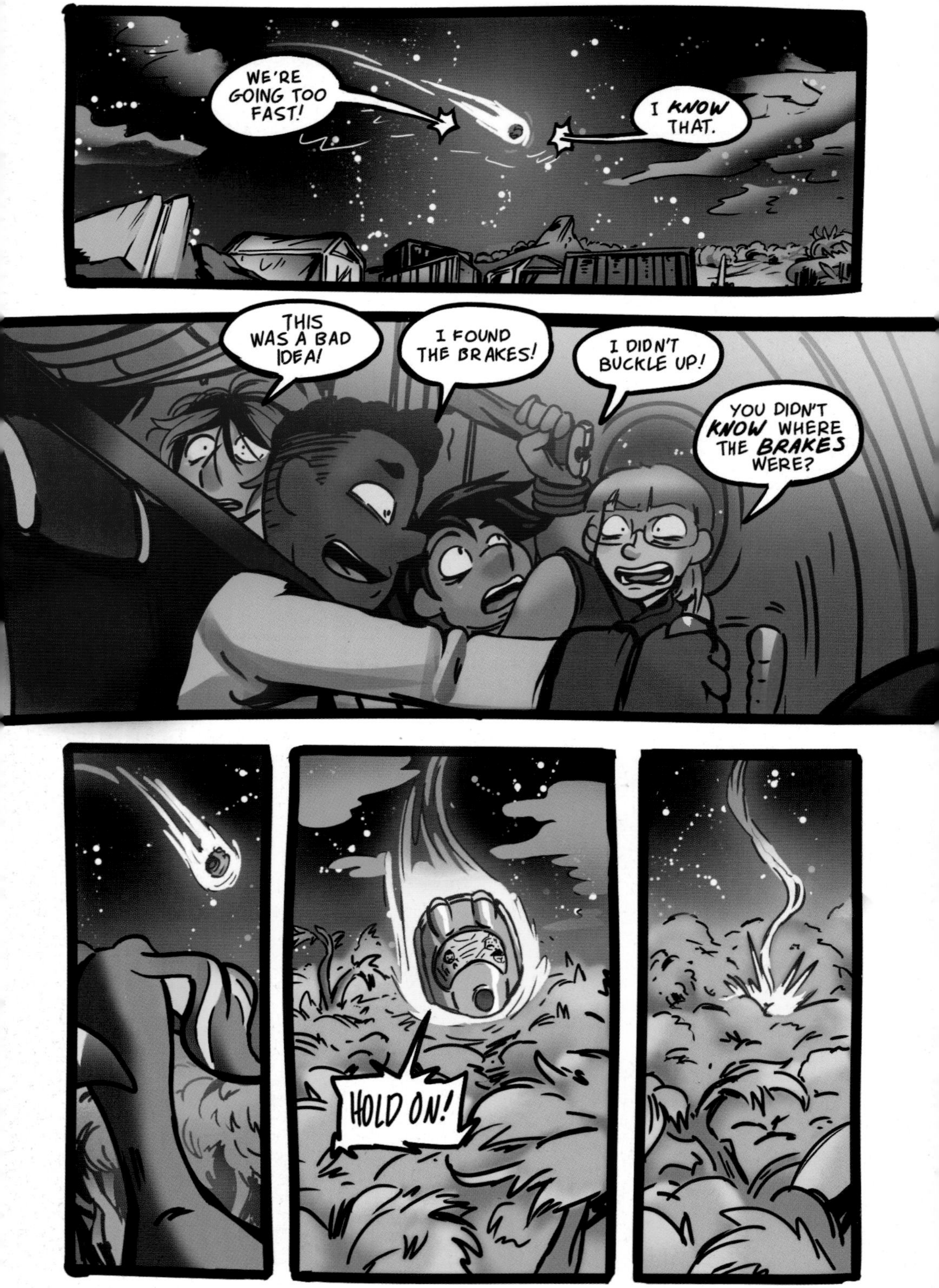
WE'RE GOING TOO FAST!
I KNOW THAT.
THIS WAS A BAD IDEA!
I FOUND THE BRAKES!
I DIDN'T BUCKLE UP!
YOU DIDN'T KNOW WHERE THE BRAKES WERE?
HOLD ON!

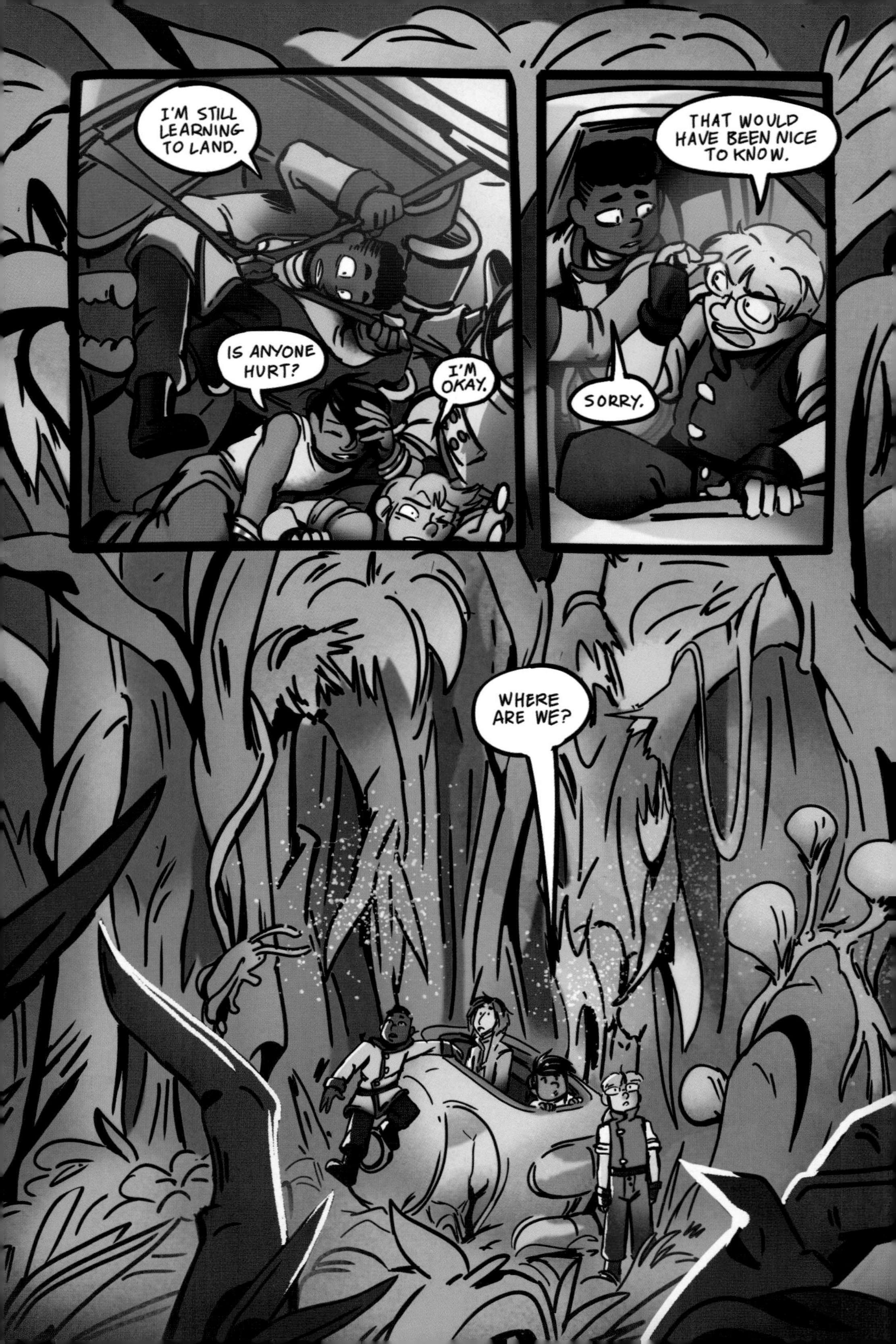
I'M STILL LEARNING TO LAND.
IS ANYONE HURT?
I'M OKAY.
THAT WOULD HAVE BEEN NICE TO KNOW.
SORRY.
WHERE ARE WE?

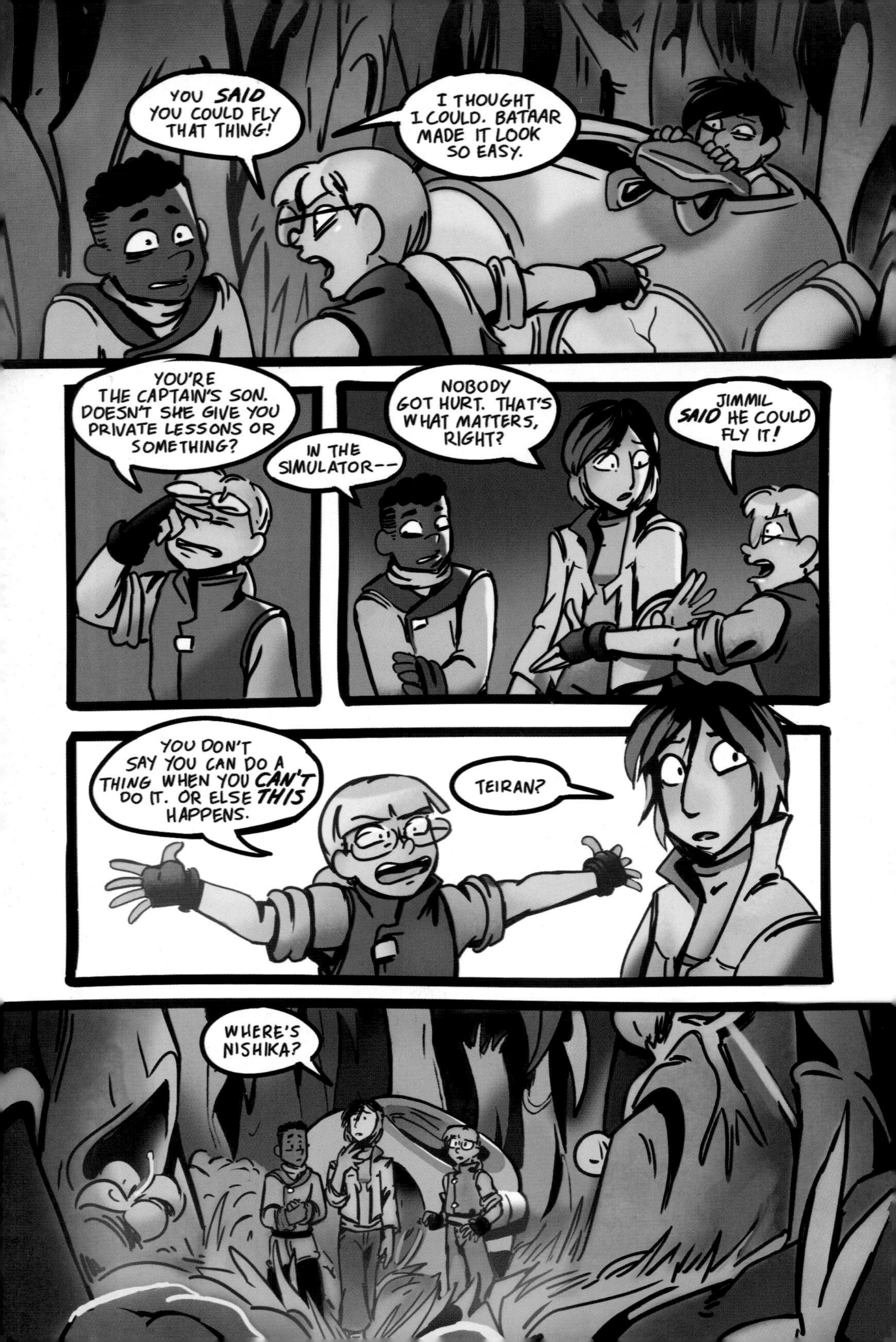
YOU SAID YOU COULD FLY THAT THING!
I THOUGHT I COULD. BATAAR MADE IT LOOK SO EASY.
YOU'RE THE CAPTAIN'S SON. DOESN'T SHE GIVE YOU PRIVATE LESSONS OR SOMETHING?
IN THE SIMULATOR--
NOBODY GOT HURT. THAT'S WHAT MATTERS, RIGHT?
JIMMIL SAID HE COULD FLY IT!
YOU DON'T SAY YOU CAN DO A THING WHEN YOU CAN'T DO IT. OR ELSE THIS HAPPENS.
TEIRAN?
WHERE'S NISHIKA?

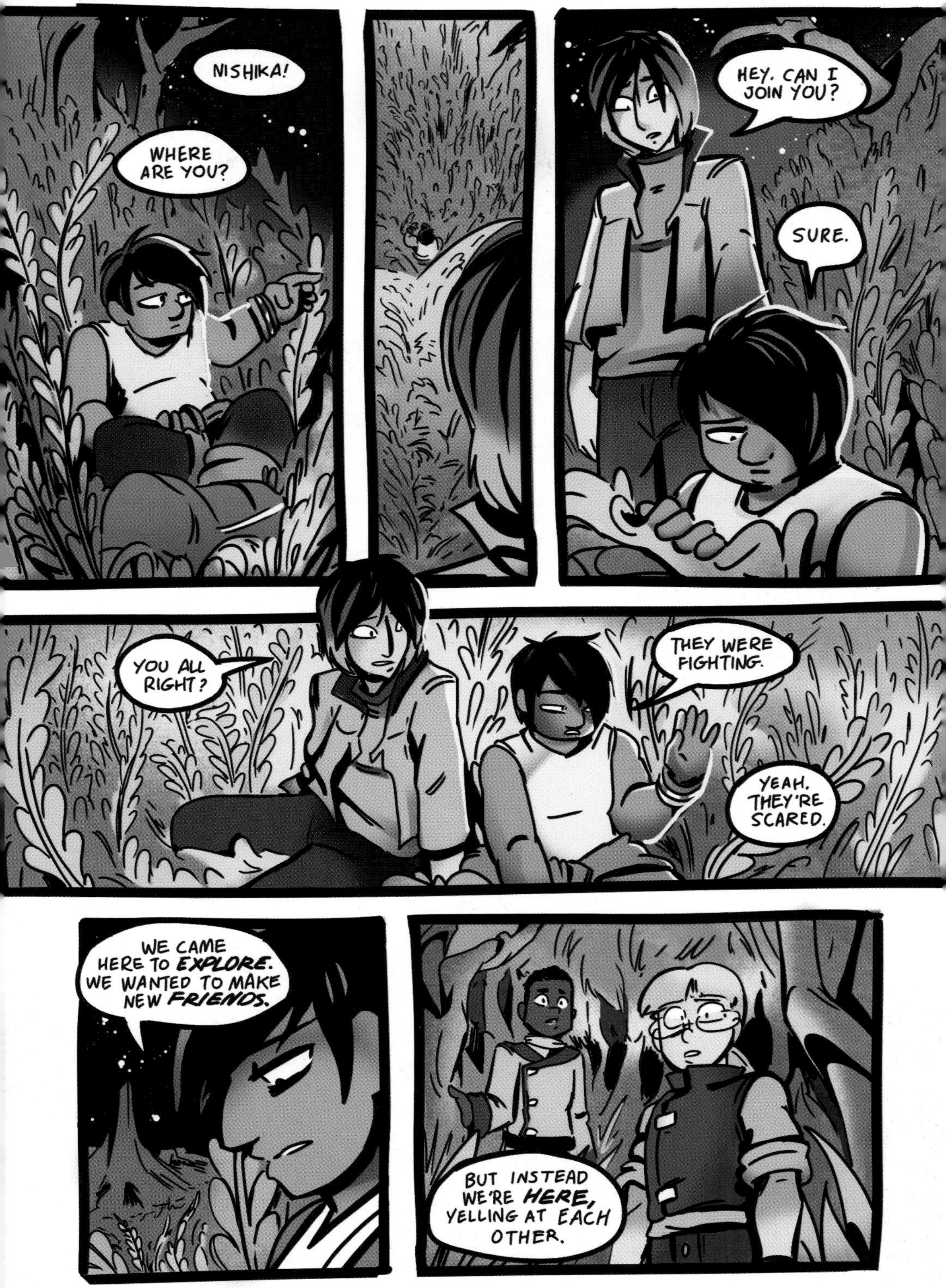
NISHIKA!
WHERE ARE YOU?
HEY. CAN I JOIN YOU?
SURE.
YOU ALL RIGHT?
THEY WERE FIGHTING.
YEAH. THEY'RE SCARED.
WE CAME HERE TO EXPLORE. WE WANTED TO MAKE NEW FRIENDS.
BUT INSTEAD WE'RE HERE, YELLING AT EACH OTHER.

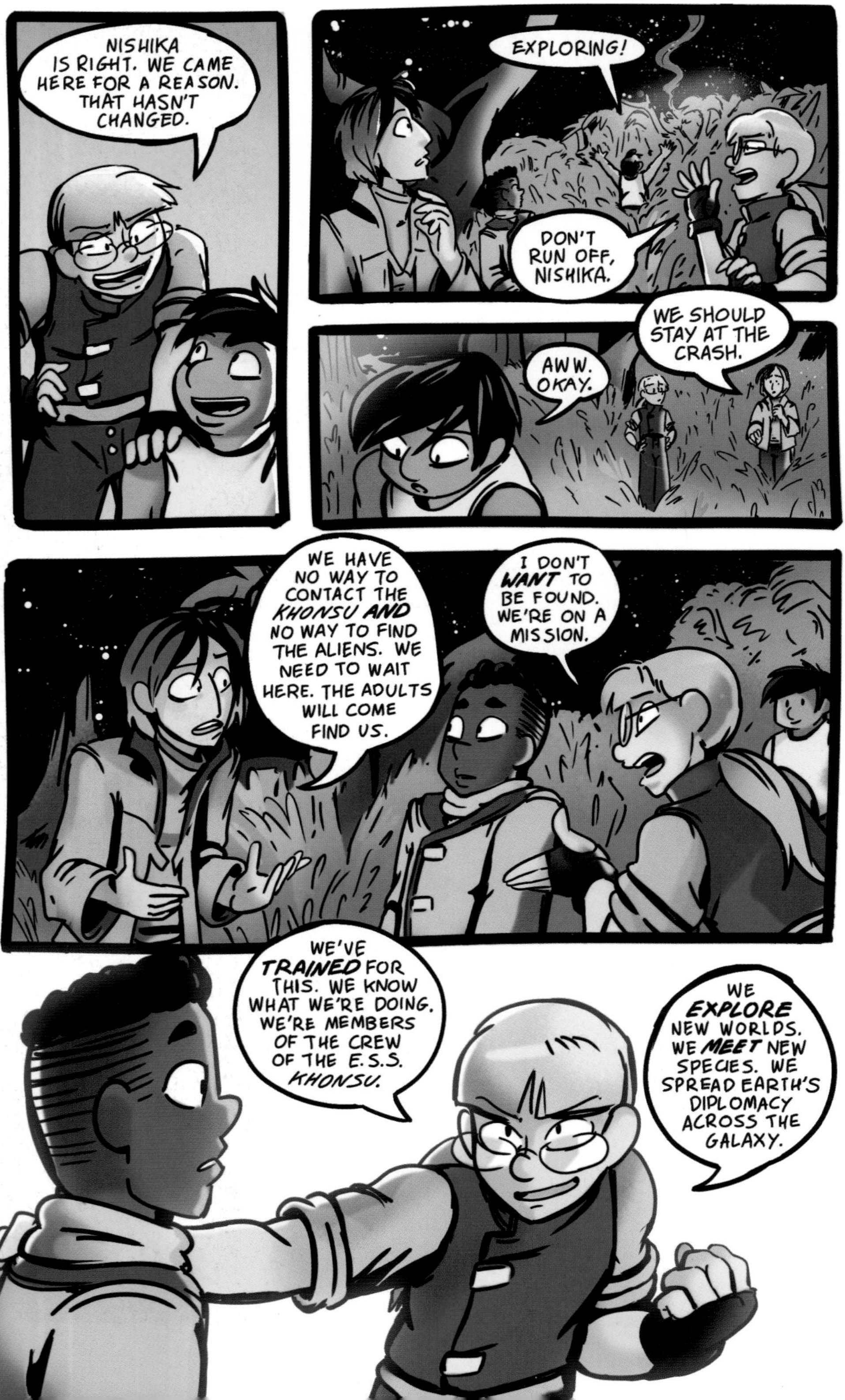
NISHIKA IS RIGHT. WE CAME HERE FOR A REASON. THAT HASN'T CHANGED.
EXPLORING!
DON'T RUN OFF, NISHIKA.
WE SHOULD STAY AT THE CRASH.
AWW. OKAY.
WE HAVE NO WAY TO CONTACT THE *KHONSU* **AND** NO WAY TO FIND THE ALIENS. WE NEED TO WAIT HERE. THE ADULTS WILL COME FIND US.
I DON'T **WANT** TO BE FOUND. WE'RE ON A MISSION.
WE'VE **TRAINED** FOR THIS. WE KNOW WHAT WE'RE DOING. WE'RE MEMBERS OF THE CREW OF THE E.S.S. *KHONSU*.
WE **EXPLORE** NEW WORLDS. WE **MEET** NEW SPECIES. WE SPREAD EARTH'S DIPLOMACY ACROSS THE GALAXY.

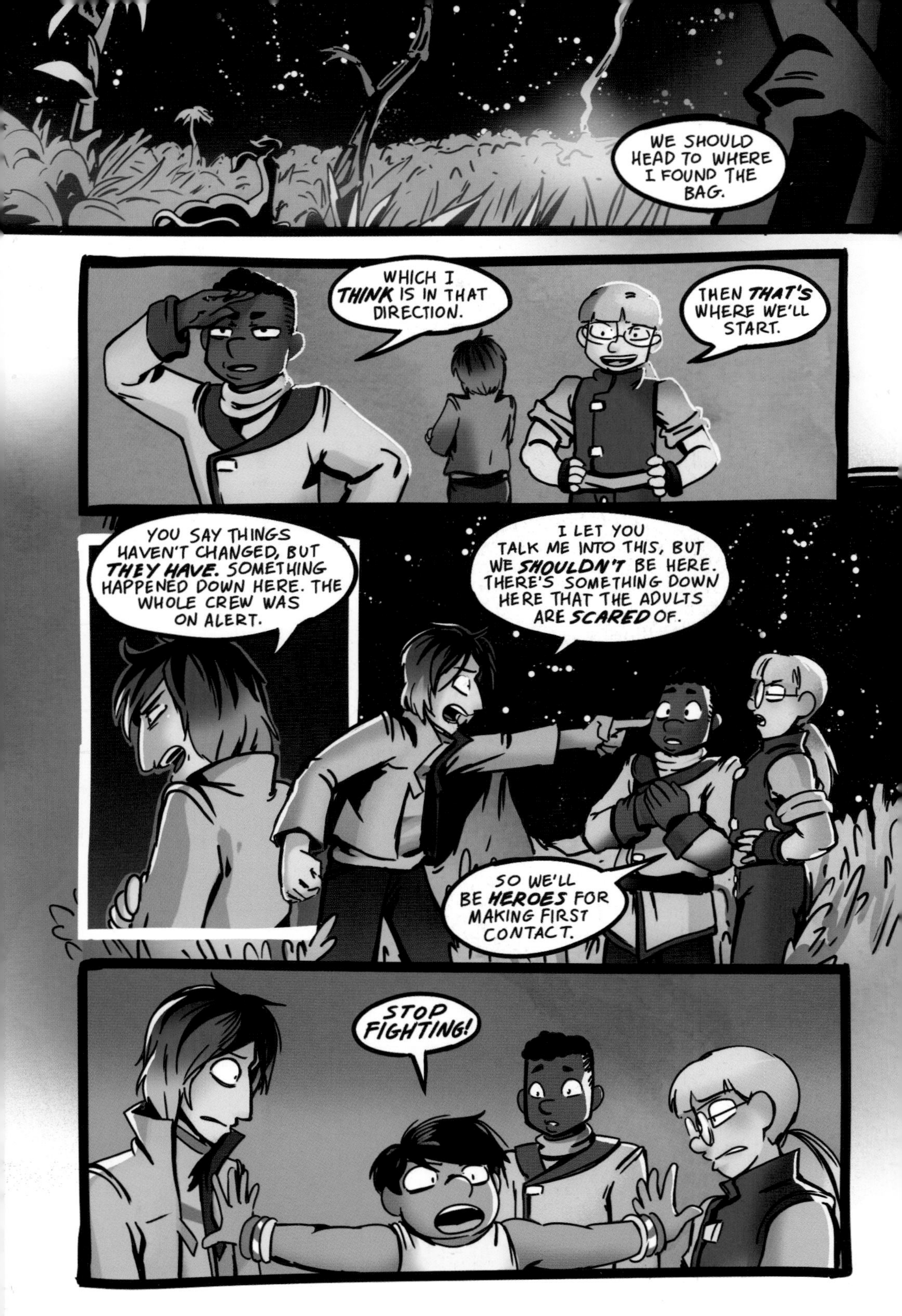
WE SHOULD HEAD TO WHERE I FOUND THE BAG.
WHICH I THINK IS IN THAT DIRECTION.
THEN THAT'S WHERE WE'LL START.
YOU SAY THINGS HAVEN'T CHANGED, BUT THEY HAVE. SOMETHING HAPPENED DOWN HERE. THE WHOLE CREW WAS ON ALERT.
I LET YOU TALK ME INTO THIS, BUT WE SHOULDN'T BE HERE. THERE'S SOMETHING DOWN HERE THAT THE ADULTS ARE SCARED OF.
SO WE'LL BE HEROES FOR MAKING FIRST CONTACT.
STOP FIGHTING!

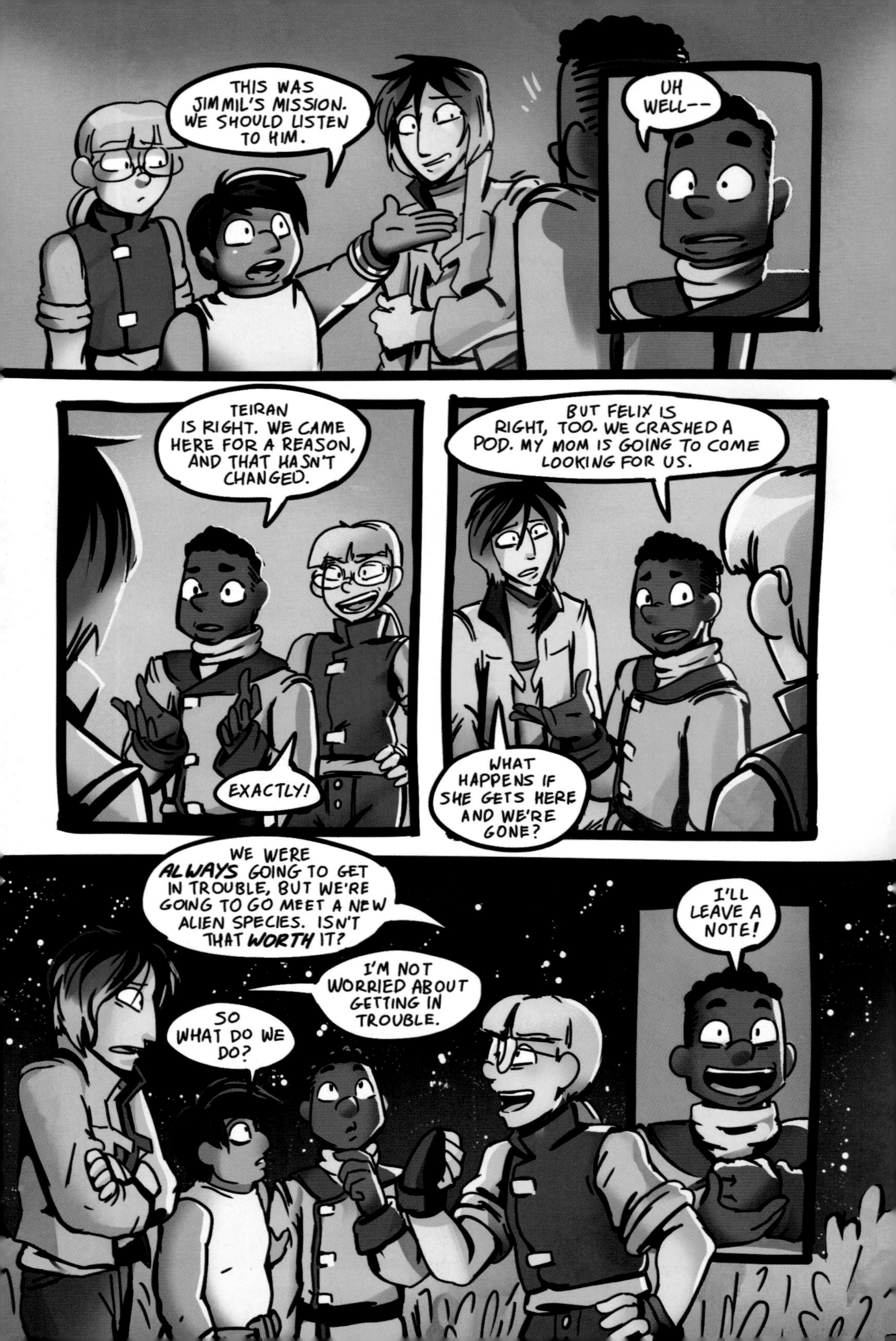
THIS WAS JIMMIL'S MISSION. WE SHOULD LISTEN TO HIM.
UH WELL--
TEIRAN IS RIGHT. WE CAME HERE FOR A REASON, AND THAT HASN'T CHANGED.
EXACTLY!
BUT FELIX IS RIGHT, TOO. WE CRASHED A POD. MY MOM IS GOING TO COME LOOKING FOR US.
WHAT HAPPENS IF SHE GETS HERE AND WE'RE GONE?
WE WERE ALWAYS GOING TO GET IN TROUBLE, BUT WE'RE GOING TO GO MEET A NEW ALIEN SPECIES. ISN'T THAT WORTH IT?
I'M NOT WORRIED ABOUT GETTING IN TROUBLE.
SO WHAT DO WE DO?
I'LL LEAVE A NOTE!

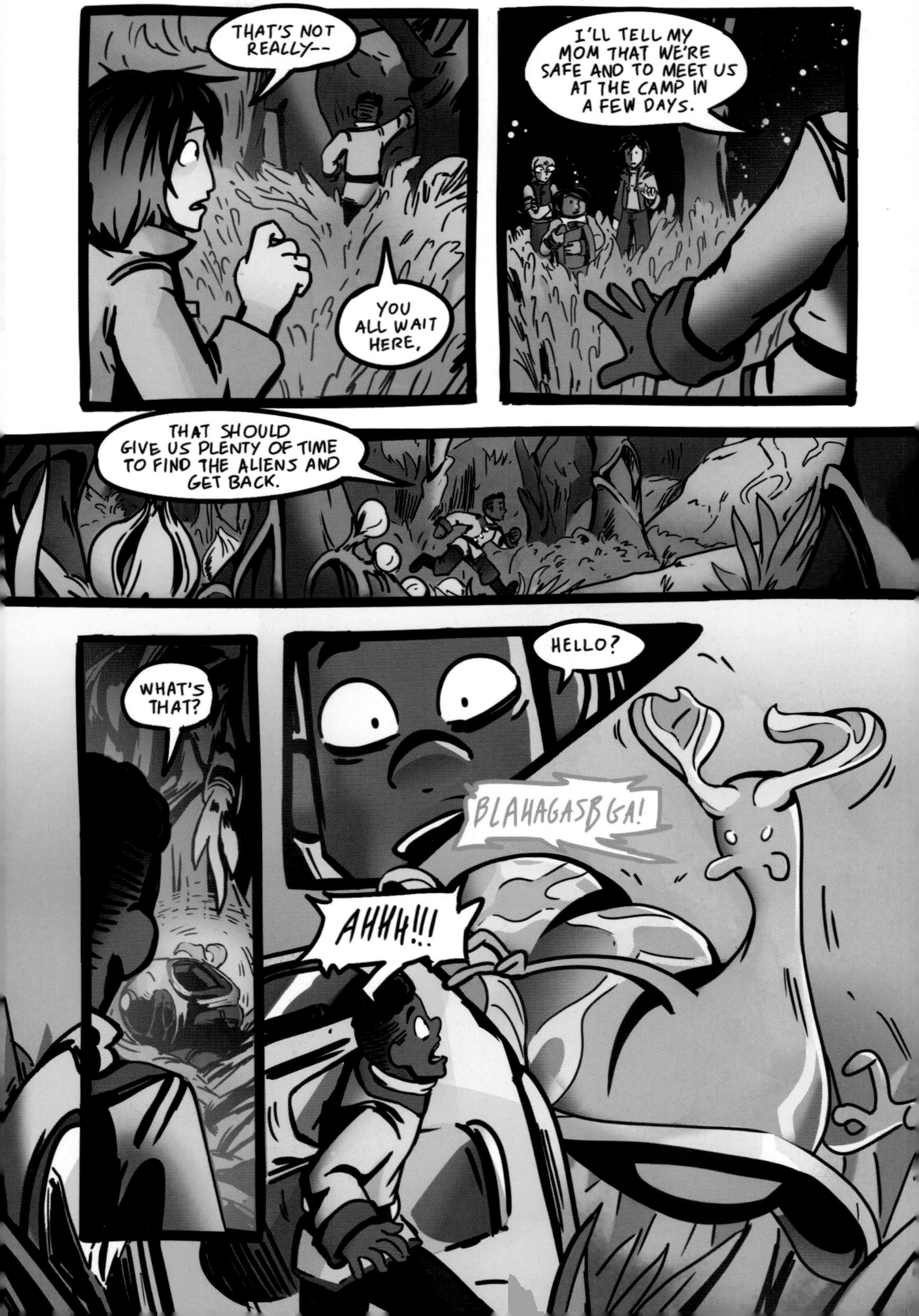
THAT'S NOT REALLY--
YOU ALL WAIT HERE.
I'LL TELL MY MOM THAT WE'RE SAFE AND TO MEET US AT THE CAMP IN A FEW DAYS.
THAT SHOULD GIVE US PLENTY OF TIME TO FIND THE ALIENS AND GET BACK.
WHAT'S THAT?
HELLO?
BLAHAGASBGA!
AHHH!!!

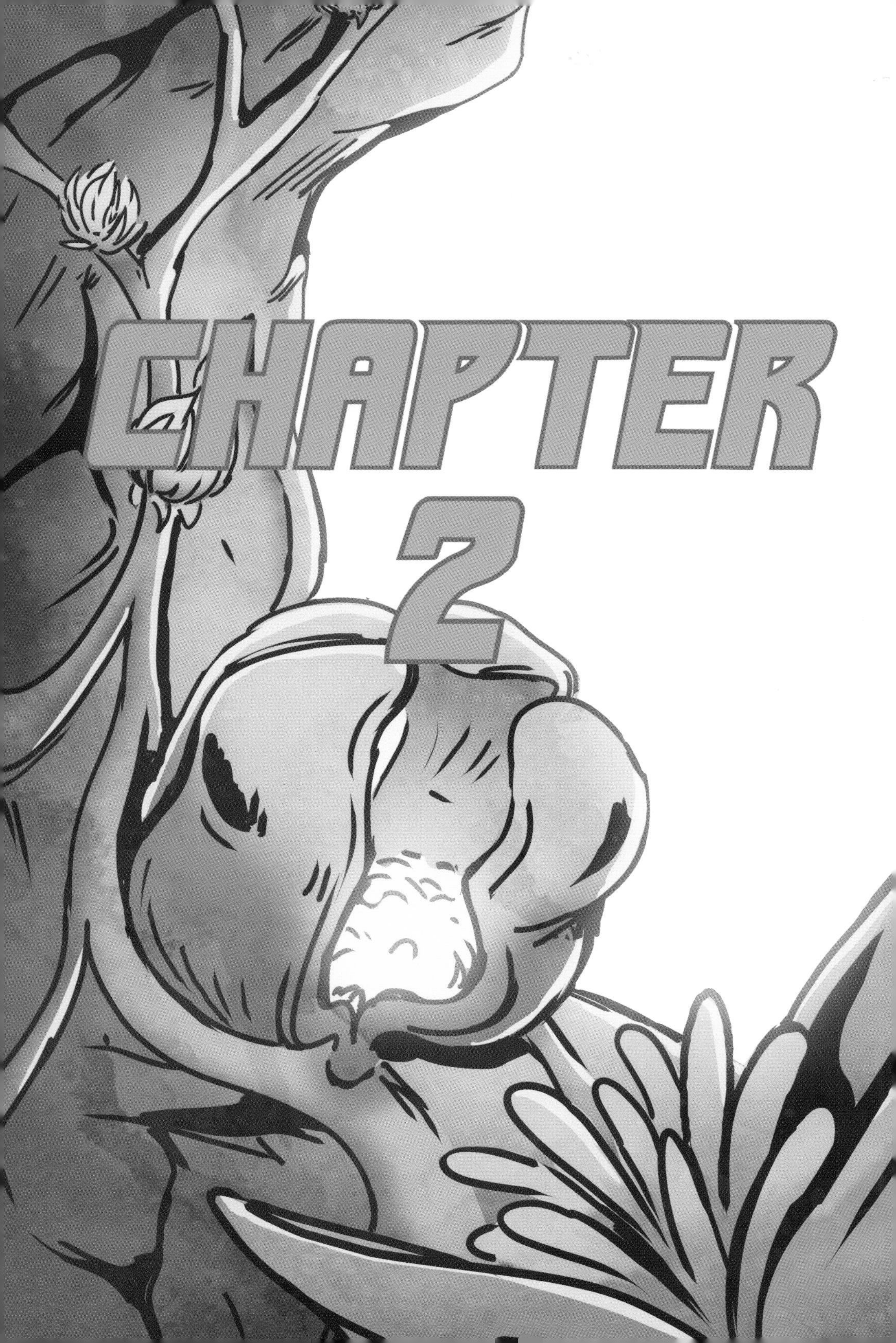
CHAPTER
2

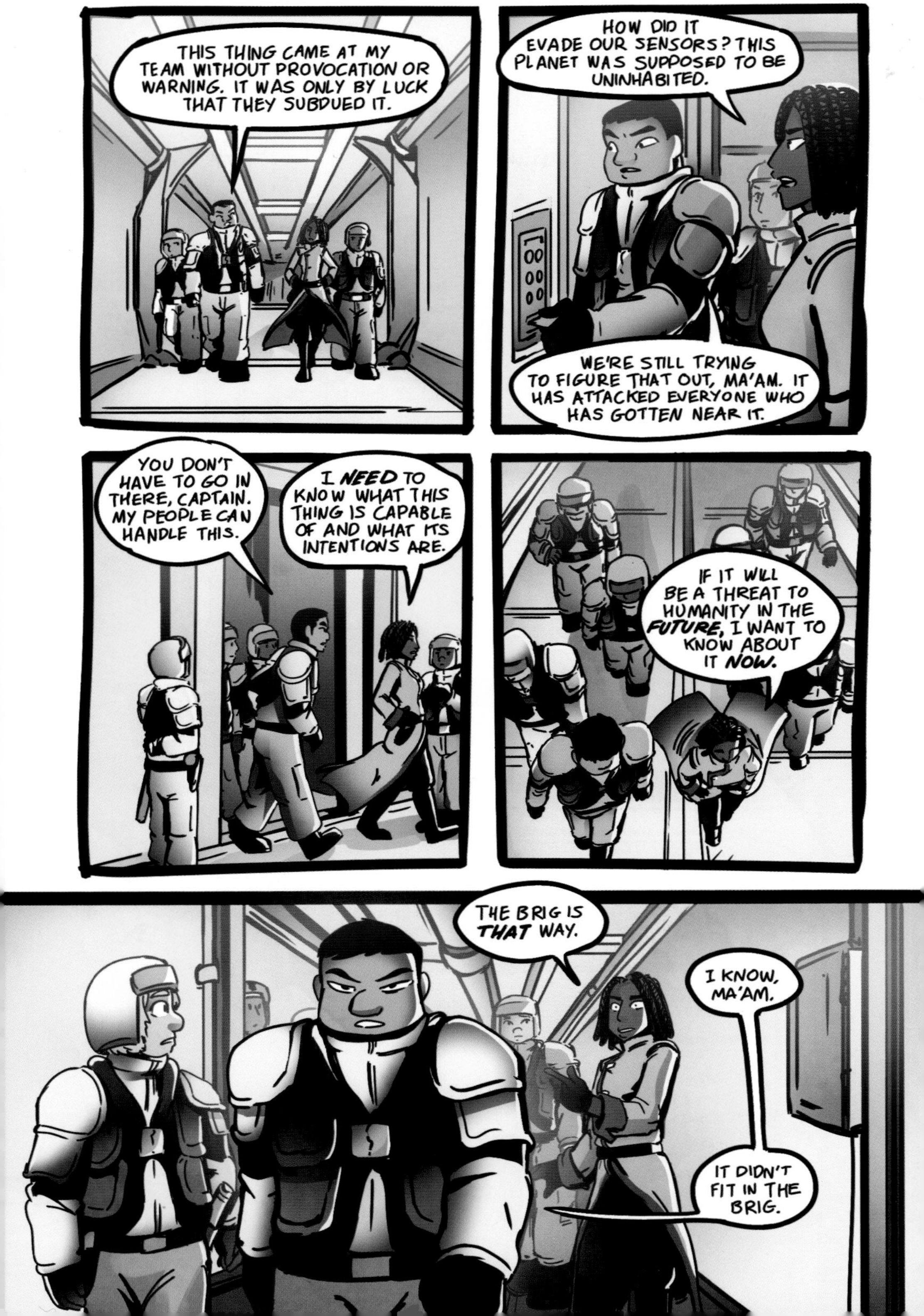
THIS THING CAME AT MY TEAM WITHOUT PROVOCATION OR WARNING. IT WAS ONLY BY LUCK THAT THEY SUBDUED IT.
HOW DID IT EVADE OUR SENSORS? THIS PLANET WAS SUPPOSED TO BE UNINHABITED.
WE'RE STILL TRYING TO FIGURE THAT OUT, MA'AM. IT HAS ATTACKED EVERYONE WHO HAS GOTTEN NEAR IT.
YOU DON'T HAVE TO GO IN THERE, CAPTAIN. MY PEOPLE CAN HANDLE THIS.
I NEED TO KNOW WHAT THIS THING IS CAPABLE OF AND WHAT ITS INTENTIONS ARE.
IF IT WILL BE A THREAT TO HUMANITY IN THE FUTURE, I WANT TO KNOW ABOUT IT NOW.
THE BRIG IS THAT WAY.
I KNOW, MA'AM.
IT DIDN'T FIT IN THE BRIG.

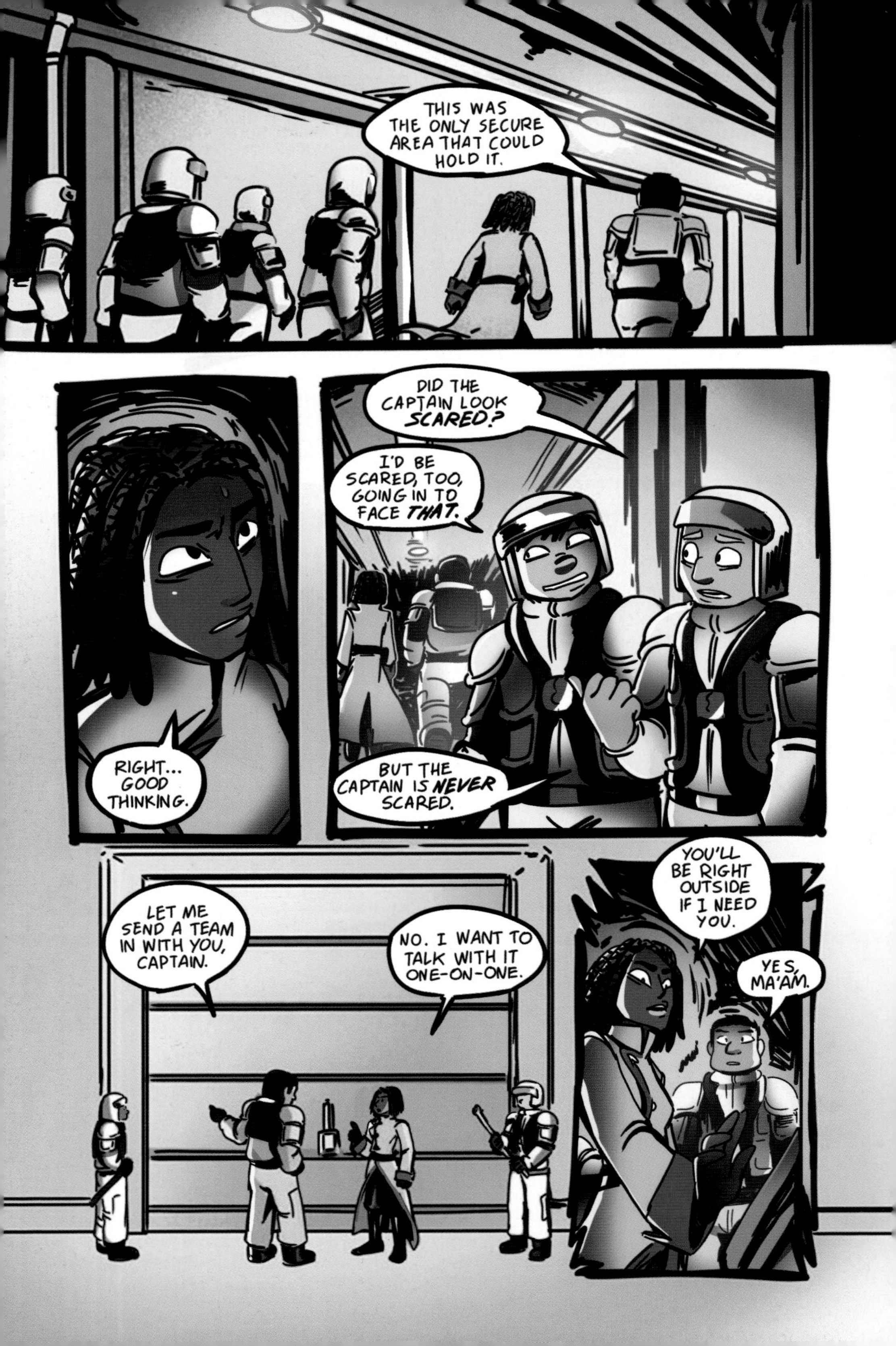
THIS WAS THE ONLY SECURE AREA THAT COULD HOLD IT.
DID THE CAPTAIN LOOK SCARED?
I'D BE SCARED, TOO, GOING IN TO FACE THAT.
RIGHT... GOOD THINKING.
BUT THE CAPTAIN IS NEVER SCARED.
LET ME SEND A TEAM IN WITH YOU, CAPTAIN.
NO. I WANT TO TALK WITH IT ONE-ON-ONE.
YOU'LL BE RIGHT OUTSIDE IF I NEED YOU.
YES, MA'AM.

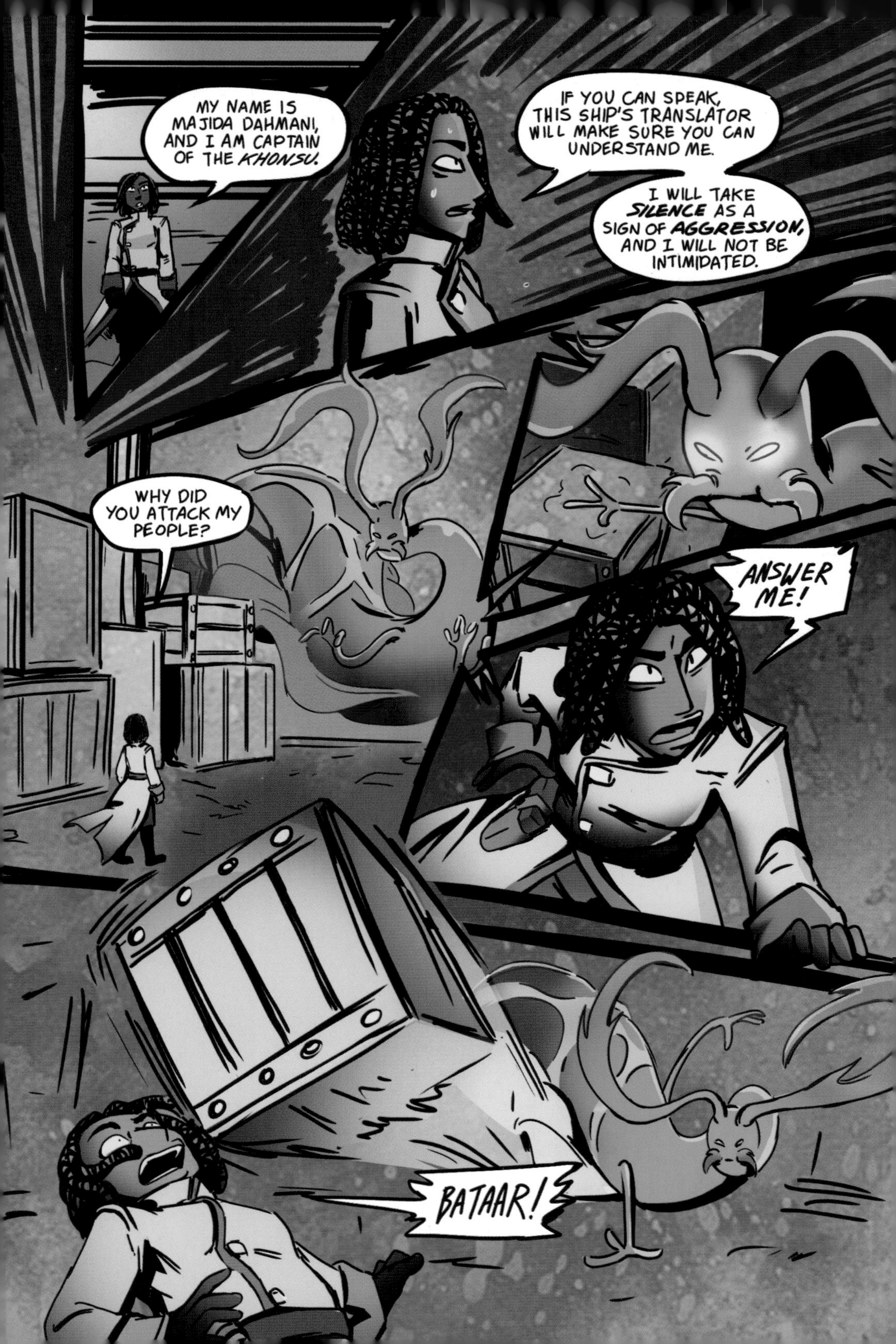
MY NAME IS MAJIDA DAHMANI, AND I AM CAPTAIN OF THE KHONSU.
IF YOU CAN SPEAK, THIS SHIP'S TRANSLATOR WILL MAKE SURE YOU CAN UNDERSTAND ME.
I WILL TAKE SILENCE AS A SIGN OF AGGRESSION, AND I WILL NOT BE INTIMIDATED.
WHY DID YOU ATTACK MY PEOPLE?
ANSWER ME!
BATAAR!

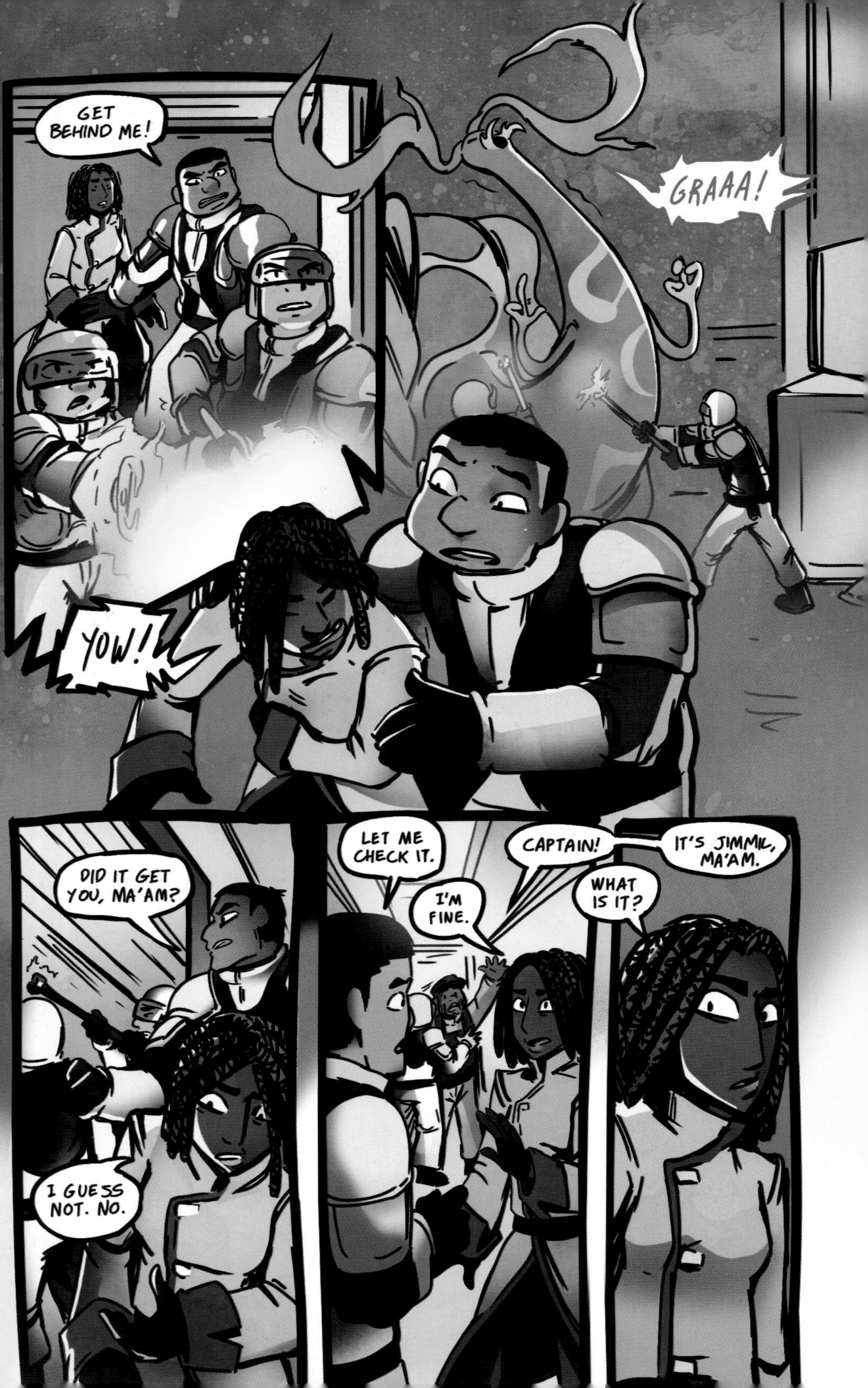
GET BEHIND ME!
GRAAA!
YOW!
DID IT GET YOU, MA'AM?
I GUESS NOT. NO.
LET ME CHECK IT.
I'M FINE.
CAPTAIN!
IT'S JIMMIL, MA'AM.
WHAT IS IT?

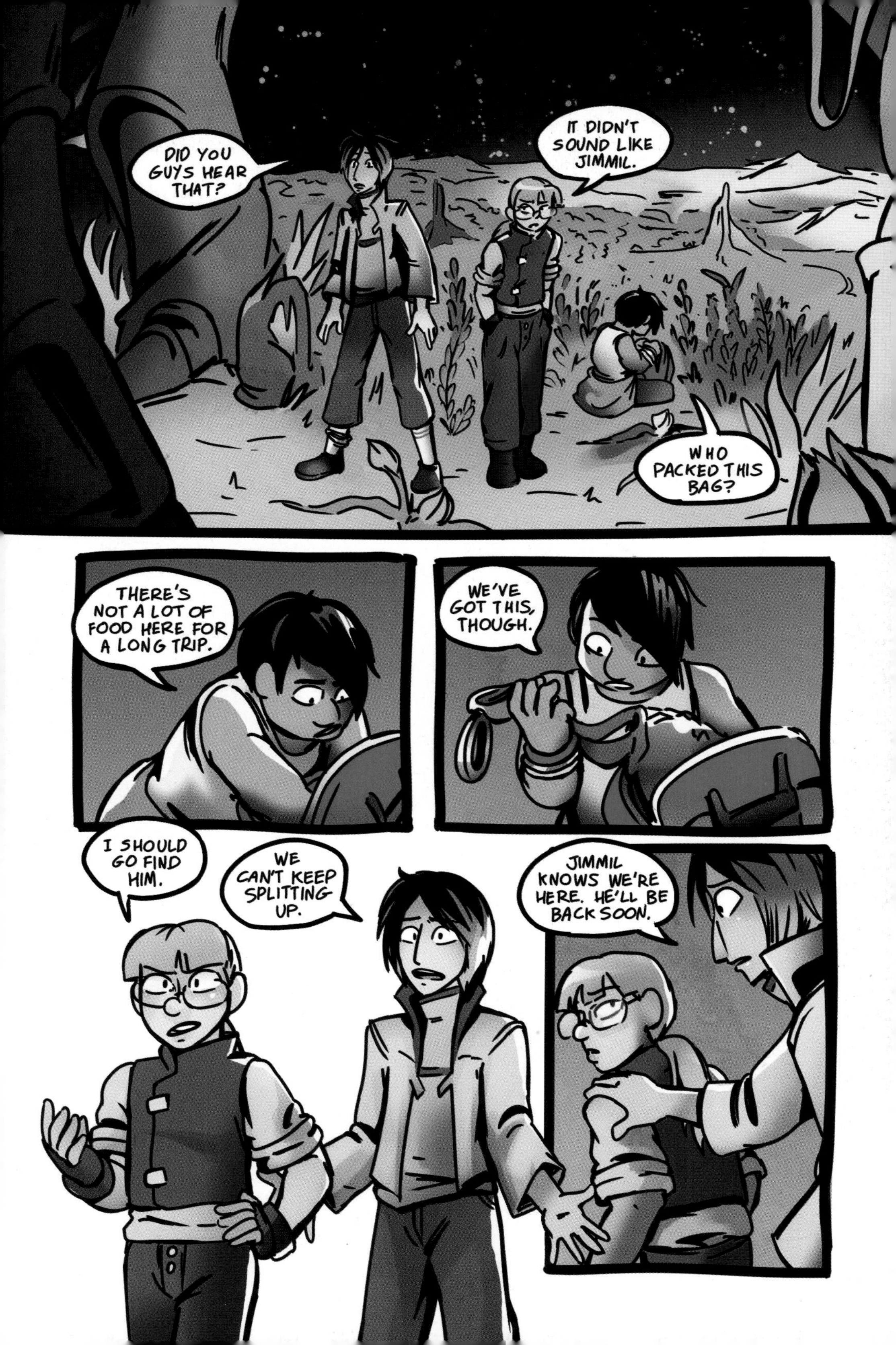
DID YOU GUYS HEAR THAT?
IT DIDN'T SOUND LIKE JIMMIL.
WHO PACKED THIS BAG?
THERE'S NOT A LOT OF FOOD HERE FOR A LONG TRIP.
WE'VE GOT THIS, THOUGH.
I SHOULD GO FIND HIM.
WE CAN'T KEEP SPLITTING UP.
JIMMIL KNOWS WE'RE HERE. HE'LL BE BACK SOON.

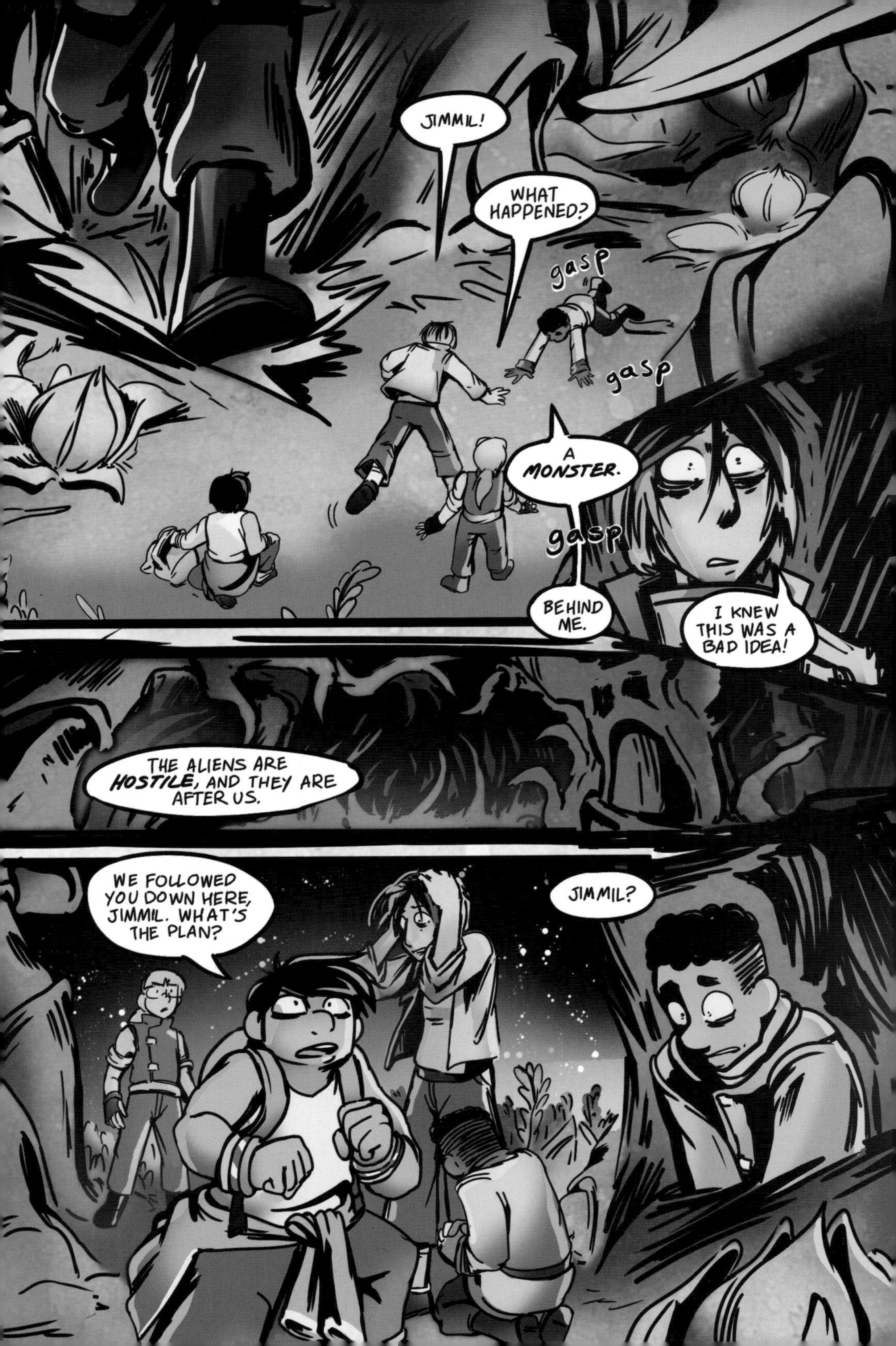
JIMMIL!
WHAT HAPPENED?
gasp
gasp
A MONSTER.
gasp
BEHIND ME.
I KNEW THIS WAS A BAD IDEA!
THE ALIENS ARE HOSTILE, AND THEY ARE AFTER US.
WE FOLLOWED YOU DOWN HERE, JIMMIL. WHAT'S THE PLAN?
JIMMIL?

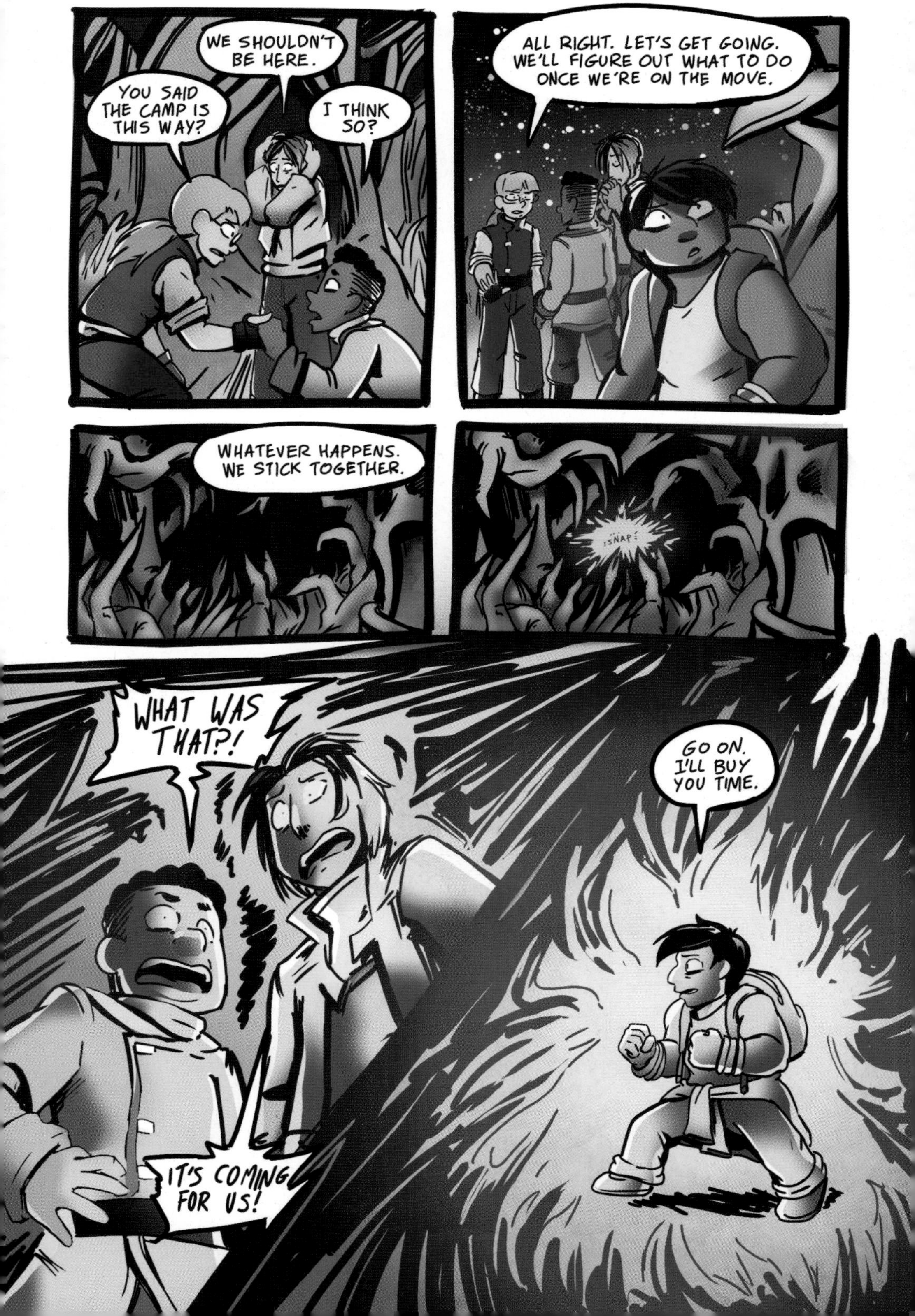
WE SHOULDN'T BE HERE.
YOU SAID THE CAMP IS THIS WAY?
I THINK SO?
ALL RIGHT. LET'S GET GOING. WE'LL FIGURE OUT WHAT TO DO ONCE WE'RE ON THE MOVE.
WHATEVER HAPPENS. WE STICK TOGETHER.
¡SNAP!
WHAT WAS THAT?!
IT'S COMING FOR US!
GO ON. I'LL BUY YOU TIME.

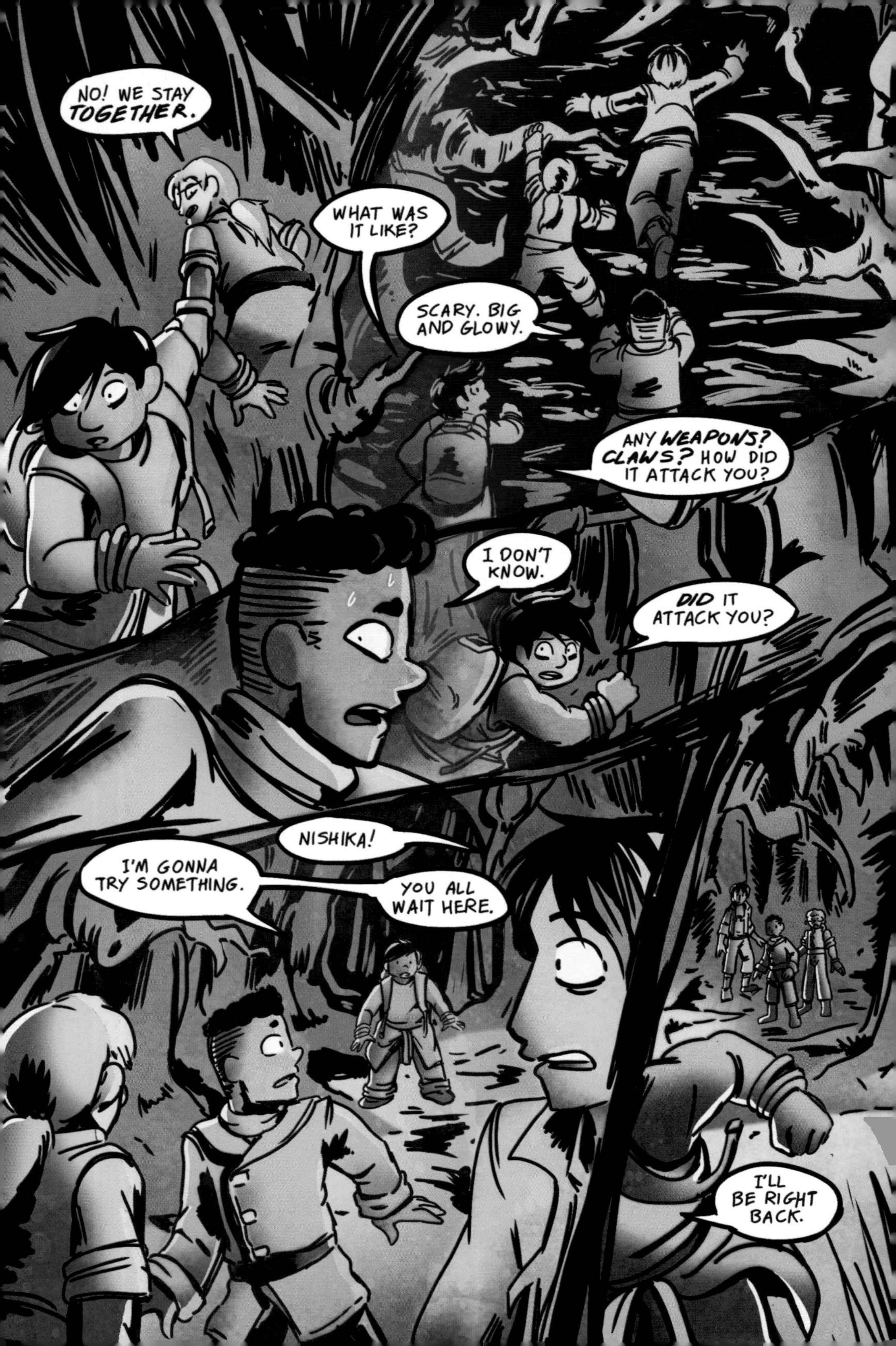
NO! WE STAY TOGETHER.
WHAT WAS IT LIKE?
SCARY. BIG AND GLOWY.
ANY WEAPONS? CLAWS? HOW DID IT ATTACK YOU?
I DON'T KNOW.
DID IT ATTACK YOU?
NISHIKA!
I'M GONNA TRY SOMETHING.
YOU ALL WAIT HERE.
I'LL BE RIGHT BACK.

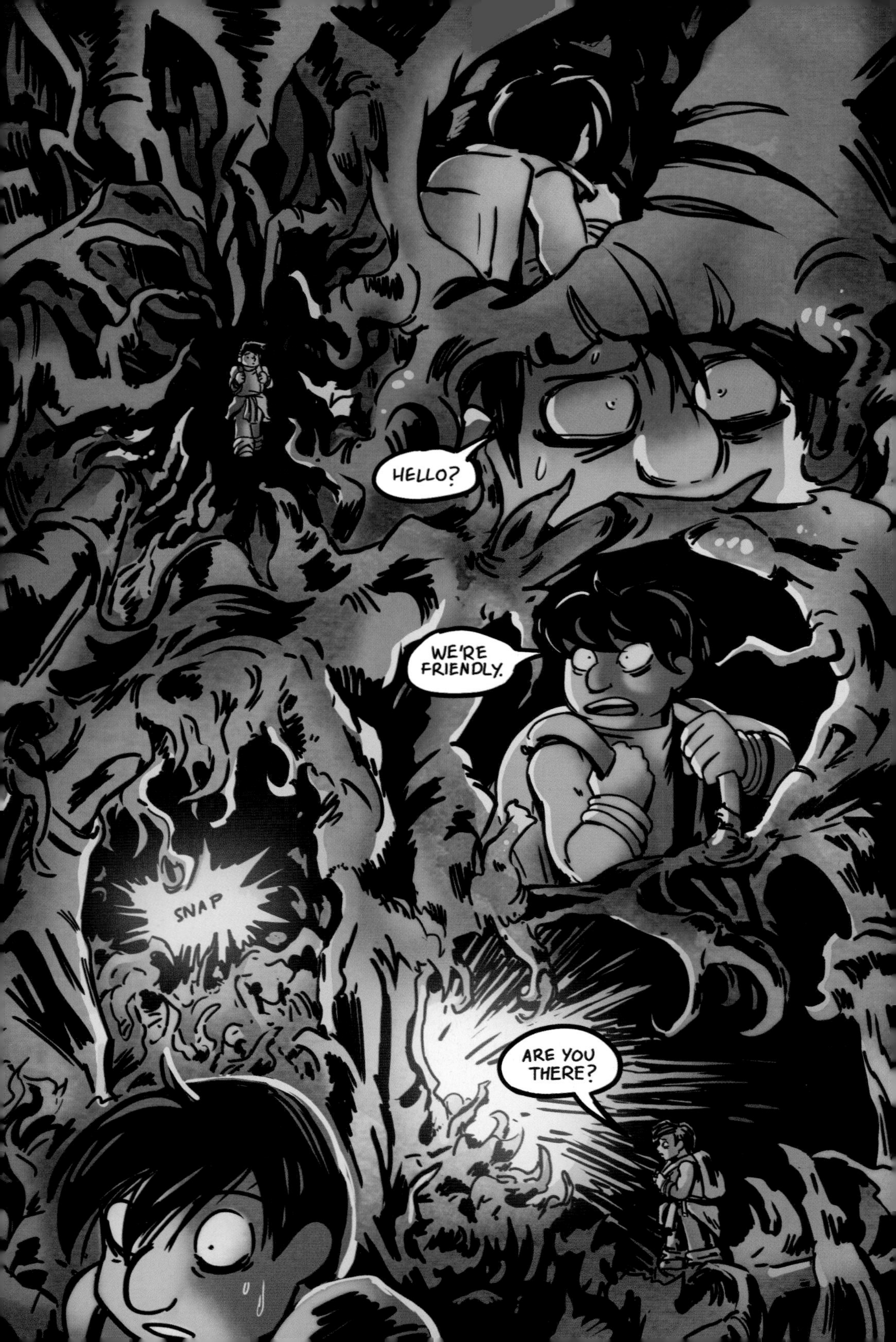
HELLO?
WE'RE FRIENDLY.
SNAP
ARE YOU THERE?

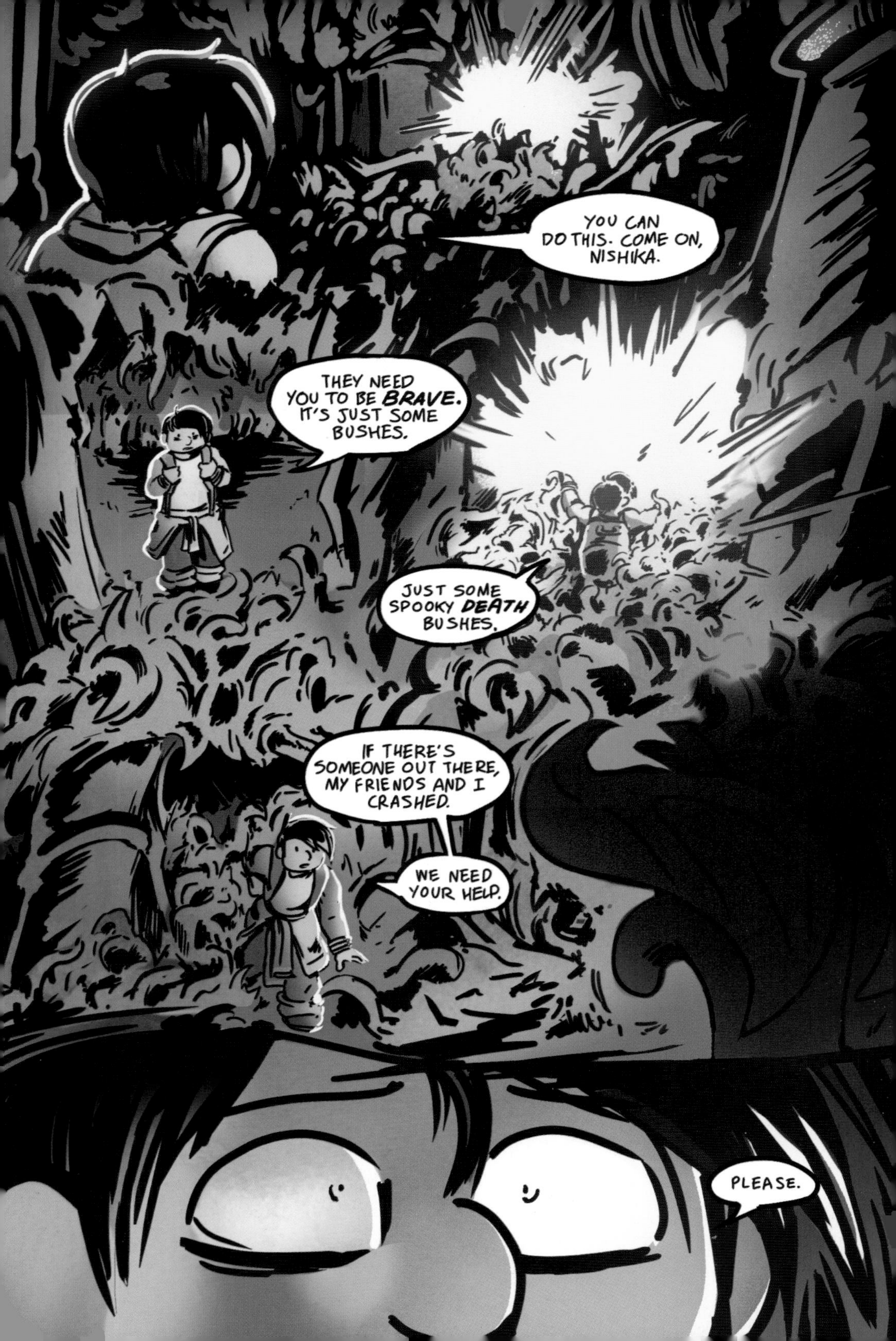
YOU CAN DO THIS. COME ON, NISHIKA.
THEY NEED YOU TO BE BRAVE. IT'S JUST SOME BUSHES.
JUST SOME SPOOKY DEATH BUSHES.
IF THERE'S SOMEONE OUT THERE, MY FRIENDS AND I CRASHED.
WE NEED YOUR HELP.
PLEASE.

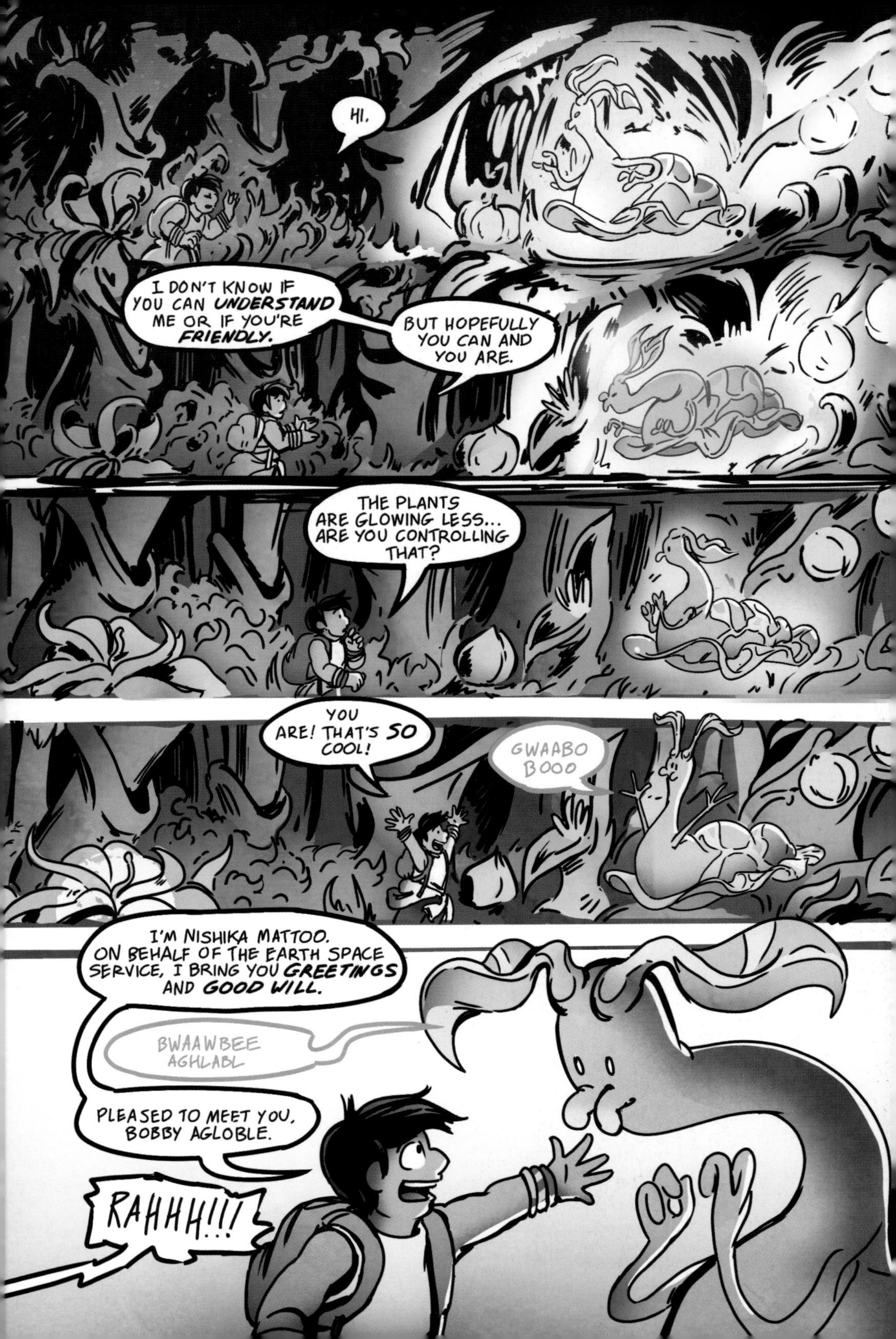
HI.
I DON'T KNOW IF YOU CAN UNDERSTAND ME OR IF YOU'RE FRIENDLY.
BUT HOPEFULLY YOU CAN AND YOU ARE.
THE PLANTS ARE GLOWING LESS... ARE YOU CONTROLLING THAT?
YOU ARE! THAT'S SO COOL!
GWAABO BOOO
I'M NISHIKA MATTOO. ON BEHALF OF THE EARTH SPACE SERVICE, I BRING YOU GREETINGS AND GOOD WILL.
BWAAWBEE AGHLABL
PLEASED TO MEET YOU, BOBBY AGLOBLE.
RAHHH!!!

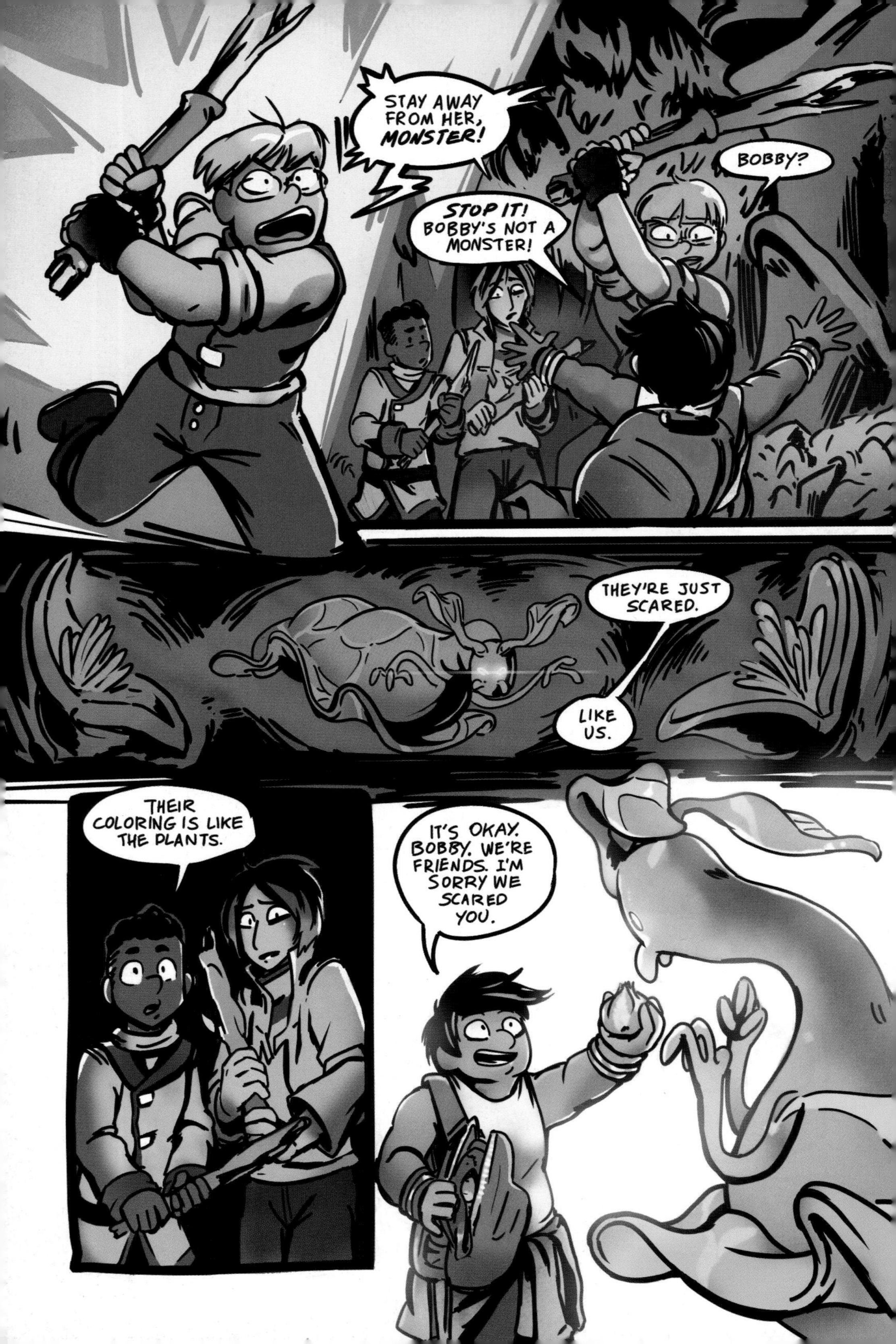
STAY AWAY FROM HER, MONSTER!
BOBBY?
STOP IT! BOBBY'S NOT A MONSTER!
THEY'RE JUST SCARED.
LIKE US.
THEIR COLORING IS LIKE THE PLANTS.
IT'S OKAY. BOBBY. WE'RE FRIENDS. I'M SORRY WE SCARED YOU.

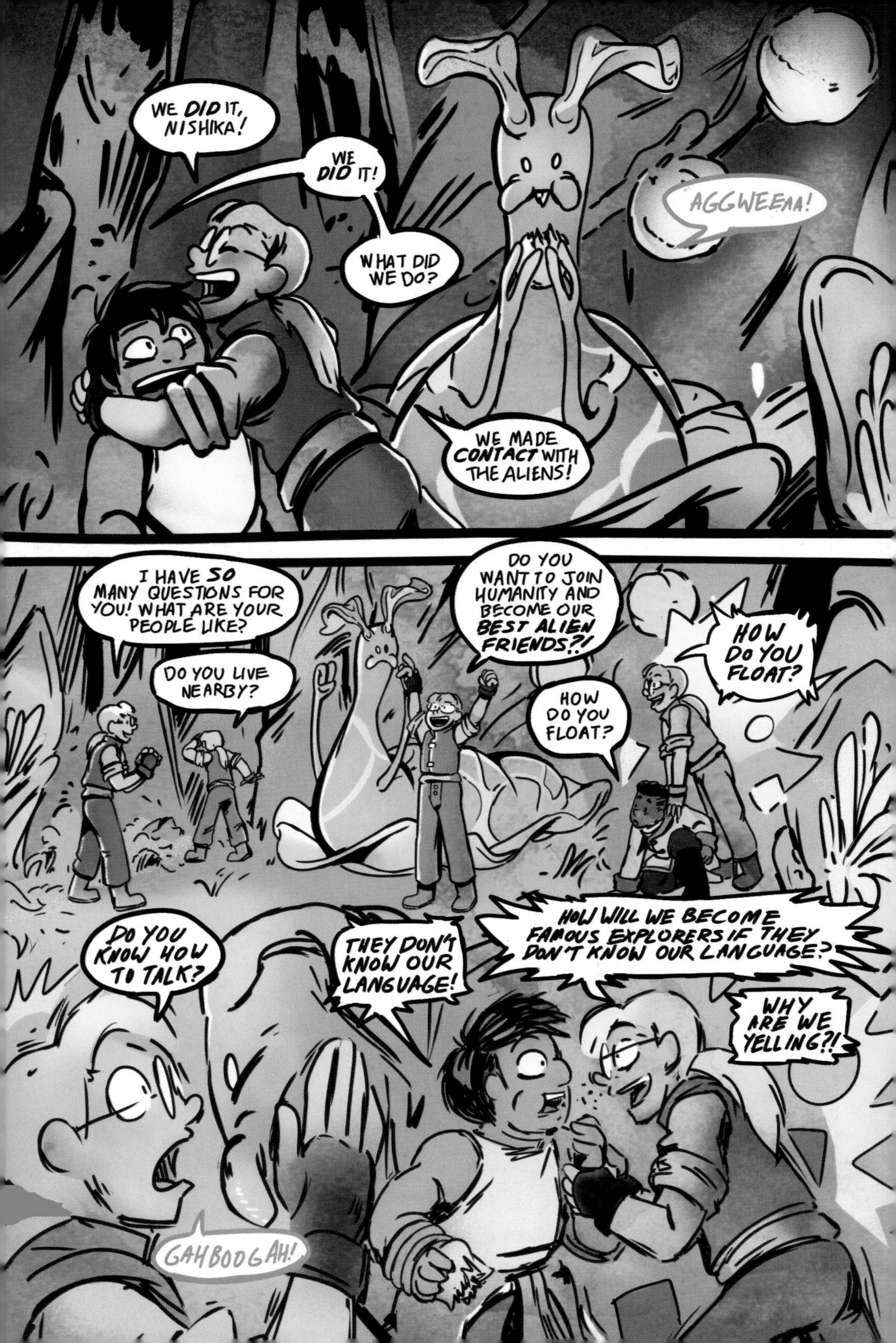
WE DID IT, NISHIKA!
WE DID IT!
WHAT DID WE DO?
AGGWEEAA!
WE MADE CONTACT WITH THE ALIENS!
I HAVE SO MANY QUESTIONS FOR YOU! WHAT ARE YOUR PEOPLE LIKE?
DO YOU LIVE NEARBY?
DO YOU WANT TO JOIN HUMANITY AND BECOME OUR BEST ALIEN FRIENDS?!
HOW DO YOU FLOAT?
HOW DO YOU FLOAT?
DO YOU KNOW HOW TO TALK?
THEY DON'T KNOW OUR LANGUAGE!
HOW WILL WE BECOME FAMOUS EXPLORERS IF THEY DON'T KNOW OUR LANGUAGE?
WHY ARE WE YELLING?!
GAHBOOGAH!

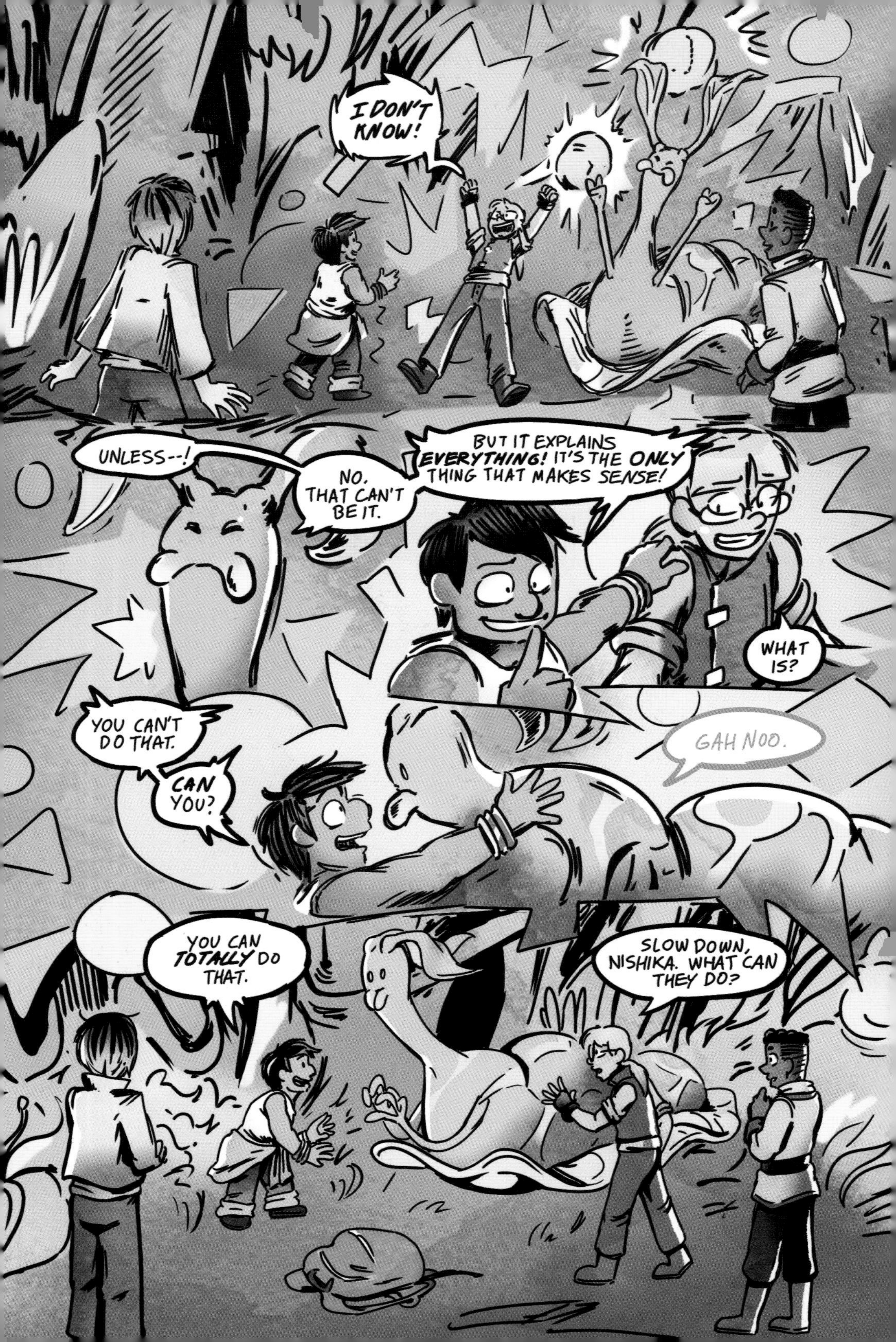
I DON'T KNOW!
UNLESS--!
NO. THAT CAN'T BE IT.
BUT IT EXPLAINS EVERYTHING! IT'S THE ONLY THING THAT MAKES SENSE!
WHAT IS?
YOU CAN'T DO THAT.
CAN YOU?
GAH NOO.
YOU CAN TOTALLY DO THAT.
SLOW DOWN, NISHIKA. WHAT CAN THEY DO?

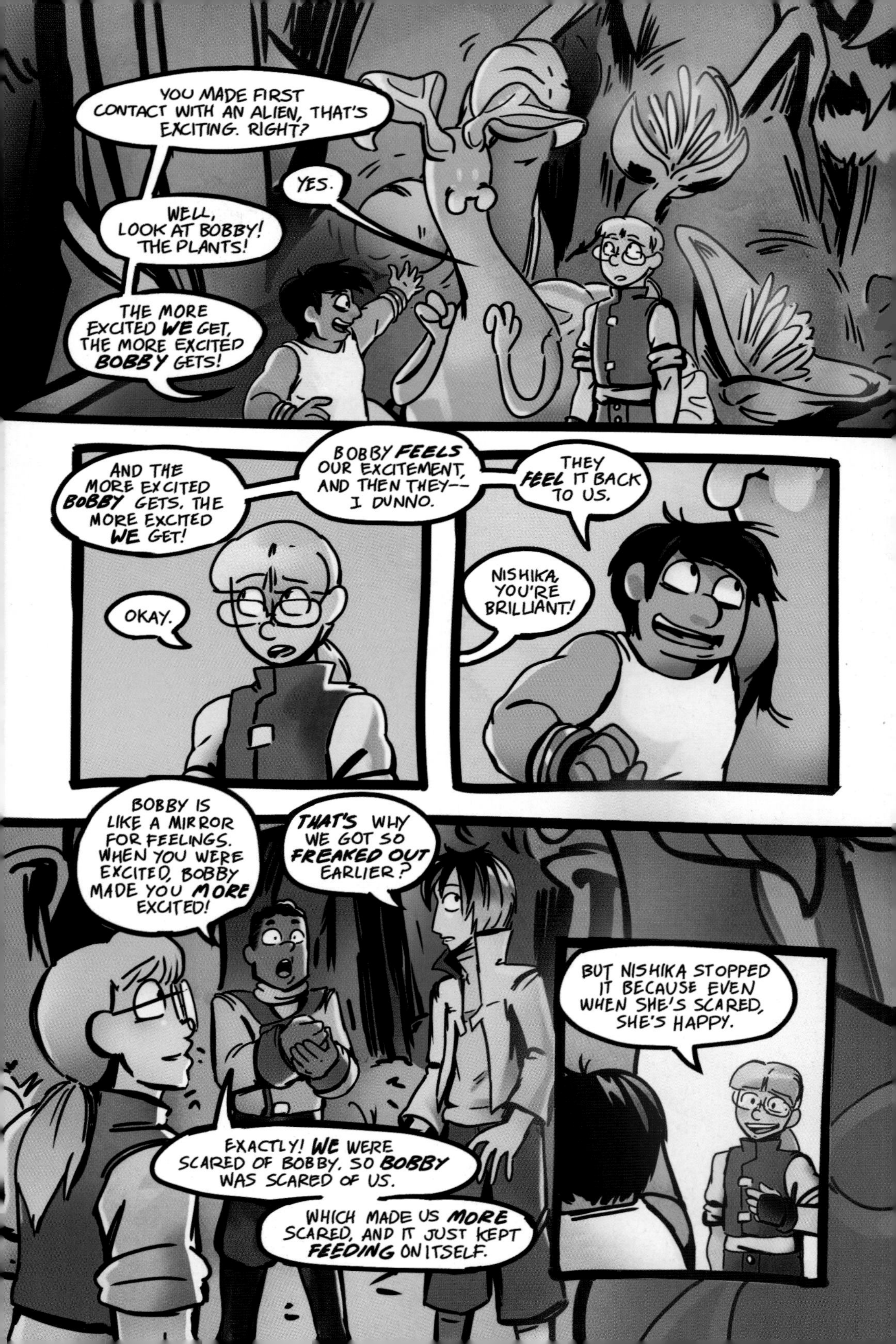
YOU MADE FIRST CONTACT WITH AN ALIEN, THAT'S EXCITING. RIGHT?
YES.
WELL, LOOK AT BOBBY! THE PLANTS!
THE MORE EXCITED **WE** GET, THE MORE EXCITED **BOBBY** GETS!
AND THE MORE EXCITED **BOBBY** GETS, THE MORE EXCITED **WE** GET!
BOBBY **FEELS** OUR EXCITEMENT, AND THEN THEY-- I DUNNO.
THEY **FEEL** IT BACK TO US.
OKAY.
NISHIKA, YOU'RE BRILLIANT!
BOBBY IS LIKE A MIRROR FOR FEELINGS. WHEN YOU WERE EXCITED, BOBBY MADE YOU **MORE** EXCITED!
THAT'S WHY WE GOT SO **FREAKED OUT** EARLIER?
EXACTLY! **WE** WERE SCARED OF BOBBY, SO **BOBBY** WAS SCARED OF US.
WHICH MADE US **MORE** SCARED, AND IT JUST KEPT **FEEDING** ON ITSELF.
BUT NISHIKA STOPPED IT BECAUSE EVEN WHEN SHE'S SCARED, SHE'S HAPPY.

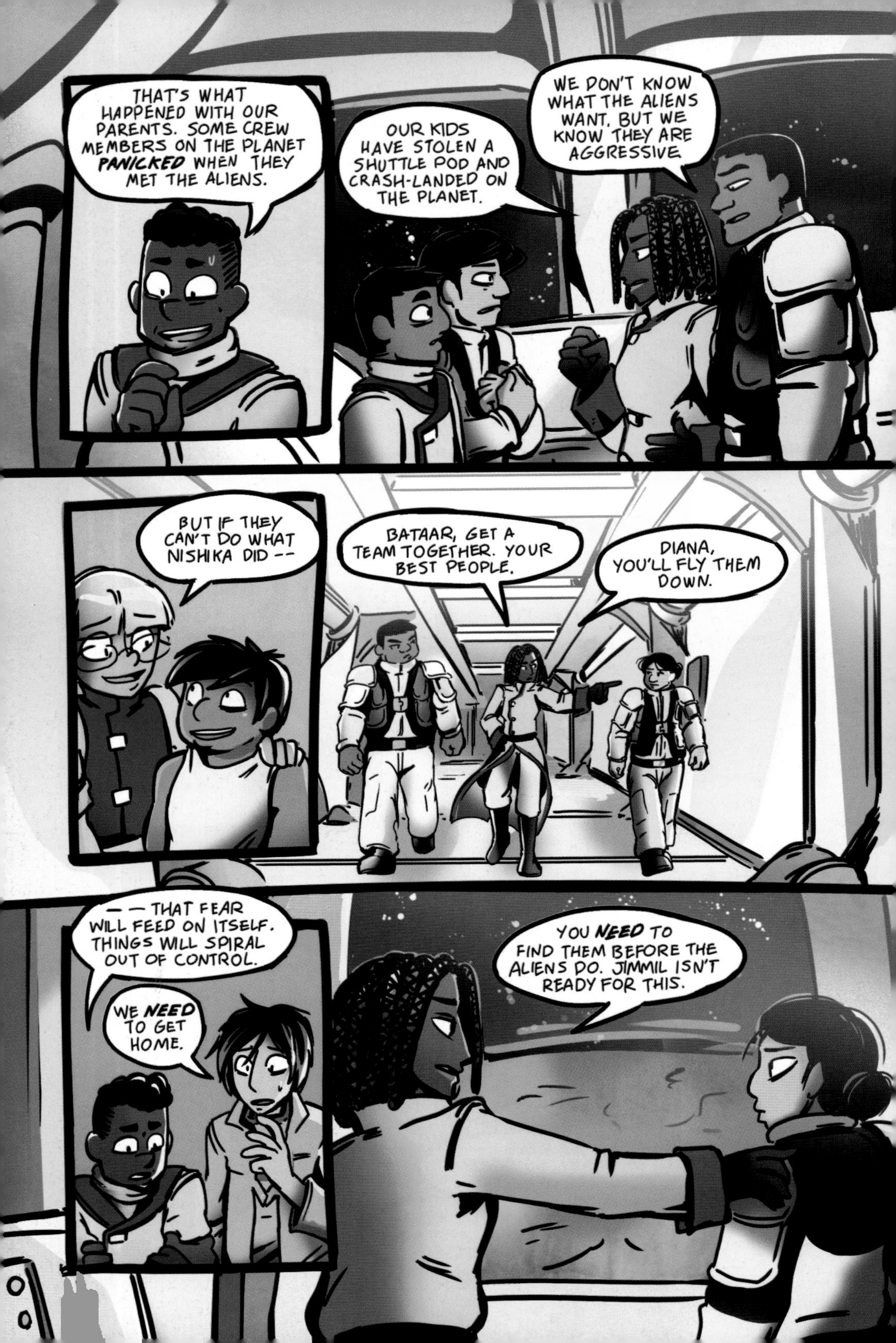
THAT'S WHAT HAPPENED WITH OUR PARENTS. SOME CREW MEMBERS ON THE PLANET **PANICKED** WHEN THEY MET THE ALIENS.
OUR KIDS HAVE STOLEN A SHUTTLE POD AND CRASH-LANDED ON THE PLANET.
WE DON'T KNOW WHAT THE ALIENS WANT, BUT WE KNOW THEY ARE AGGRESSIVE
BUT IF THEY CAN'T DO WHAT NISHIKA DID --
BATAAR, GET A TEAM TOGETHER. YOUR BEST PEOPLE.
DIANA, YOU'LL FLY THEM DOWN.
-- THAT FEAR WILL FEED ON ITSELF. THINGS WILL SPIRAL OUT OF CONTROL.
WE **NEED** TO GET HOME.
YOU **NEED** TO FIND THEM BEFORE THE ALIENS DO. JIMMIL ISN'T READY FOR THIS.

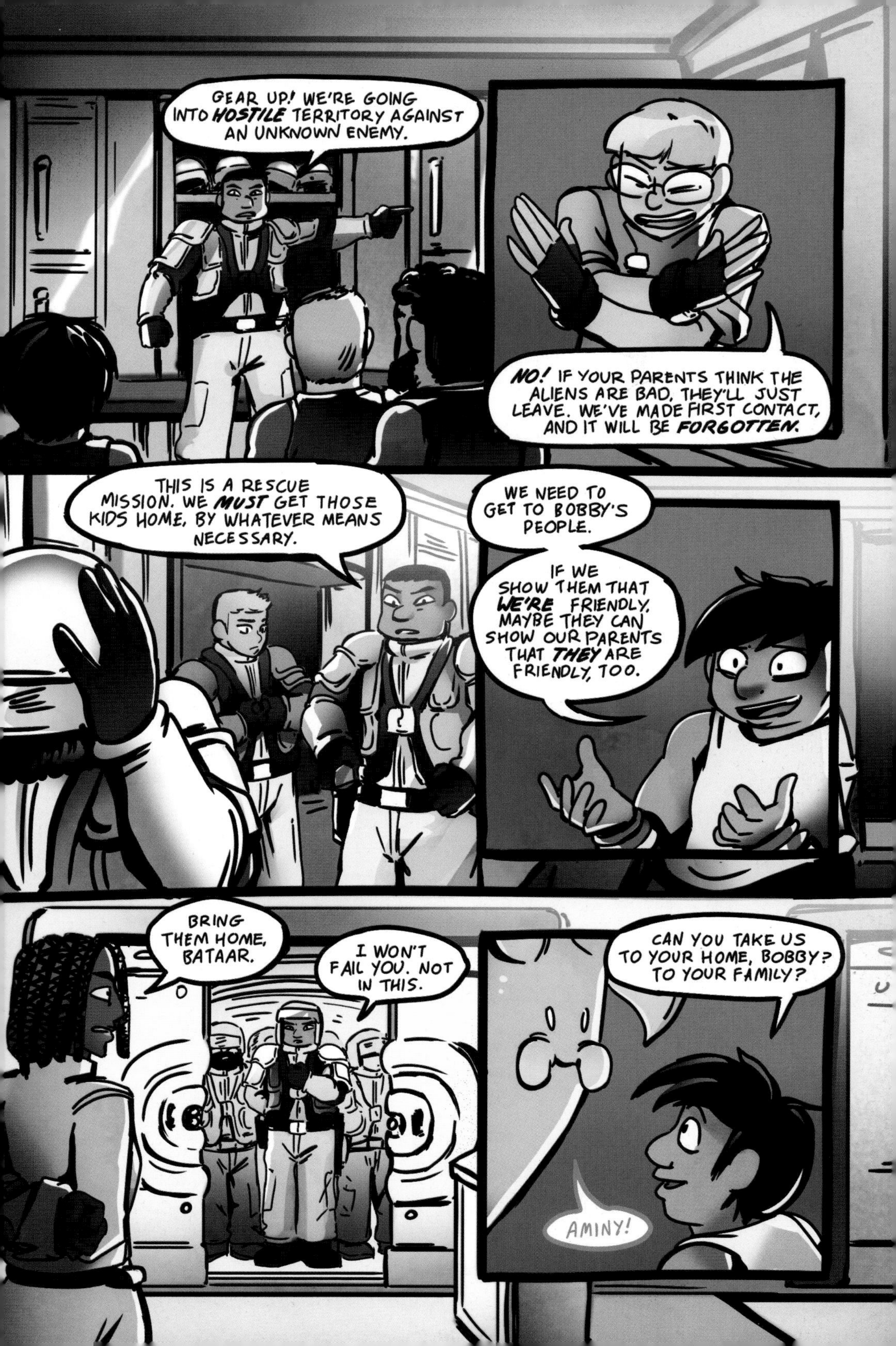
GEAR UP! WE'RE GOING INTO HOSTILE TERRITORY AGAINST AN UNKNOWN ENEMY.
NO! IF YOUR PARENTS THINK THE ALIENS ARE BAD, THEY'LL JUST LEAVE. WE'VE MADE FIRST CONTACT, AND IT WILL BE FORGOTTEN.
THIS IS A RESCUE MISSION. WE MUST GET THOSE KIDS HOME, BY WHATEVER MEANS NECESSARY.
WE NEED TO GET TO BOBBY'S PEOPLE.
IF WE SHOW THEM THAT WE'RE FRIENDLY, MAYBE THEY CAN SHOW OUR PARENTS THAT THEY ARE FRIENDLY, TOO.
BRING THEM HOME, BATAAR.
I WON'T FAIL YOU. NOT IN THIS.
CAN YOU TAKE US TO YOUR HOME, BOBBY? TO YOUR FAMILY?
AMINY!

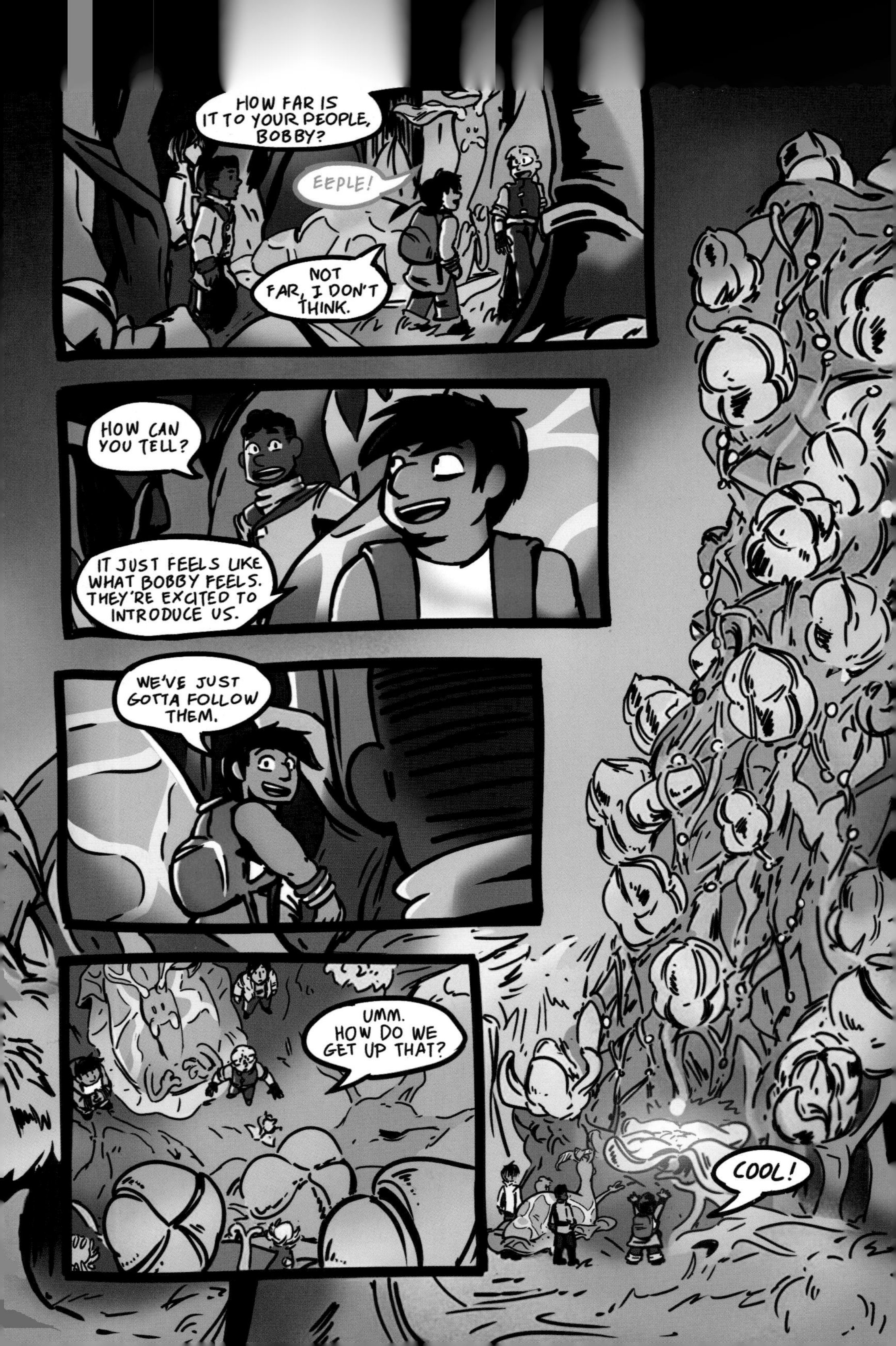
HOW FAR IS IT TO YOUR PEOPLE, BOBBY?
EEPLE!
NOT FAR, I DON'T THINK.
HOW CAN YOU TELL?
IT JUST FEELS LIKE WHAT BOBBY FEELS. THEY'RE EXCITED TO INTRODUCE US.
WE'VE JUST GOTTA FOLLOW THEM.
UMM. HOW DO WE GET UP THAT?
COOL!

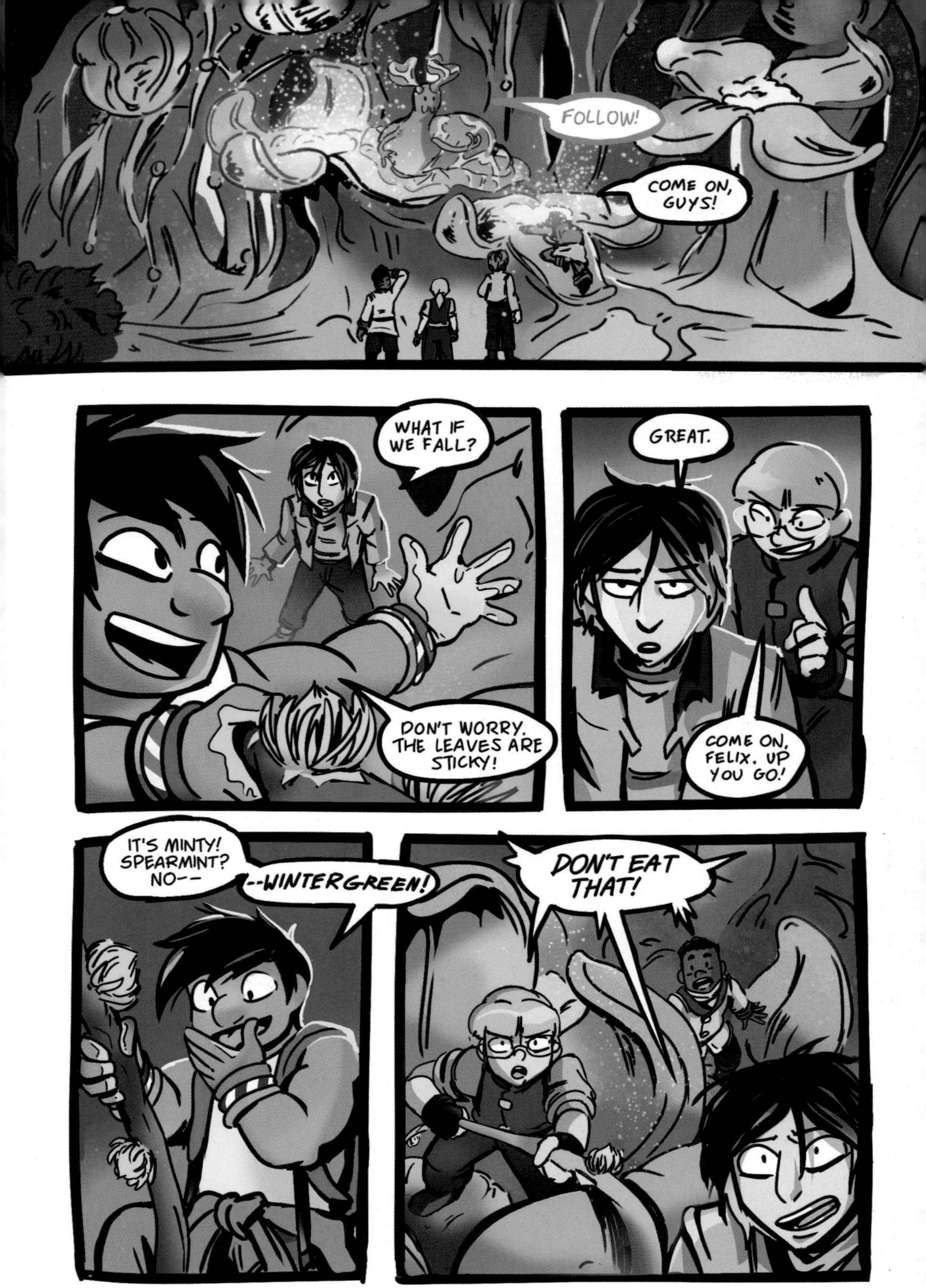
FOLLOW!
COME ON, GUYS!
WHAT IF WE FALL?
DON'T WORRY. THE LEAVES ARE STICKY!
GREAT.
COME ON, FELIX. UP YOU GO!
IT'S MINTY! SPEARMINT? NO--
--WINTERGREEN!
DON'T EAT THAT!

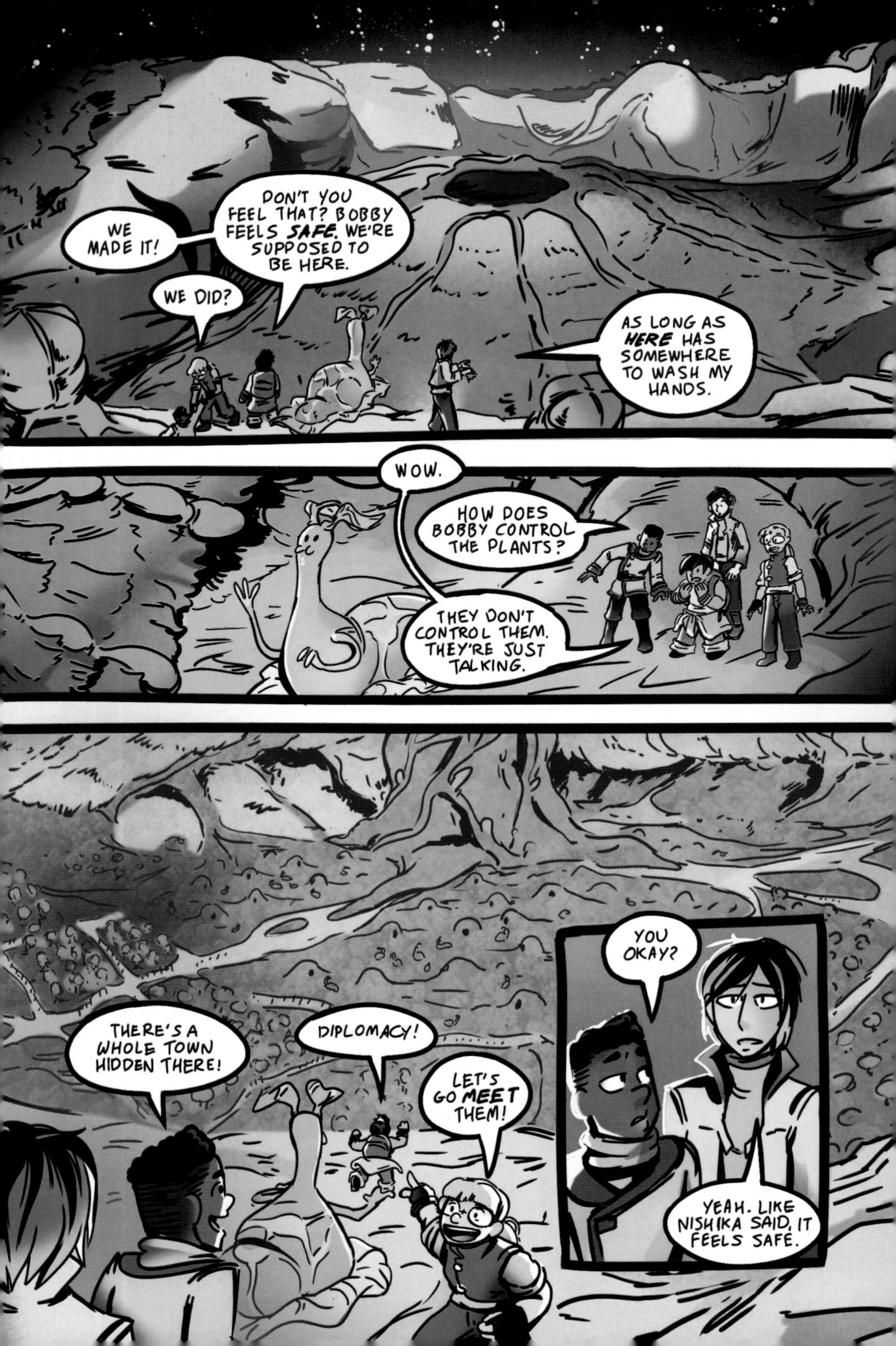
WE MADE IT!
DON'T YOU FEEL THAT? BOBBY FEELS SAFE. WE'RE SUPPOSED TO BE HERE.
WE DID?
AS LONG AS HERE HAS SOMEWHERE TO WASH MY HANDS.
WOW.
HOW DOES BOBBY CONTROL THE PLANTS?
THEY DON'T CONTROL THEM. THEY'RE JUST TALKING.
THERE'S A WHOLE TOWN HIDDEN THERE!
DIPLOMACY!
LET'S GO MEET THEM!
YOU OKAY?
YEAH. LIKE NISHIKA SAID, IT FEELS SAFE.

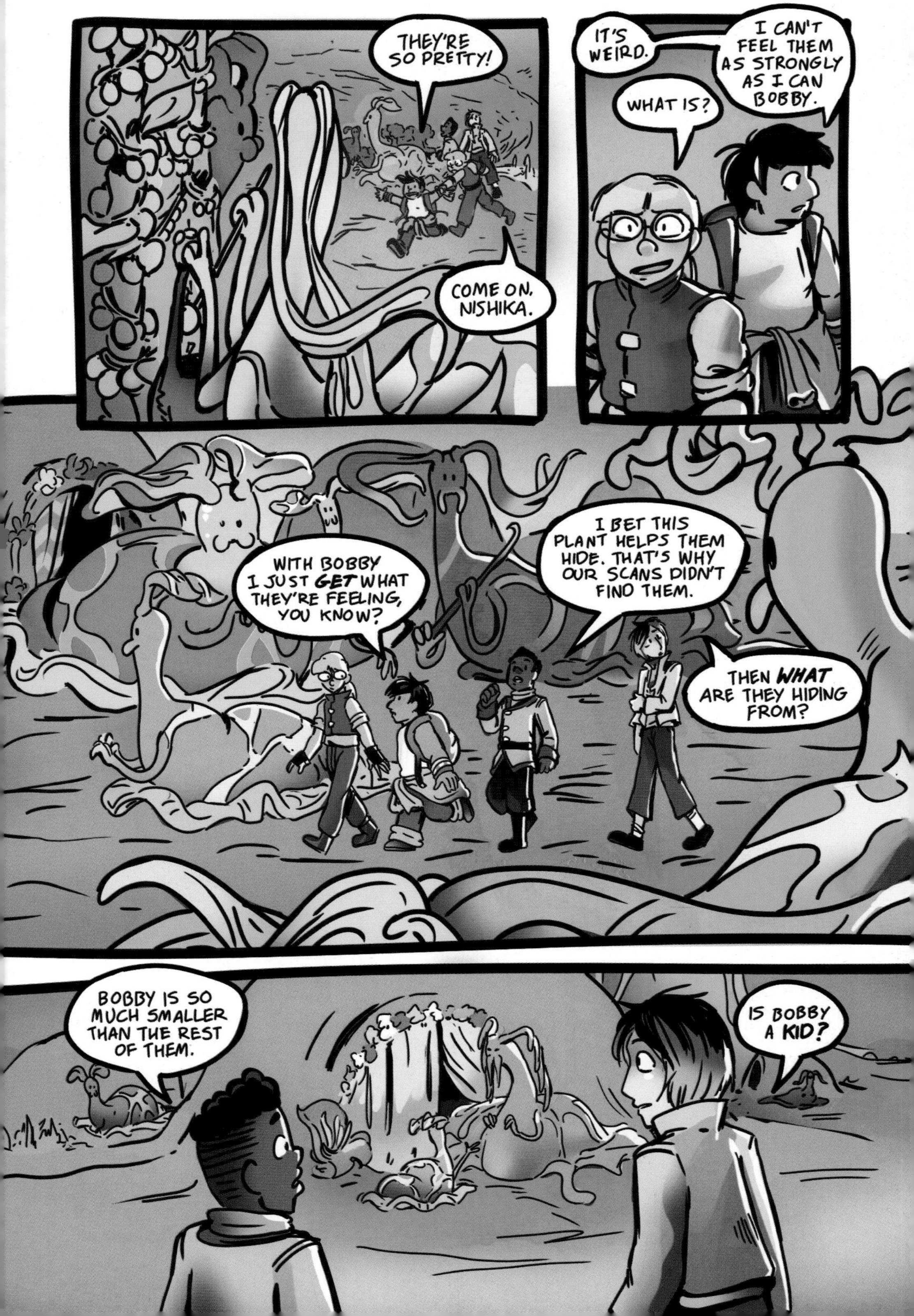
THEY'RE SO PRETTY!
COME ON, NISHIKA.
IT'S WEIRD.
I CAN'T FEEL THEM AS STRONGLY AS I CAN BOBBY.
WHAT IS?
WITH BOBBY I JUST **GET** WHAT THEY'RE FEELING, YOU KNOW?
I BET THIS PLANT HELPS THEM HIDE. THAT'S WHY OUR SCANS DIDN'T FIND THEM.
THEN **WHAT** ARE THEY HIDING FROM?
BOBBY IS SO MUCH SMALLER THAN THE REST OF THEM.
IS BOBBY A **KID?**

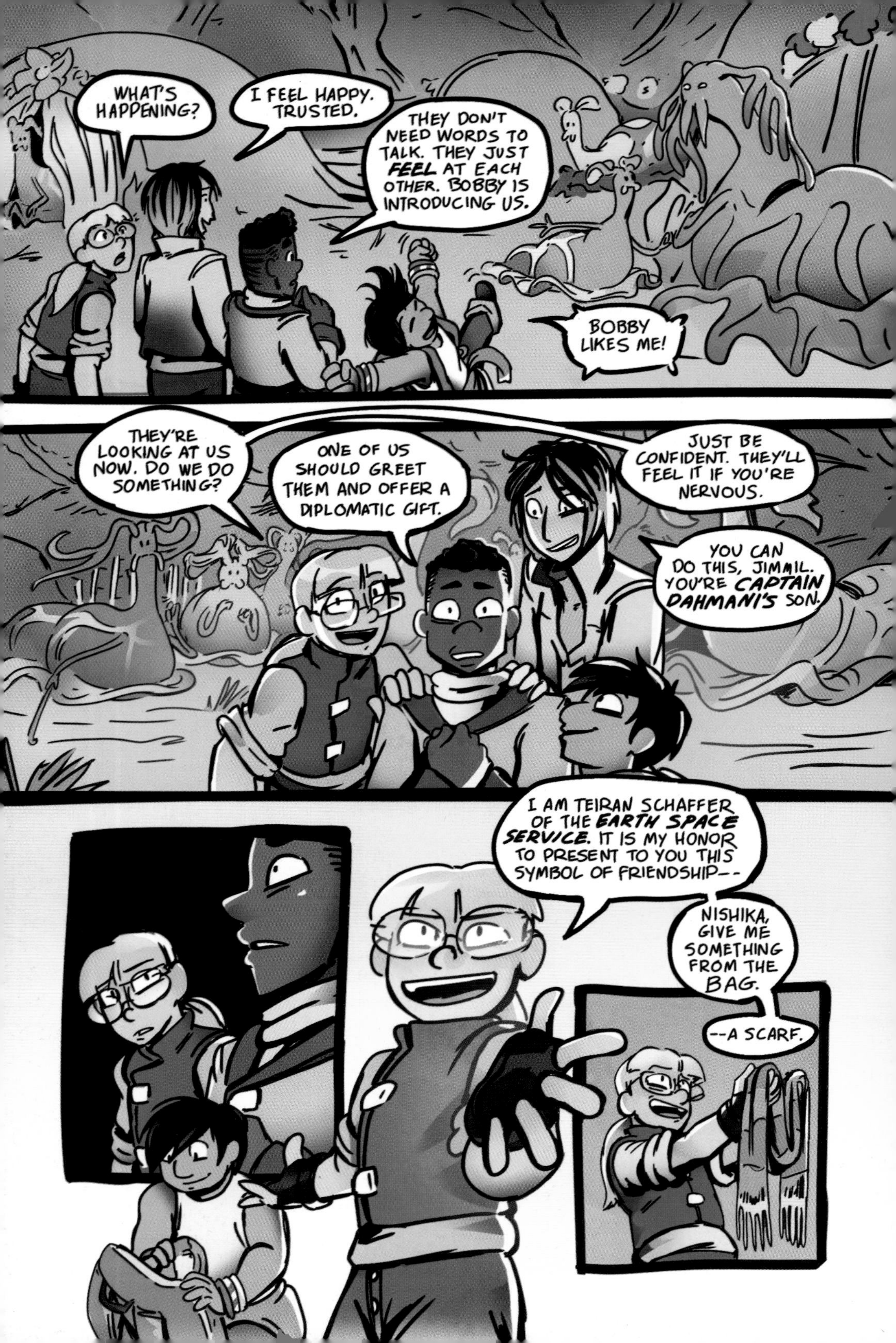
WHAT'S HAPPENING?
I FEEL HAPPY. TRUSTED.
THEY DON'T NEED WORDS TO TALK. THEY JUST FEEL AT EACH OTHER. BOBBY IS INTRODUCING US.
BOBBY LIKES ME!
THEY'RE LOOKING AT US NOW. DO WE DO SOMETHING?
ONE OF US SHOULD GREET THEM AND OFFER A DIPLOMATIC GIFT.
JUST BE CONFIDENT. THEY'LL FEEL IT IF YOU'RE NERVOUS.
YOU CAN DO THIS, JIMMIL. YOU'RE CAPTAIN DAHMANI'S SON.
I AM TEIRAN SCHAFFER OF THE EARTH SPACE SERVICE. IT IS MY HONOR TO PRESENT TO YOU THIS SYMBOL OF FRIENDSHIP--
NISHIKA, GIVE ME SOMETHING FROM THE BAG.
--A SCARF.

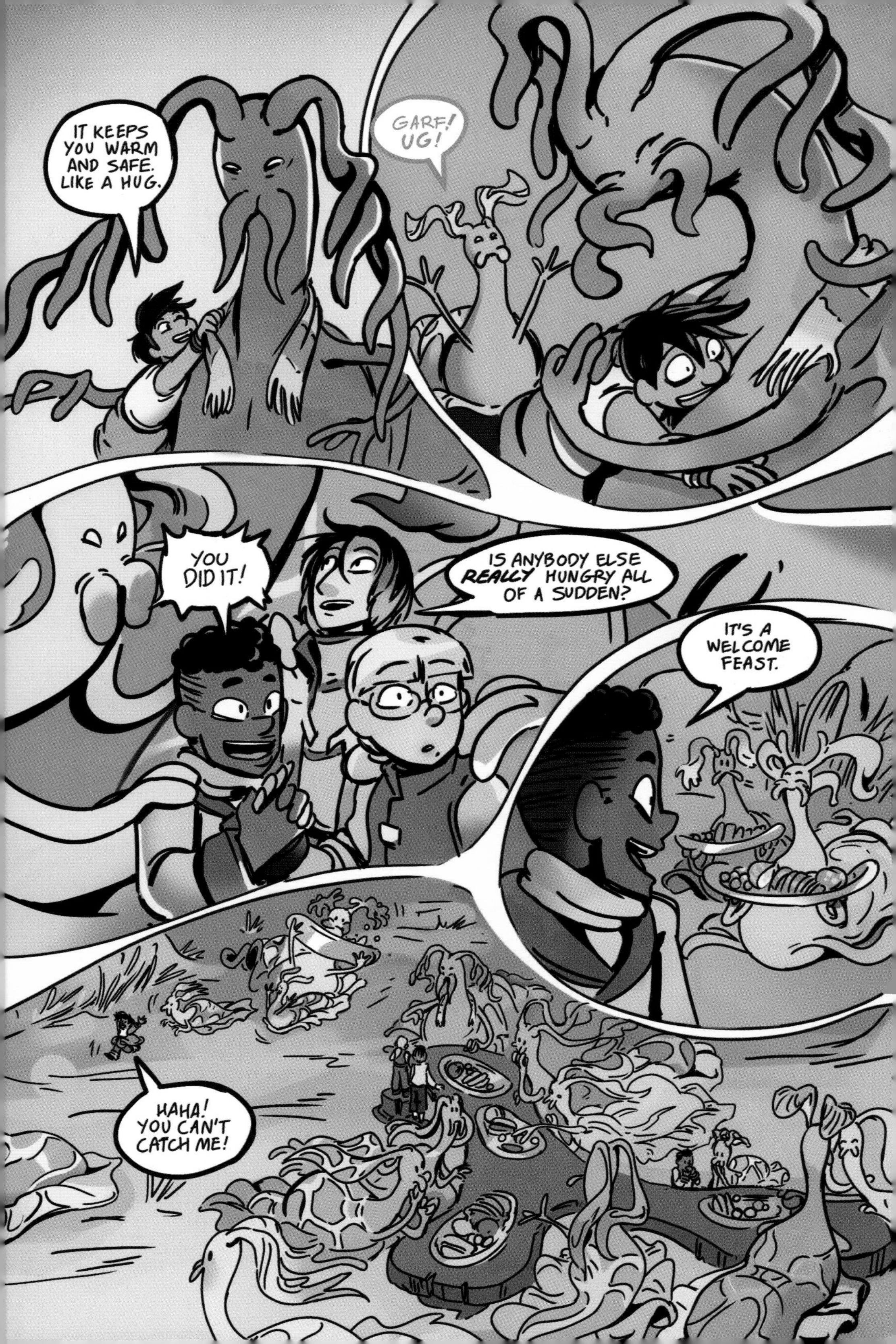
IT KEEPS YOU WARM AND SAFE. LIKE A HUG.
GARF! UG!
YOU DID IT!
IS ANYBODY ELSE REALLY HUNGRY ALL OF A SUDDEN?
IT'S A WELCOME FEAST.
HAHA! YOU CAN'T CATCH ME!

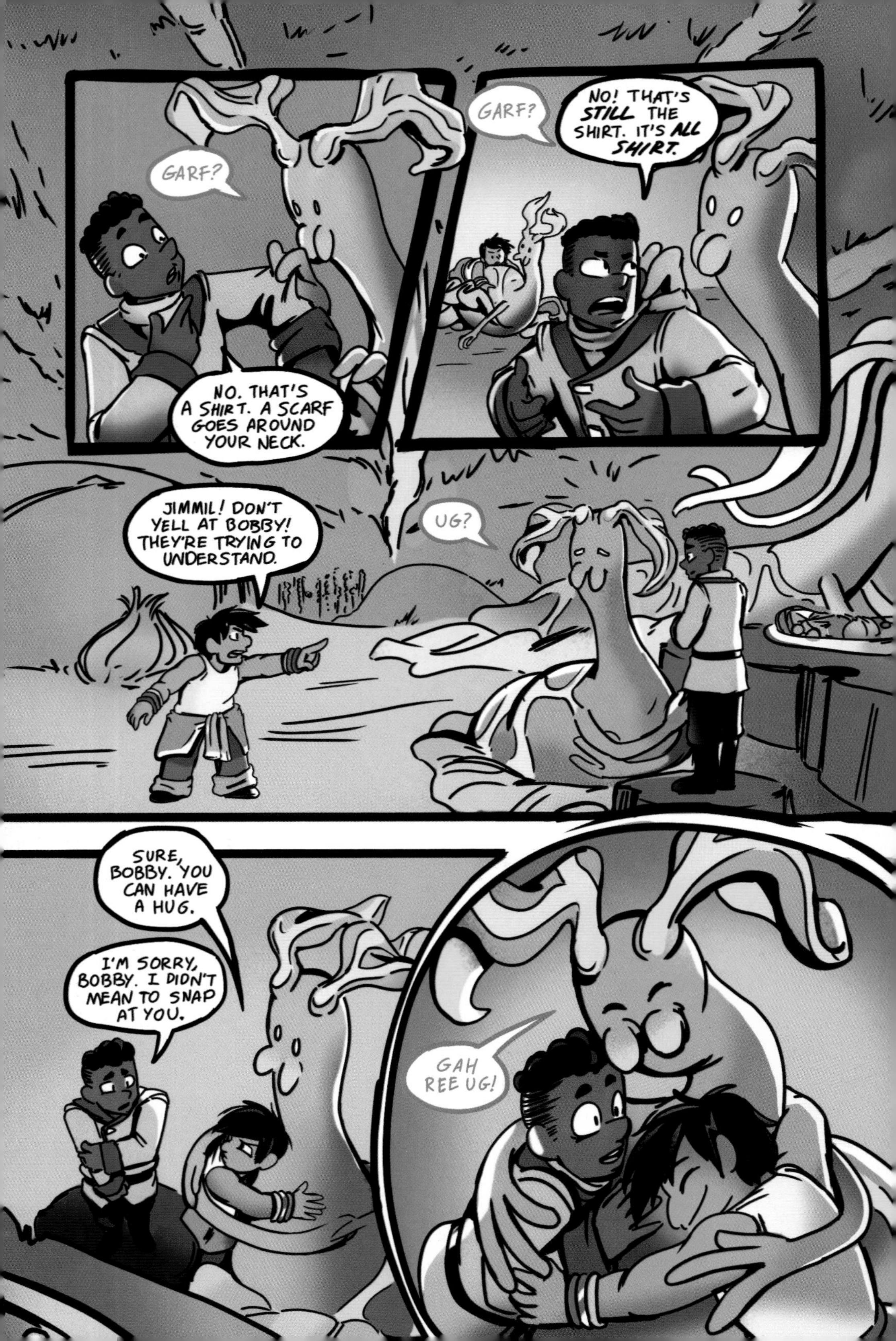
GARF?
NO. THAT'S A SHIRT. A SCARF GOES AROUND YOUR NECK.
GARF?
NO! THAT'S **STILL** THE SHIRT. IT'S **ALL SHIRT.**
JIMMIL! DON'T YELL AT BOBBY! THEY'RE TRYING TO UNDERSTAND.
UG?
SURE, BOBBY. YOU CAN HAVE A HUG.
I'M SORRY, BOBBY. I DIDN'T MEAN TO SNAP AT YOU.
GAH REE UG!

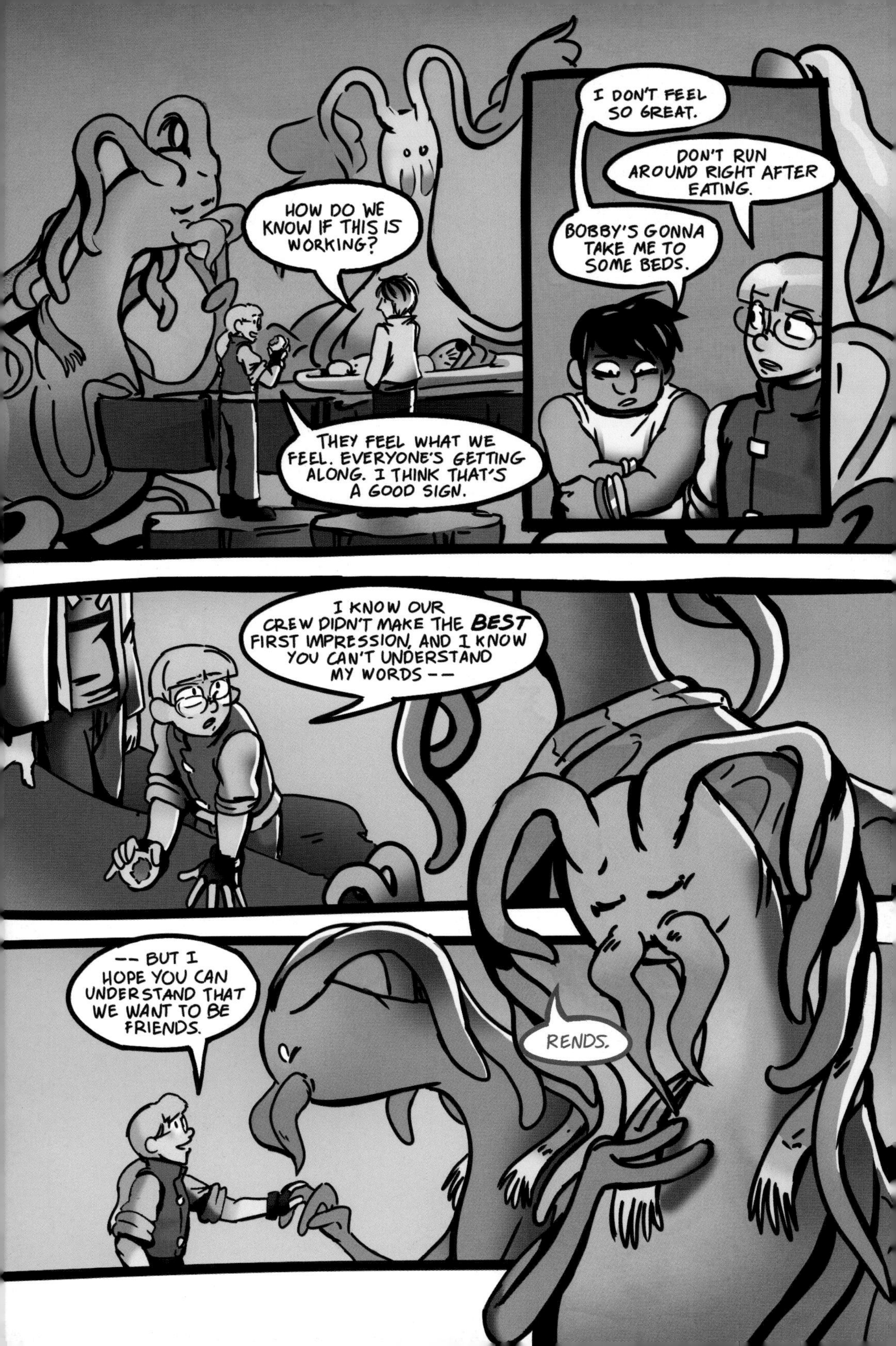
HOW DO WE KNOW IF THIS IS WORKING?
THEY FEEL WHAT WE FEEL. EVERYONE'S GETTING ALONG. I THINK THAT'S A GOOD SIGN.
I DON'T FEEL SO GREAT.
DON'T RUN AROUND RIGHT AFTER EATING.
BOBBY'S GONNA TAKE ME TO SOME BEDS.
I KNOW OUR CREW DIDN'T MAKE THE BEST FIRST IMPRESSION, AND I KNOW YOU CAN'T UNDERSTAND MY WORDS --
-- BUT I HOPE YOU CAN UNDERSTAND THAT WE WANT TO BE FRIENDS.
RENDS.

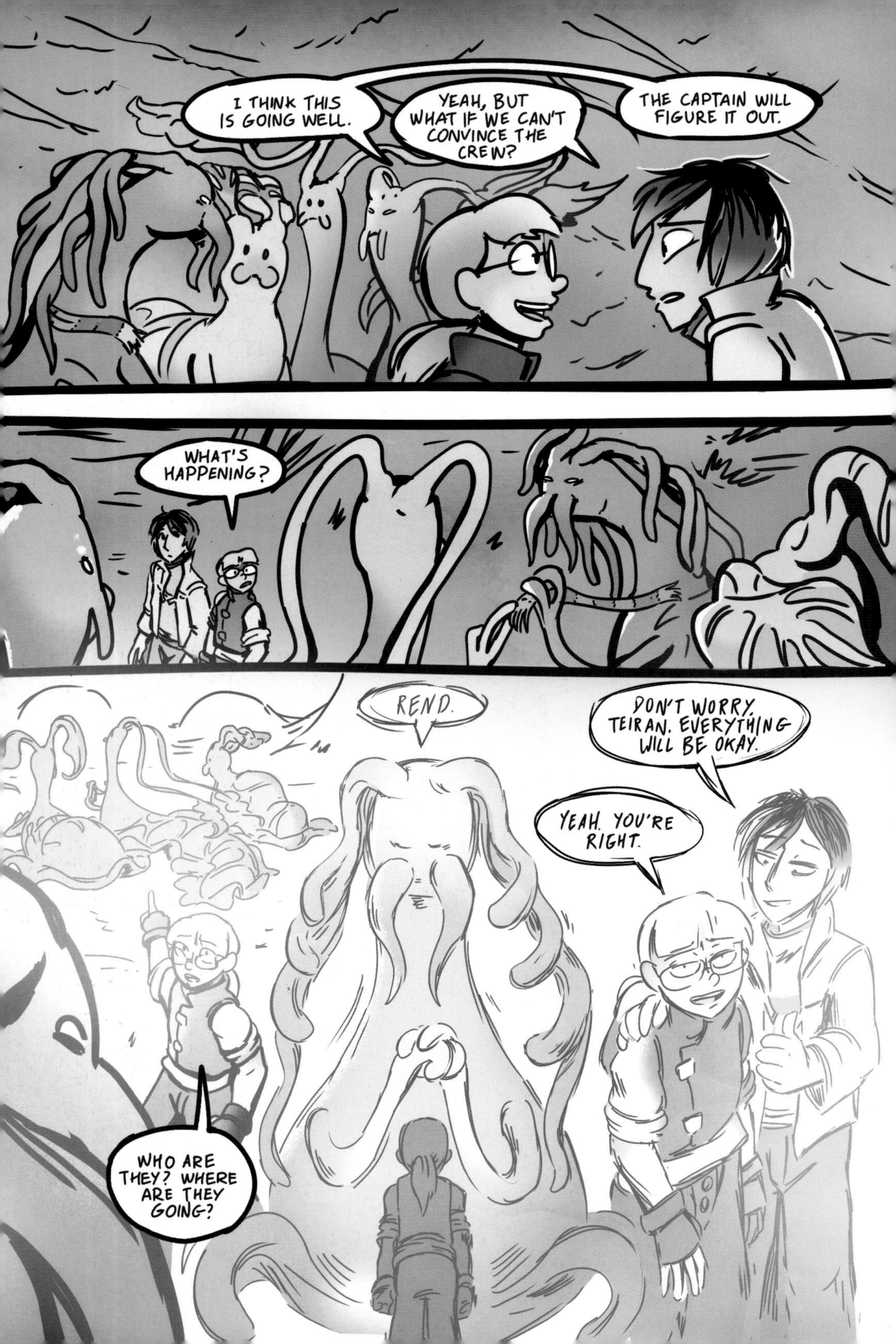
I THINK THIS IS GOING WELL.
YEAH, BUT WHAT IF WE CAN'T CONVINCE THE CREW?
THE CAPTAIN WILL FIGURE IT OUT.
WHAT'S HAPPENING?
REND.
DON'T WORRY, TEIRAN. EVERYTHING WILL BE OKAY.
YEAH. YOU'RE RIGHT.
WHO ARE THEY? WHERE ARE THEY GOING?

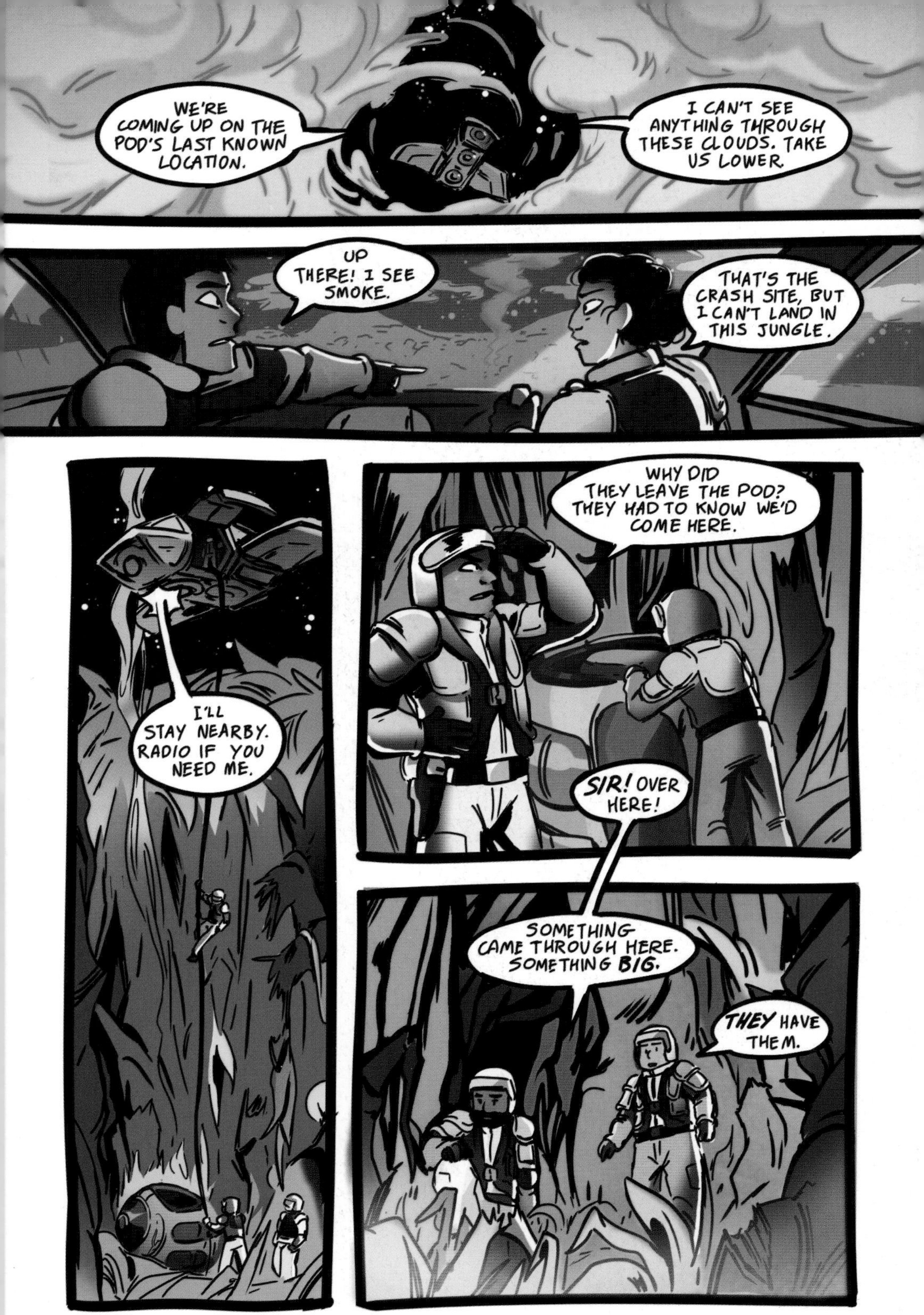
WE'RE COMING UP ON THE POD'S LAST KNOWN LOCATION.
I CAN'T SEE ANYTHING THROUGH THESE CLOUDS. TAKE US LOWER.
UP THERE! I SEE SMOKE.
THAT'S THE CRASH SITE, BUT I CAN'T LAND IN THIS JUNGLE.
I'LL STAY NEARBY. RADIO IF YOU NEED ME.
WHY DID THEY LEAVE THE POD? THEY HAD TO KNOW WE'D COME HERE.
SIR! OVER HERE!
SOMETHING CAME THROUGH HERE. SOMETHING BIG.
THEY HAVE THEM.

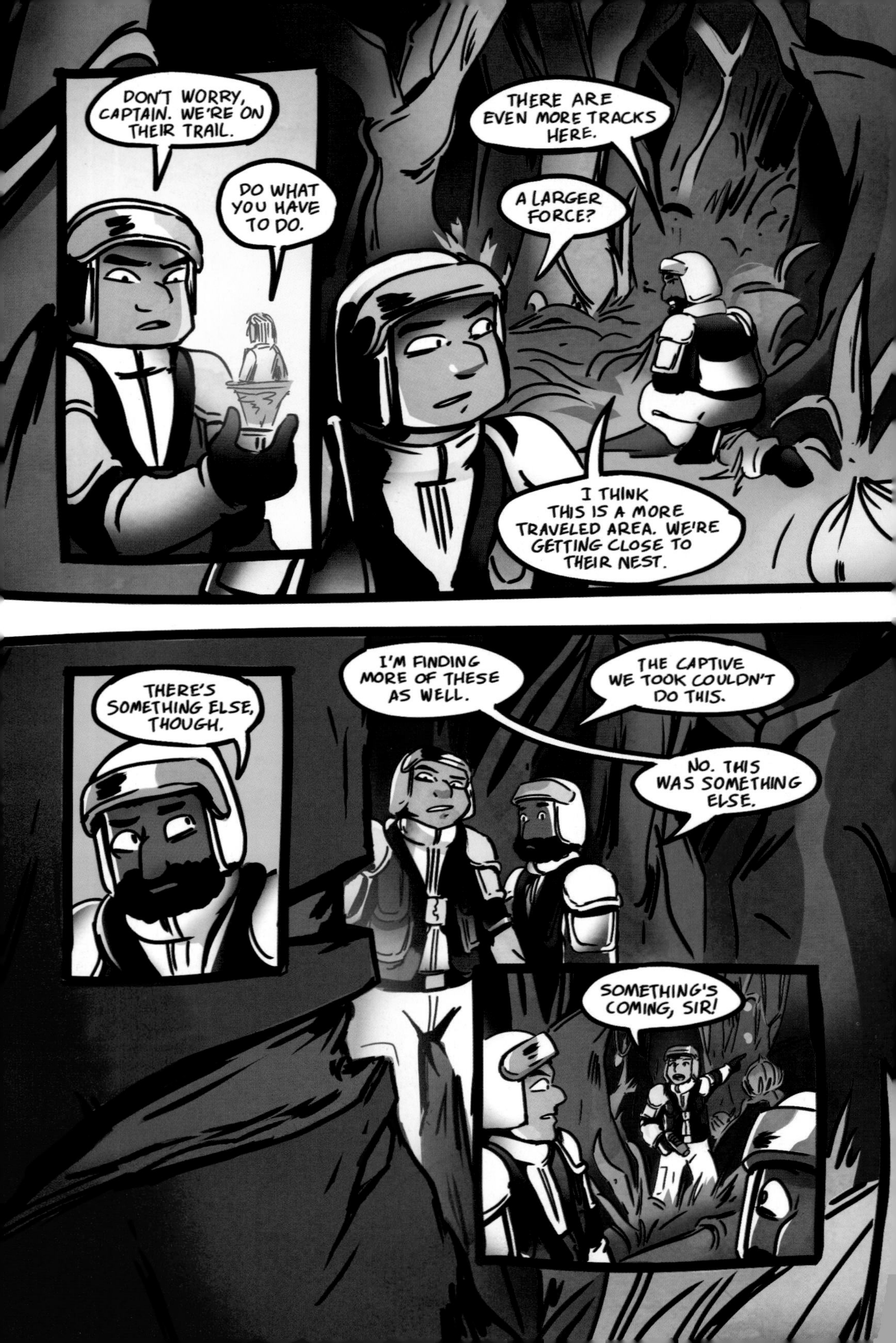
DON'T WORRY, CAPTAIN. WE'RE ON THEIR TRAIL.
DO WHAT YOU HAVE TO DO.
THERE ARE EVEN MORE TRACKS HERE.
A LARGER FORCE?
I THINK THIS IS A MORE TRAVELED AREA. WE'RE GETTING CLOSE TO THEIR NEST.
THERE'S SOMETHING ELSE, THOUGH.
I'M FINDING MORE OF THESE AS WELL.
THE CAPTIVE WE TOOK COULDN'T DO THIS.
NO. THIS WAS SOMETHING ELSE.
SOMETHING'S COMING, SIR!

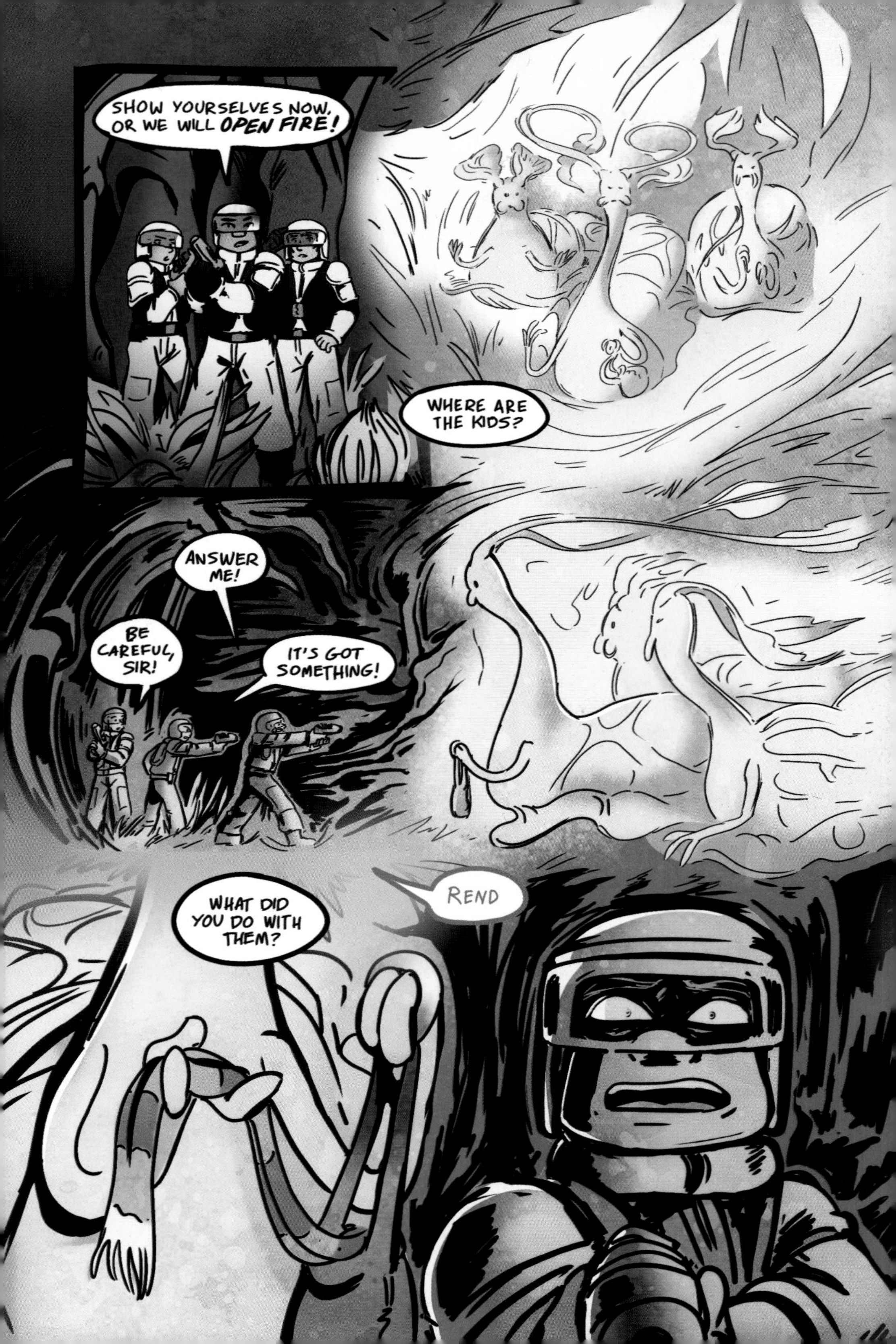
SHOW YOURSELVES NOW, OR WE WILL OPEN FIRE!
WHERE ARE THE KIDS?
ANSWER ME!
BE CAREFUL, SIR!
IT'S GOT SOMETHING!
WHAT DID YOU DO WITH THEM?
REND

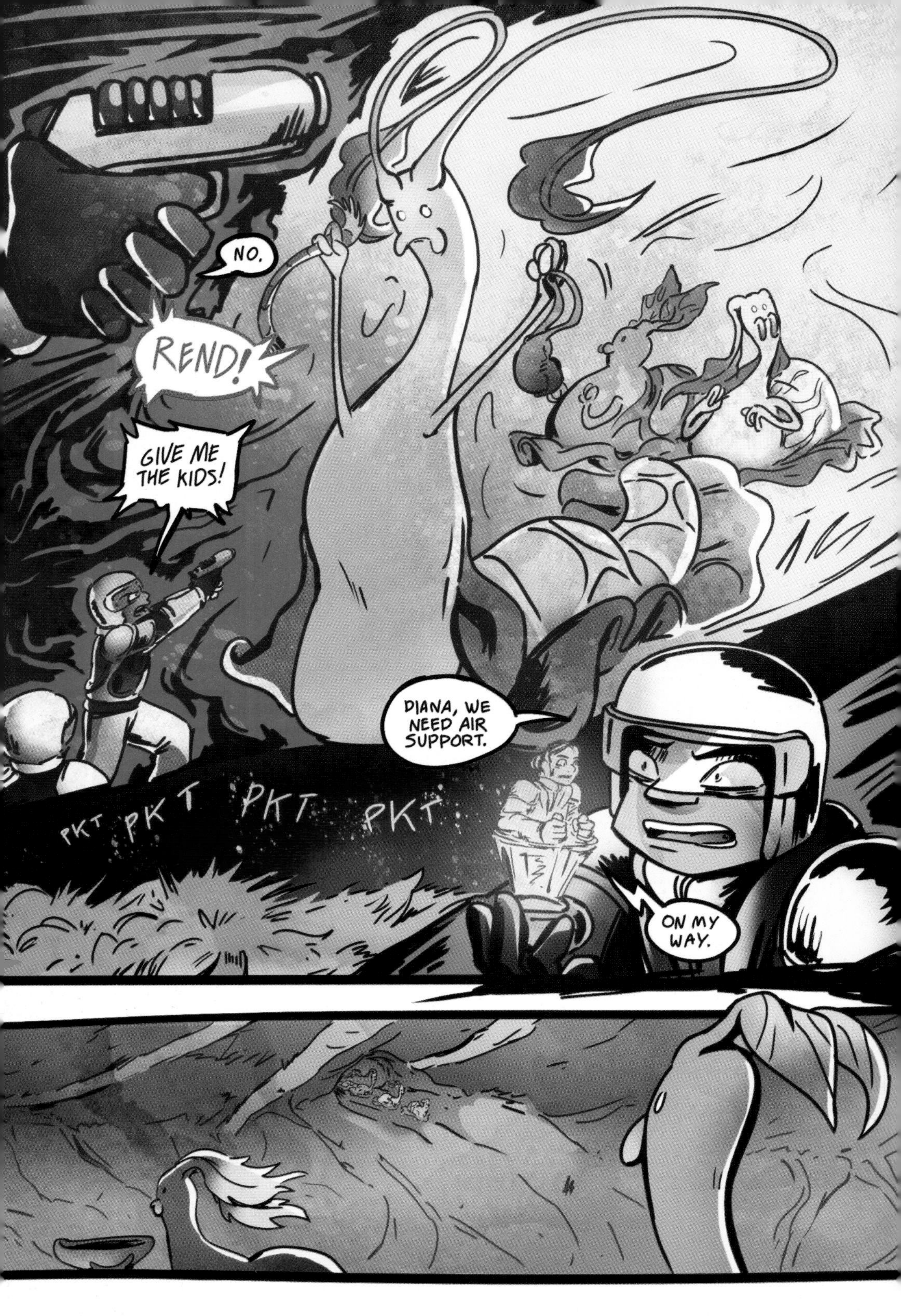
NO.
REND!
GIVE ME THE KIDS!
DIANA, WE NEED AIR SUPPORT.
PKT PKT PKT PKT
ON MY WAY.

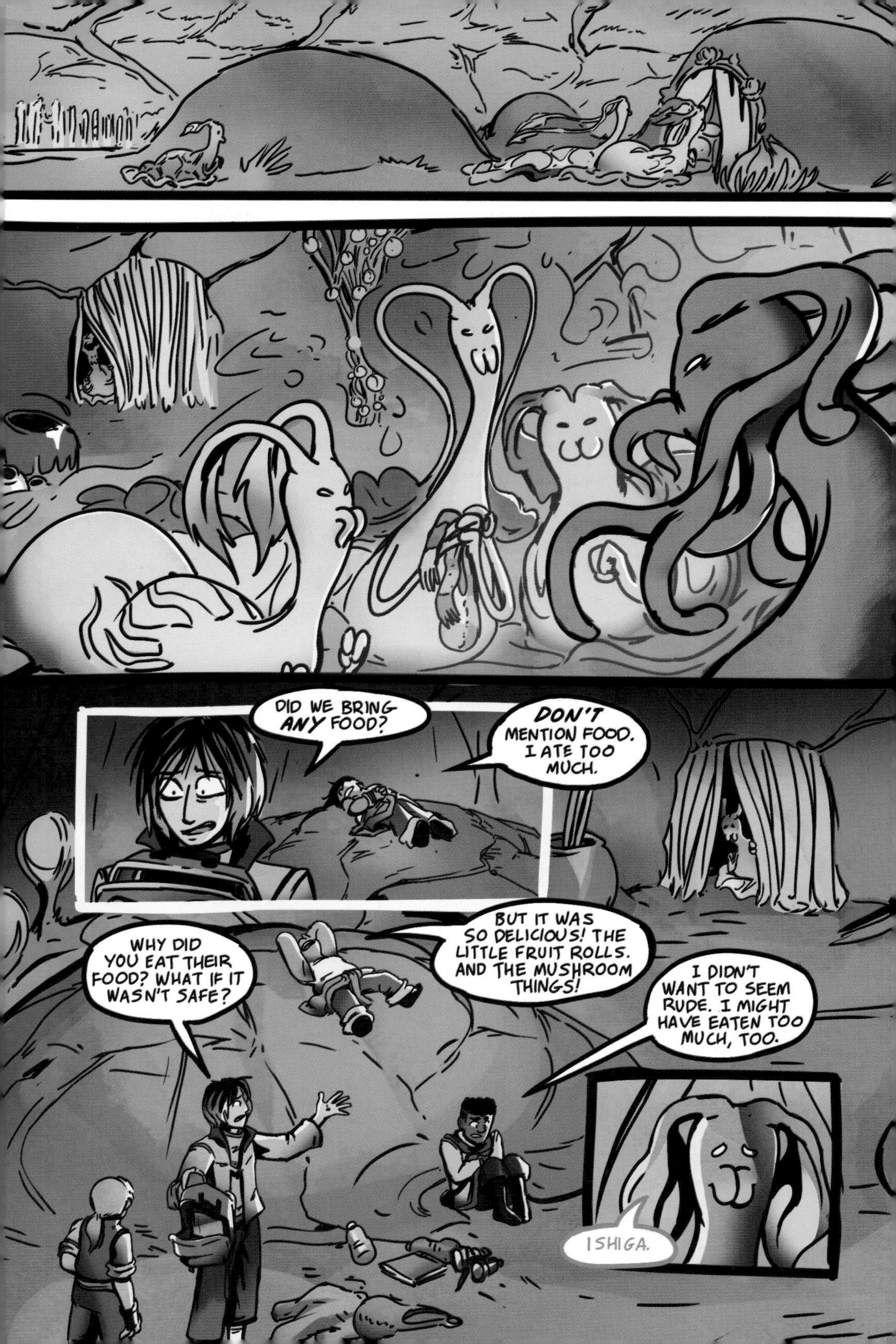
DID WE BRING ANY FOOD?
DON'T MENTION FOOD. I ATE TOO MUCH.
WHY DID YOU EAT THEIR FOOD? WHAT IF IT WASN'T SAFE?
BUT IT WAS SO DELICIOUS! THE LITTLE FRUIT ROLLS. AND THE MUSHROOM THINGS!
I DIDN'T WANT TO SEEM RUDE. I MIGHT HAVE EATEN TOO MUCH, TOO.
ISHIGA.

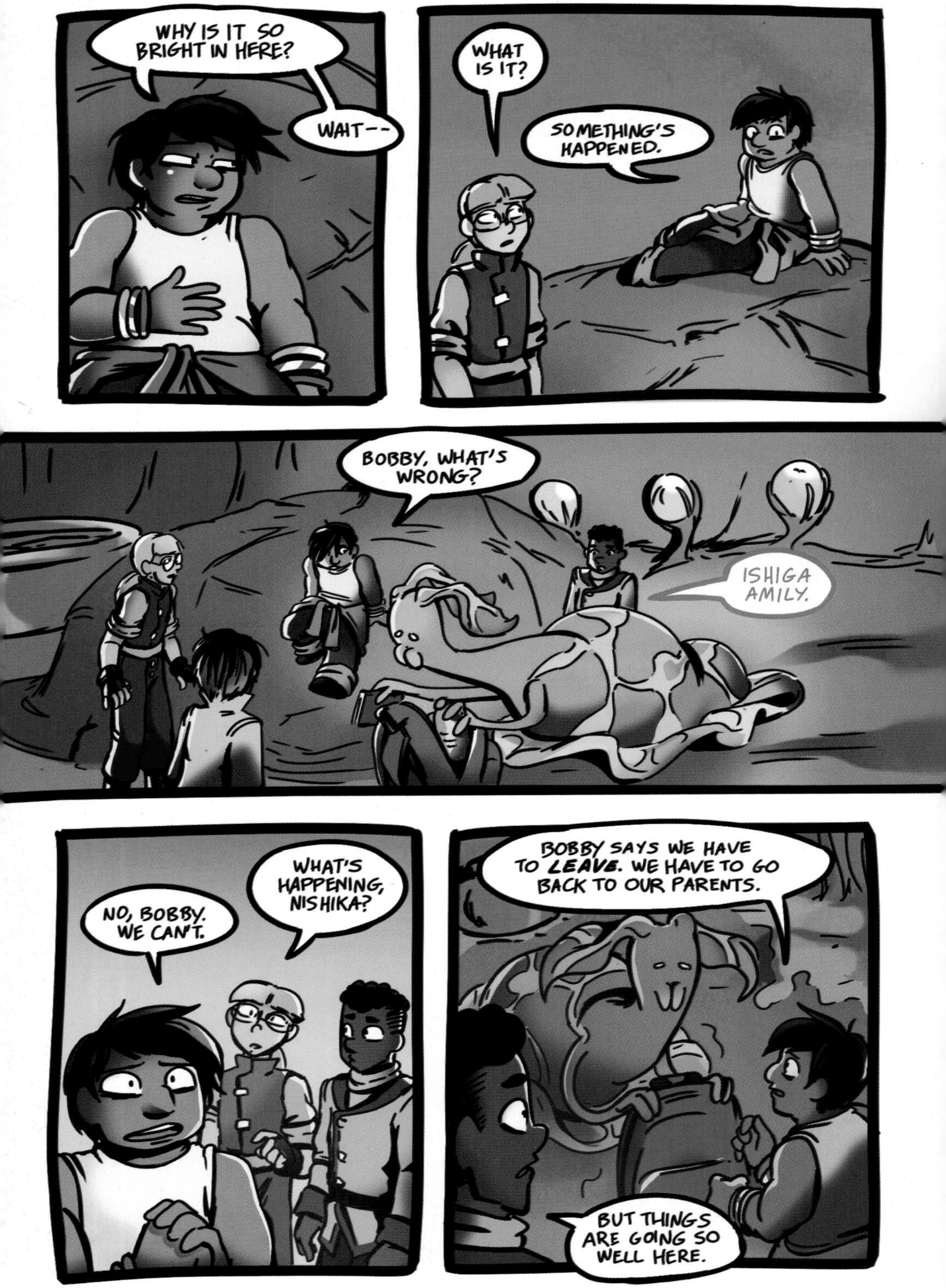
WHY IS IT SO BRIGHT IN HERE?
WAIT--
WHAT IS IT?
SOMETHING'S HAPPENED.
BOBBY, WHAT'S WRONG?
ISHIGA AMILY.
NO, BOBBY. WE CAN'T.
WHAT'S HAPPENING, NISHIKA?
BOBBY SAYS WE HAVE TO *LEAVE*. WE HAVE TO GO BACK TO OUR PARENTS.
BUT THINGS ARE GOING SO WELL HERE.

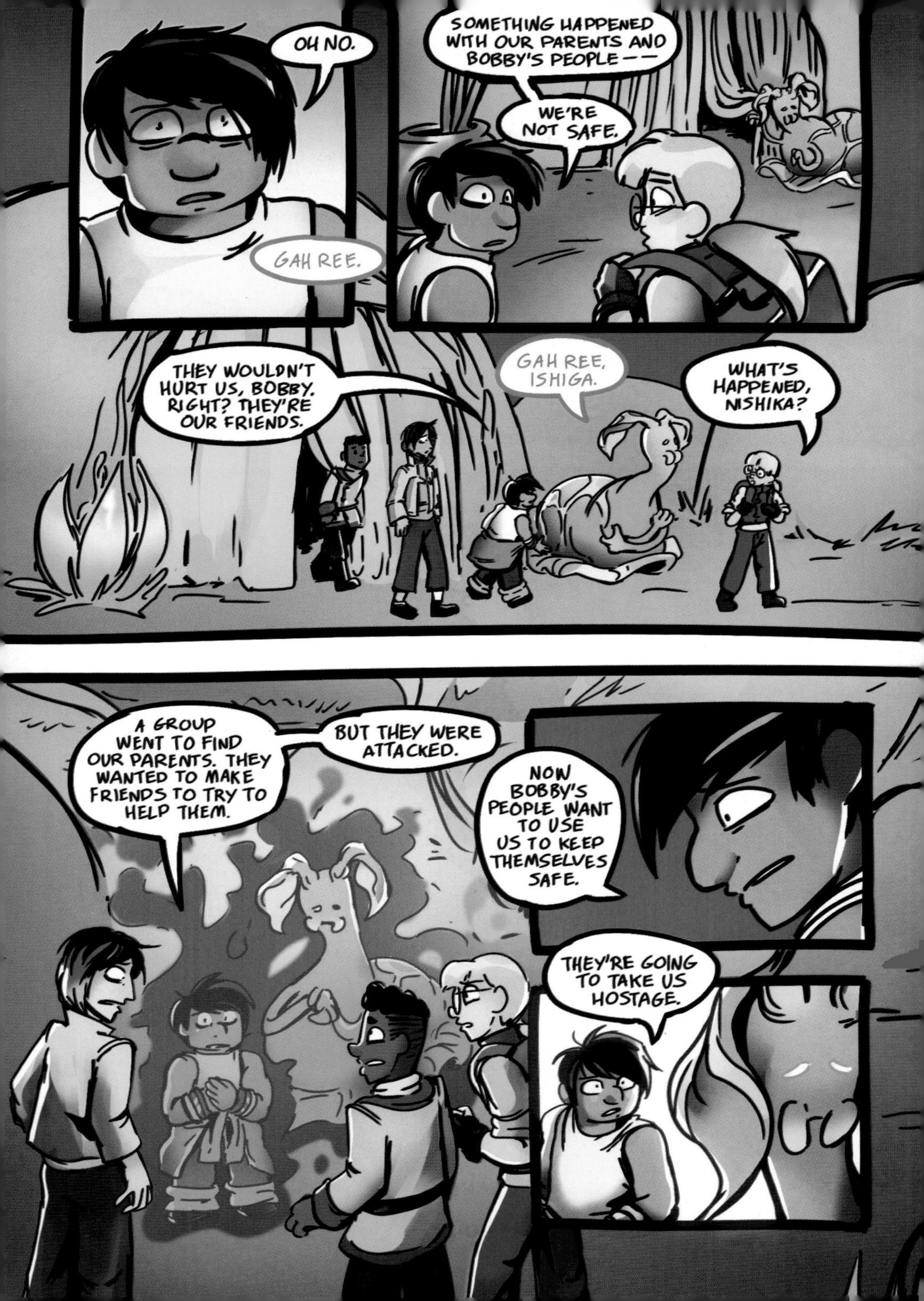
OH NO.
GAH REE.
SOMETHING HAPPENED WITH OUR PARENTS AND BOBBY'S PEOPLE--
WE'RE NOT SAFE.
THEY WOULDN'T HURT US, BOBBY. RIGHT? THEY'RE OUR FRIENDS.
GAH REE, ISHIGA.
WHAT'S HAPPENED, NISHIKA?
A GROUP WENT TO FIND OUR PARENTS. THEY WANTED TO MAKE FRIENDS TO TRY TO HELP THEM.
BUT THEY WERE ATTACKED.
NOW BOBBY'S PEOPLE WANT TO USE US TO KEEP THEMSELVES SAFE.
THEY'RE GOING TO TAKE US HOSTAGE.

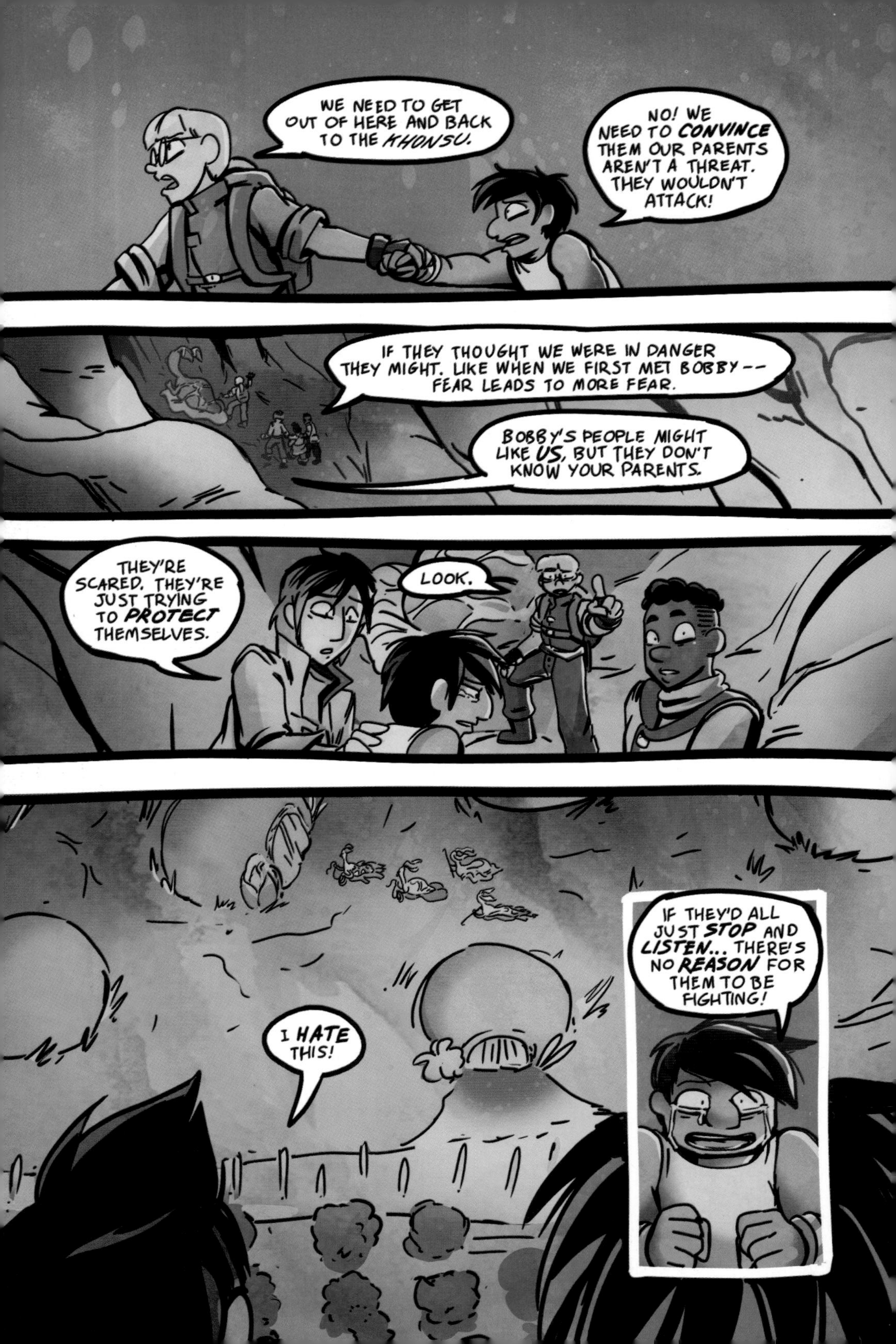
WE NEED TO GET OUT OF HERE AND BACK TO THE KHONSU.
NO! WE NEED TO CONVINCE THEM OUR PARENTS AREN'T A THREAT. THEY WOULDN'T ATTACK!
IF THEY THOUGHT WE WERE IN DANGER THEY MIGHT. LIKE WHEN WE FIRST MET BOBBY-- FEAR LEADS TO MORE FEAR.
BOBBY'S PEOPLE MIGHT LIKE US, BUT THEY DON'T KNOW YOUR PARENTS.
THEY'RE SCARED. THEY'RE JUST TRYING TO PROTECT THEMSELVES.
LOOK.
IF THEY'D ALL JUST STOP AND LISTEN... THERE'S NO REASON FOR THEM TO BE FIGHTING!
I HATE THIS!

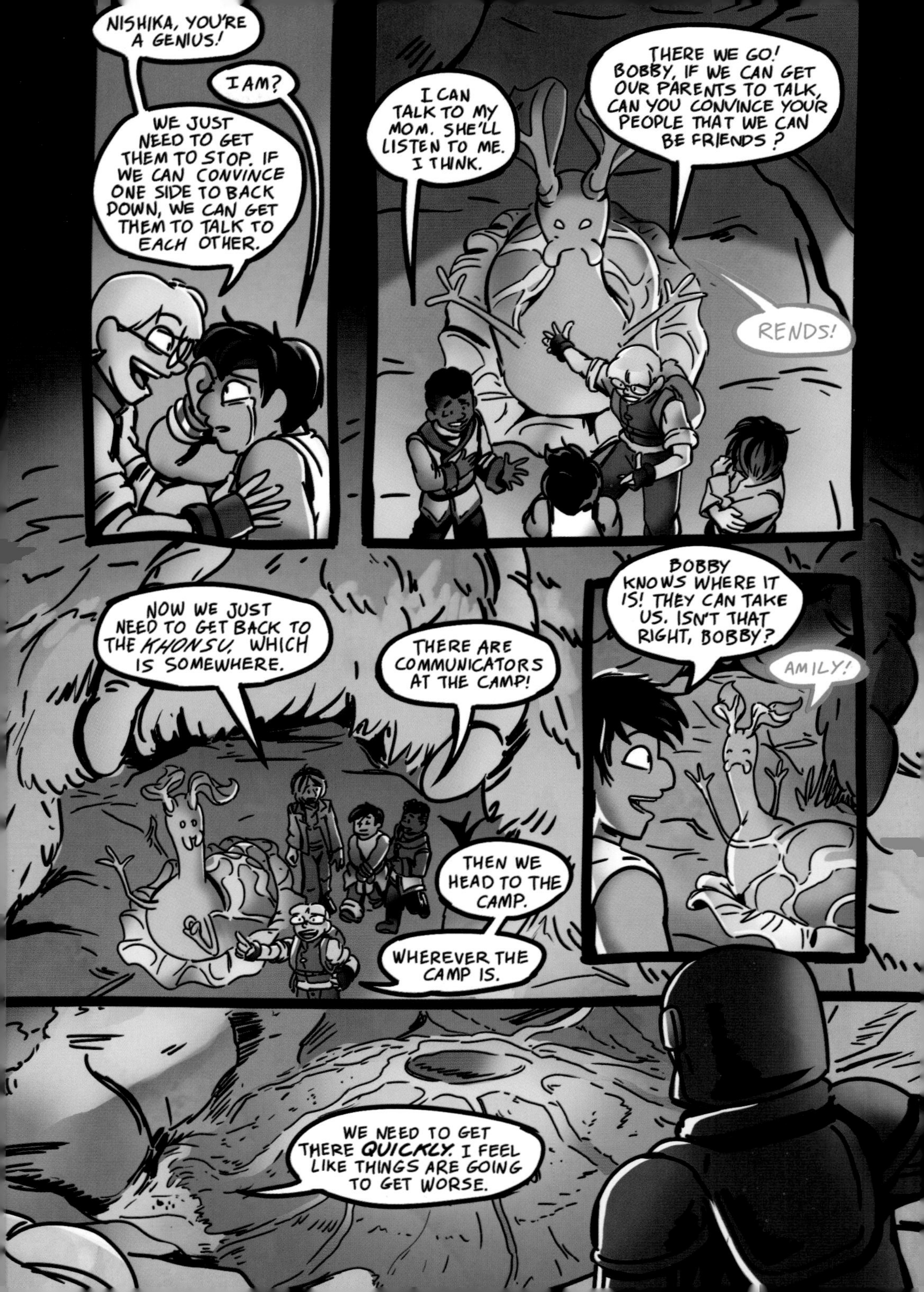
NISHIKA, YOU'RE A GENIUS!
I AM?
WE JUST NEED TO GET THEM TO STOP. IF WE CAN CONVINCE ONE SIDE TO BACK DOWN, WE CAN GET THEM TO TALK TO EACH OTHER.
I CAN TALK TO MY MOM. SHE'LL LISTEN TO ME. I THINK.
THERE WE GO! BOBBY, IF WE CAN GET OUR PARENTS TO TALK, CAN YOU CONVINCE YOUR PEOPLE THAT WE CAN BE FRIENDS?
RENDS!
NOW WE JUST NEED TO GET BACK TO THE *KHONSU,* WHICH IS SOMEWHERE.
THERE ARE COMMUNICATORS AT THE CAMP!
THEN WE HEAD TO THE CAMP.
WHEREVER THE CAMP IS.
BOBBY KNOWS WHERE IT IS! THEY CAN TAKE US. ISN'T THAT RIGHT, BOBBY?
AMILY!
WE NEED TO GET THERE ***QUICKLY.*** I FEEL LIKE THINGS ARE GOING TO GET WORSE.

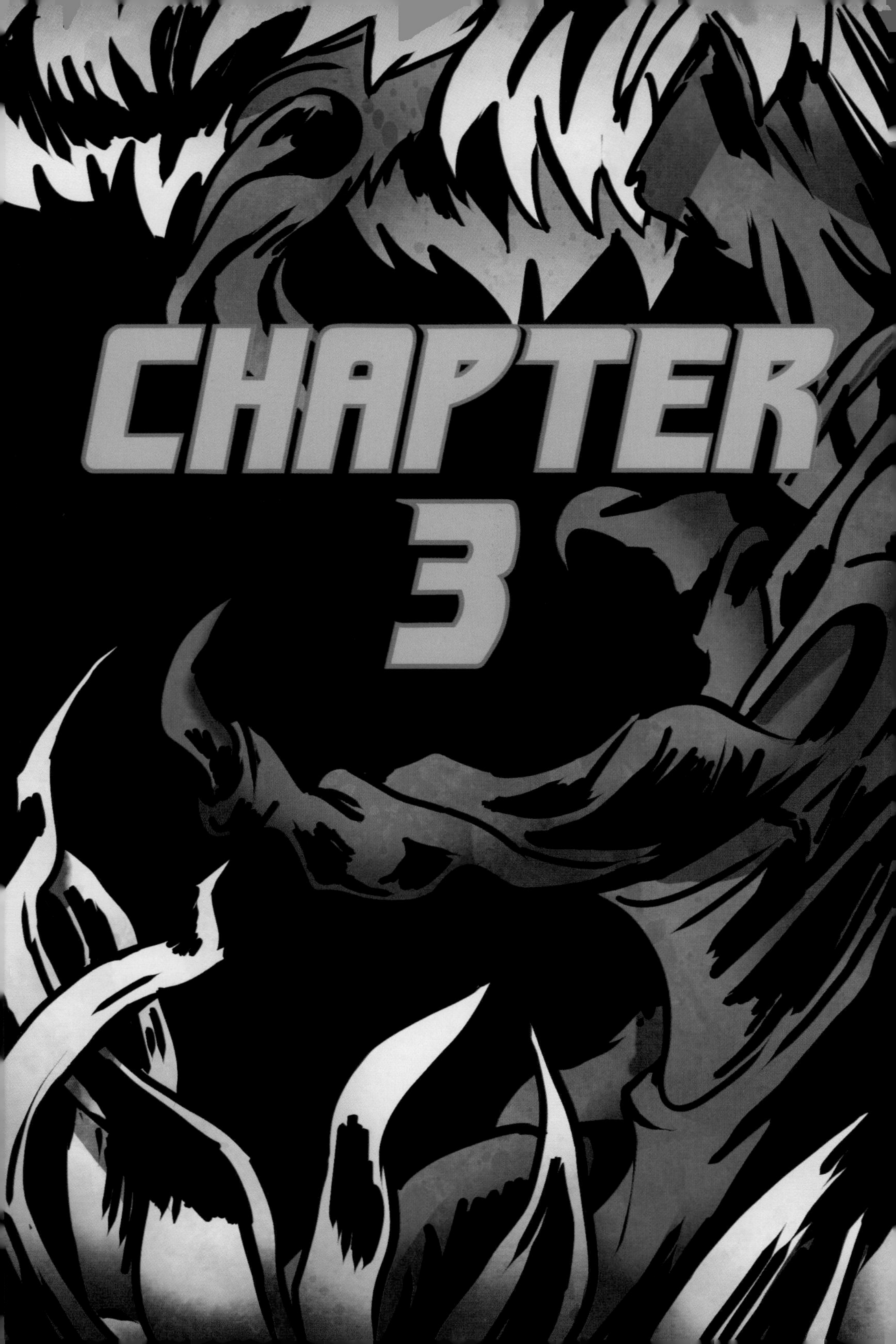
CHAPTER
3

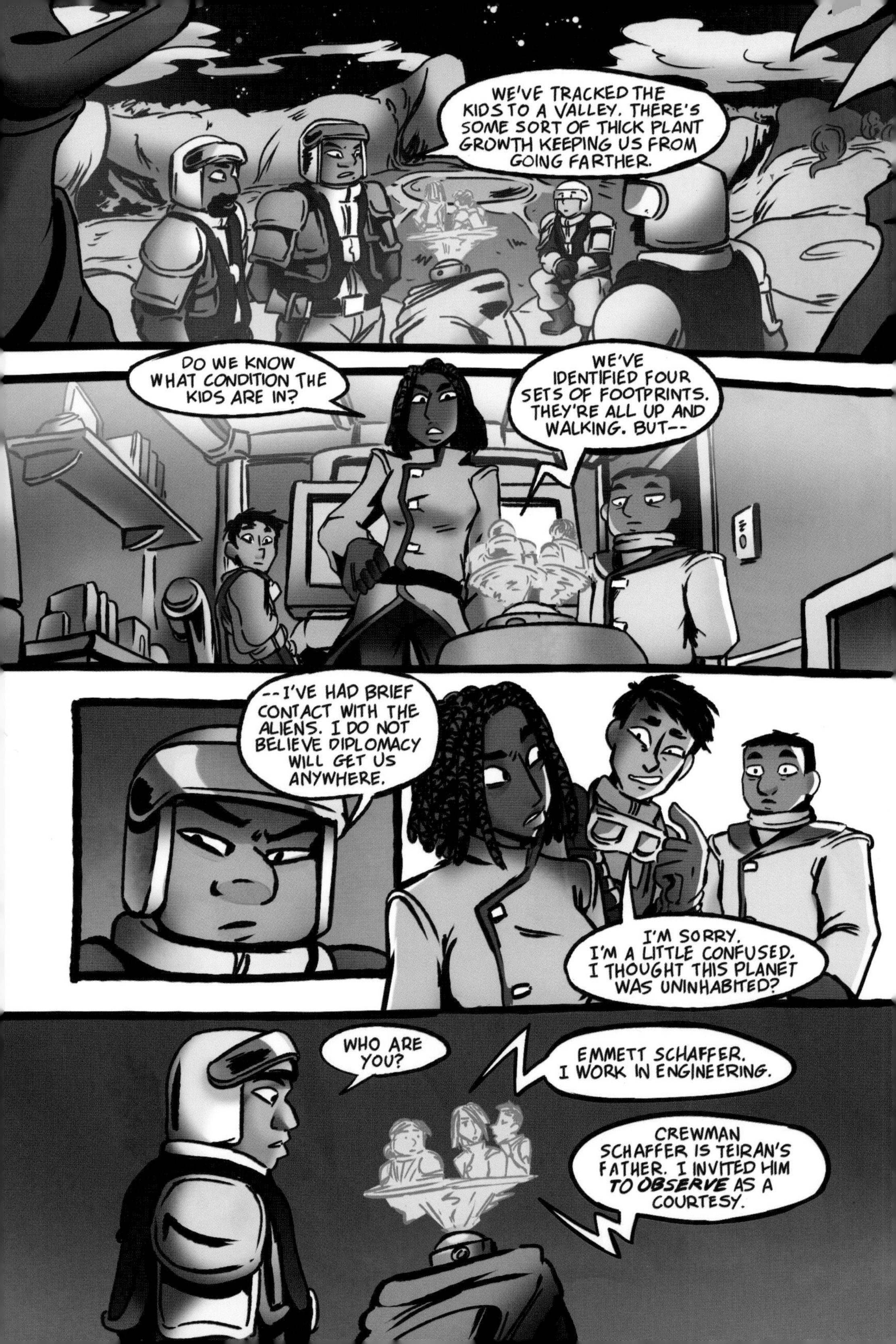
WE'VE TRACKED THE KIDS TO A VALLEY. THERE'S SOME SORT OF THICK PLANT GROWTH KEEPING US FROM GOING FARTHER.
DO WE KNOW WHAT CONDITION THE KIDS ARE IN?
WE'VE IDENTIFIED FOUR SETS OF FOOTPRINTS. THEY'RE ALL UP AND WALKING. BUT--
--I'VE HAD BRIEF CONTACT WITH THE ALIENS. I DO NOT BELIEVE DIPLOMACY WILL GET US ANYWHERE.
I'M SORRY. I'M A LITTLE CONFUSED. I THOUGHT THIS PLANET WAS UNINHABITED?
WHO ARE YOU?
EMMETT SCHAFFER. I WORK IN ENGINEERING.
CREWMAN SCHAFFER IS TEIRAN'S FATHER. I INVITED HIM *TO OBSERVE* AS A COURTESY.

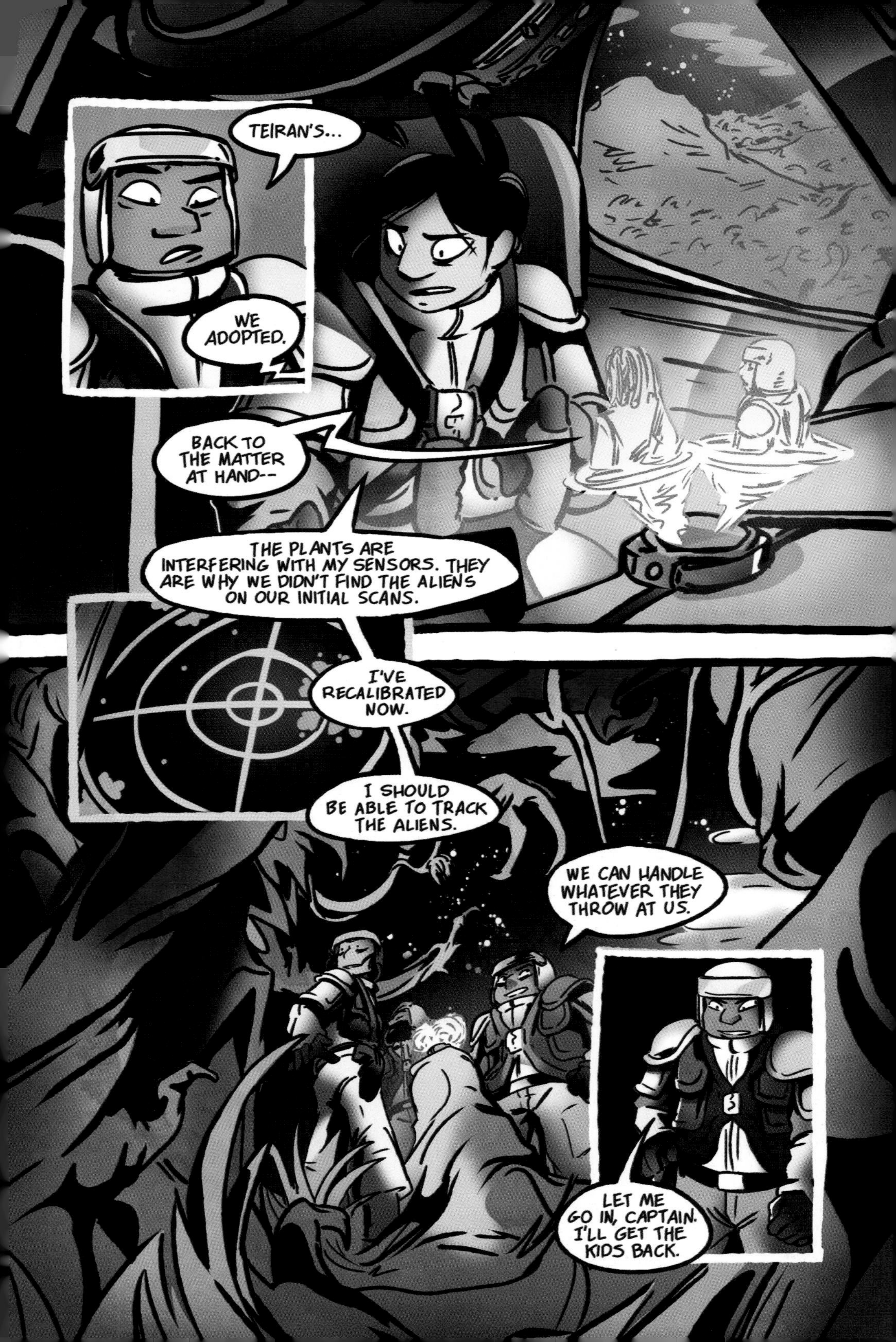
TEIRAN'S...
WE ADOPTED.
BACK TO THE MATTER AT HAND--
THE PLANTS ARE INTERFERING WITH MY SENSORS. THEY ARE WHY WE DIDN'T FIND THE ALIENS ON OUR INITIAL SCANS.
I'VE RECALIBRATED NOW.
I SHOULD BE ABLE TO TRACK THE ALIENS.
WE CAN HANDLE WHATEVER THEY THROW AT US.
LET ME GO IN, CAPTAIN. I'LL GET THE KIDS BACK.

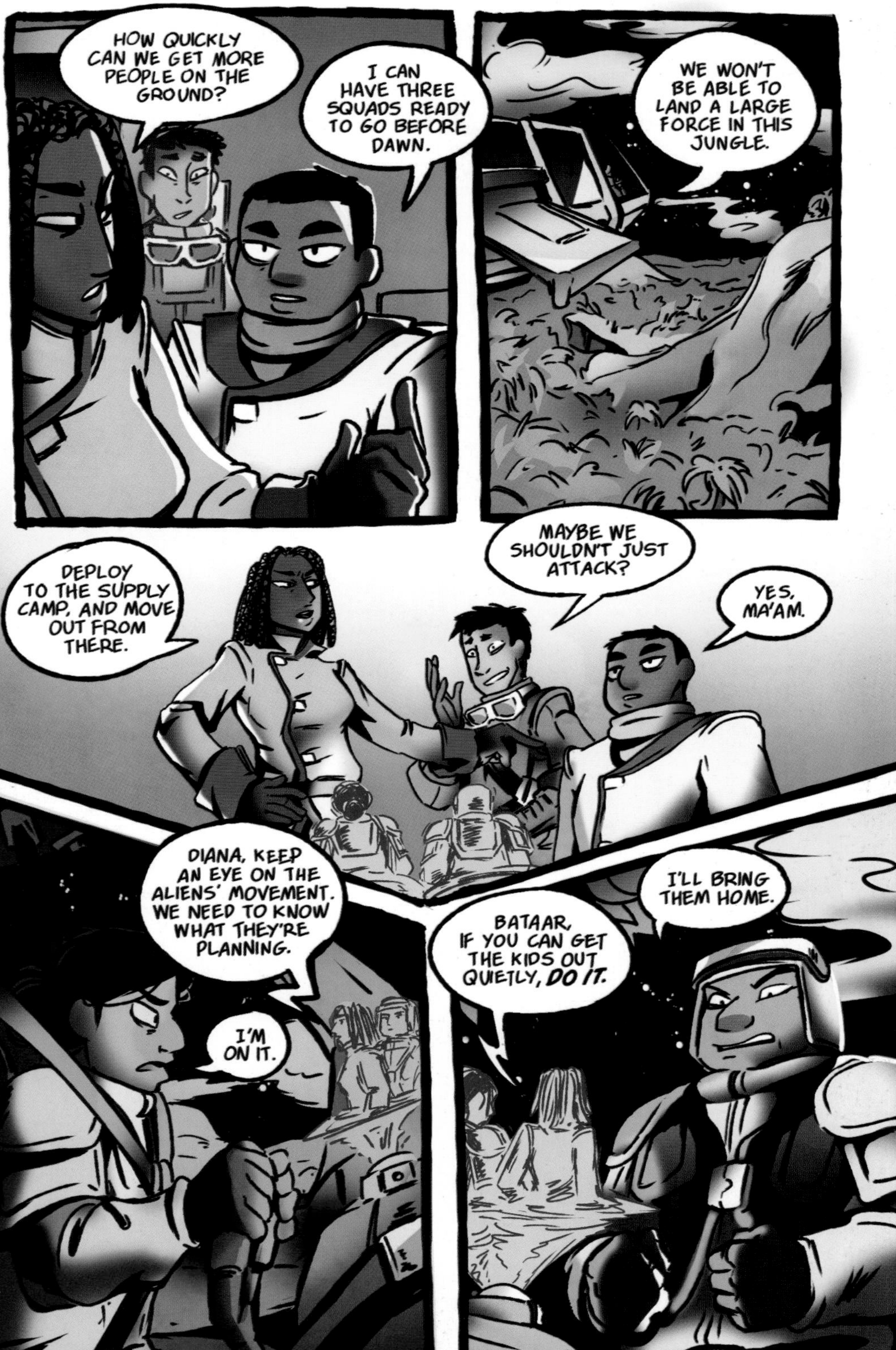
HOW QUICKLY CAN WE GET MORE PEOPLE ON THE GROUND?
I CAN HAVE THREE SQUADS READY TO GO BEFORE DAWN.
WE WON'T BE ABLE TO LAND A LARGE FORCE IN THIS JUNGLE.
DEPLOY TO THE SUPPLY CAMP, AND MOVE OUT FROM THERE.
MAYBE WE SHOULDN'T JUST ATTACK?
YES, MA'AM.
DIANA, KEEP AN EYE ON THE ALIENS' MOVEMENT. WE NEED TO KNOW WHAT THEY'RE PLANNING.
I'M ON IT.
BATAAR, IF YOU CAN GET THE KIDS OUT QUIETLY, ***DO IT.***
I'LL BRING THEM HOME.

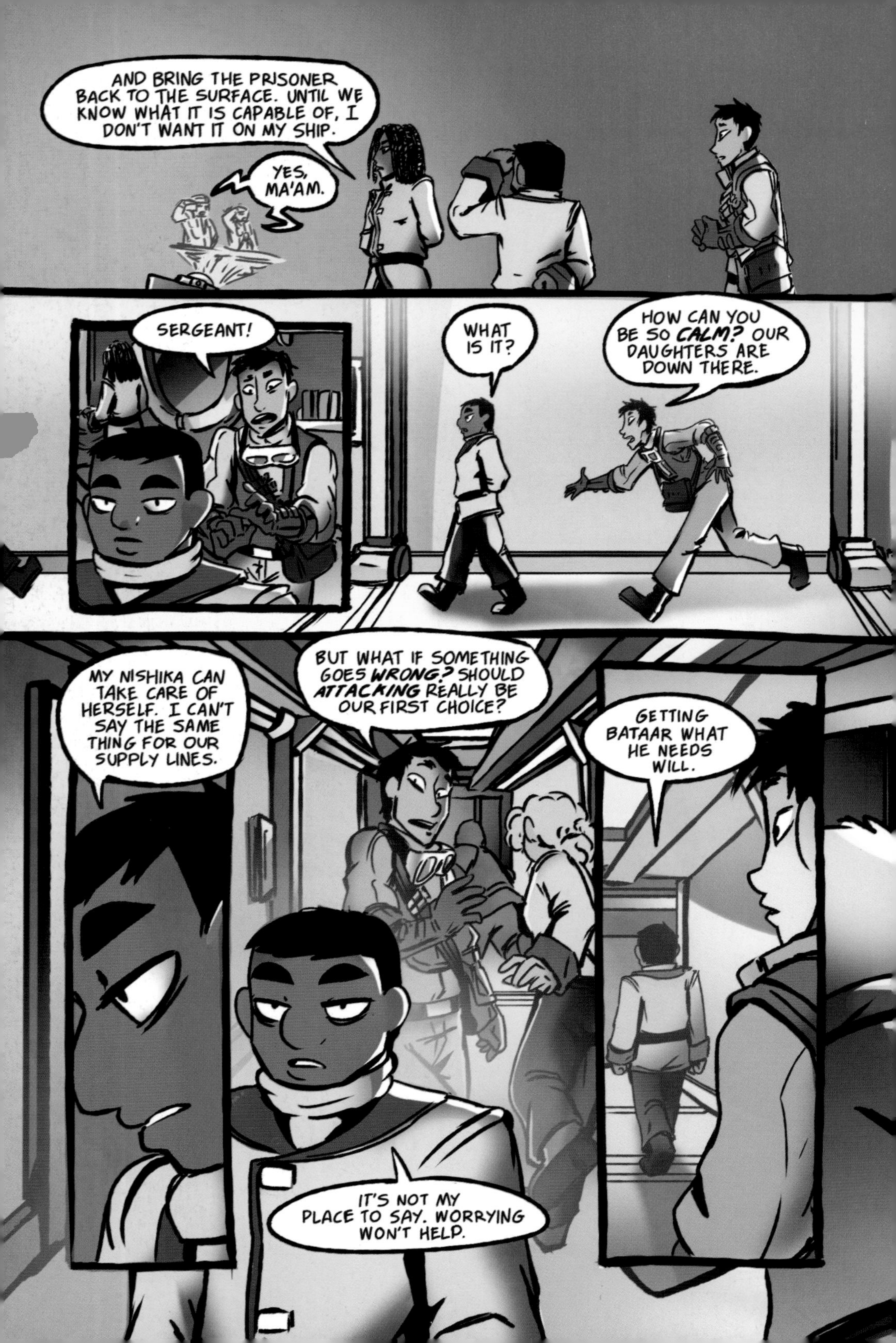
AND BRING THE PRISONER BACK TO THE SURFACE. UNTIL WE KNOW WHAT IT IS CAPABLE OF, I DON'T WANT IT ON MY SHIP.
YES, MA'AM.
SERGEANT!
WHAT IS IT?
HOW CAN YOU BE SO CALM? OUR DAUGHTERS ARE DOWN THERE.
MY NISHIKA CAN TAKE CARE OF HERSELF. I CAN'T SAY THE SAME THING FOR OUR SUPPLY LINES.
BUT WHAT IF SOMETHING GOES WRONG? SHOULD ATTACKING REALLY BE OUR FIRST CHOICE?
GETTING BATAAR WHAT HE NEEDS WILL.
IT'S NOT MY PLACE TO SAY. WORRYING WON'T HELP.

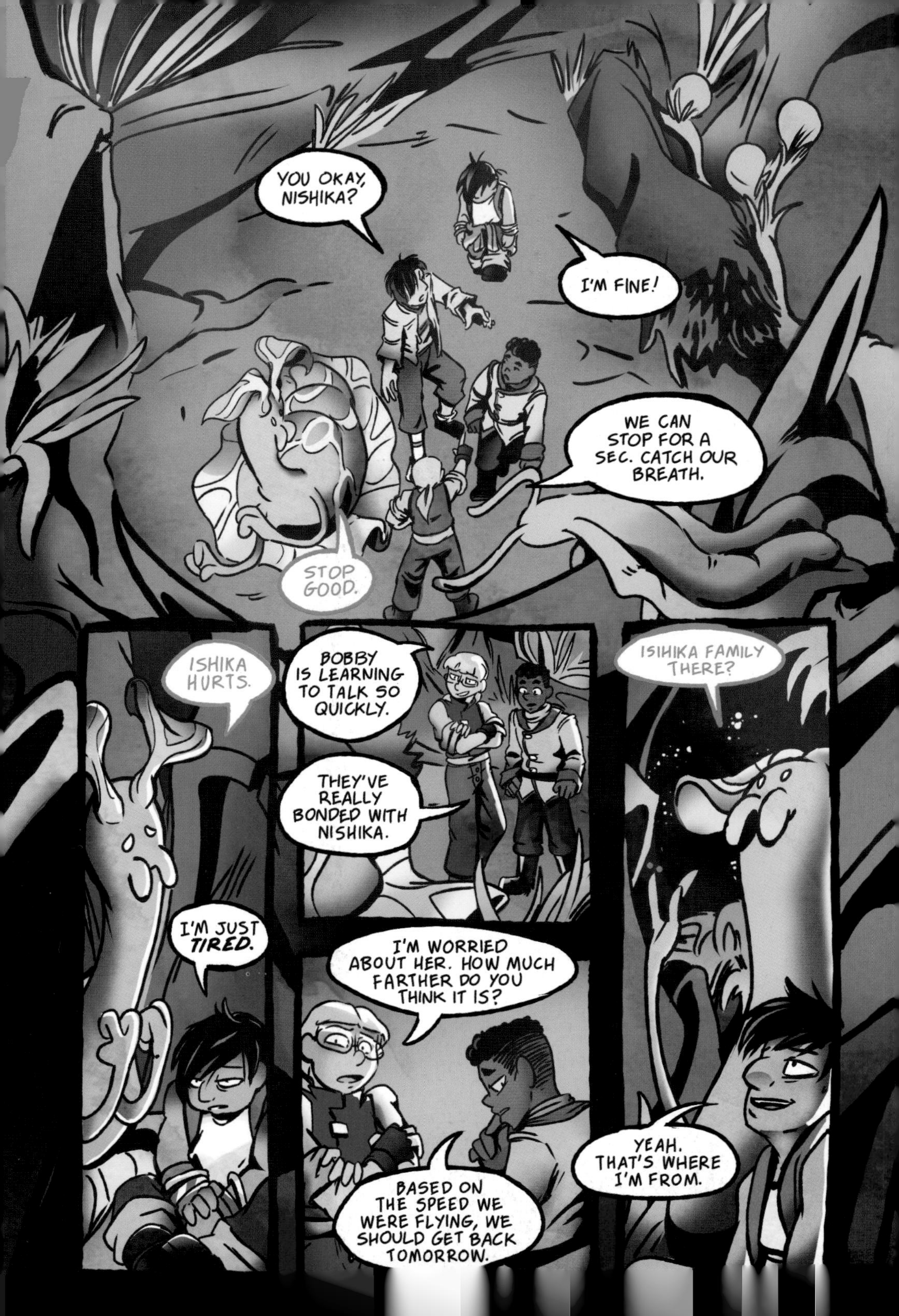
YOU OKAY, NISHIKA?
I'M FINE!
WE CAN STOP FOR A SEC. CATCH OUR BREATH.
STOP GOOD.
ISHIKA HURTS.
I'M JUST TIRED.
BOBBY IS LEARNING TO TALK SO QUICKLY.
THEY'VE REALLY BONDED WITH NISHIKA.
I'M WORRIED ABOUT HER. HOW MUCH FARTHER DO YOU THINK IT IS?
BASED ON THE SPEED WE WERE FLYING, WE SHOULD GET BACK TOMORROW.
ISIHIKA FAMILY THERE?
YEAH. THAT'S WHERE I'M FROM.

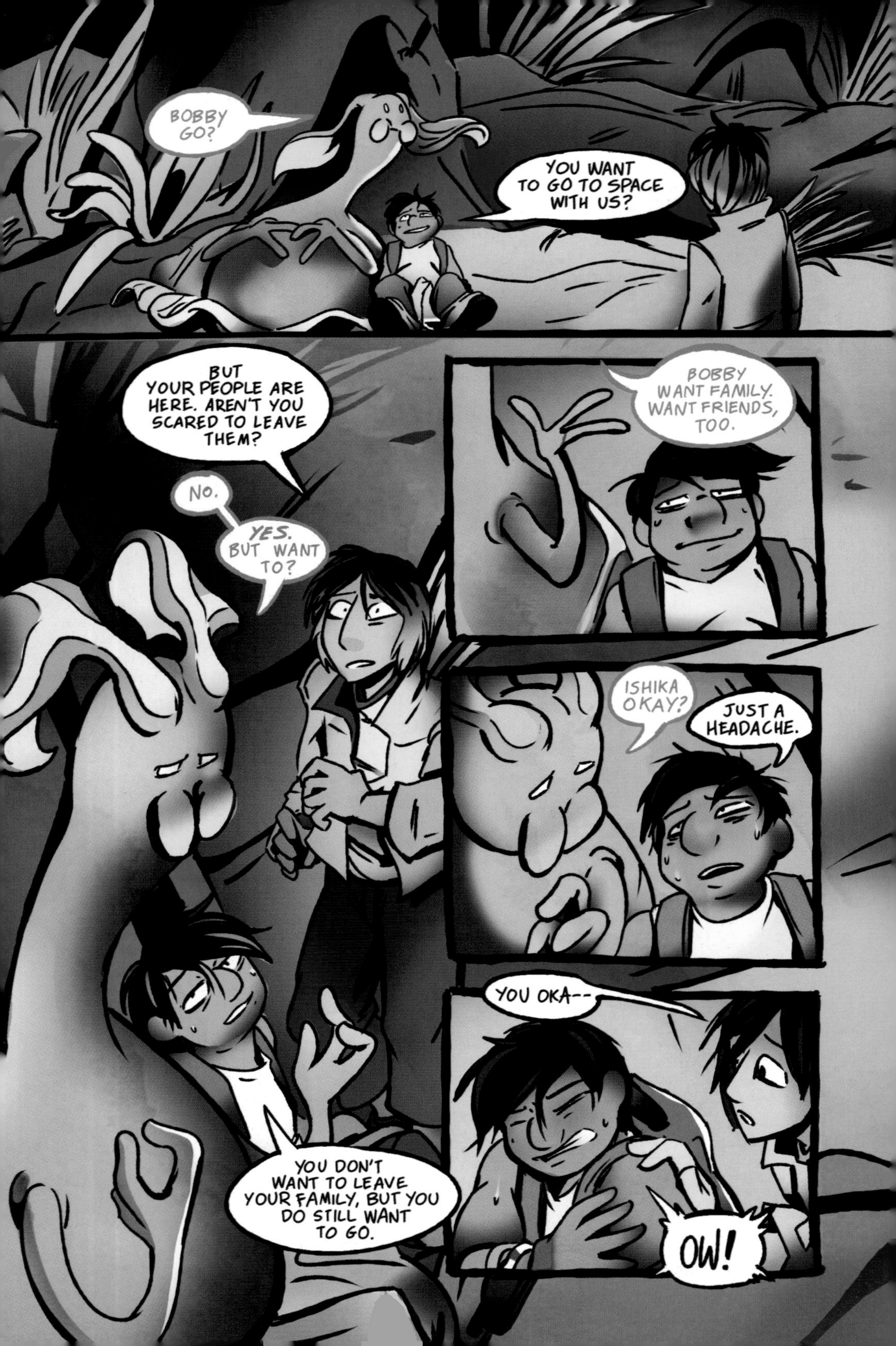
BOBBY GO?
YOU WANT TO GO TO SPACE WITH US?
BUT YOUR PEOPLE ARE HERE. AREN'T YOU SCARED TO LEAVE THEM?
NO.
YES. BUT WANT TO?
YOU DON'T WANT TO LEAVE YOUR FAMILY, BUT YOU DO STILL WANT TO GO.
BOBBY WANT FAMILY. WANT FRIENDS, TOO.
ISHIKA OKAY?
JUST A HEADACHE.
YOU OKA--
OW!

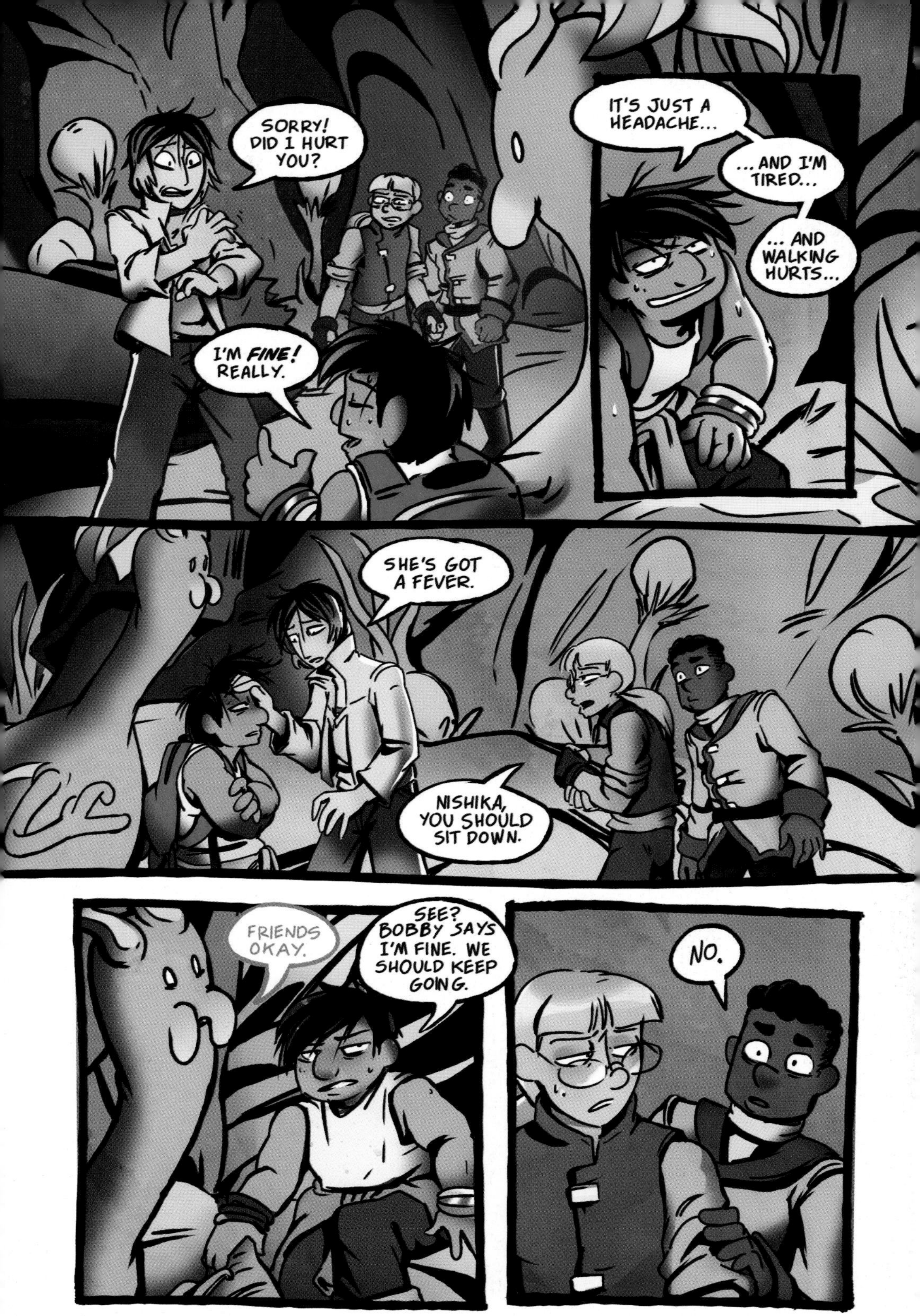
SORRY! DID I HURT YOU?
I'M FINE! REALLY.
IT'S JUST A HEADACHE...
...AND I'M TIRED...
...AND WALKING HURTS...
SHE'S GOT A FEVER.
NISHIKA, YOU SHOULD SIT DOWN.
FRIENDS OKAY.
SEE? BOBBY SAYS I'M FINE. WE SHOULD KEEP GOING.
NO.

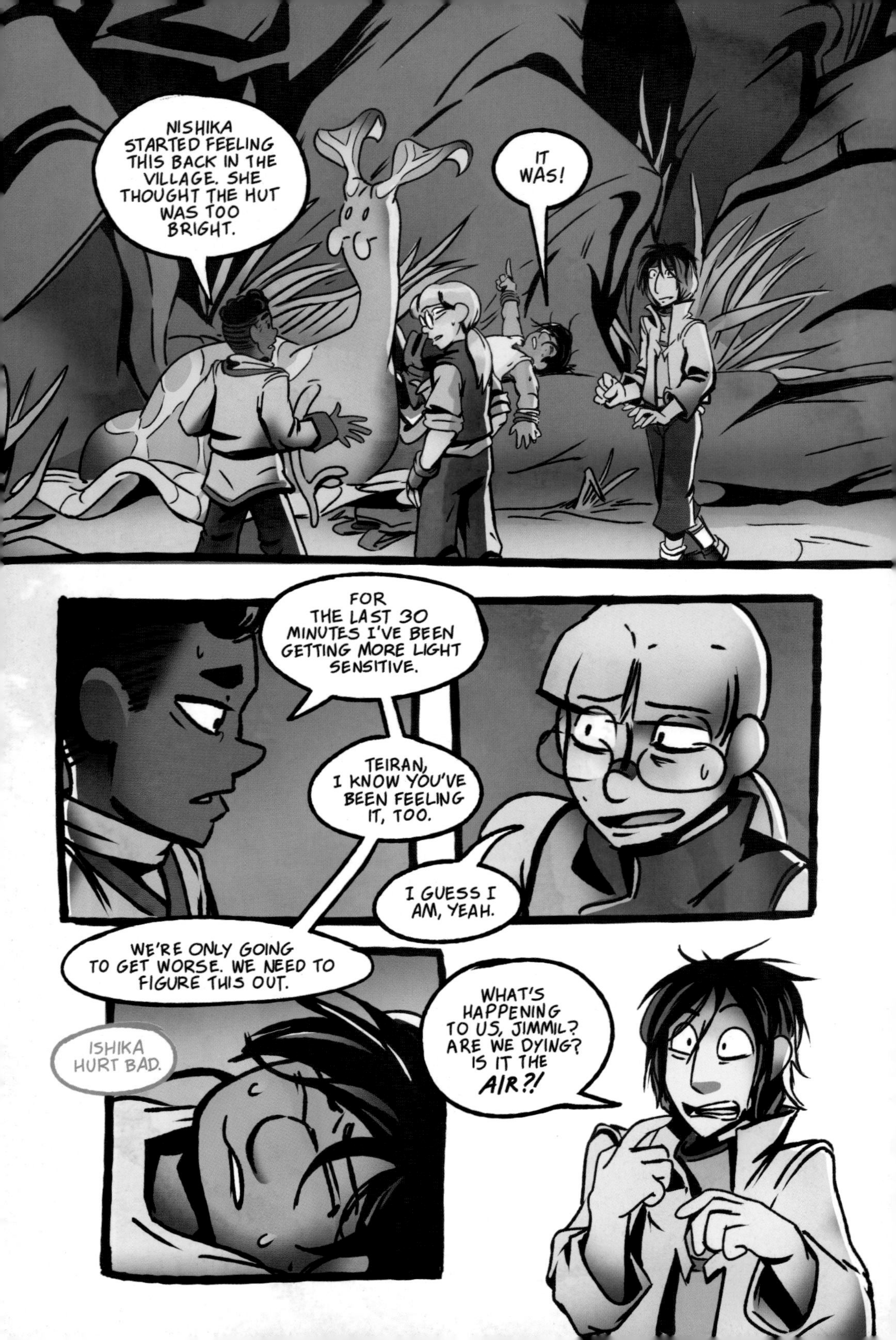
NISHIKA STARTED FEELING THIS BACK IN THE VILLAGE. SHE THOUGHT THE HUT WAS TOO BRIGHT.
IT WAS!
FOR THE LAST 30 MINUTES I'VE BEEN GETTING MORE LIGHT SENSITIVE.
TEIRAN, I KNOW YOU'VE BEEN FEELING IT, TOO.
I GUESS I AM, YEAH.
WE'RE ONLY GOING TO GET WORSE. WE NEED TO FIGURE THIS OUT.
ISHIKA HURT BAD.
WHAT'S HAPPENING TO US, JIMMIL? ARE WE DYING? IS IT THE AIR?!

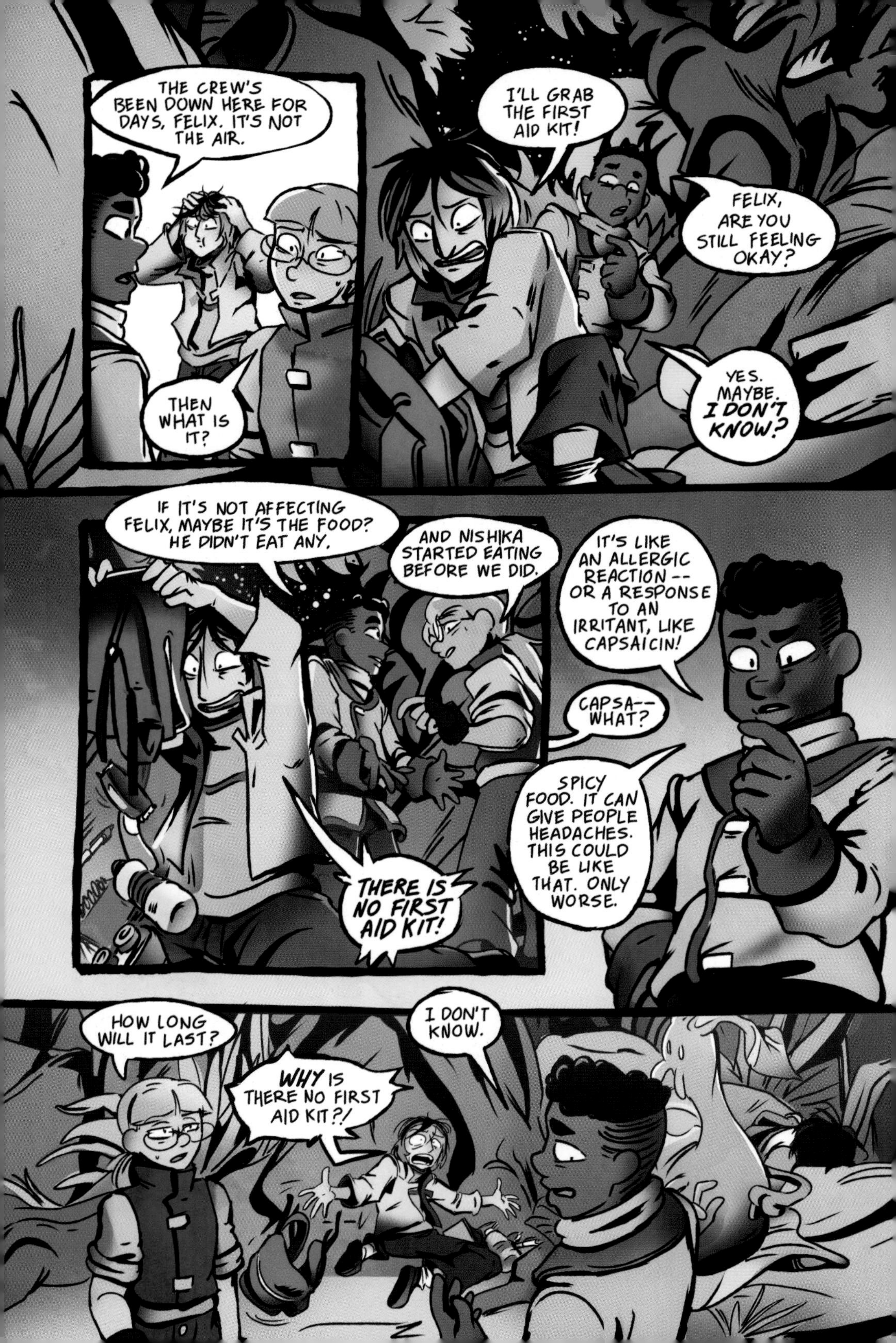
THE CREW'S BEEN DOWN HERE FOR DAYS, FELIX. IT'S NOT THE AIR.
THEN WHAT IS IT?
I'LL GRAB THE FIRST AID KIT!
FELIX, ARE YOU STILL FEELING OKAY?
YES. MAYBE. I DON'T KNOW?
IF IT'S NOT AFFECTING FELIX, MAYBE IT'S THE FOOD? HE DIDN'T EAT ANY.
AND NISHIKA STARTED EATING BEFORE WE DID.
IT'S LIKE AN ALLERGIC REACTION -- OR A RESPONSE TO AN IRRITANT, LIKE CAPSAICIN!
CAPSA-- WHAT?
SPICY FOOD. IT CAN GIVE PEOPLE HEADACHES. THIS COULD BE LIKE THAT. ONLY WORSE.
THERE IS NO FIRST AID KIT!
HOW LONG WILL IT LAST?
I DON'T KNOW.
WHY IS THERE NO FIRST AID KIT?!

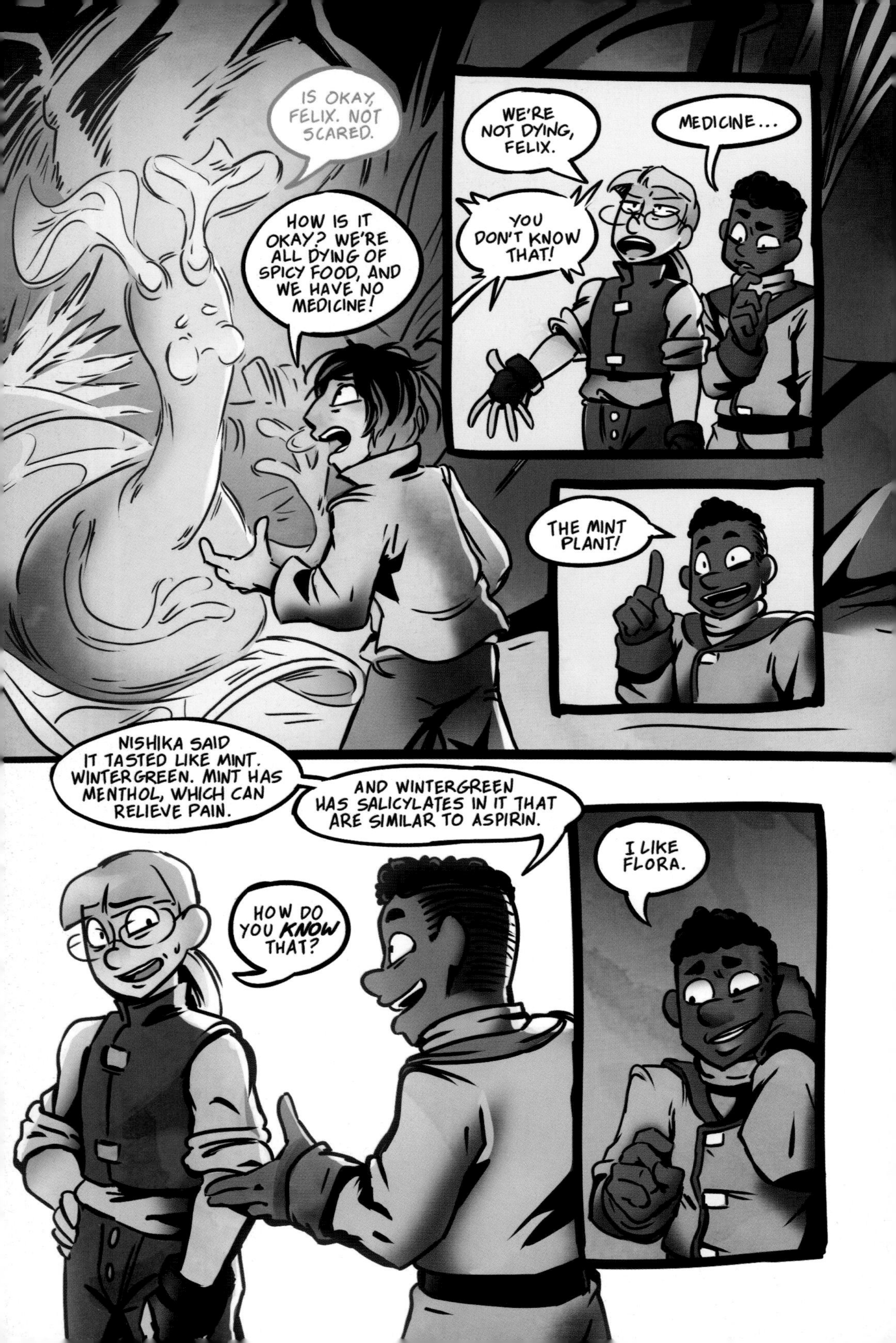
IS OKAY, FELIX. NOT SCARED.
HOW IS IT OKAY? WE'RE ALL DYING OF SPICY FOOD, AND WE HAVE NO MEDICINE!
WE'RE NOT DYING, FELIX.
MEDICINE...
YOU DON'T KNOW THAT!
THE MINT PLANT!
NISHIKA SAID IT TASTED LIKE MINT. WINTERGREEN. MINT HAS MENTHOL, WHICH CAN RELIEVE PAIN.
AND WINTERGREEN HAS SALICYLATES IN IT THAT ARE SIMILAR TO ASPIRIN.
HOW DO YOU KNOW THAT?
I LIKE FLORA.

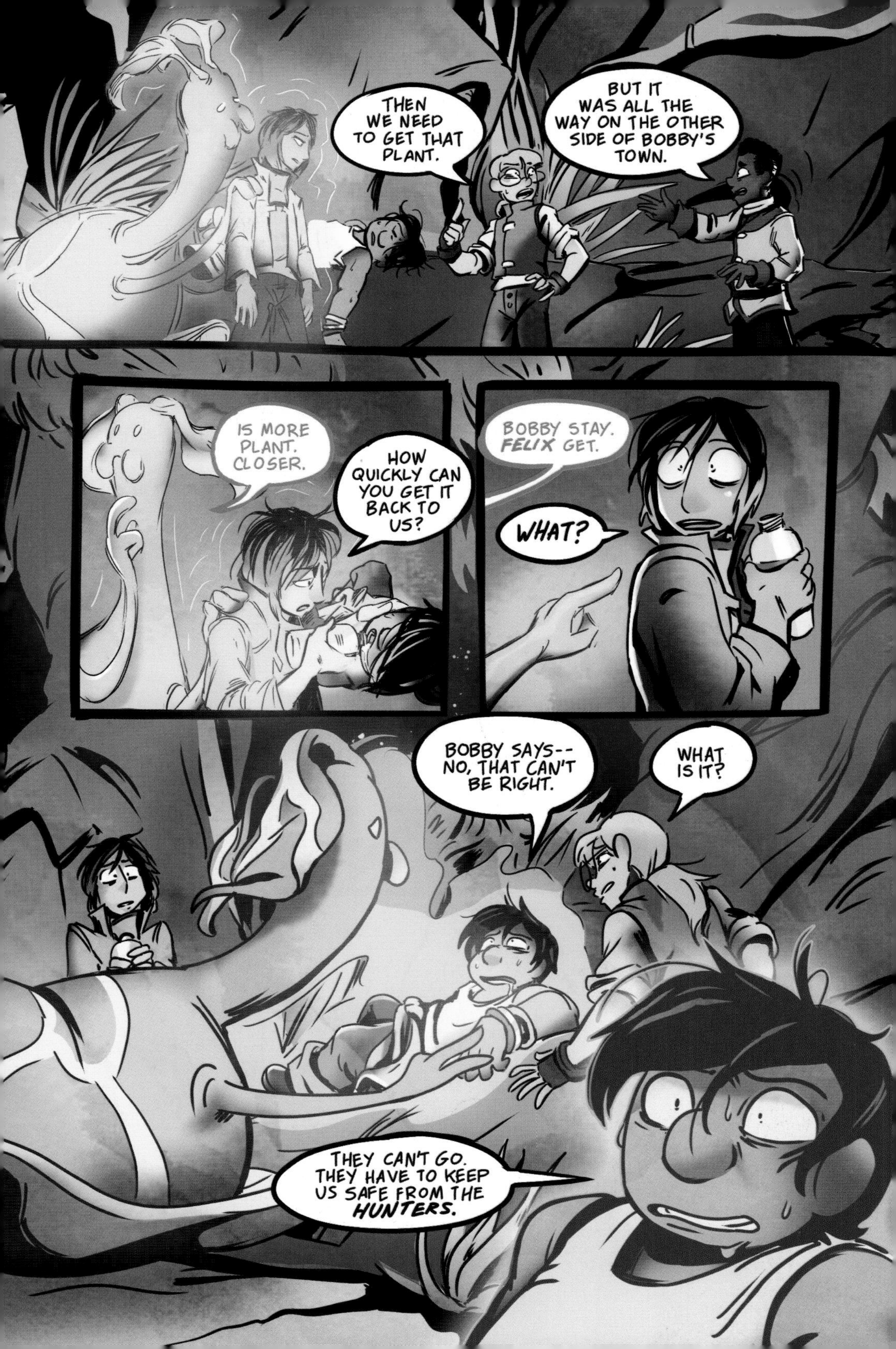
THEN WE NEED TO GET THAT PLANT.
BUT IT WAS ALL THE WAY ON THE OTHER SIDE OF BOBBY'S TOWN.
IS MORE PLANT. CLOSER.
HOW QUICKLY CAN YOU GET IT BACK TO US?
BOBBY STAY. *FELIX* GET.
WHAT?
BOBBY SAYS-- NO, THAT CAN'T BE RIGHT.
WHAT IS IT?
THEY CAN'T GO. THEY HAVE TO KEEP US SAFE FROM THE *HUNTERS.*

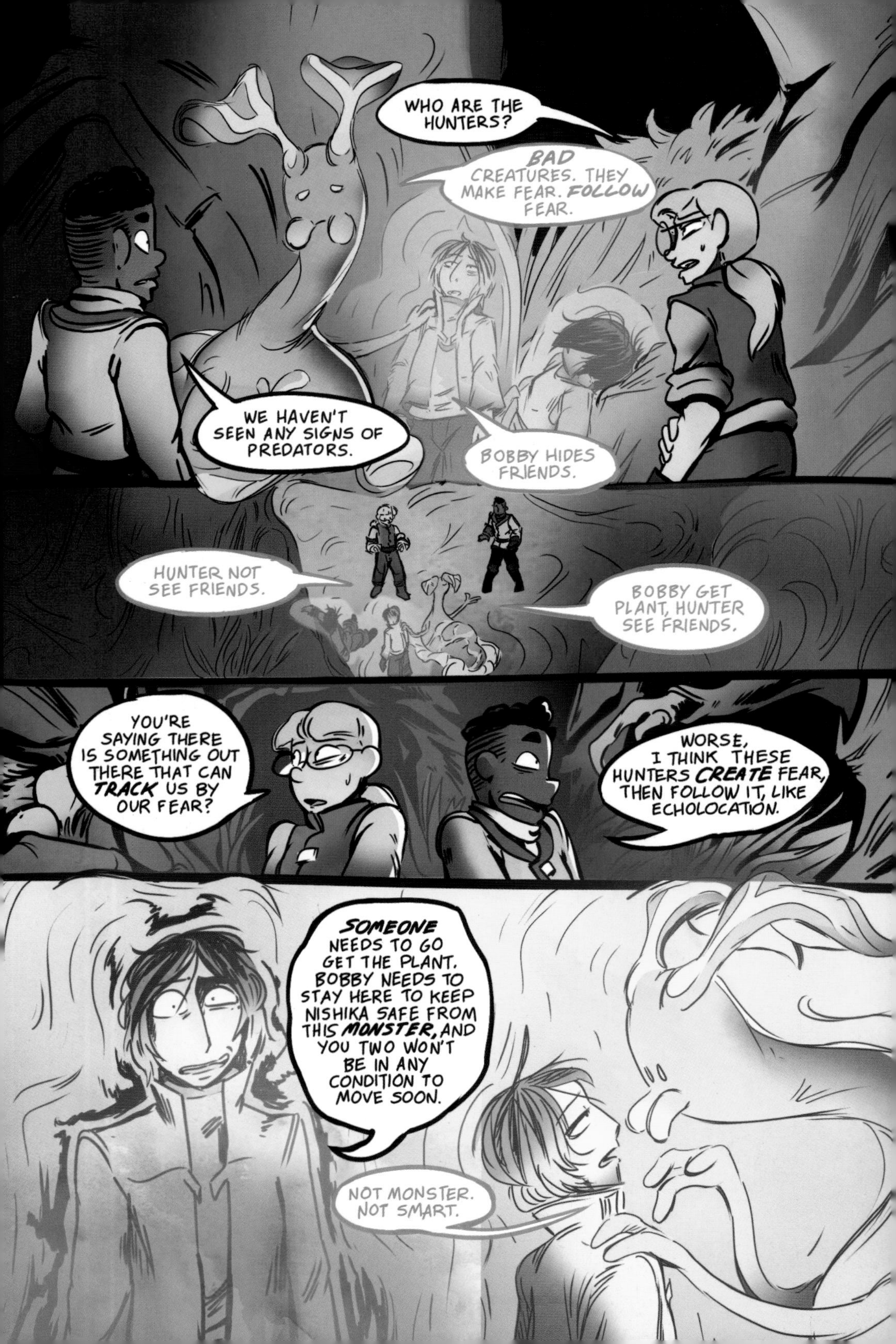
WHO ARE THE HUNTERS?
BAD CREATURES. THEY MAKE FEAR. FOLLOW FEAR.
WE HAVEN'T SEEN ANY SIGNS OF PREDATORS.
BOBBY HIDES FRIENDS.
HUNTER NOT SEE FRIENDS.
BOBBY GET PLANT, HUNTER SEE FRIENDS.
YOU'RE SAYING THERE IS SOMETHING OUT THERE THAT CAN TRACK US BY OUR FEAR?
WORSE, I THINK THESE HUNTERS CREATE FEAR, THEN FOLLOW IT, LIKE ECHOLOCATION.
SOMEONE NEEDS TO GO GET THE PLANT. BOBBY NEEDS TO STAY HERE TO KEEP NISHIKA SAFE FROM THIS MONSTER, AND YOU TWO WON'T BE IN ANY CONDITION TO MOVE SOON.
NOT MONSTER. NOT SMART.

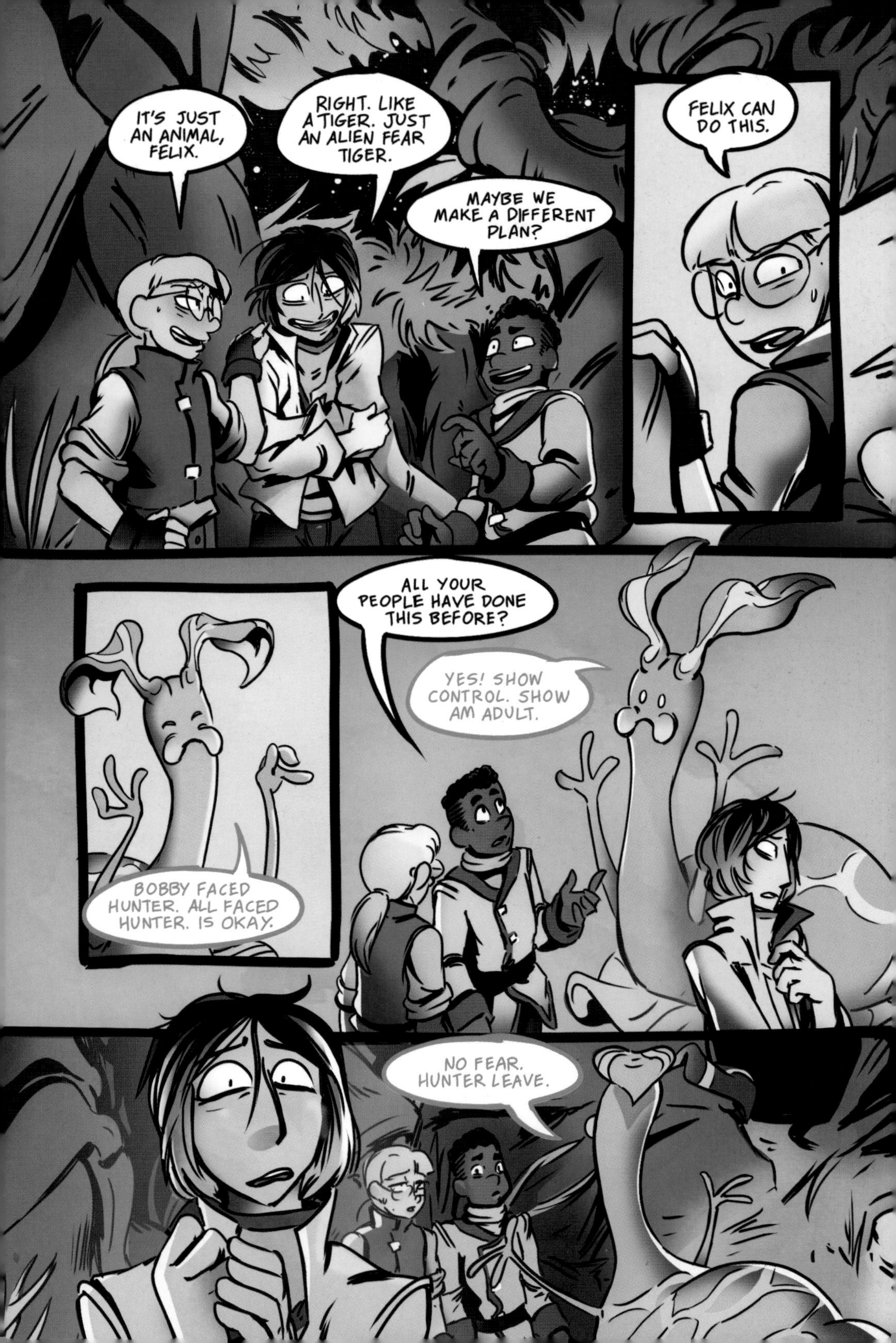
IT'S JUST AN ANIMAL, FELIX.
RIGHT. LIKE A TIGER. JUST AN ALIEN FEAR TIGER.
MAYBE WE MAKE A DIFFERENT PLAN?
FELIX CAN DO THIS.
BOBBY FACED HUNTER. ALL FACED HUNTER. IS OKAY.
ALL YOUR PEOPLE HAVE DONE THIS BEFORE?
YES! SHOW CONTROL. SHOW AM ADULT.
NO FEAR. HUNTER LEAVE.

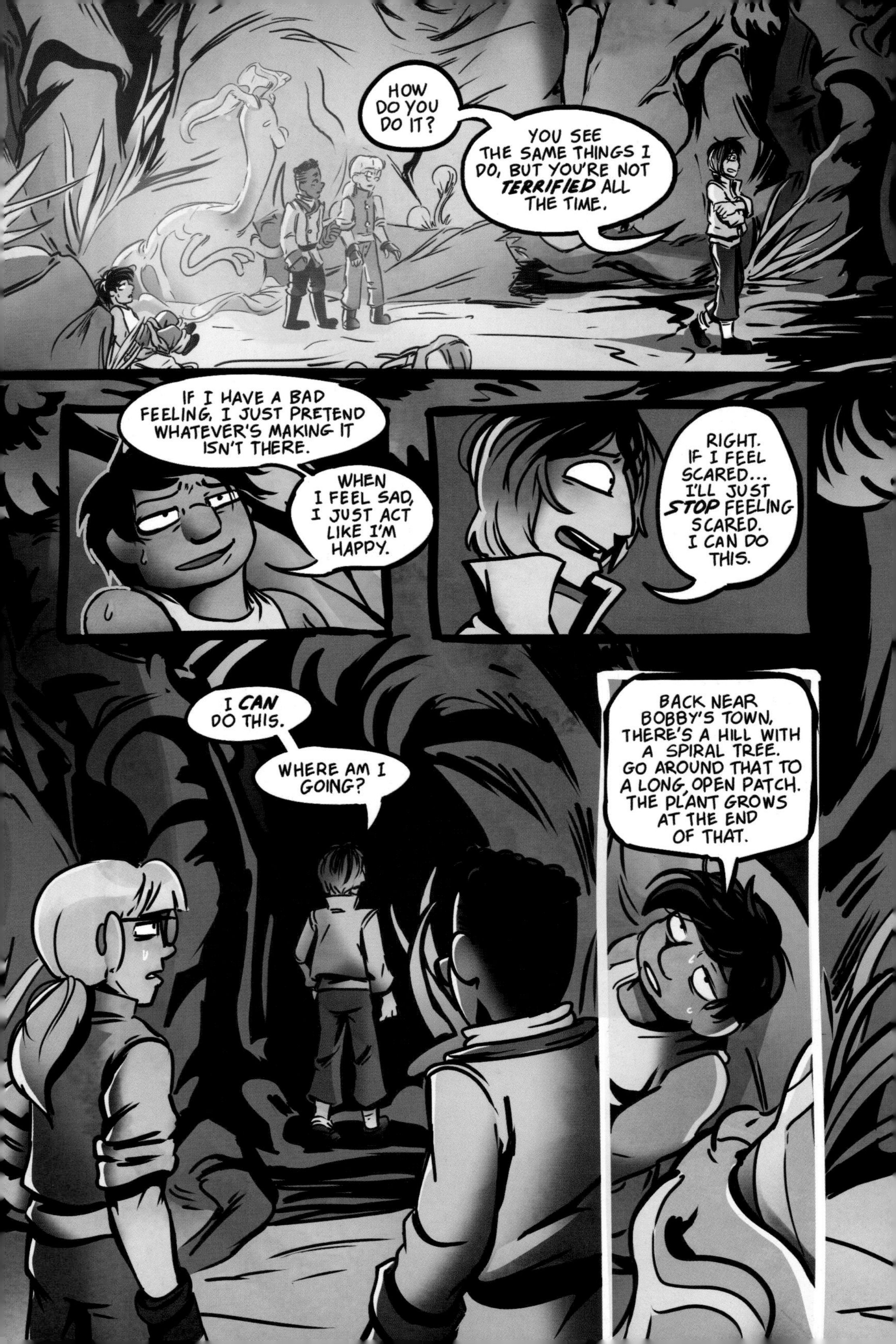
HOW DO YOU DO IT?
YOU SEE THE SAME THINGS I DO, BUT YOU'RE NOT TERRIFIED ALL THE TIME.
IF I HAVE A BAD FEELING, I JUST PRETEND WHATEVER'S MAKING IT ISN'T THERE.
WHEN I FEEL SAD, I JUST ACT LIKE I'M HAPPY.
RIGHT. IF I FEEL SCARED... I'LL JUST STOP FEELING SCARED. I CAN DO THIS.
I CAN DO THIS.
WHERE AM I GOING?
BACK NEAR BOBBY'S TOWN, THERE'S A HILL WITH A SPIRAL TREE. GO AROUND THAT TO A LONG, OPEN PATCH. THE PLANT GROWS AT THE END OF THAT.

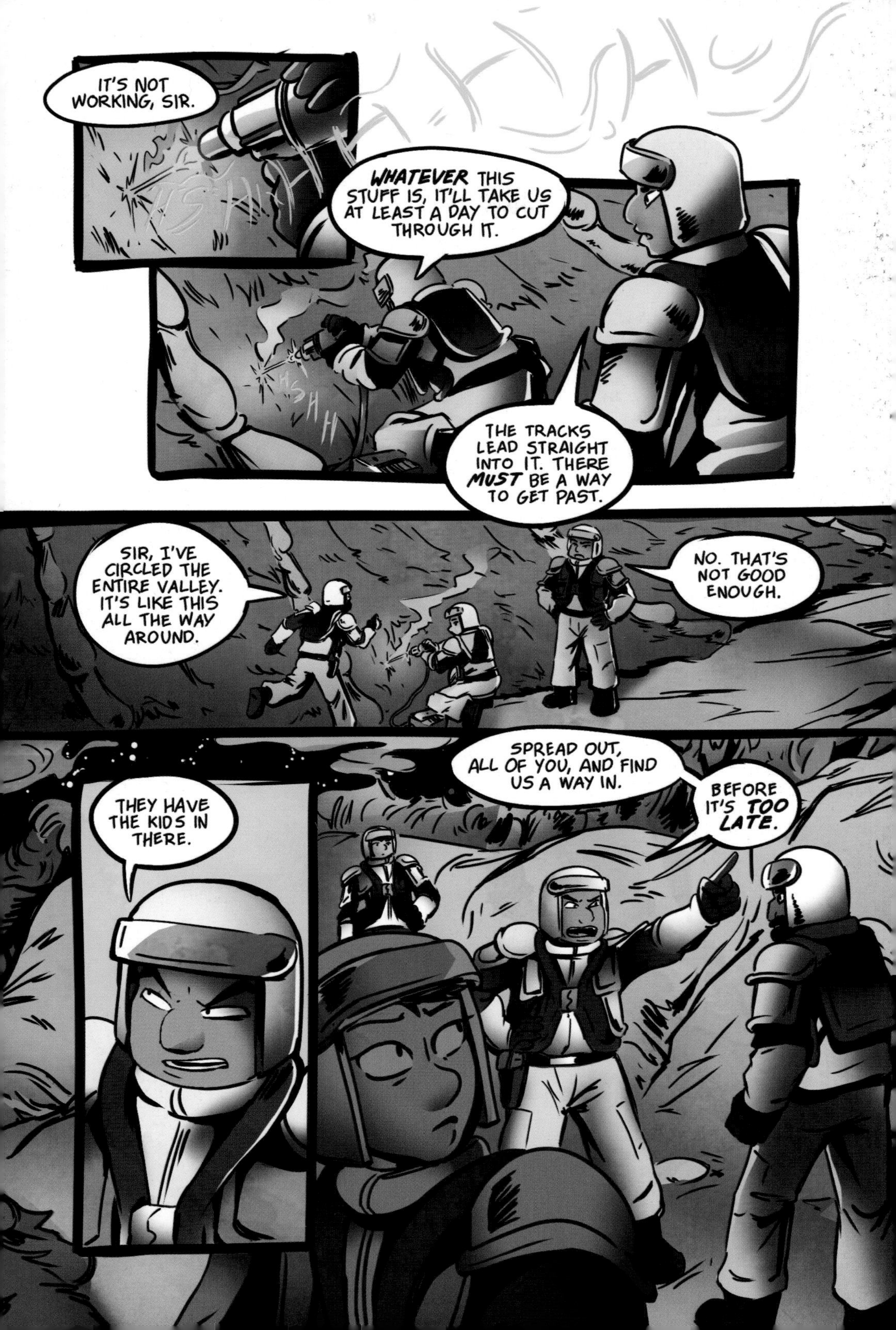
IT'S NOT WORKING, SIR.
WHATEVER THIS STUFF IS, IT'LL TAKE US AT LEAST A DAY TO CUT THROUGH IT.
THE TRACKS LEAD STRAIGHT INTO IT. THERE MUST BE A WAY TO GET PAST.
SIR, I'VE CIRCLED THE ENTIRE VALLEY. IT'S LIKE THIS ALL THE WAY AROUND.
NO. THAT'S NOT GOOD ENOUGH.
THEY HAVE THE KIDS IN THERE.
SPREAD OUT, ALL OF YOU, AND FIND US A WAY IN.
BEFORE IT'S TOO LATE.

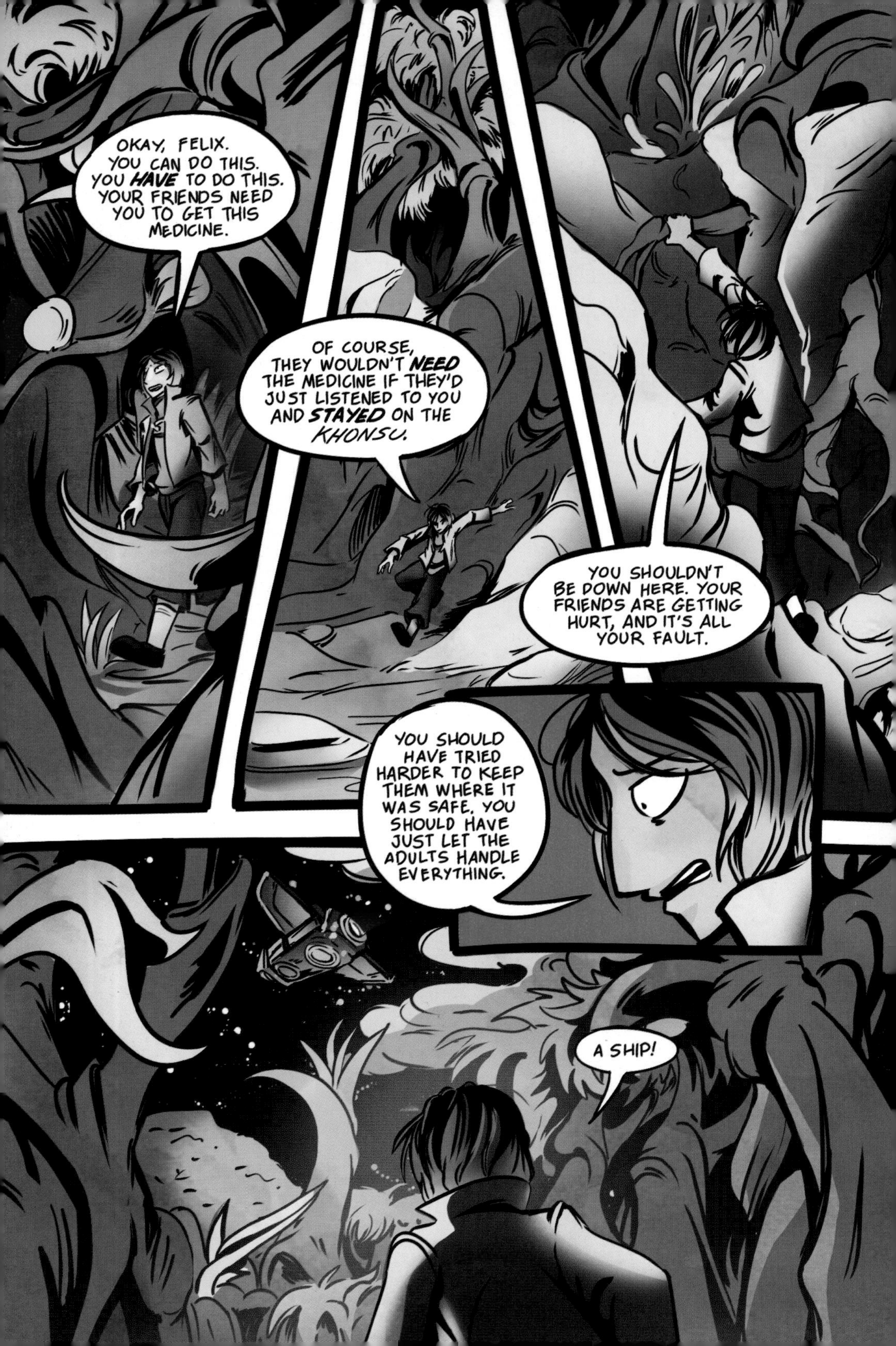
OKAY, FELIX. YOU CAN DO THIS. YOU ***HAVE*** TO DO THIS. YOUR FRIENDS NEED YOU TO GET THIS MEDICINE.
OF COURSE, THEY WOULDN'T ***NEED*** THE MEDICINE IF THEY'D JUST LISTENED TO YOU AND ***STAYED*** ON THE *KHONSU*.
YOU SHOULDN'T BE DOWN HERE. YOUR FRIENDS ARE GETTING HURT, AND IT'S ALL YOUR FAULT.
YOU SHOULD HAVE TRIED HARDER TO KEEP THEM WHERE IT WAS SAFE. YOU SHOULD HAVE JUST LET THE ADULTS HANDLE EVERYTHING.
A SHIP!

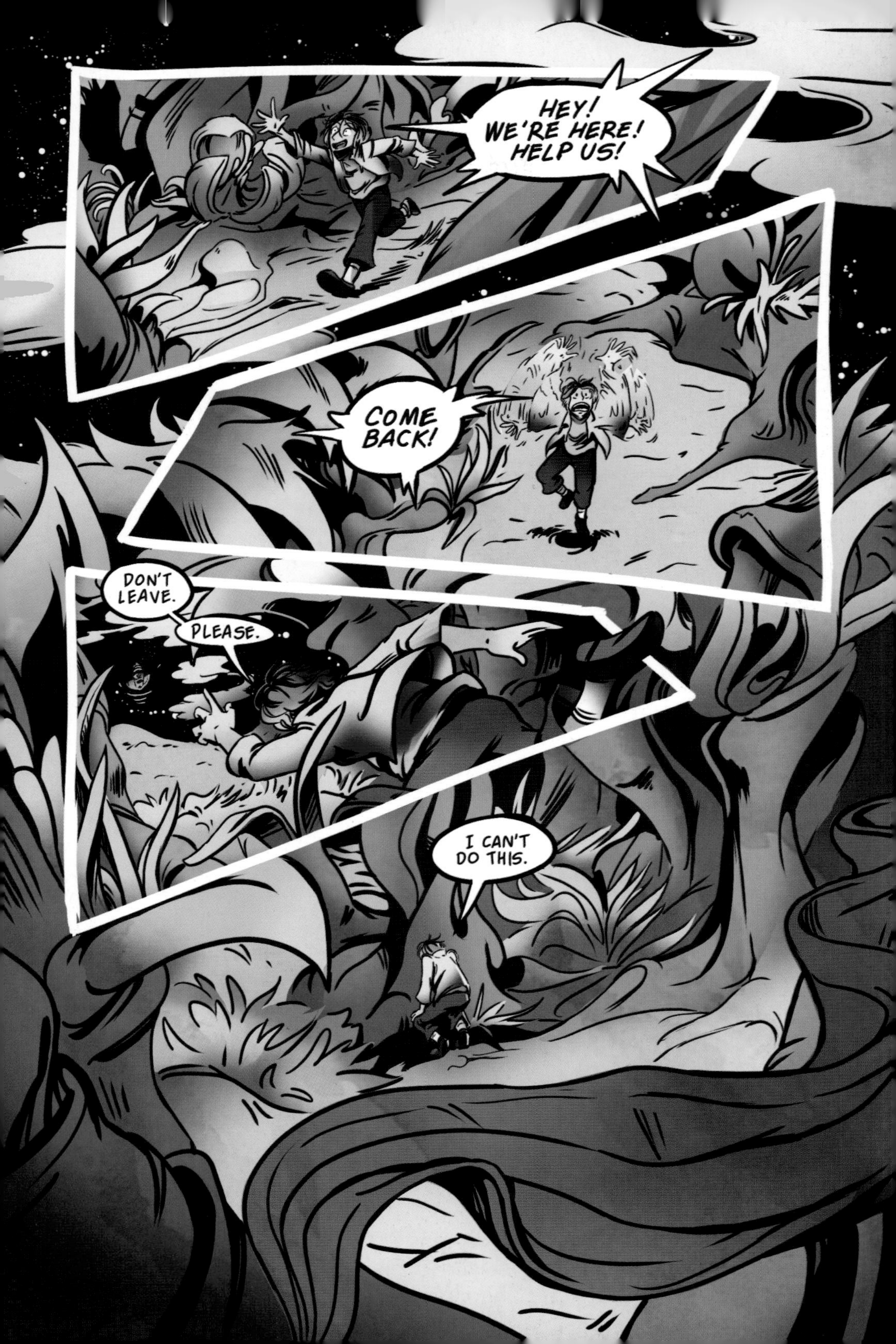
HEY! WE'RE HERE! HELP US!
COME BACK!
DON'T LEAVE.
PLEASE.
I CAN'T DO THIS.

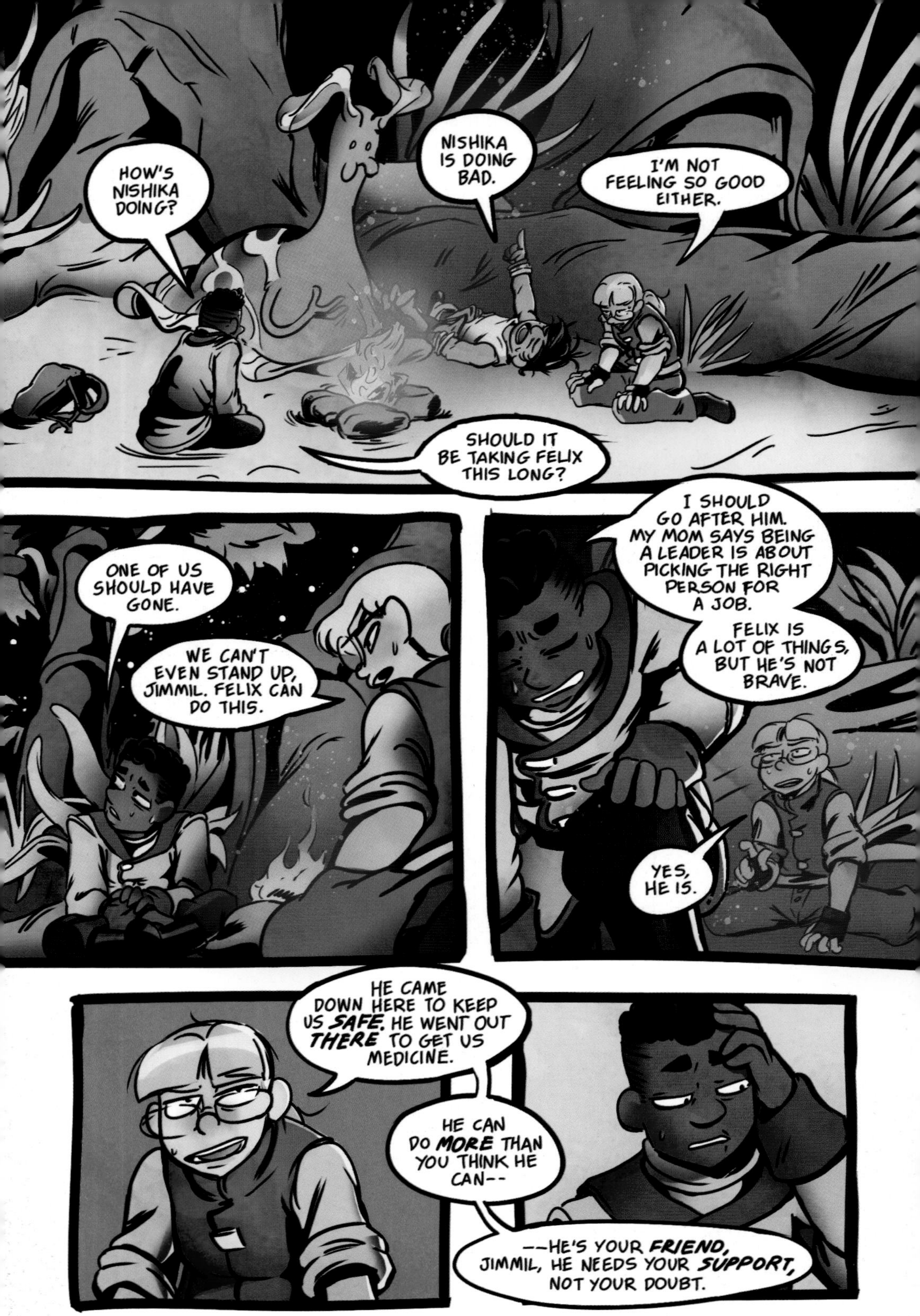
HOW'S NISHIKA DOING?
NISHIKA IS DOING BAD.
I'M NOT FEELING SO GOOD EITHER.
SHOULD IT BE TAKING FELIX THIS LONG?
ONE OF US SHOULD HAVE GONE.
WE CAN'T EVEN STAND UP, JIMMIL. FELIX CAN DO THIS.
I SHOULD GO AFTER HIM. MY MOM SAYS BEING A LEADER IS ABOUT PICKING THE RIGHT PERSON FOR A JOB.
FELIX IS A LOT OF THINGS, BUT HE'S NOT BRAVE.
YES, HE IS.
HE CAME DOWN HERE TO KEEP US SAFE. HE WENT OUT THERE TO GET US MEDICINE.
HE CAN DO MORE THAN YOU THINK HE CAN--
--HE'S YOUR FRIEND, JIMMIL, HE NEEDS YOUR SUPPORT, NOT YOUR DOUBT.

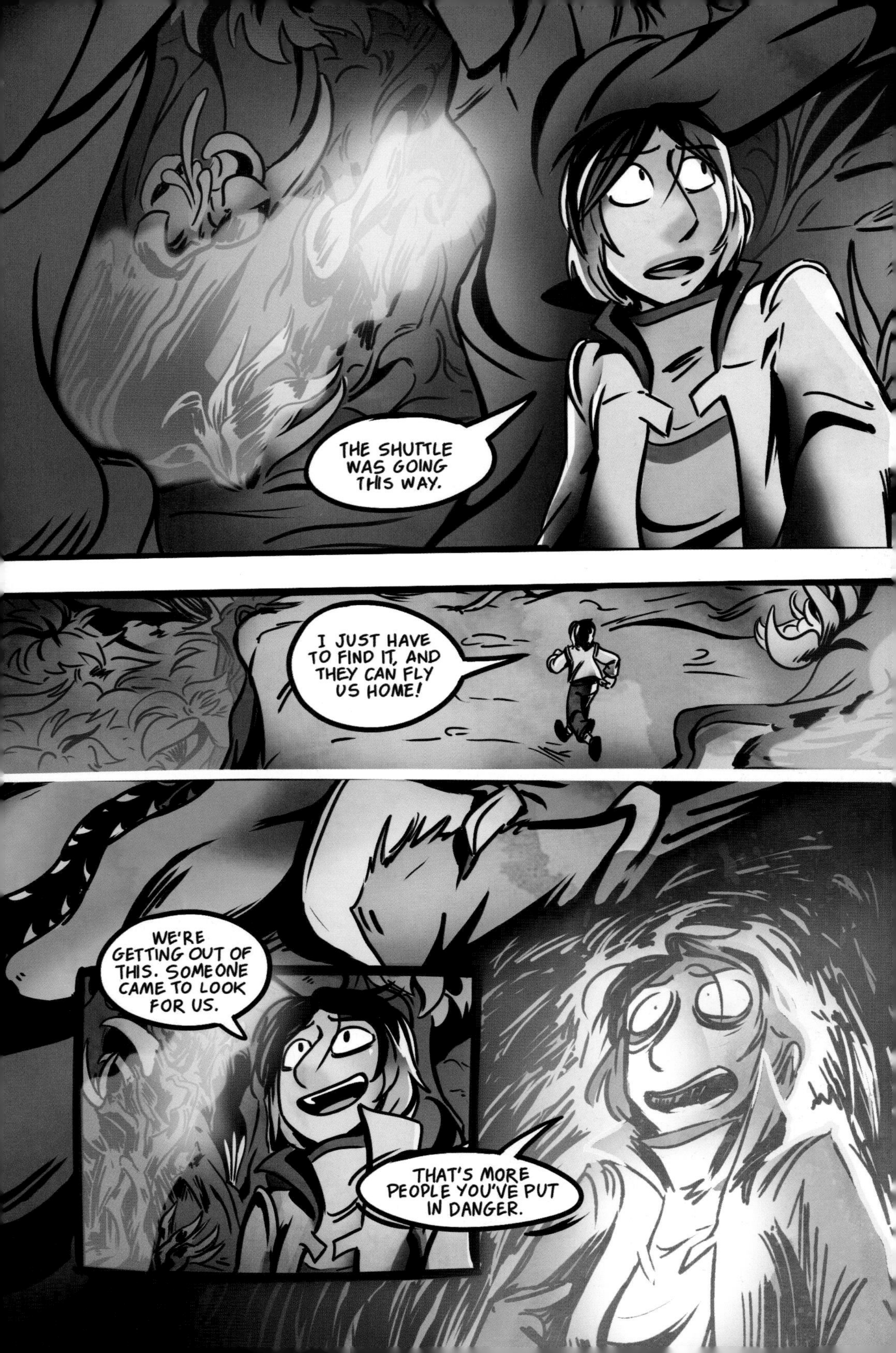
THE SHUTTLE WAS GOING THIS WAY.
I JUST HAVE TO FIND IT, AND THEY CAN FLY US HOME!
WE'RE GETTING OUT OF THIS. SOMEONE CAME TO LOOK FOR US.
THAT'S MORE PEOPLE YOU'VE PUT IN DANGER.

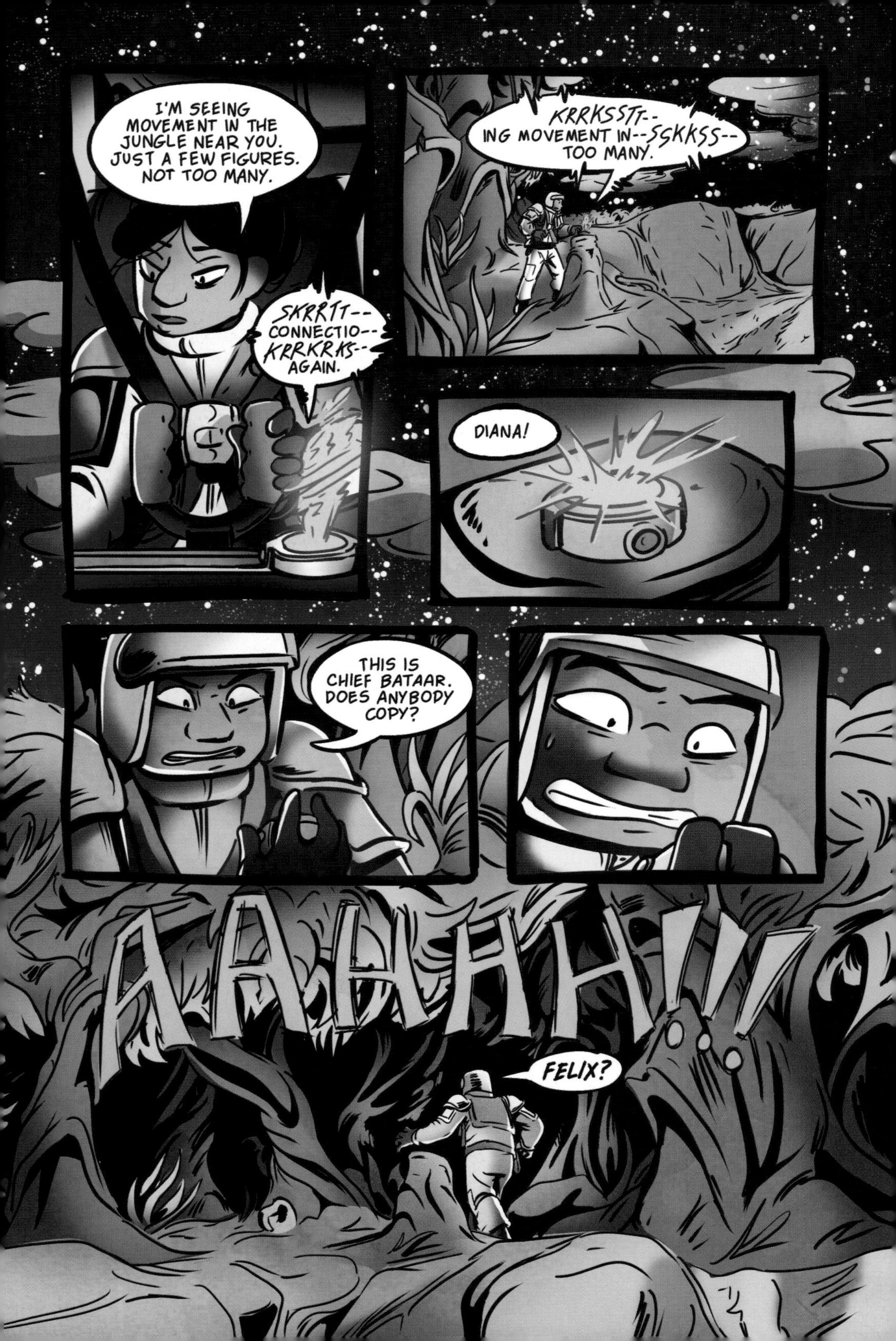
I'M SEEING MOVEMENT IN THE JUNGLE NEAR YOU. JUST A FEW FIGURES. NOT TOO MANY.
KRRKSSTT-- ING MOVEMENT IN--SSKKSS-- TOO MANY.
SKRRTT-- CONNECTIO-- KRRKRKS-- AGAIN.
DIANA!
THIS IS CHIEF BATAAR. DOES ANYBODY COPY?
AAAHHH!!!
FELIX?

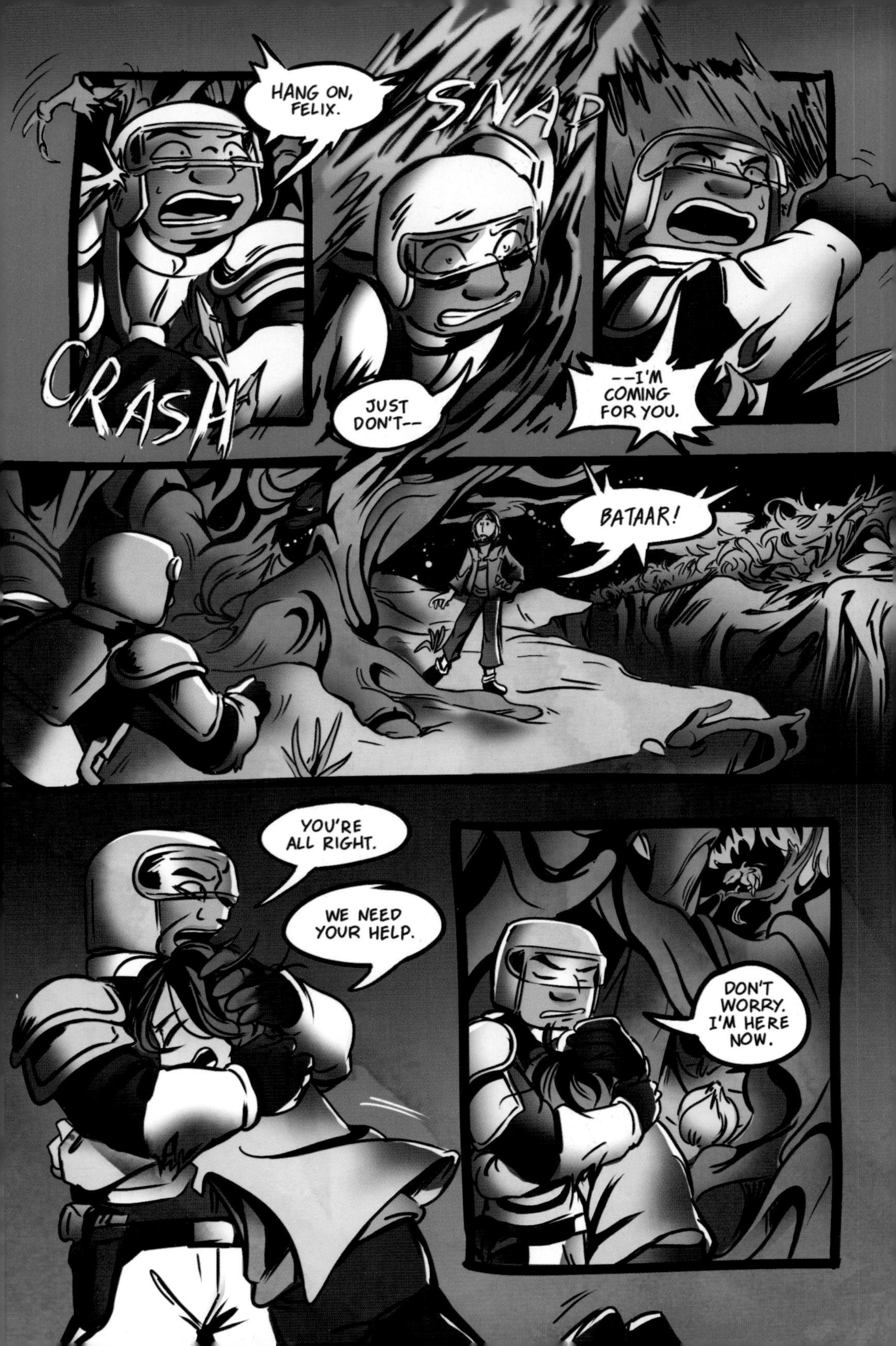

HANG ON, FELIX.
SNAP
CRASH
JUST DON'T--
--I'M COMING FOR YOU.
BATAAR!
YOU'RE ALL RIGHT.
WE NEED YOUR HELP.
DON'T WORRY. I'M HERE NOW.

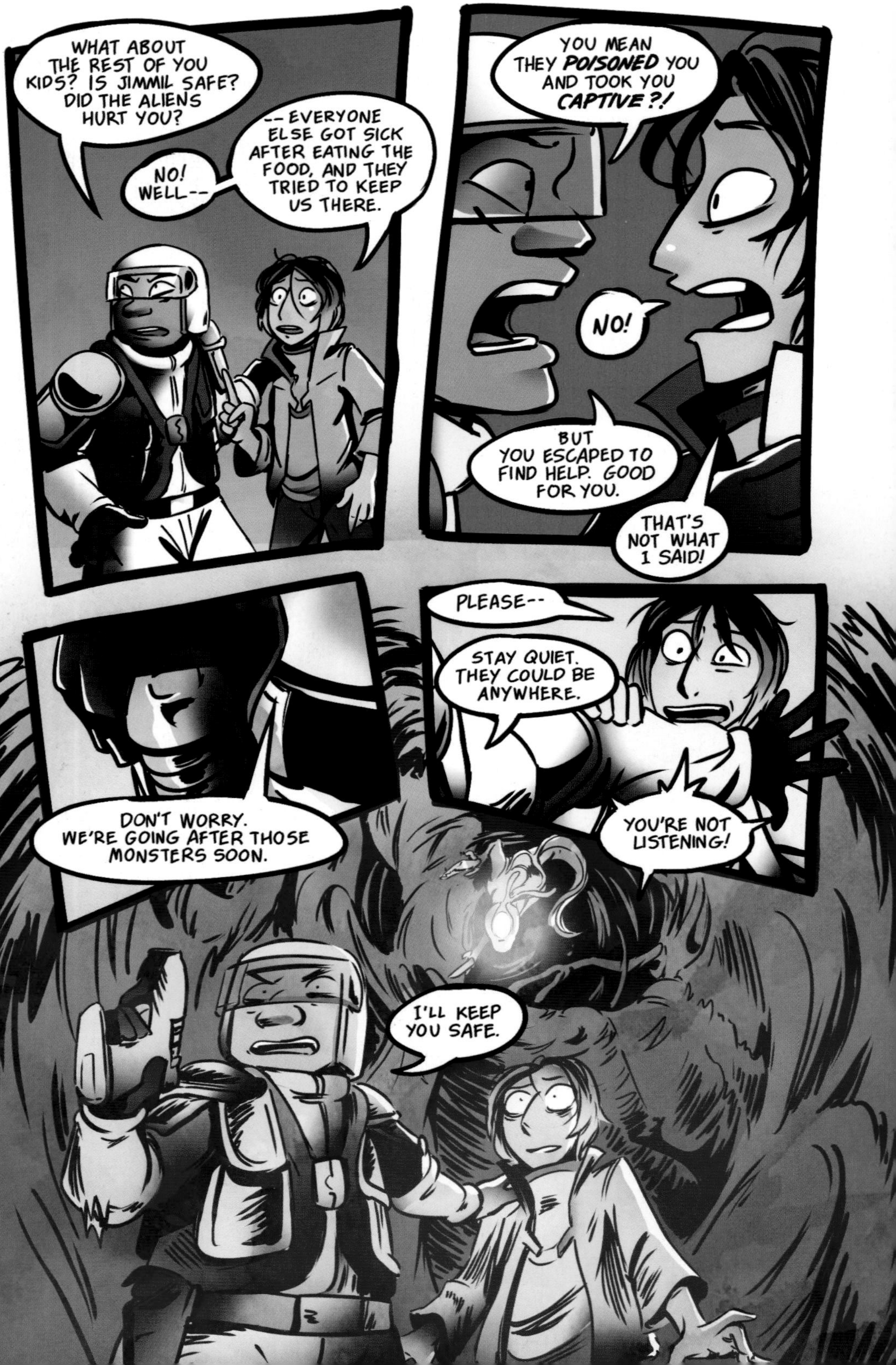
WHAT ABOUT THE REST OF YOU KIDS? IS JIMMIL SAFE? DID THE ALIENS HURT YOU?
NO! WELL--
--EVERYONE ELSE GOT SICK AFTER EATING THE FOOD, AND THEY TRIED TO KEEP US THERE.
YOU MEAN THEY POISONED YOU AND TOOK YOU CAPTIVE?!
NO!
BUT YOU ESCAPED TO FIND HELP. GOOD FOR YOU.
THAT'S NOT WHAT I SAID!
DON'T WORRY. WE'RE GOING AFTER THOSE MONSTERS SOON.
PLEASE--
STAY QUIET. THEY COULD BE ANYWHERE.
YOU'RE NOT LISTENING!
I'LL KEEP YOU SAFE.

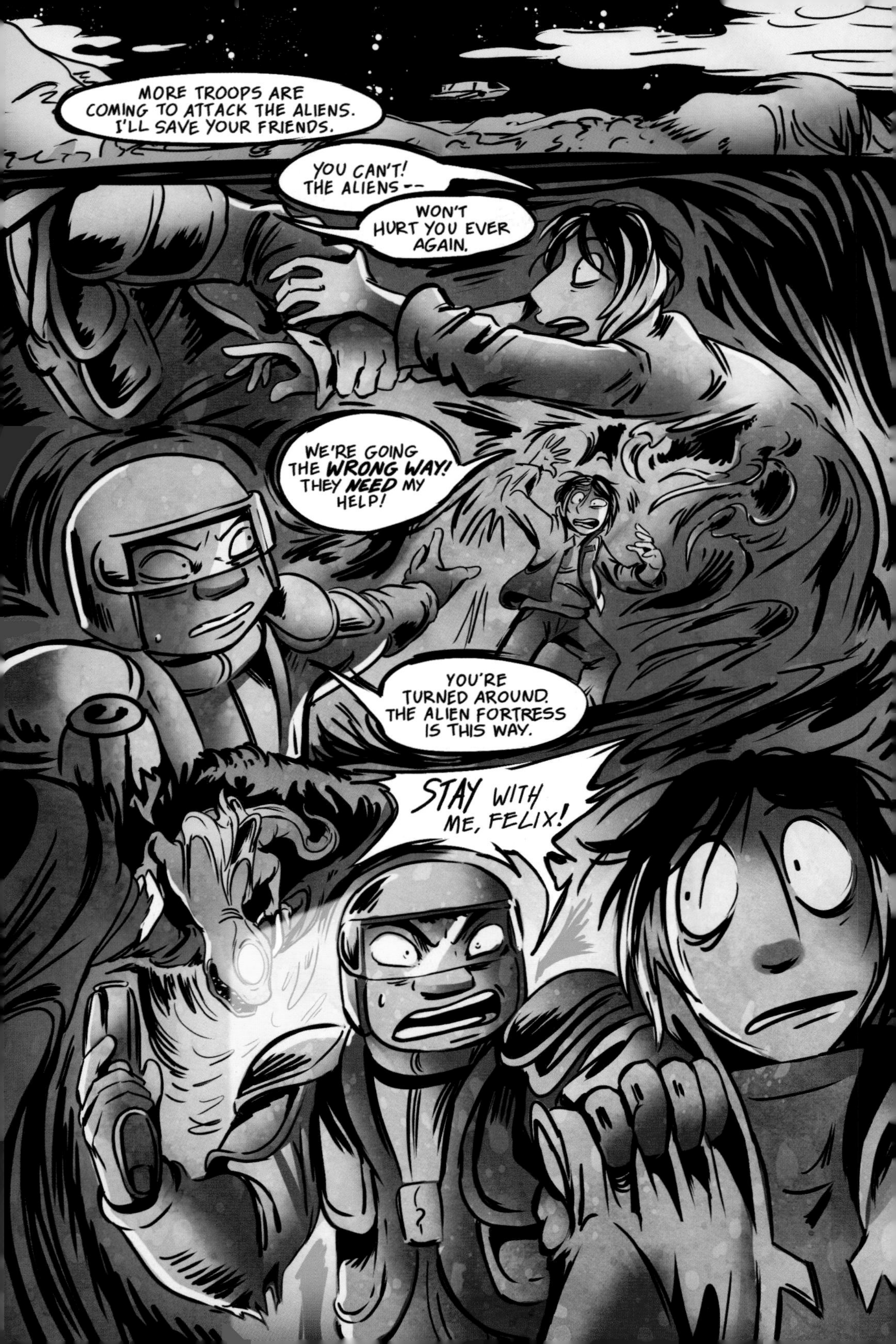

MORE TROOPS ARE COMING TO ATTACK THE ALIENS. I'LL SAVE YOUR FRIENDS.
YOU CAN'T! THE ALIENS --
WON'T HURT YOU EVER AGAIN.
WE'RE GOING THE **WRONG WAY!** THEY **NEED** MY HELP!
YOU'RE TURNED AROUND. THE ALIEN FORTRESS IS THIS WAY.
STAY WITH ME, FELIX!

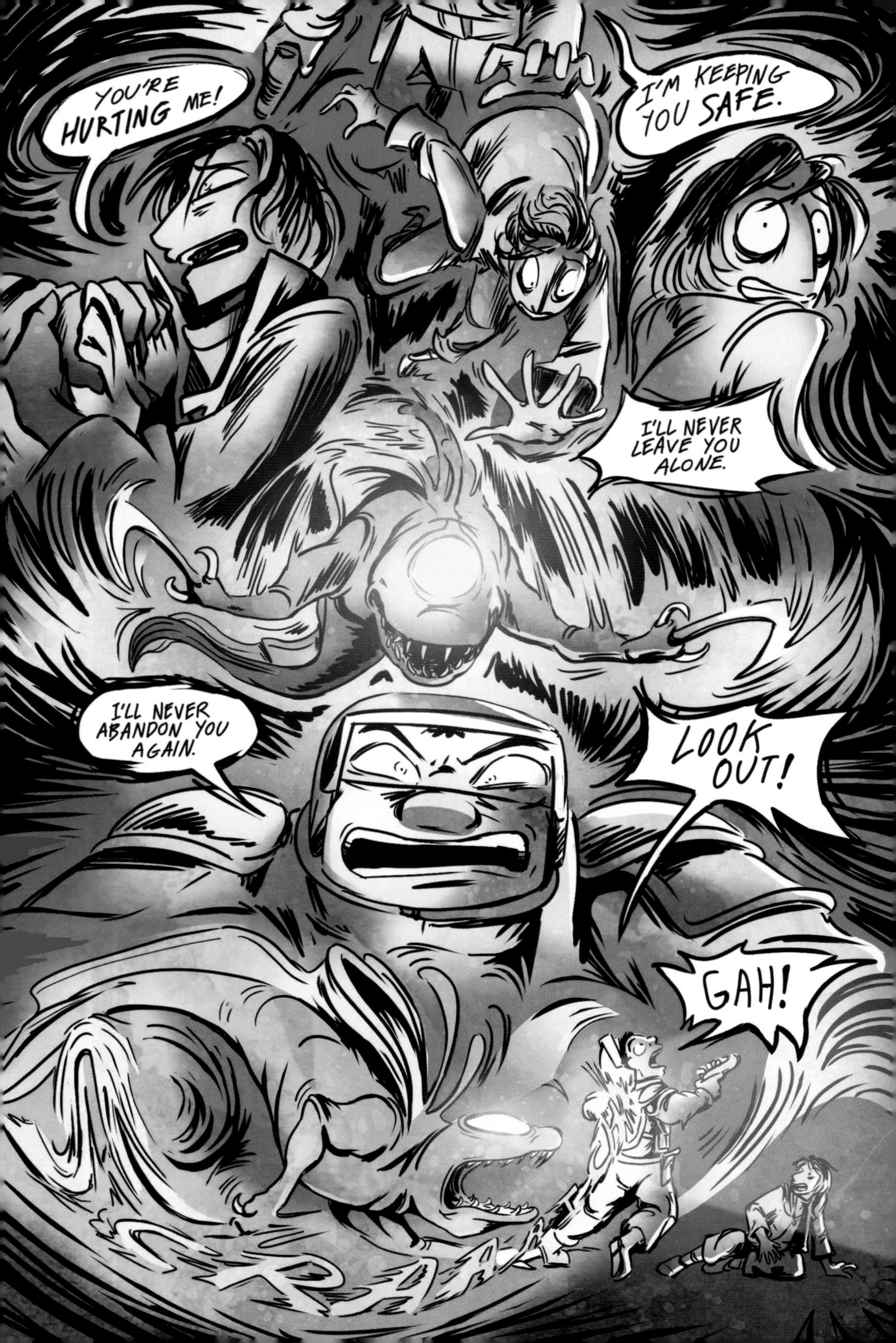
YOU'RE HURTING ME!
I'M KEEPING YOU SAFE.
I'LL NEVER LEAVE YOU ALONE.
I'LL NEVER ABANDON YOU AGAIN.
LOOK OUT!
GAH!

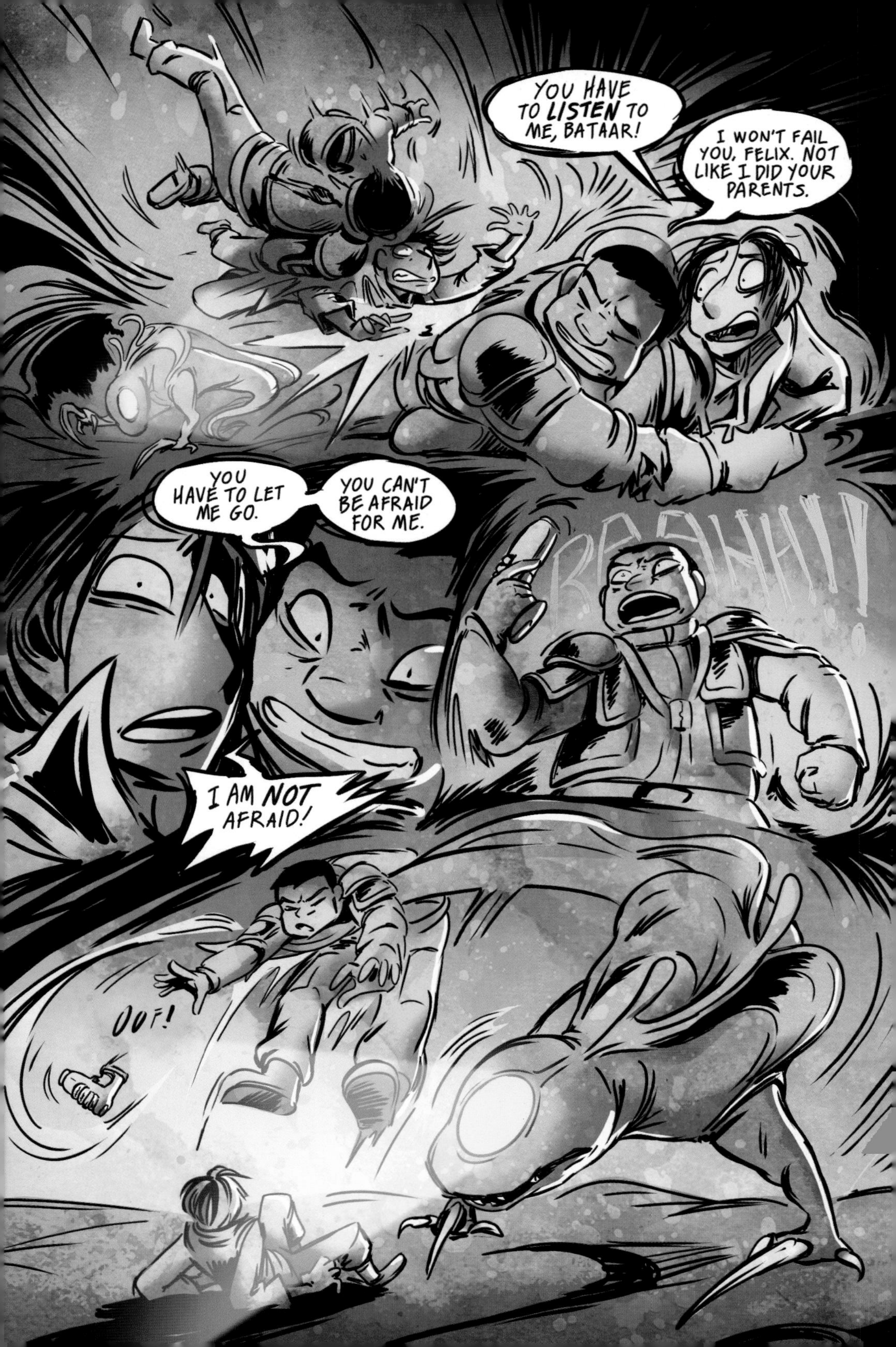
YOU HAVE TO LISTEN TO ME, BATAAR!
I WON'T FAIL YOU, FELIX. NOT LIKE I DID YOUR PARENTS.
YOU HAVE TO LET ME GO.
YOU CAN'T BE AFRAID FOR ME.
I AM NOT AFRAID!
OOF!

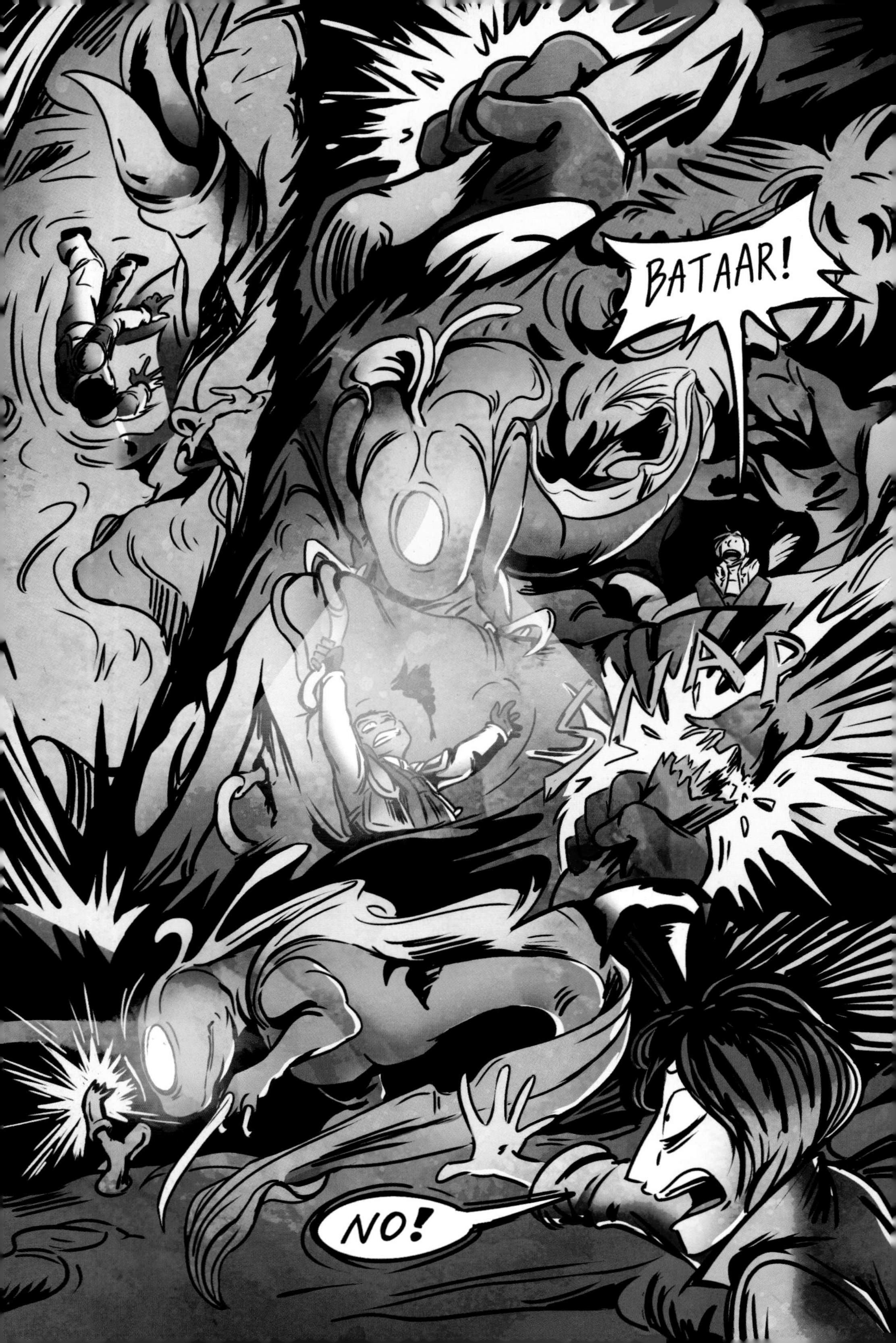
BATAAR!
SNAP
NO!

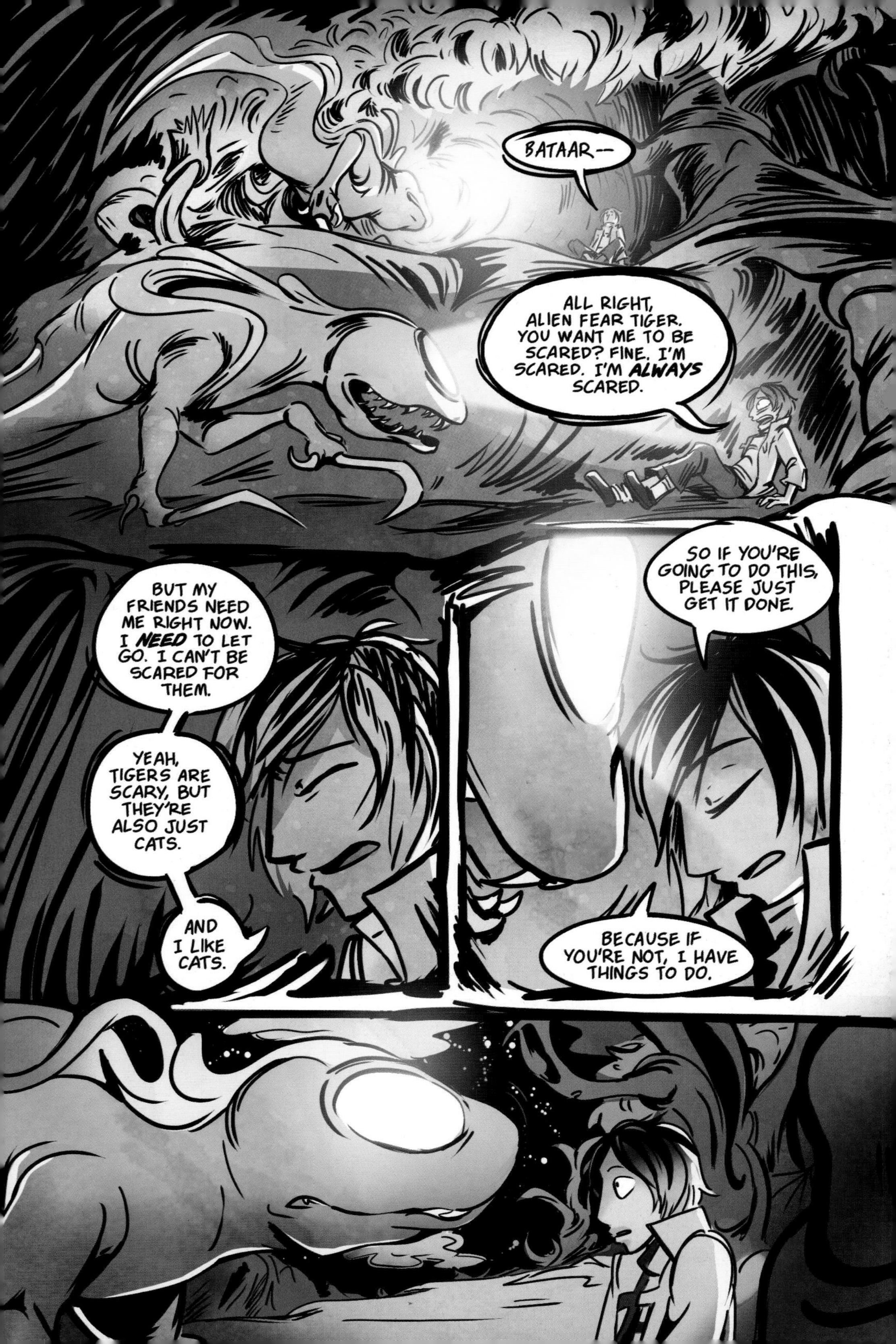
BATAAR--
ALL RIGHT, ALIEN FEAR TIGER. YOU WANT ME TO BE SCARED? FINE. I'M SCARED. I'M ALWAYS SCARED.
BUT MY FRIENDS NEED ME RIGHT NOW. I NEED TO LET GO. I CAN'T BE SCARED FOR THEM.
YEAH, TIGERS ARE SCARY, BUT THEY'RE ALSO JUST CATS.
AND I LIKE CATS.
SO IF YOU'RE GOING TO DO THIS, PLEASE JUST GET IT DONE.
BECAUSE IF YOU'RE NOT, I HAVE THINGS TO DO.

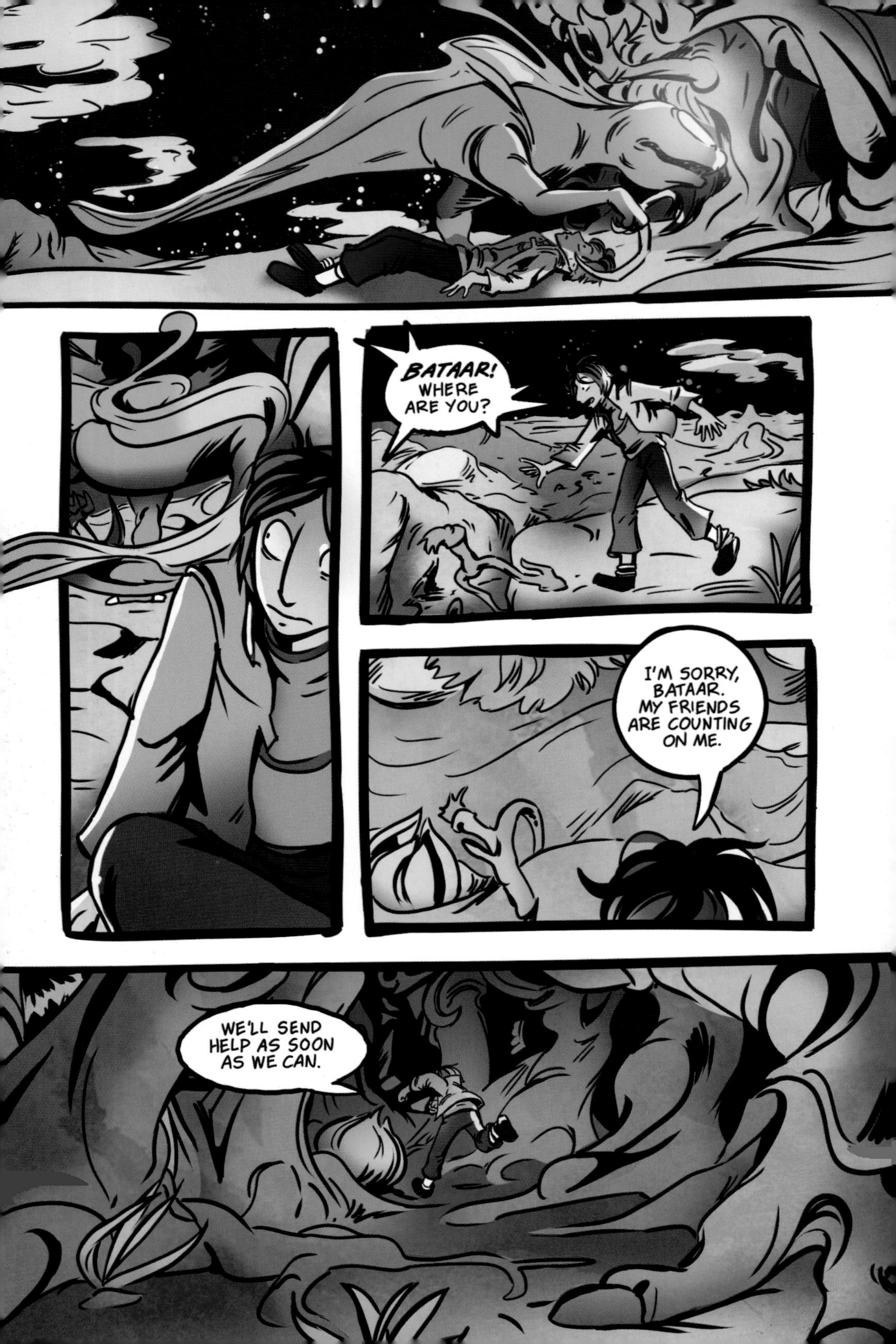
BATAAR! WHERE ARE YOU?
I'M SORRY, BATAAR. MY FRIENDS ARE COUNTING ON ME.
WE'LL SEND HELP AS SOON AS WE CAN.

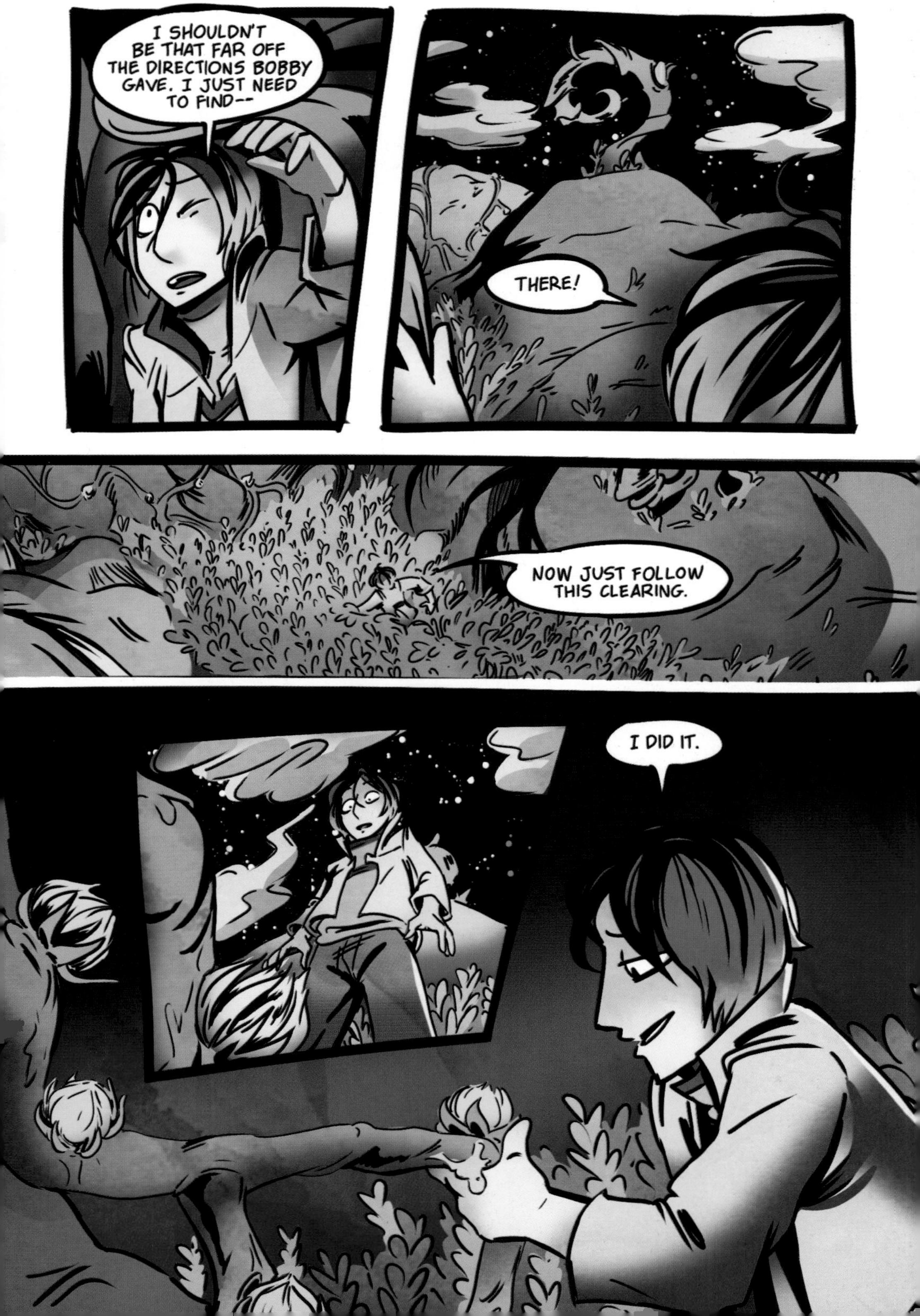
I SHOULDN'T BE THAT FAR OFF THE DIRECTIONS BOBBY GAVE. I JUST NEED TO FIND--
THERE!
NOW JUST FOLLOW THIS CLEARING.
I DID IT.

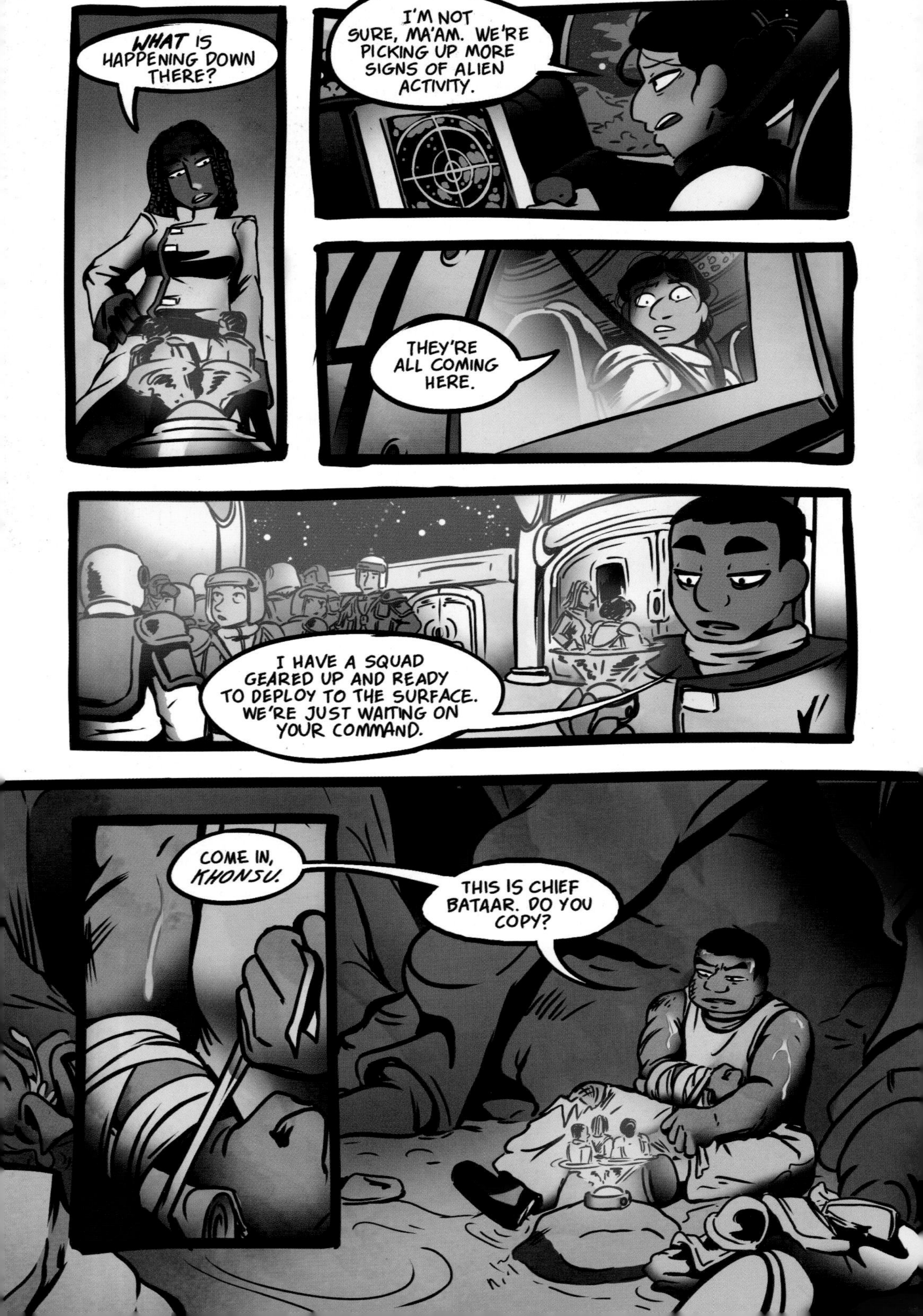
WHAT IS HAPPENING DOWN THERE?
I'M NOT SURE, MA'AM. WE'RE PICKING UP MORE SIGNS OF ALIEN ACTIVITY.
THEY'RE ALL COMING HERE.
I HAVE A SQUAD GEARED UP AND READY TO DEPLOY TO THE SURFACE. WE'RE JUST WAITING ON YOUR COMMAND.
COME IN, KHONSU.
THIS IS CHIEF BATAAR. DO YOU COPY?

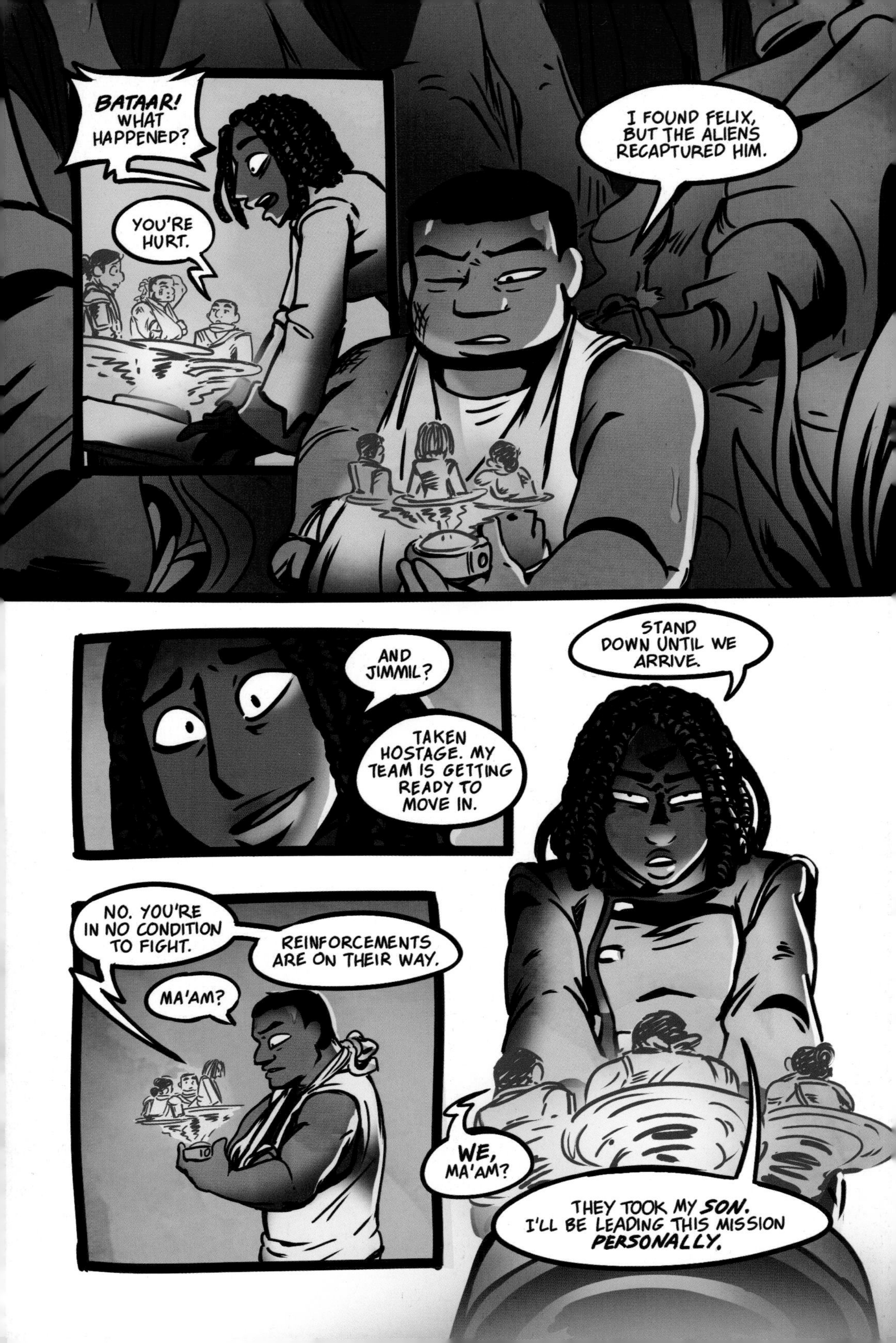
BATAAR! WHAT HAPPENED?
YOU'RE HURT.
I FOUND FELIX, BUT THE ALIENS RECAPTURED HIM.
AND JIMMIL?
TAKEN HOSTAGE. MY TEAM IS GETTING READY TO MOVE IN.
STAND DOWN UNTIL WE ARRIVE.
NO. YOU'RE IN NO CONDITION TO FIGHT.
REINFORCEMENTS ARE ON THEIR WAY.
MA'AM?
WE, MA'AM?
THEY TOOK MY SON. I'LL BE LEADING THIS MISSION PERSONALLY.

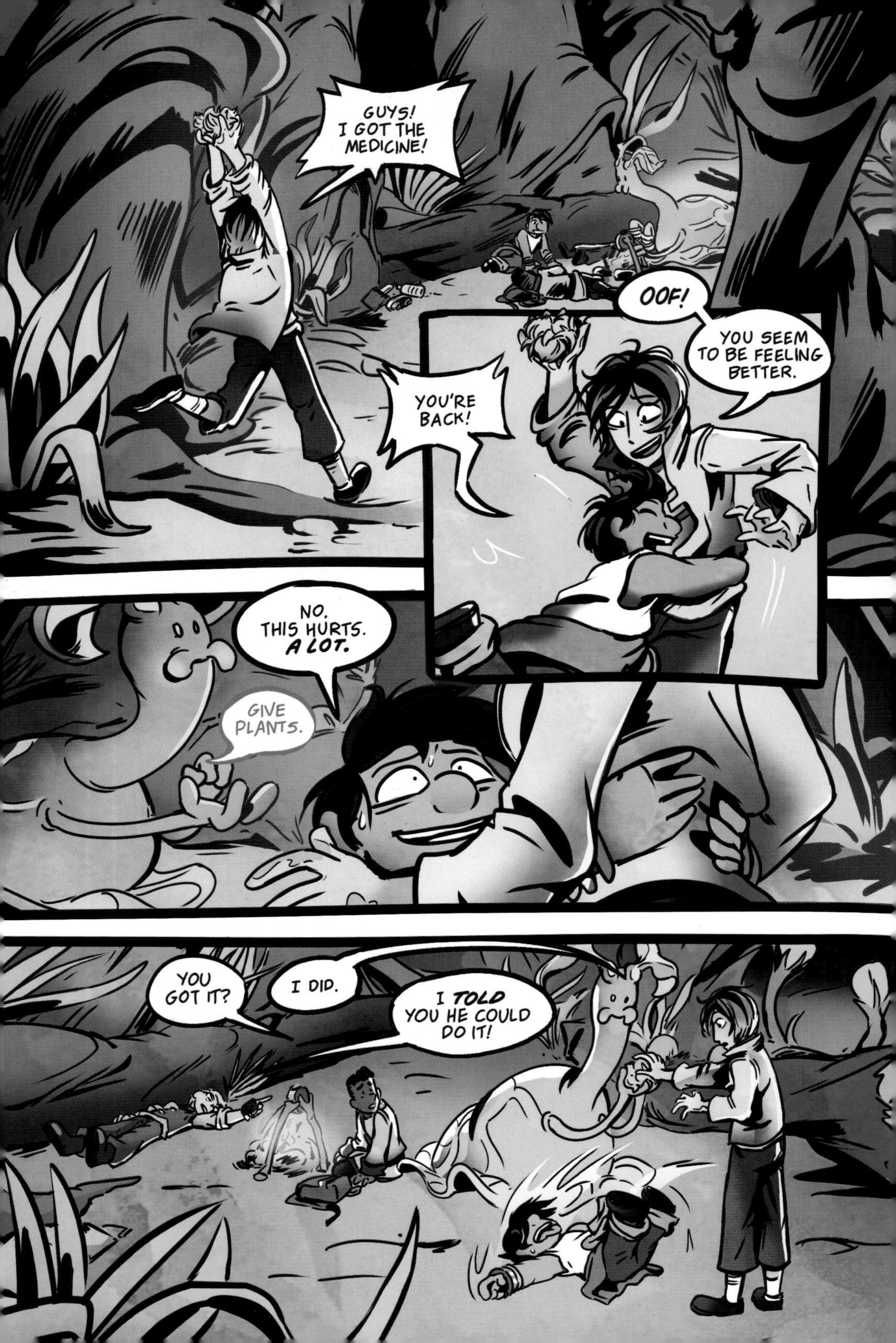
GUYS! I GOT THE MEDICINE!
OOF!
YOU SEEM TO BE FEELING BETTER.
YOU'RE BACK!
NO. THIS HURTS. A LOT.
GIVE PLANTS.
YOU GOT IT?
I DID.
I TOLD YOU HE COULD DO IT!

YOU DIDN'T THINK I COULD DO IT?

I...

I'M SORRY.

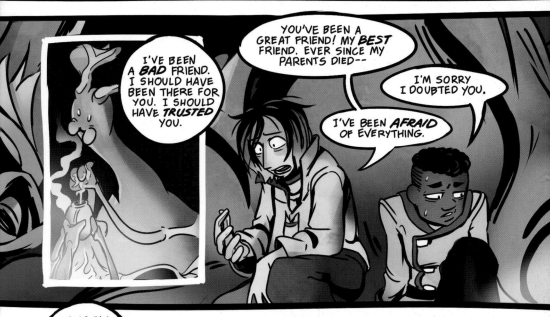

I'VE BEEN A *BAD* FRIEND. I SHOULD HAVE BEEN THERE FOR YOU. I SHOULD HAVE *TRUSTED* YOU.

YOU'VE BEEN A GREAT FRIEND! MY *BEST* FRIEND. EVER SINCE MY PARENTS DIED--

I'M SORRY I DOUBTED YOU.

I'VE BEEN *AFRAID* OF EVERYTHING.

BUT I'M *DONE* BEING SCARED.

THEY'D BE *PROUD* OF YOU.

THE MEDICINE IS READY.

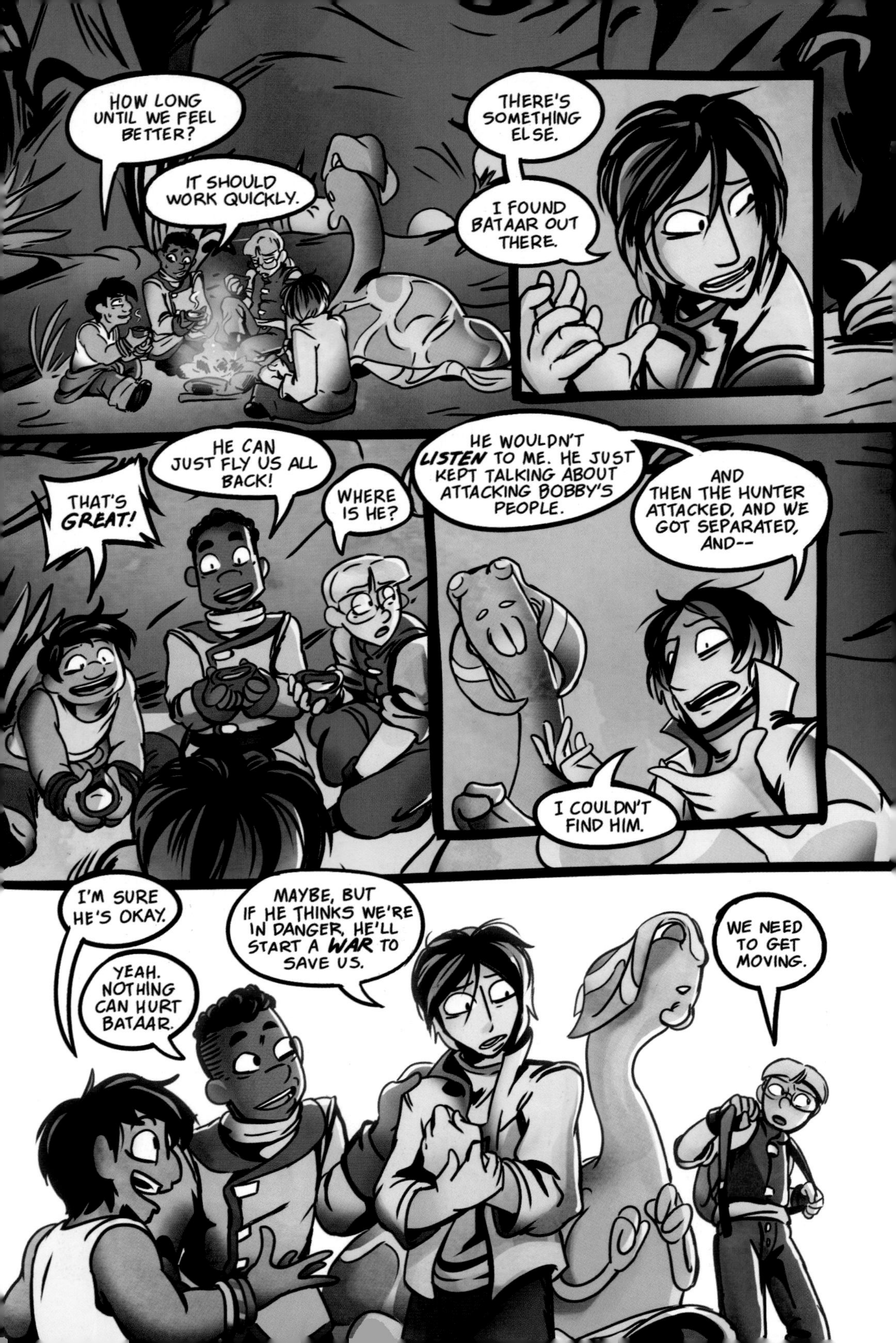
HOW LONG UNTIL WE FEEL BETTER?
IT SHOULD WORK QUICKLY.
THERE'S SOMETHING ELSE.
I FOUND BATAAR OUT THERE.
THAT'S **GREAT!**
HE CAN JUST FLY US ALL BACK!
WHERE IS HE?
HE WOULDN'T ***LISTEN*** TO ME. HE JUST KEPT TALKING ABOUT ATTACKING BOBBY'S PEOPLE.
AND THEN THE HUNTER ATTACKED, AND WE GOT SEPARATED, AND--
I COULDN'T FIND HIM.
I'M SURE HE'S OKAY.
YEAH. NOTHING CAN HURT BATAAR.
MAYBE, BUT IF HE THINKS WE'RE IN DANGER, HE'LL START A ***WAR*** TO SAVE US.
WE NEED TO GET MOVING.

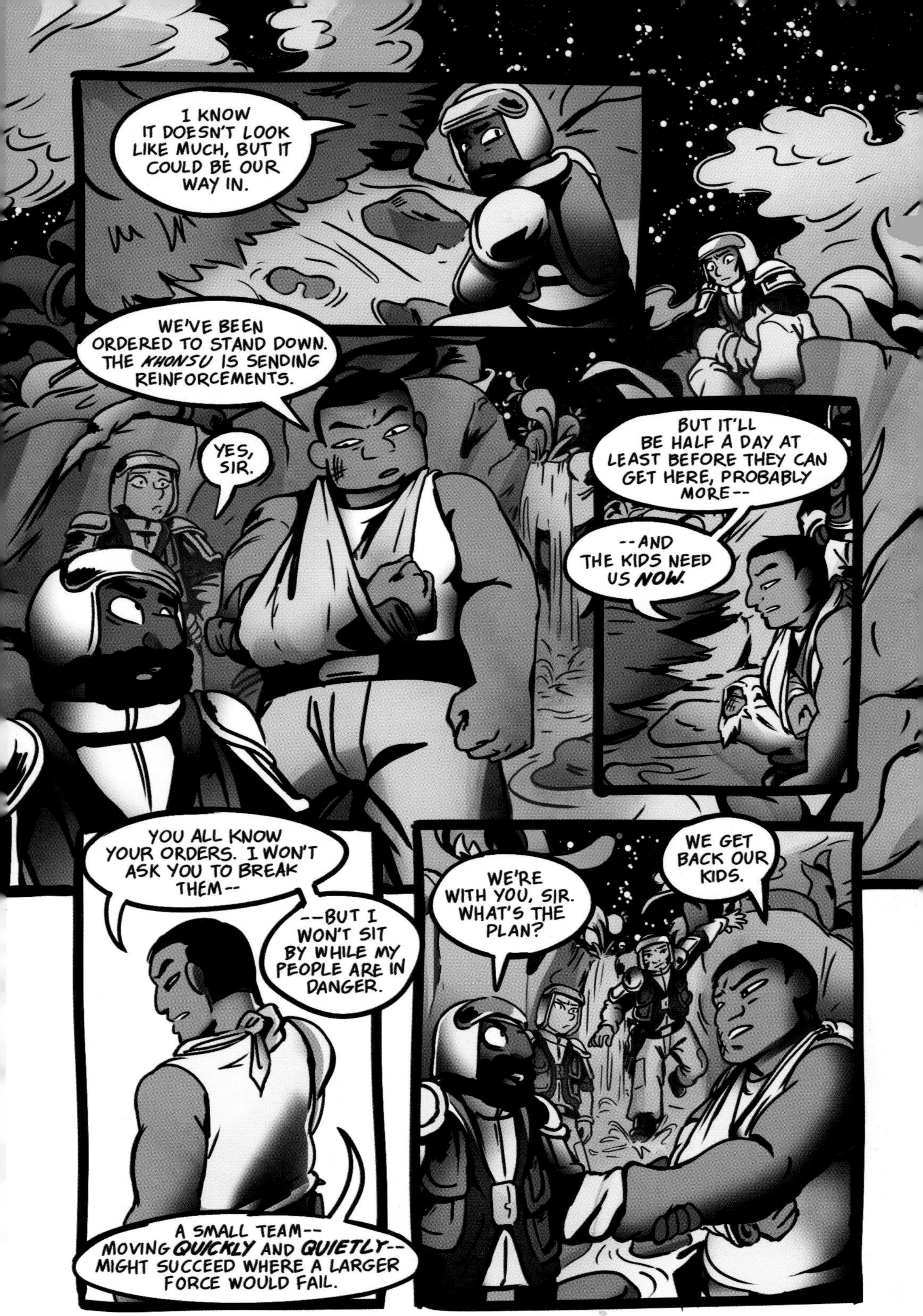

I KNOW IT DOESN'T LOOK LIKE MUCH, BUT IT COULD BE OUR WAY IN.
WE'VE BEEN ORDERED TO STAND DOWN. THE *KHONSU* IS SENDING REINFORCEMENTS.
YES, SIR.
BUT IT'LL BE HALF A DAY AT LEAST BEFORE THEY CAN GET HERE, PROBABLY MORE--
--AND THE KIDS NEED US ***NOW.***
YOU ALL KNOW YOUR ORDERS. I WON'T ASK YOU TO BREAK THEM--
--BUT I WON'T SIT BY WHILE MY PEOPLE ARE IN DANGER.
A SMALL TEAM-- MOVING ***QUICKLY*** AND ***QUIETLY***-- MIGHT SUCCEED WHERE A LARGER FORCE WOULD FAIL.
WE'RE WITH YOU, SIR. WHAT'S THE PLAN?
WE GET BACK OUR KIDS.

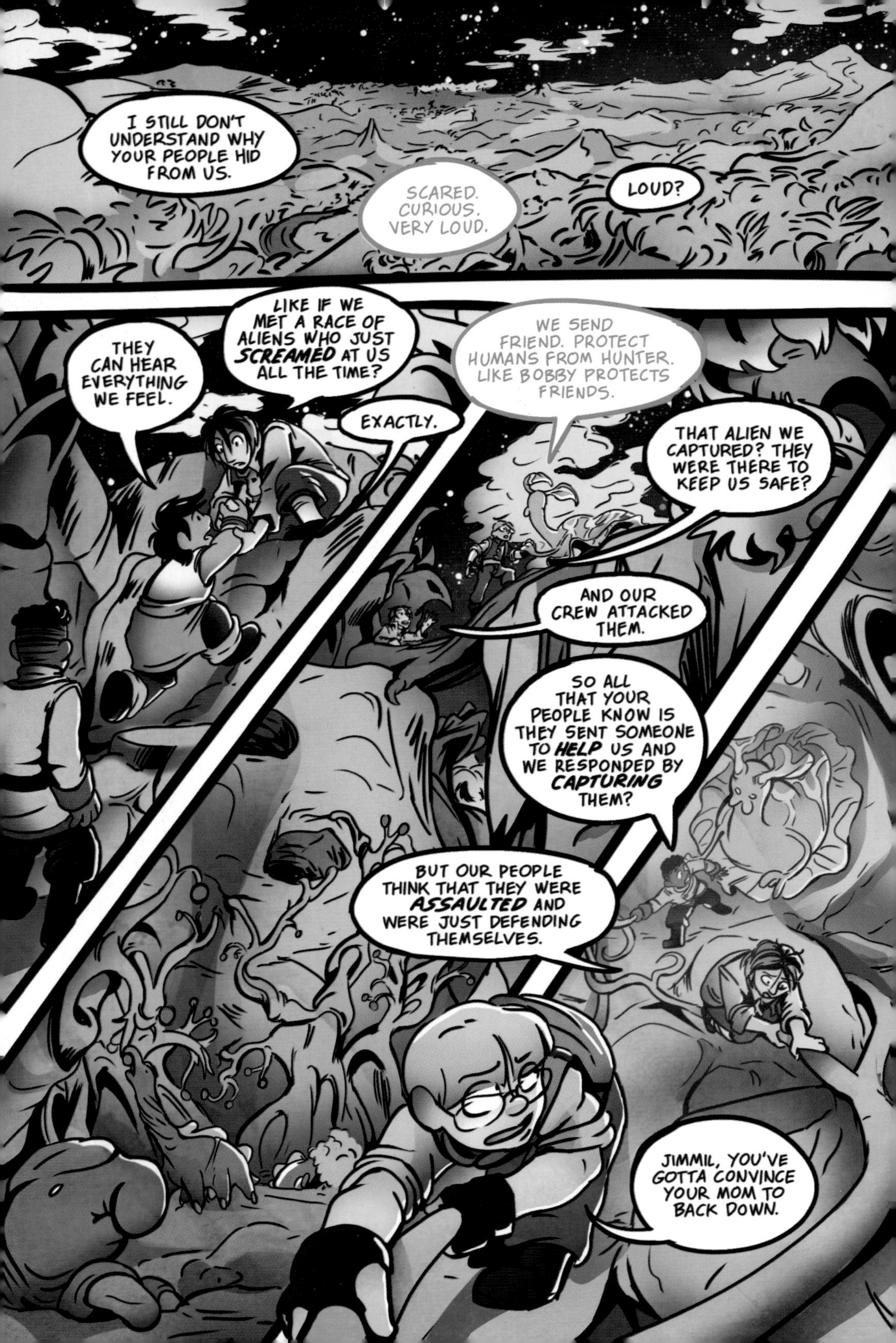
I STILL DON'T UNDERSTAND WHY YOUR PEOPLE HID FROM US.
SCARED. CURIOUS. VERY LOUD.
LOUD?
THEY CAN HEAR EVERYTHING WE FEEL.
LIKE IF WE MET A RACE OF ALIENS WHO JUST SCREAMED AT US ALL THE TIME?
EXACTLY.
WE SEND FRIEND. PROTECT HUMANS FROM HUNTER. LIKE BOBBY PROTECTS FRIENDS.
THAT ALIEN WE CAPTURED? THEY WERE THERE TO KEEP US SAFE?
AND OUR CREW ATTACKED THEM.
SO ALL THAT YOUR PEOPLE KNOW IS THEY SENT SOMEONE TO HELP US AND WE RESPONDED BY CAPTURING THEM?
BUT OUR PEOPLE THINK THAT THEY WERE ASSAULTED AND WERE JUST DEFENDING THEMSELVES.
JIMMIL, YOU'VE GOTTA CONVINCE YOUR MOM TO BACK DOWN.

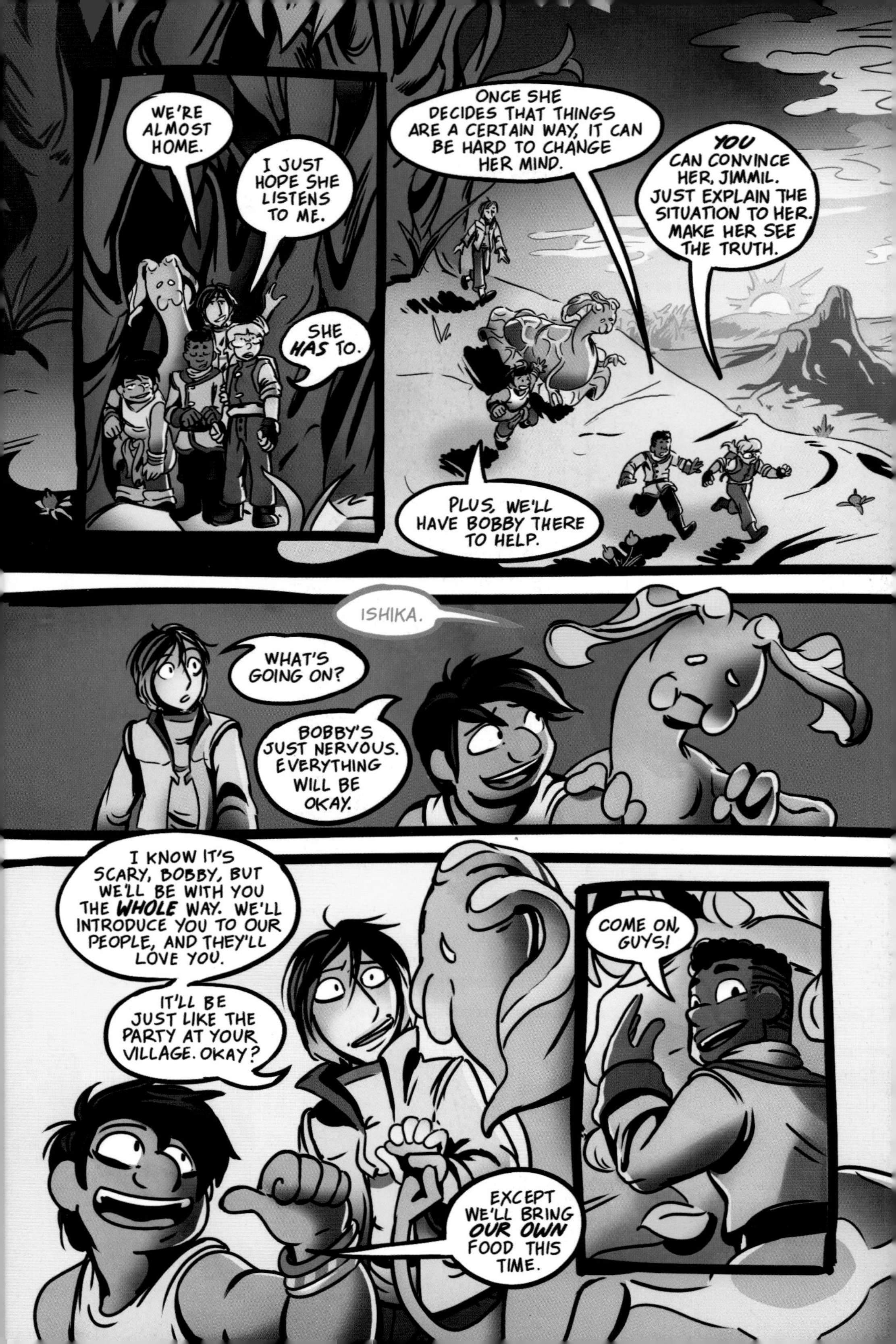

WE'RE ALMOST HOME.
I JUST HOPE SHE LISTENS TO ME.
SHE *HAS* TO.
ONCE SHE DECIDES THAT THINGS ARE A CERTAIN WAY, IT CAN BE HARD TO CHANGE HER MIND.
YOU CAN CONVINCE HER, JIMMIL. JUST EXPLAIN THE SITUATION TO HER. MAKE HER SEE THE TRUTH.
PLUS, WE'LL HAVE BOBBY THERE TO HELP.
ISHIKA.
WHAT'S GOING ON?
BOBBY'S JUST NERVOUS. EVERYTHING WILL BE OKAY.
I KNOW IT'S SCARY, BOBBY, BUT WE'LL BE WITH YOU THE *WHOLE* WAY. WE'LL INTRODUCE YOU TO OUR PEOPLE, AND THEY'LL LOVE YOU.
IT'LL BE JUST LIKE THE PARTY AT YOUR VILLAGE. OKAY?
COME ON, GUYS!
EXCEPT WE'LL BRING *OUR OWN* FOOD THIS TIME.

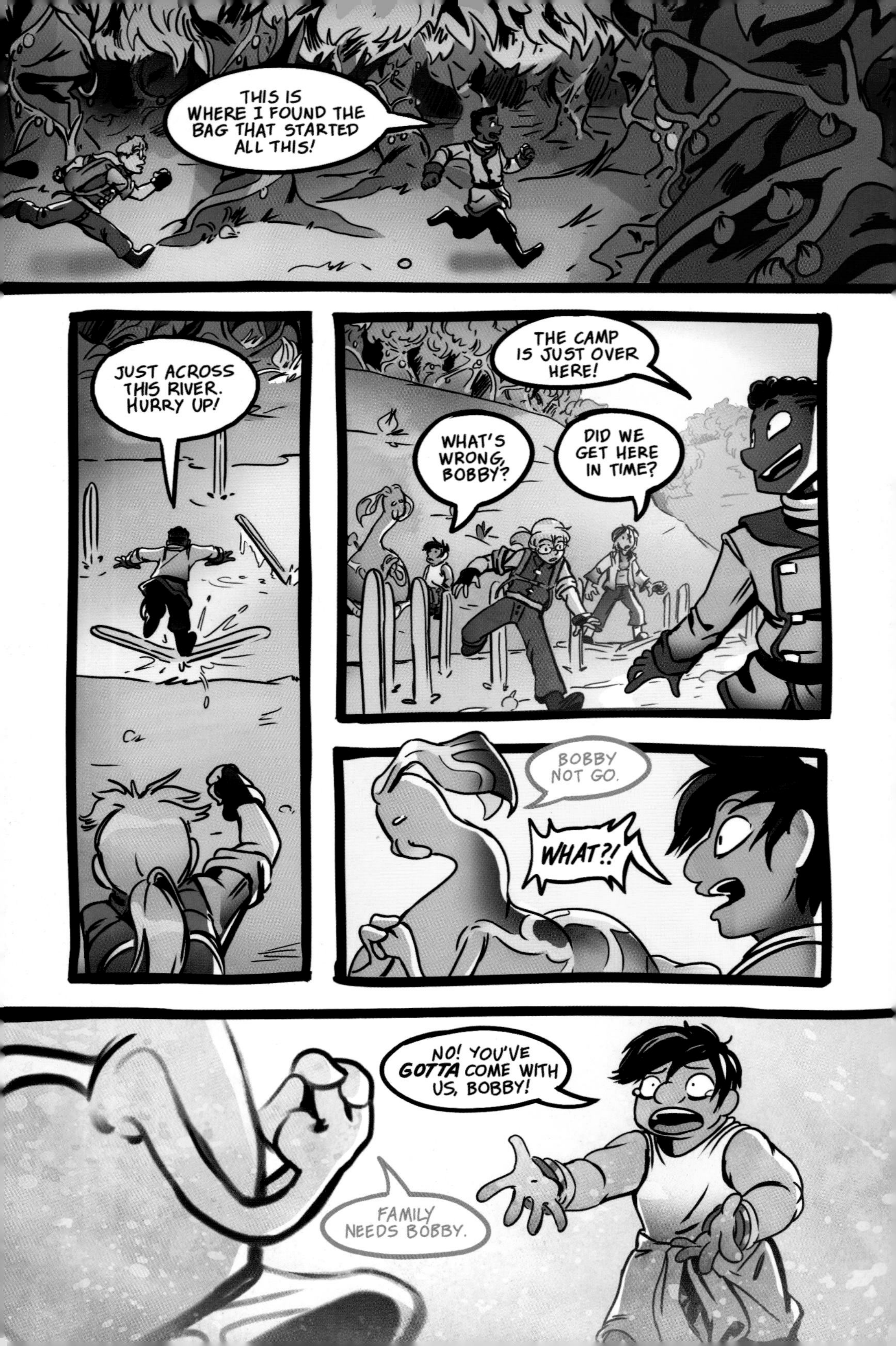
THIS IS WHERE I FOUND THE BAG THAT STARTED ALL THIS!
JUST ACROSS THIS RIVER. HURRY UP!
THE CAMP IS JUST OVER HERE!
WHAT'S WRONG, BOBBY?
DID WE GET HERE IN TIME?
BOBBY NOT GO.
WHAT?!
NO! YOU'VE GOTTA COME WITH US, BOBBY!
FAMILY NEEDS BOBBY.

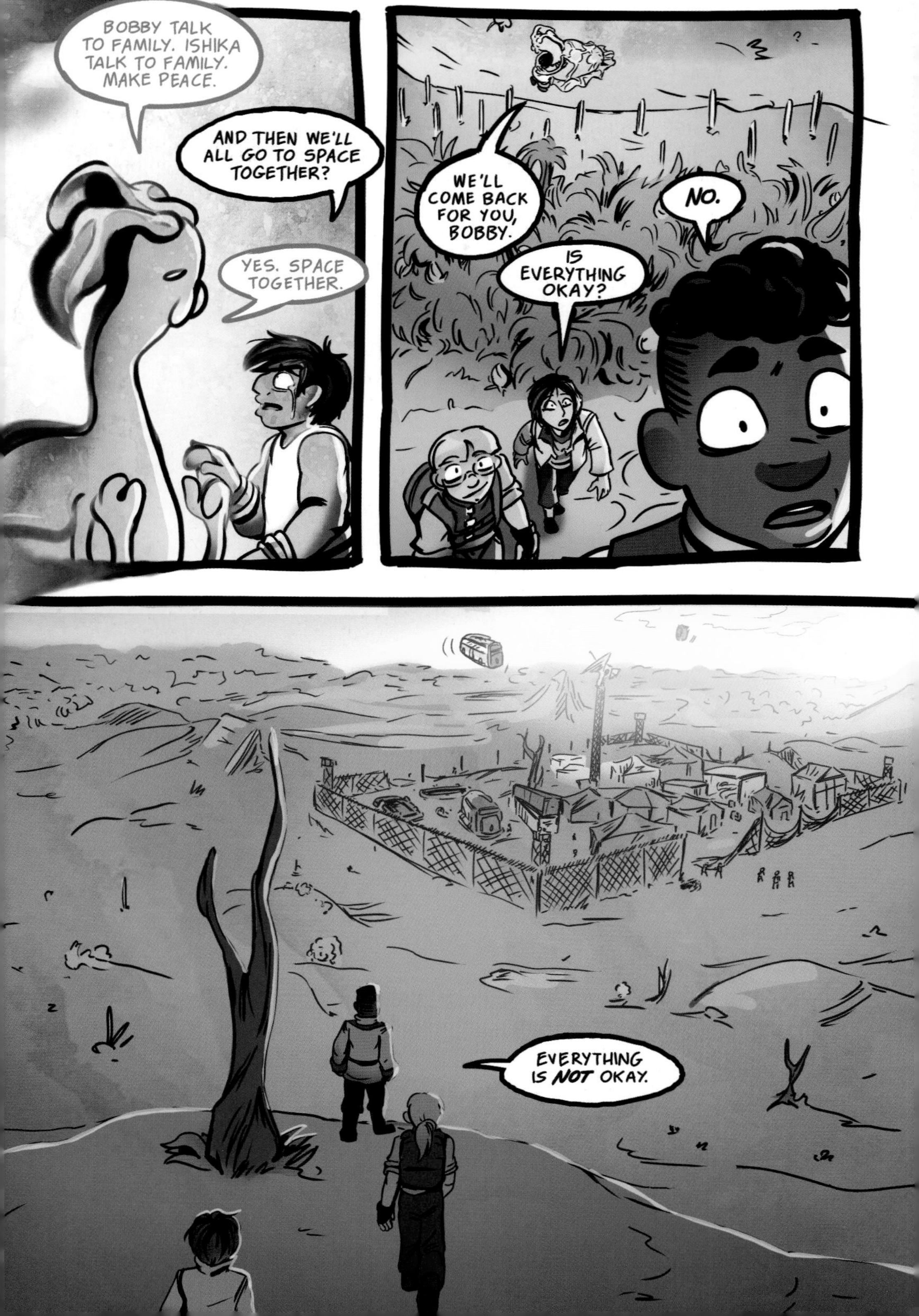
BOBBY TALK TO FAMILY. ISHIKA TALK TO FAMILY. MAKE PEACE.
AND THEN WE'LL ALL GO TO SPACE TOGETHER?
YES. SPACE TOGETHER.
WE'LL COME BACK FOR YOU, BOBBY.
NO.
IS EVERYTHING OKAY?
EVERYTHING IS NOT OKAY.

CHAPTER 4

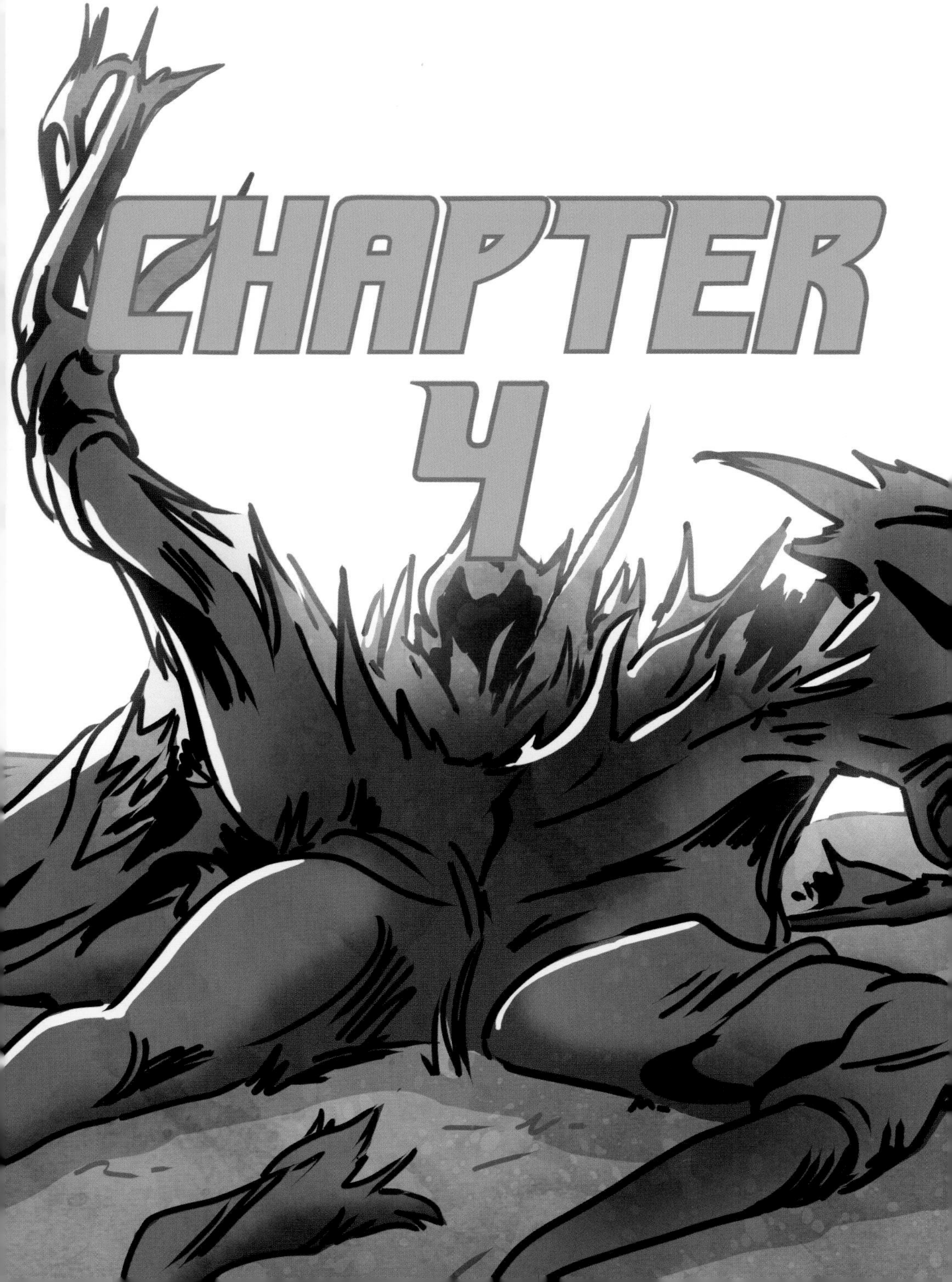

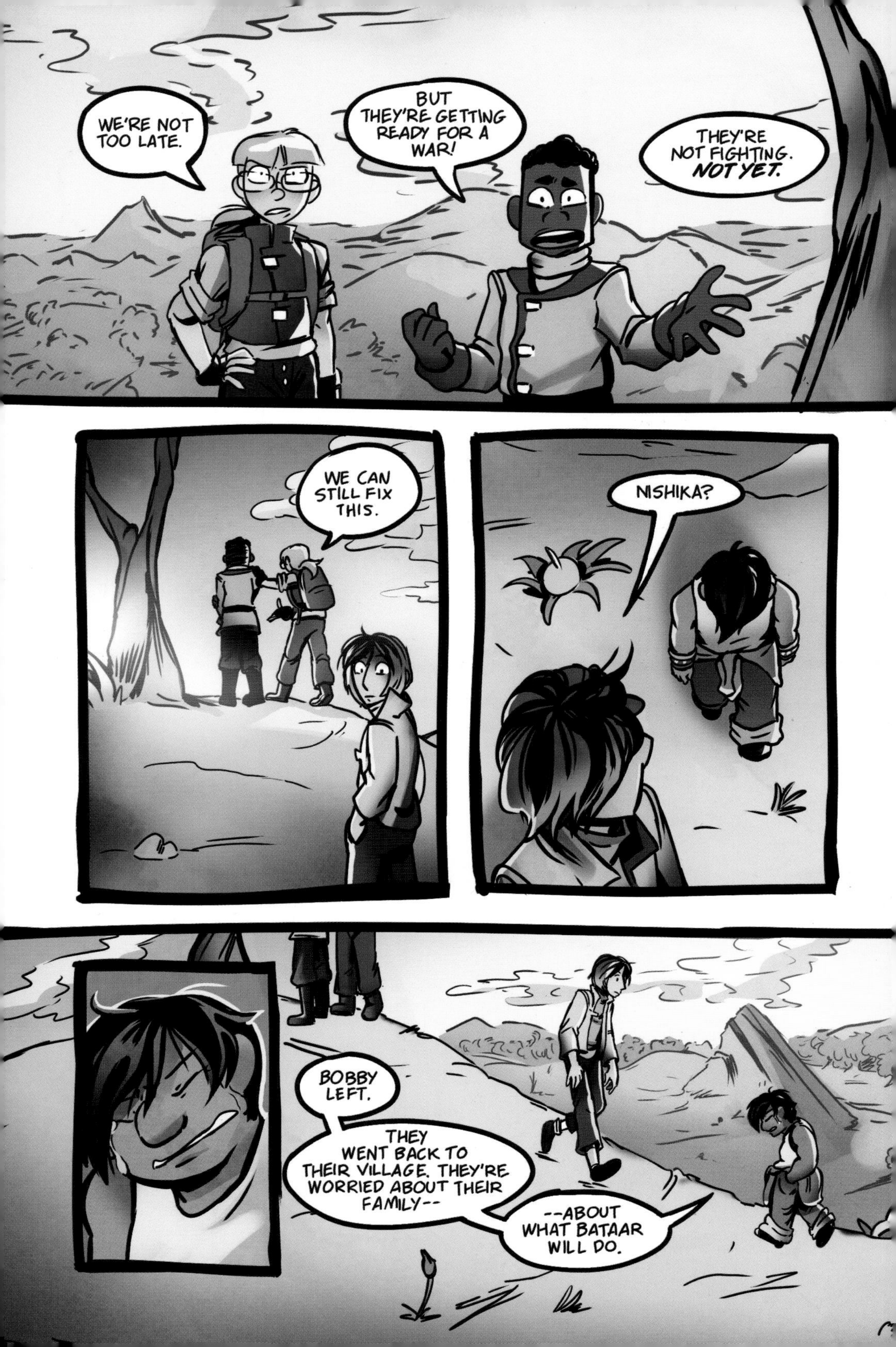
WE'RE NOT TOO LATE.
BUT THEY'RE GETTING READY FOR A WAR!
THEY'RE NOT FIGHTING. *NOT YET.*
WE CAN STILL FIX THIS.
NISHIKA?
BOBBY LEFT.
THEY WENT BACK TO THEIR VILLAGE. THEY'RE WORRIED ABOUT THEIR FAMILY--
--ABOUT WHAT BATAAR WILL DO.

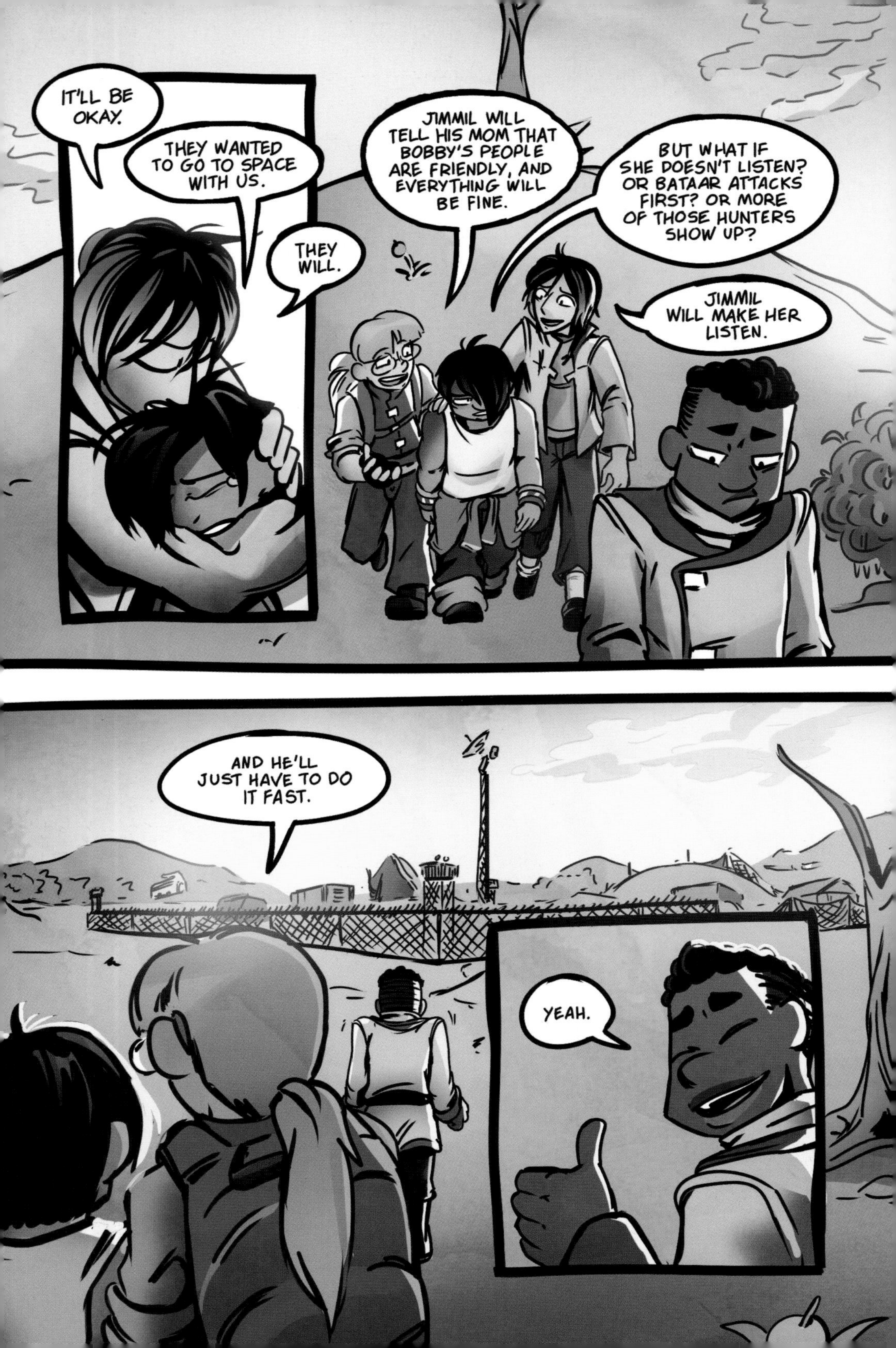
IT'LL BE OKAY.
THEY WANTED TO GO TO SPACE WITH US.
THEY WILL.
JIMMIL WILL TELL HIS MOM THAT BOBBY'S PEOPLE ARE FRIENDLY, AND EVERYTHING WILL BE FINE.
BUT WHAT IF SHE DOESN'T LISTEN? OR BATAAR ATTACKS FIRST? OR MORE OF THOSE HUNTERS SHOW UP?
JIMMIL WILL MAKE HER LISTEN.
AND HE'LL JUST HAVE TO DO IT FAST.
YEAH.

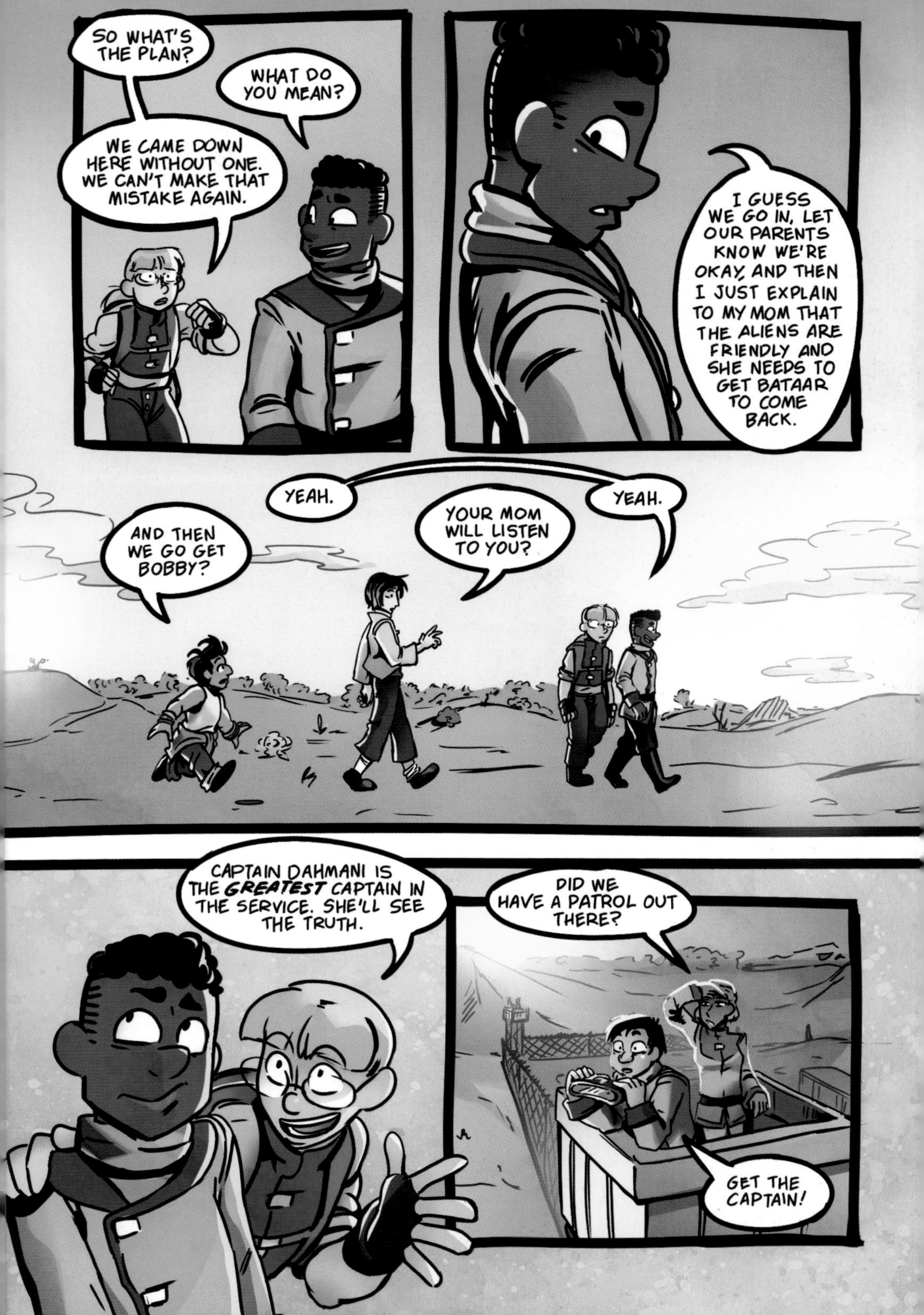

SO WHAT'S THE PLAN?
WHAT DO YOU MEAN?
WE CAME DOWN HERE WITHOUT ONE. WE CAN'T MAKE THAT MISTAKE AGAIN.
I GUESS WE GO IN, LET OUR PARENTS KNOW WE'RE OKAY, AND THEN I JUST EXPLAIN TO MY MOM THAT THE ALIENS ARE FRIENDLY AND SHE NEEDS TO GET BATAAR TO COME BACK.
AND THEN WE GO GET BOBBY?
YEAH.
YEAH.
YOUR MOM WILL LISTEN TO YOU?
CAPTAIN DAHMANI IS THE *GREATEST* CAPTAIN IN THE SERVICE. SHE'LL SEE THE TRUTH.
DID WE HAVE A PATROL OUT THERE?
GET THE CAPTAIN!

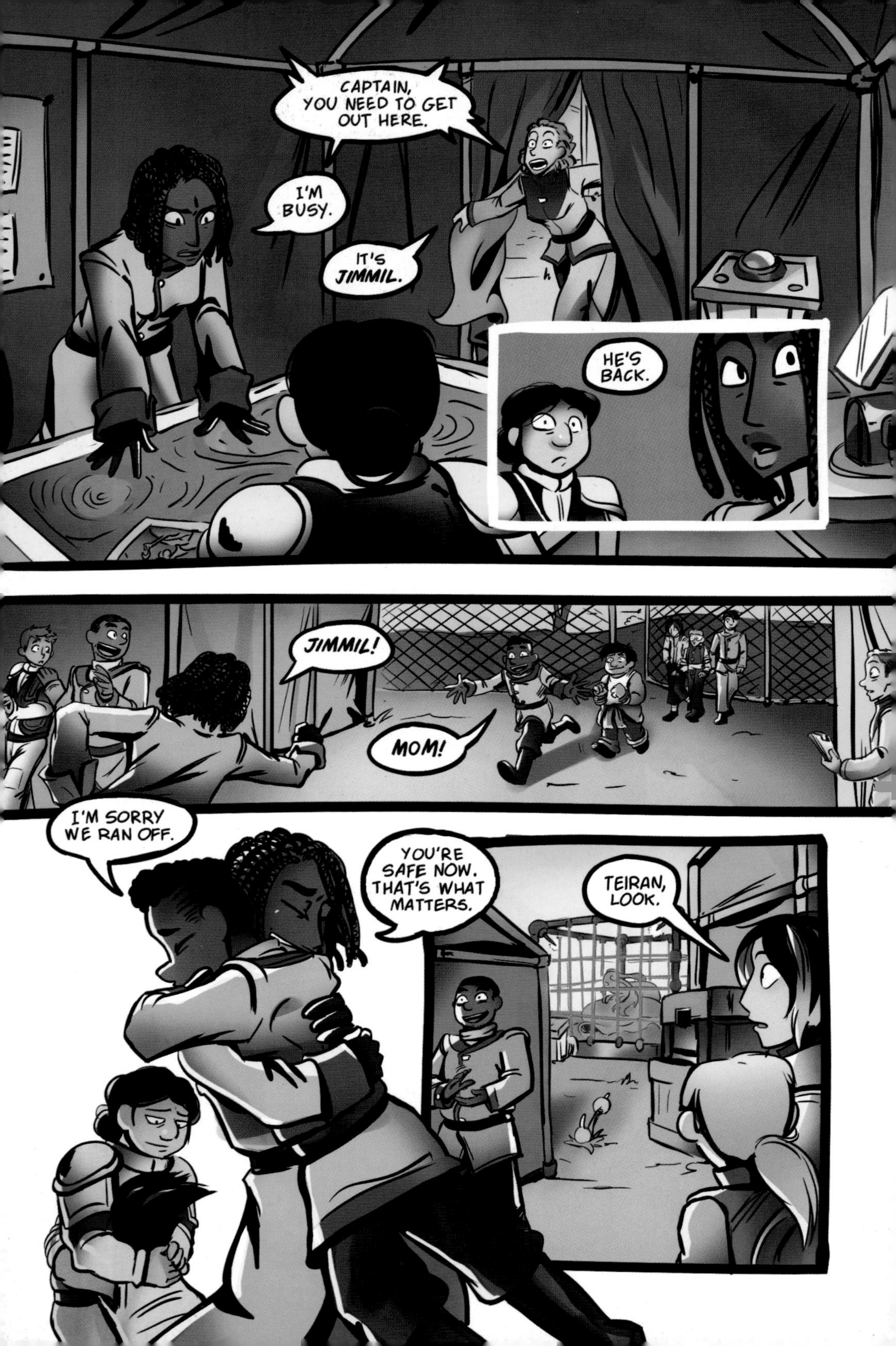
CAPTAIN, YOU NEED TO GET OUT HERE.
I'M BUSY.
IT'S JIMMIL.
HE'S BACK.
JIMMIL!
MOM!
I'M SORRY WE RAN OFF.
YOU'RE SAFE NOW. THAT'S WHAT MATTERS.
TEIRAN, LOOK.

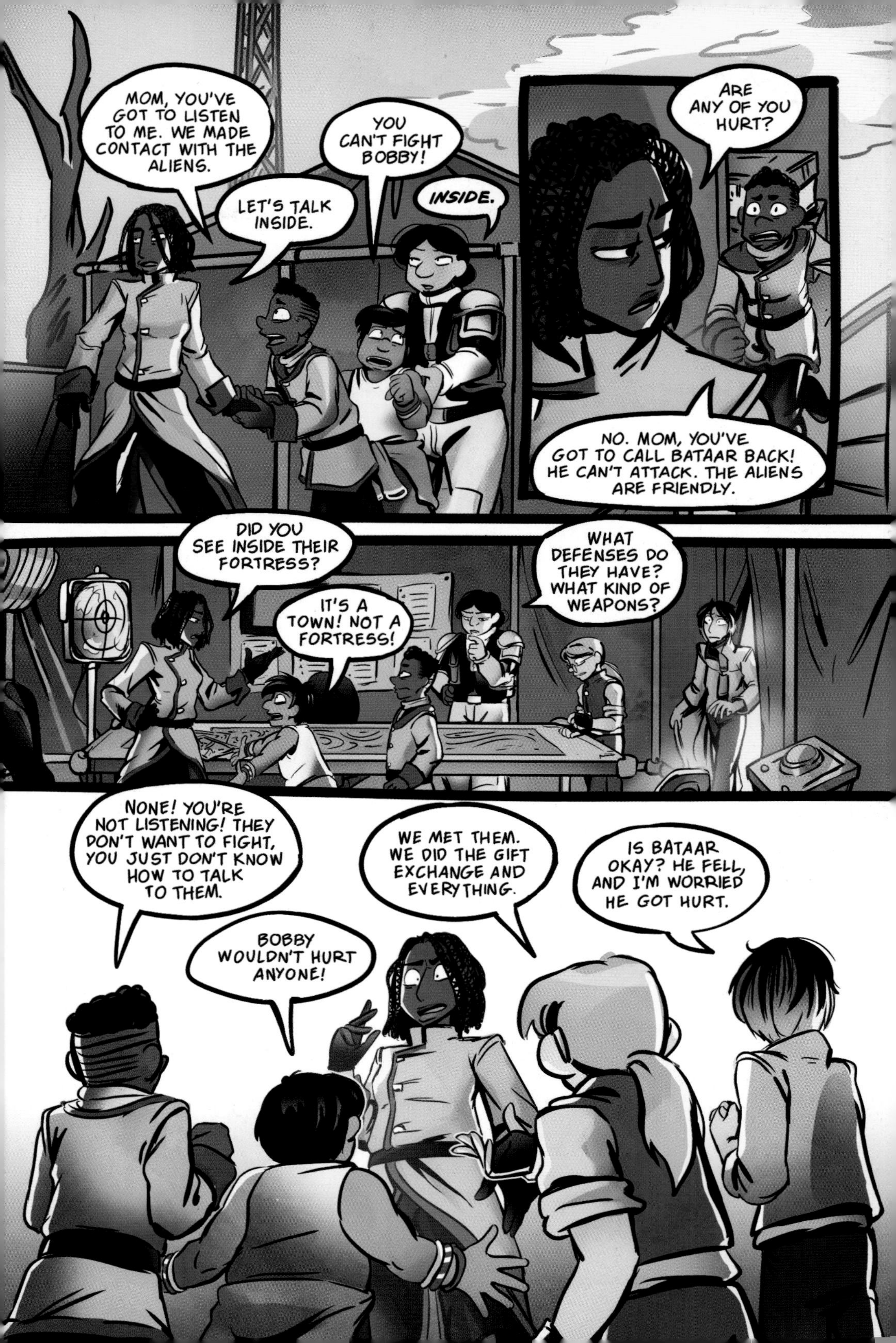
MOM, YOU'VE GOT TO LISTEN TO ME. WE MADE CONTACT WITH THE ALIENS.
LET'S TALK INSIDE.
YOU CAN'T FIGHT BOBBY!
INSIDE.
ARE ANY OF YOU HURT?
NO. MOM, YOU'VE GOT TO CALL BATAAR BACK! HE CAN'T ATTACK. THE ALIENS ARE FRIENDLY.
DID YOU SEE INSIDE THEIR FORTRESS?
IT'S A TOWN! NOT A FORTRESS!
WHAT DEFENSES DO THEY HAVE? WHAT KIND OF WEAPONS?
NONE! YOU'RE NOT LISTENING! THEY DON'T WANT TO FIGHT, YOU JUST DON'T KNOW HOW TO TALK TO THEM.
BOBBY WOULDN'T HURT ANYONE!
WE MET THEM. WE DID THE GIFT EXCHANGE AND EVERYTHING.
IS BATAAR OKAY? HE FELL, AND I'M WORRIED HE GOT HURT.

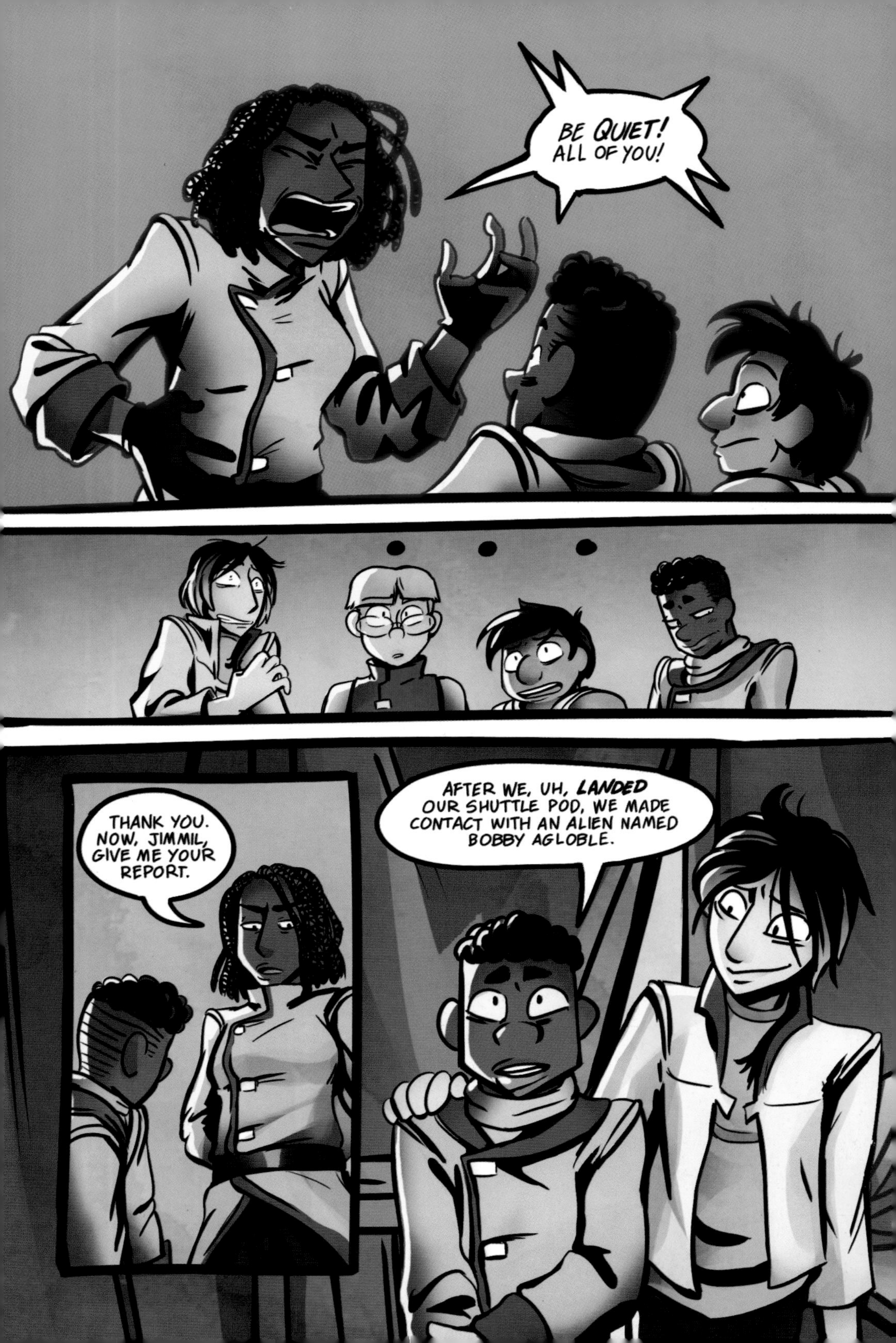
BE QUIET! ALL OF YOU!
THANK YOU. NOW, JIMMIL, GIVE ME YOUR REPORT.
AFTER WE, UH, LANDED OUR SHUTTLE POD, WE MADE CONTACT WITH AN ALIEN NAMED BOBBY AGLOBLE.

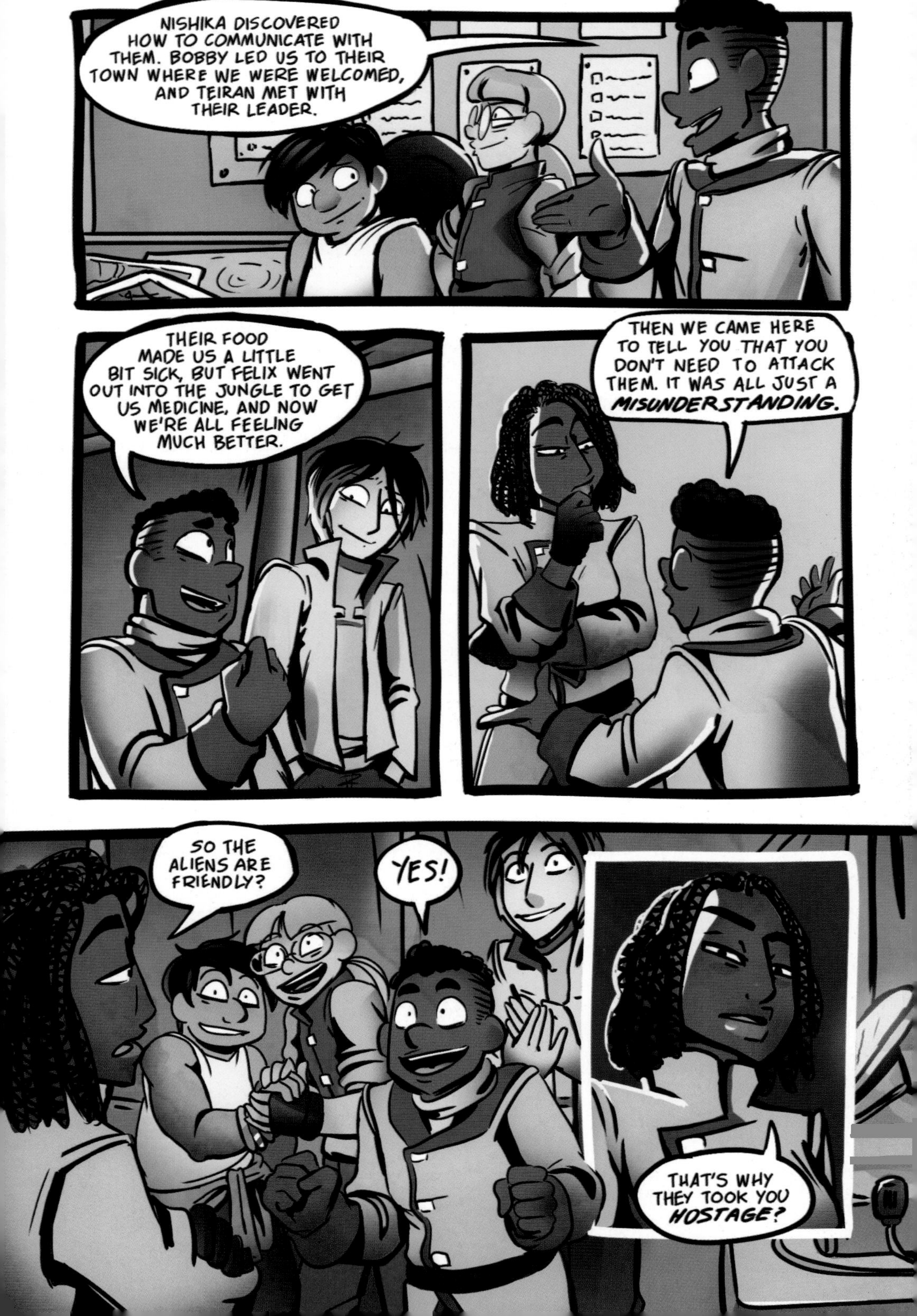
NISHIKA DISCOVERED HOW TO COMMUNICATE WITH THEM. BOBBY LED US TO THEIR TOWN WHERE WE WERE WELCOMED, AND TEIRAN MET WITH THEIR LEADER.
THEIR FOOD MADE US A LITTLE BIT SICK, BUT FELIX WENT OUT INTO THE JUNGLE TO GET US MEDICINE, AND NOW WE'RE ALL FEELING MUCH BETTER.
THEN WE CAME HERE TO TELL YOU THAT YOU DON'T NEED TO ATTACK THEM. IT WAS ALL JUST A *MISUNDERSTANDING*.
SO THE ALIENS ARE FRIENDLY?
YES!
THAT'S WHY THEY TOOK YOU *HOSTAGE*?

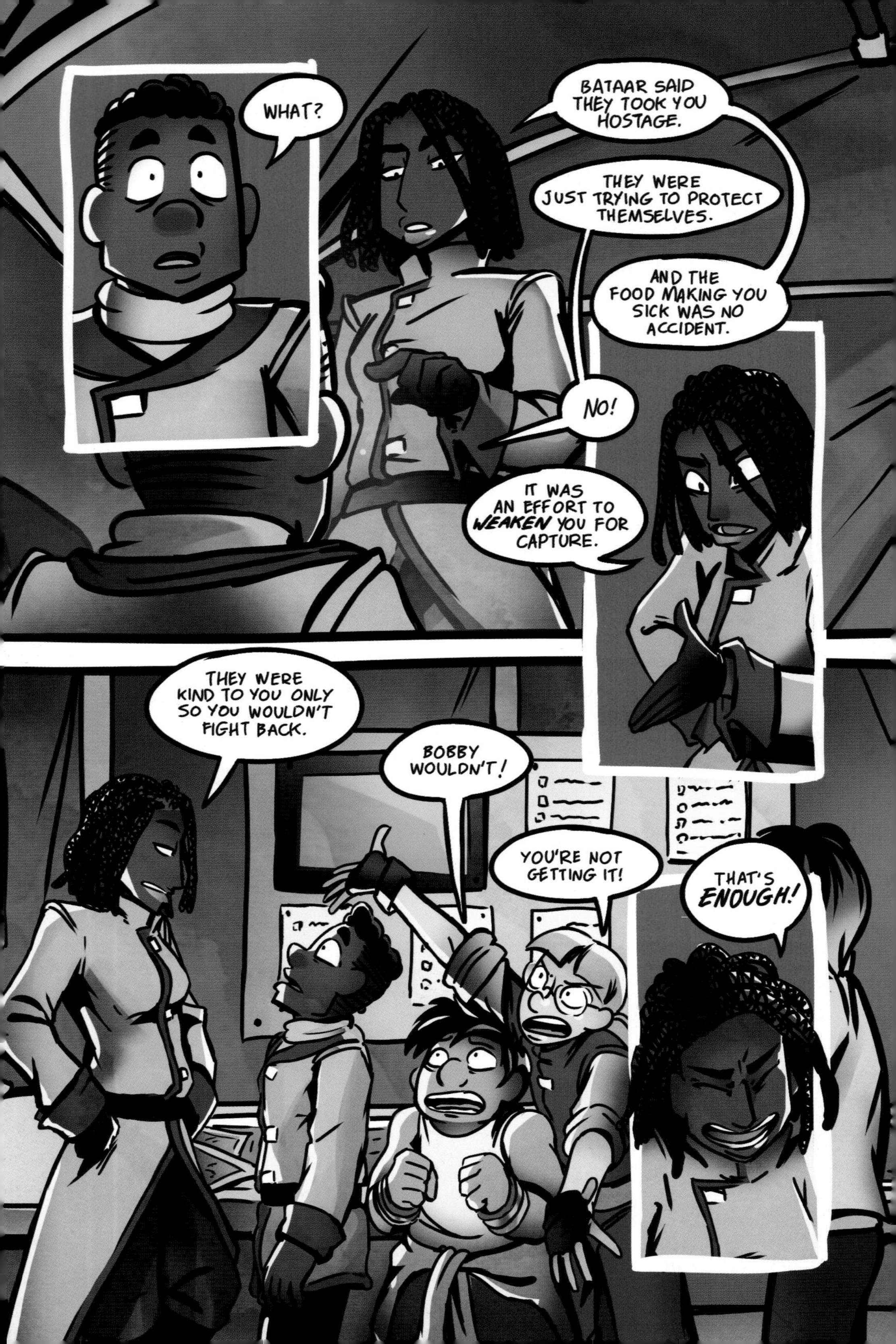
WHAT?
BATAAR SAID THEY TOOK YOU HOSTAGE.
THEY WERE JUST TRYING TO PROTECT THEMSELVES.
AND THE FOOD MAKING YOU SICK WAS NO ACCIDENT.
NO!
IT WAS AN EFFORT TO WEAKEN YOU FOR CAPTURE.
THEY WERE KIND TO YOU ONLY SO YOU WOULDN'T FIGHT BACK.
BOBBY WOULDN'T!
YOU'RE NOT GETTING IT!
THAT'S ENOUGH!

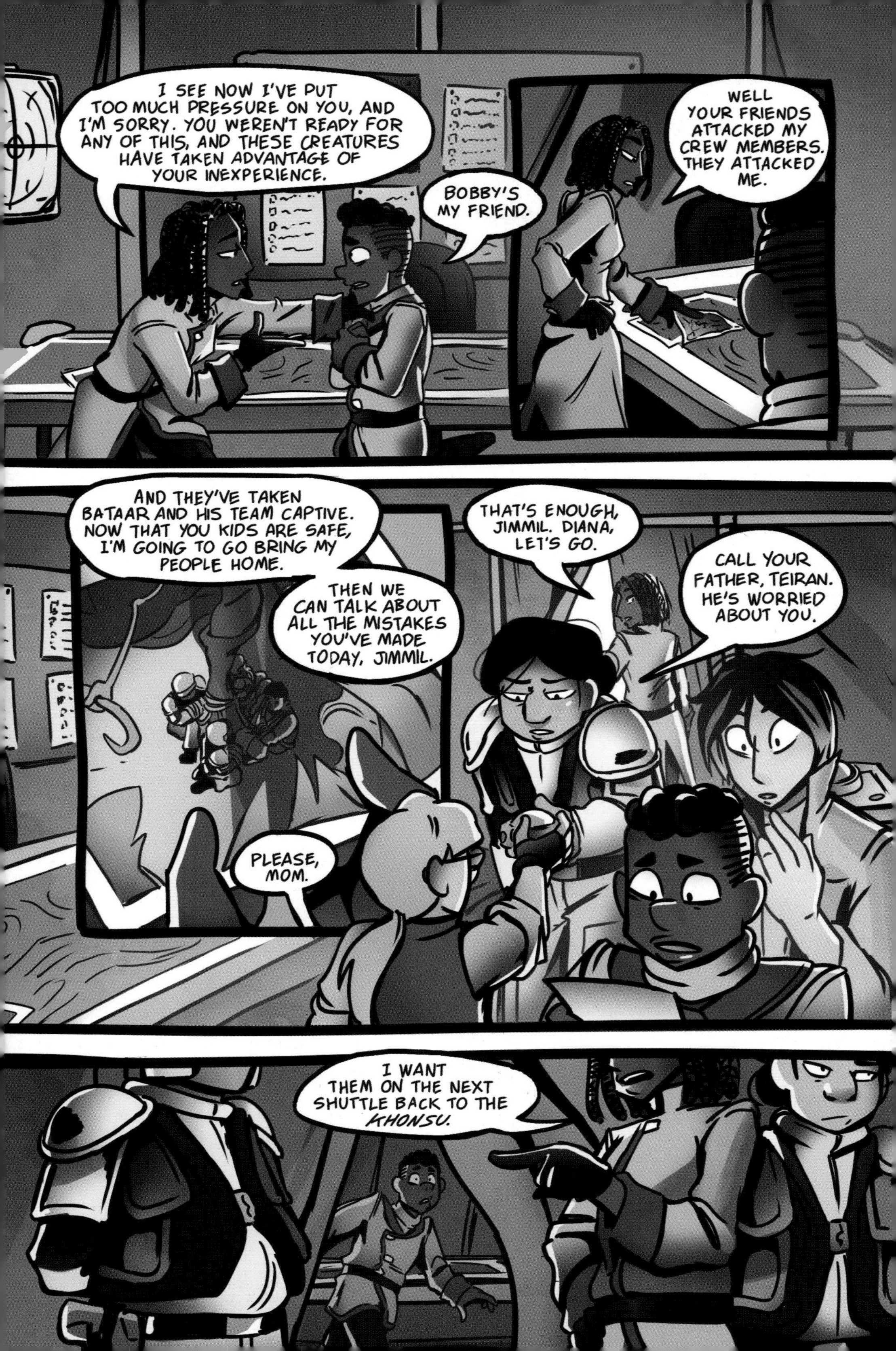
I SEE NOW I'VE PUT TOO MUCH PRESSURE ON YOU, AND I'M SORRY. YOU WEREN'T READY FOR ANY OF THIS, AND THESE CREATURES HAVE TAKEN ADVANTAGE OF YOUR INEXPERIENCE.
BOBBY'S MY FRIEND.
WELL YOUR FRIENDS ATTACKED MY CREW MEMBERS. THEY ATTACKED ME.
AND THEY'VE TAKEN BATAAR AND HIS TEAM CAPTIVE. NOW THAT YOU KIDS ARE SAFE, I'M GOING TO GO BRING MY PEOPLE HOME.
THEN WE CAN TALK ABOUT ALL THE MISTAKES YOU'VE MADE TODAY, JIMMIL.
PLEASE, MOM.
THAT'S ENOUGH, JIMMIL. DIANA, LET'S GO.
CALL YOUR FATHER, TEIRAN. HE'S WORRIED ABOUT YOU.
I WANT THEM ON THE NEXT SHUTTLE BACK TO THE *KHONSU*.

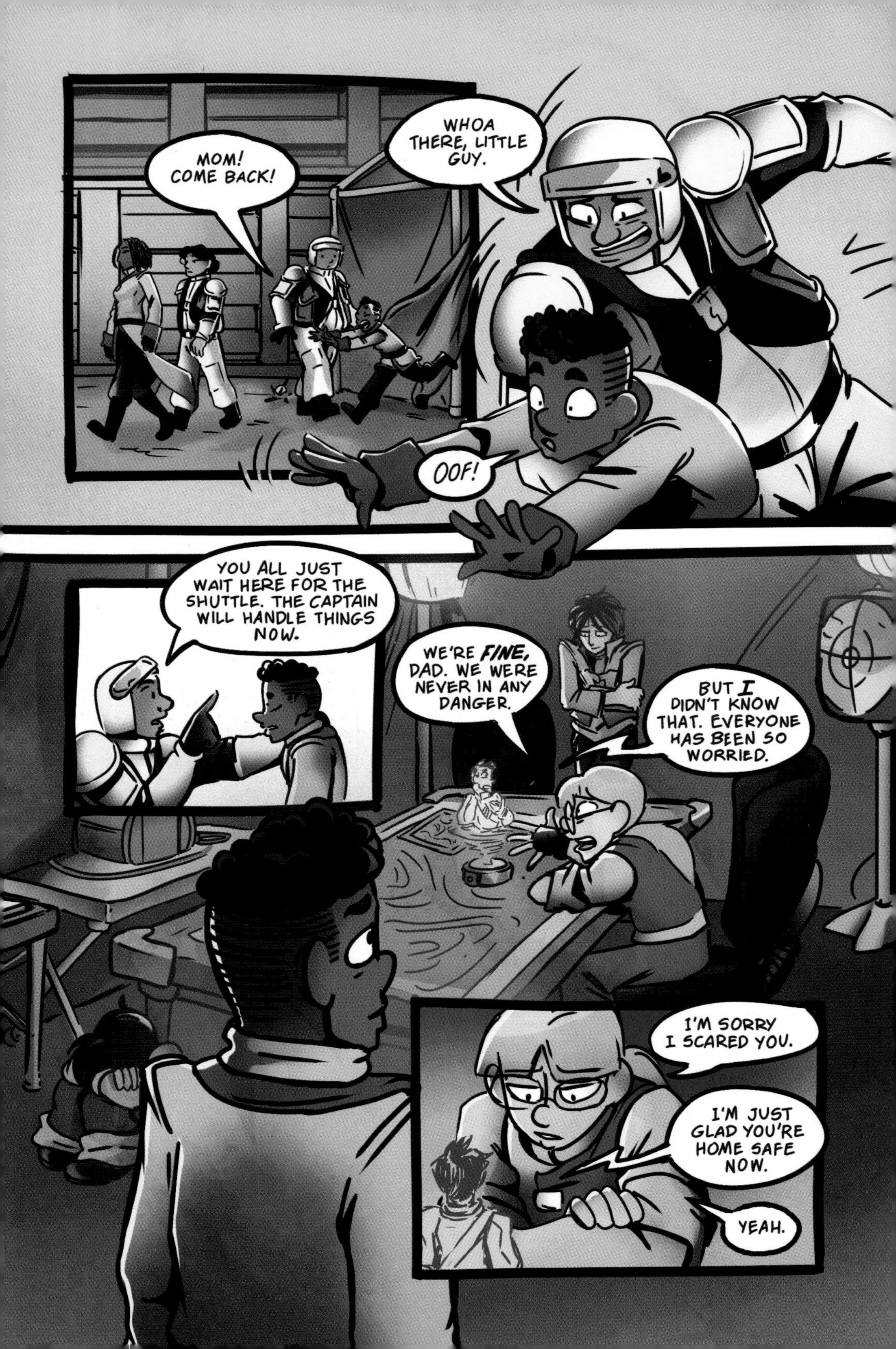
MOM! COME BACK!
WHOA THERE, LITTLE GUY.
OOF!
YOU ALL JUST WAIT HERE FOR THE SHUTTLE. THE CAPTAIN WILL HANDLE THINGS NOW.
WE'RE FINE, DAD. WE WERE NEVER IN ANY DANGER.
BUT I DIDN'T KNOW THAT. EVERYONE HAS BEEN SO WORRIED.
I'M SORRY I SCARED YOU.
I'M JUST GLAD YOU'RE HOME SAFE NOW.
YEAH.

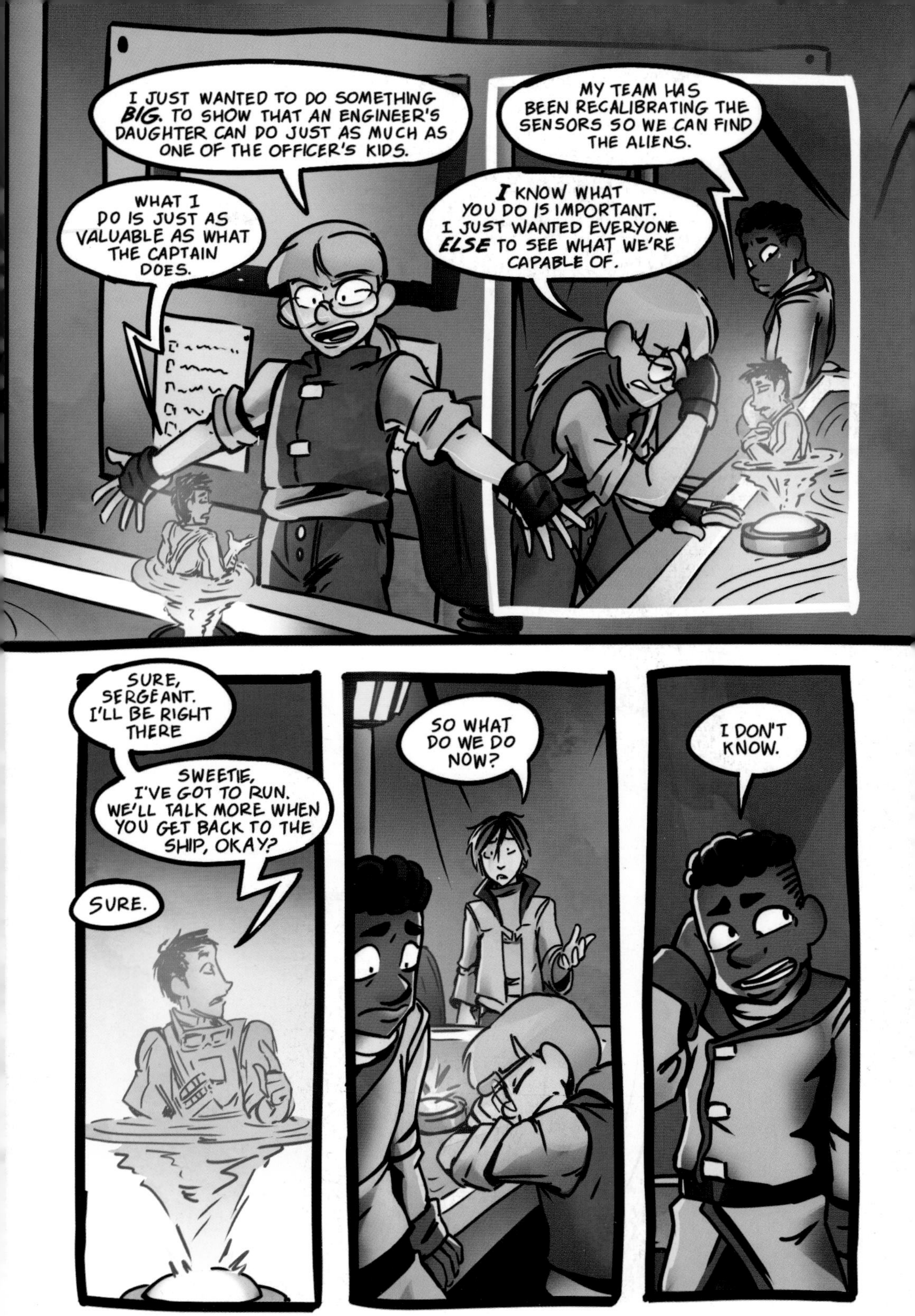
I JUST WANTED TO DO SOMETHING BIG. TO SHOW THAT AN ENGINEER'S DAUGHTER CAN DO JUST AS MUCH AS ONE OF THE OFFICER'S KIDS.
WHAT I DO IS JUST AS VALUABLE AS WHAT THE CAPTAIN DOES.
MY TEAM HAS BEEN RECALIBRATING THE SENSORS SO WE CAN FIND THE ALIENS.
I KNOW WHAT YOU DO IS IMPORTANT. I JUST WANTED EVERYONE ELSE TO SEE WHAT WE'RE CAPABLE OF.
SURE, SERGEANT. I'LL BE RIGHT THERE
SWEETIE, I'VE GOT TO RUN. WE'LL TALK MORE WHEN YOU GET BACK TO THE SHIP, OKAY?
SURE.
SO WHAT DO WE DO NOW?
I DON'T KNOW.

WE CAN'T DO *NOTHING*.

I KNOW.

BOBBY-- THEY'RE GOING TO ATTACK BOBBY.

WE WON'T LET THAT HAPPEN.

BUT HOW? THE CAPTAIN WOULDN'T LISTEN--

WE CAME HERE TO SPREAD DIPLOMACY, RIGHT? THAT'S THE MISSION. THE CAPTAIN IS ABOUT TO MAKE A TERRIBLE MISTAKE, AND WE'RE THE ONLY ONES WHO CAN STOP HER.

OUR FRIENDS NEED US. OUR FAMILIES NEED US. WE DON'T HAVE TIME TO WASTE.

BUT IF JIMMIL COULDN'T CONVINCE HIS MOM--

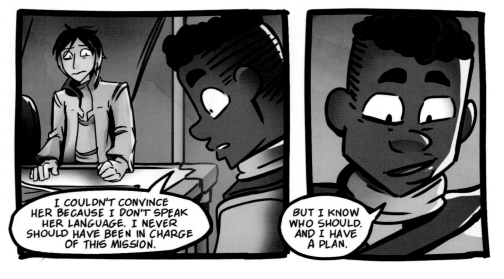

I COULDN'T CONVINCE HER BECAUSE I DON'T SPEAK HER LANGUAGE. I NEVER SHOULD HAVE BEEN IN CHARGE OF THIS MISSION.

BUT I KNOW WHO SHOULD. AND I HAVE A PLAN.

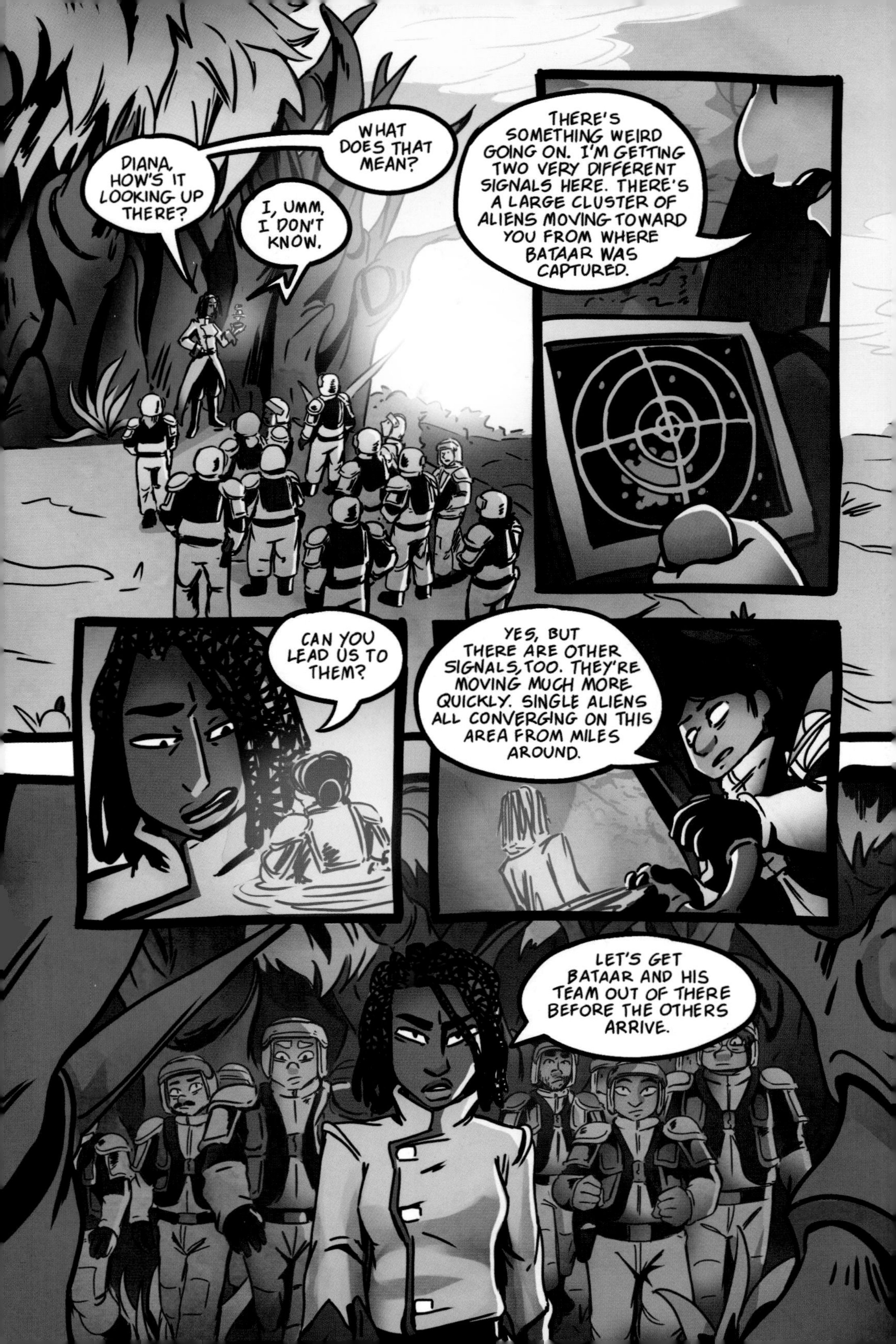
DIANA, HOW'S IT LOOKING UP THERE?
I, UMM, I DON'T KNOW.
WHAT DOES THAT MEAN?
THERE'S SOMETHING WEIRD GOING ON. I'M GETTING TWO VERY DIFFERENT SIGNALS HERE. THERE'S A LARGE CLUSTER OF ALIENS MOVING TOWARD YOU FROM WHERE BATAAR WAS CAPTURED.
CAN YOU LEAD US TO THEM?
YES, BUT THERE ARE OTHER SIGNALS, TOO. THEY'RE MOVING MUCH MORE QUICKLY. SINGLE ALIENS ALL CONVERGING ON THIS AREA FROM MILES AROUND.
LET'S GET BATAAR AND HIS TEAM OUT OF THERE BEFORE THE OTHERS ARRIVE.

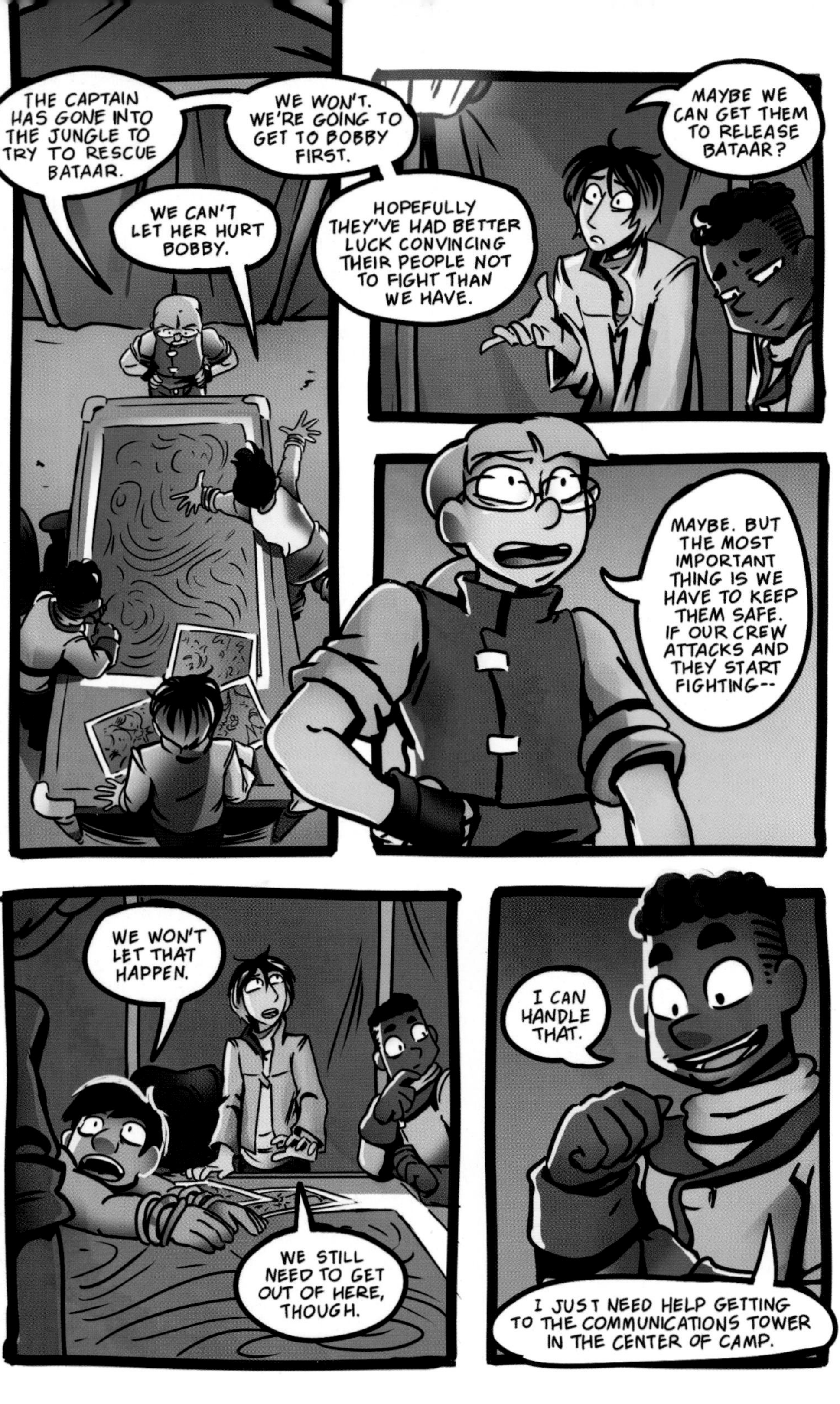
THE CAPTAIN HAS GONE INTO THE JUNGLE TO TRY TO RESCUE BATAAR.
WE WON'T. WE'RE GOING TO GET TO BOBBY FIRST.
WE CAN'T LET HER HURT BOBBY.
HOPEFULLY THEY'VE HAD BETTER LUCK CONVINCING THEIR PEOPLE NOT TO FIGHT THAN WE HAVE.
MAYBE WE CAN GET THEM TO RELEASE BATAAR?
MAYBE. BUT THE MOST IMPORTANT THING IS WE HAVE TO KEEP THEM SAFE. IF OUR CREW ATTACKS AND THEY START FIGHTING--
WE WON'T LET THAT HAPPEN.
WE STILL NEED TO GET OUT OF HERE, THOUGH.
I CAN HANDLE THAT.
I JUST NEED HELP GETTING TO THE COMMUNICATIONS TOWER IN THE CENTER OF CAMP.

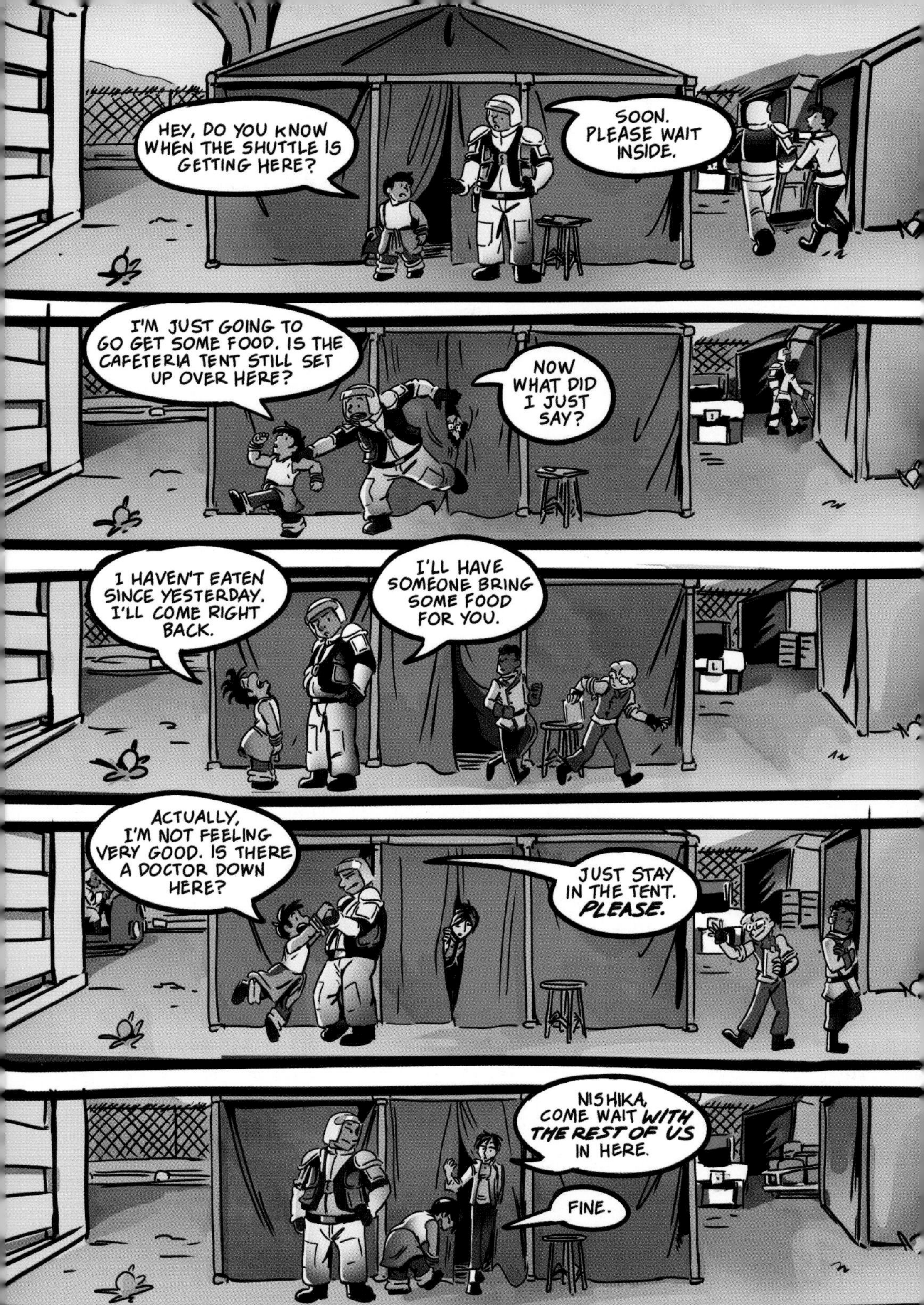
HEY, DO YOU KNOW WHEN THE SHUTTLE IS GETTING HERE?
SOON. PLEASE WAIT INSIDE.
I'M JUST GOING TO GO GET SOME FOOD. IS THE CAFETERIA TENT STILL SET UP OVER HERE?
NOW WHAT DID I JUST SAY?
I HAVEN'T EATEN SINCE YESTERDAY. I'LL COME RIGHT BACK.
I'LL HAVE SOMEONE BRING SOME FOOD FOR YOU.
ACTUALLY, I'M NOT FEELING VERY GOOD. IS THERE A DOCTOR DOWN HERE?
JUST STAY IN THE TENT. PLEASE.
NISHIKA, COME WAIT WITH THE REST OF US IN HERE.
FINE.

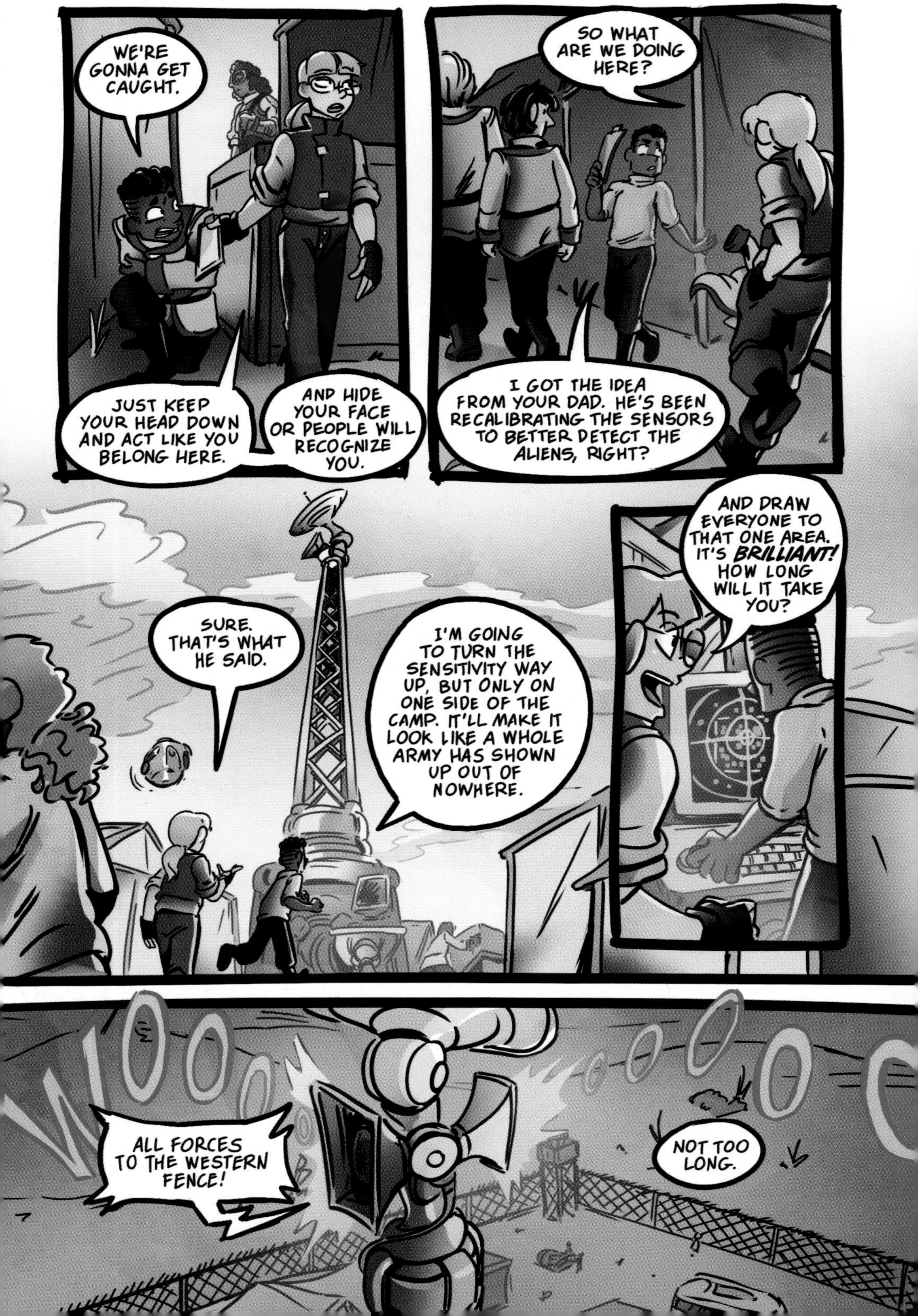
WE'RE GONNA GET CAUGHT.
JUST KEEP YOUR HEAD DOWN AND ACT LIKE YOU BELONG HERE.
AND HIDE YOUR FACE OR PEOPLE WILL RECOGNIZE YOU.
SO WHAT ARE WE DOING HERE?
I GOT THE IDEA FROM YOUR DAD. HE'S BEEN RECALIBRATING THE SENSORS TO BETTER DETECT THE ALIENS, RIGHT?
SURE. THAT'S WHAT HE SAID.
I'M GOING TO TURN THE SENSITIVITY WAY UP, BUT ONLY ON ONE SIDE OF THE CAMP. IT'LL MAKE IT LOOK LIKE A WHOLE ARMY HAS SHOWN UP OUT OF NOWHERE.
AND DRAW EVERYONE TO THAT ONE AREA. IT'S BRILLIANT! HOW LONG WILL IT TAKE YOU?
WOOOOOOOOO
ALL FORCES TO THE WESTERN FENCE!
NOT TOO LONG.

IT'S CLEAR. LET'S GO!

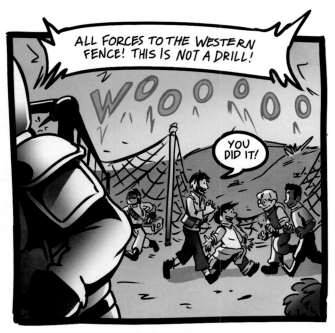

ALL FORCES TO THE WESTERN FENCE! THIS IS NOT A DRILL!

YOU DID IT!

HURRY UP!

WAIT.

WE CAN'T LEAVE YET.

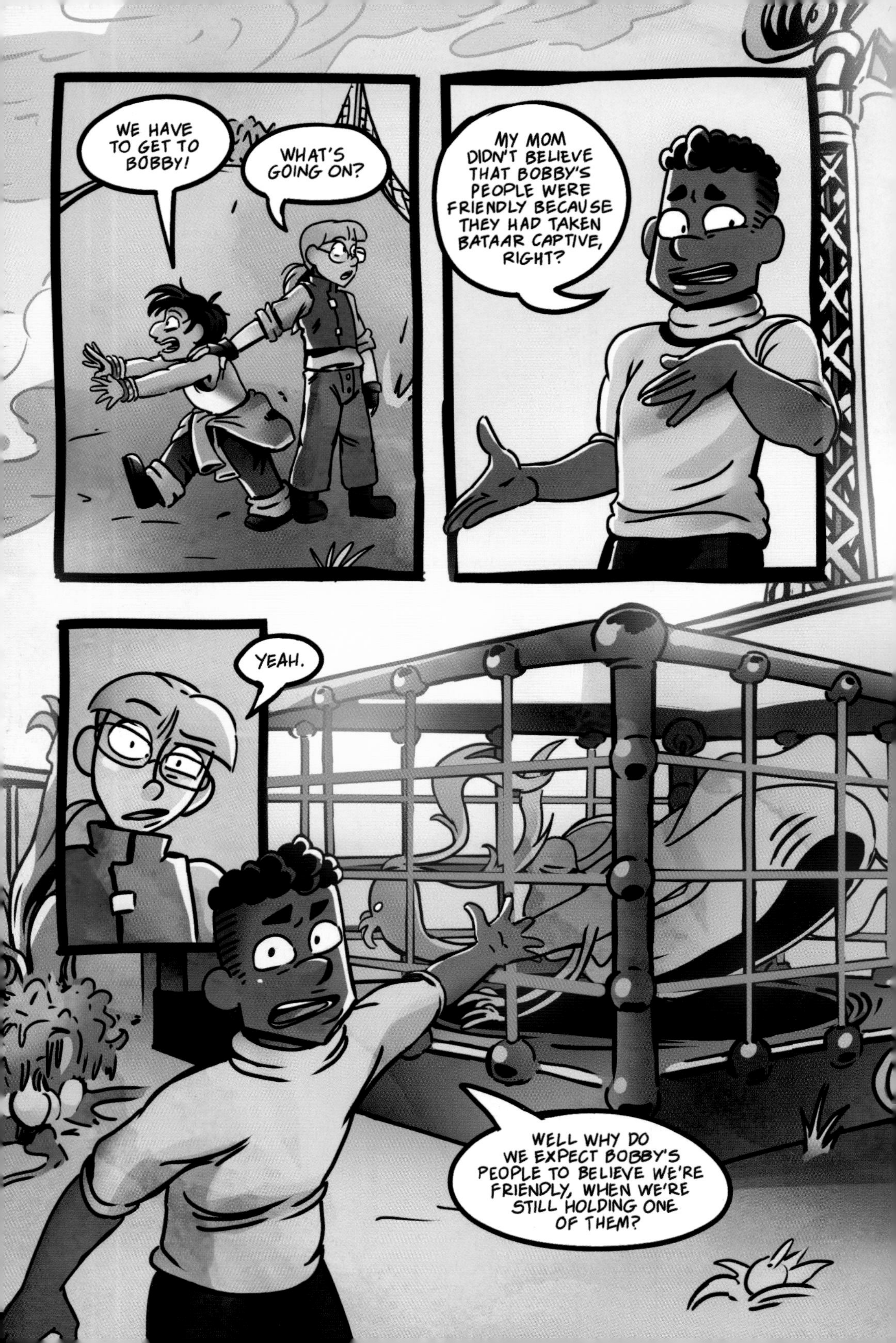
WE HAVE TO GET TO BOBBY!
WHAT'S GOING ON?
MY MOM DIDN'T BELIEVE THAT BOBBY'S PEOPLE WERE FRIENDLY BECAUSE THEY HAD TAKEN BATAAR CAPTIVE, RIGHT?
YEAH.
WELL WHY DO WE EXPECT BOBBY'S PEOPLE TO BELIEVE WE'RE FRIENDLY, WHEN WE'RE STILL HOLDING ONE OF THEM?

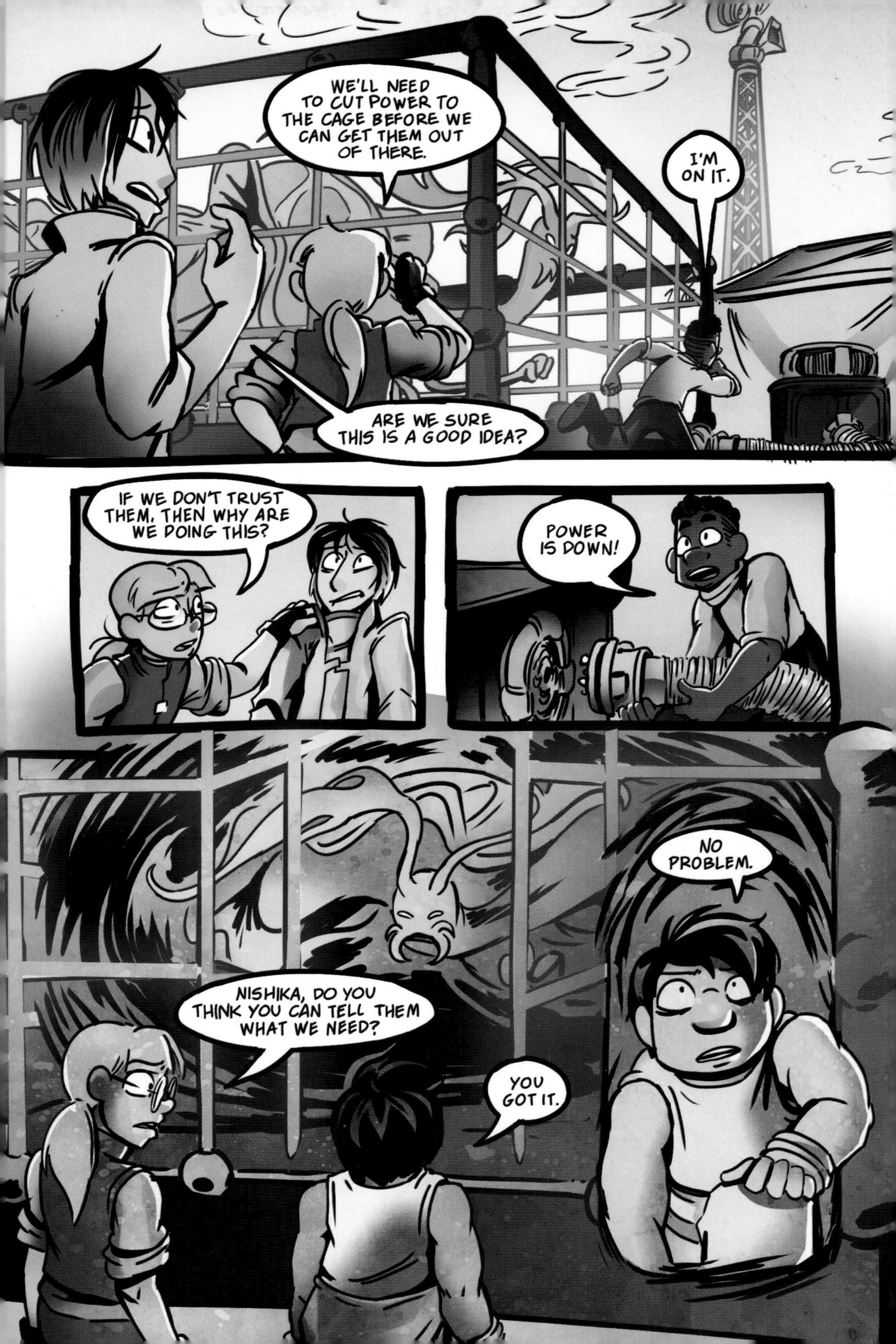
WE'LL NEED TO CUT POWER TO THE CAGE BEFORE WE CAN GET THEM OUT OF THERE.
I'M ON IT.
ARE WE SURE THIS IS A GOOD IDEA?
IF WE DON'T TRUST THEM, THEN WHY ARE WE DOING THIS?
POWER IS DOWN!
NO PROBLEM.
NISHIKA, DO YOU THINK YOU CAN TELL THEM WHAT WE NEED?
YOU GOT IT.

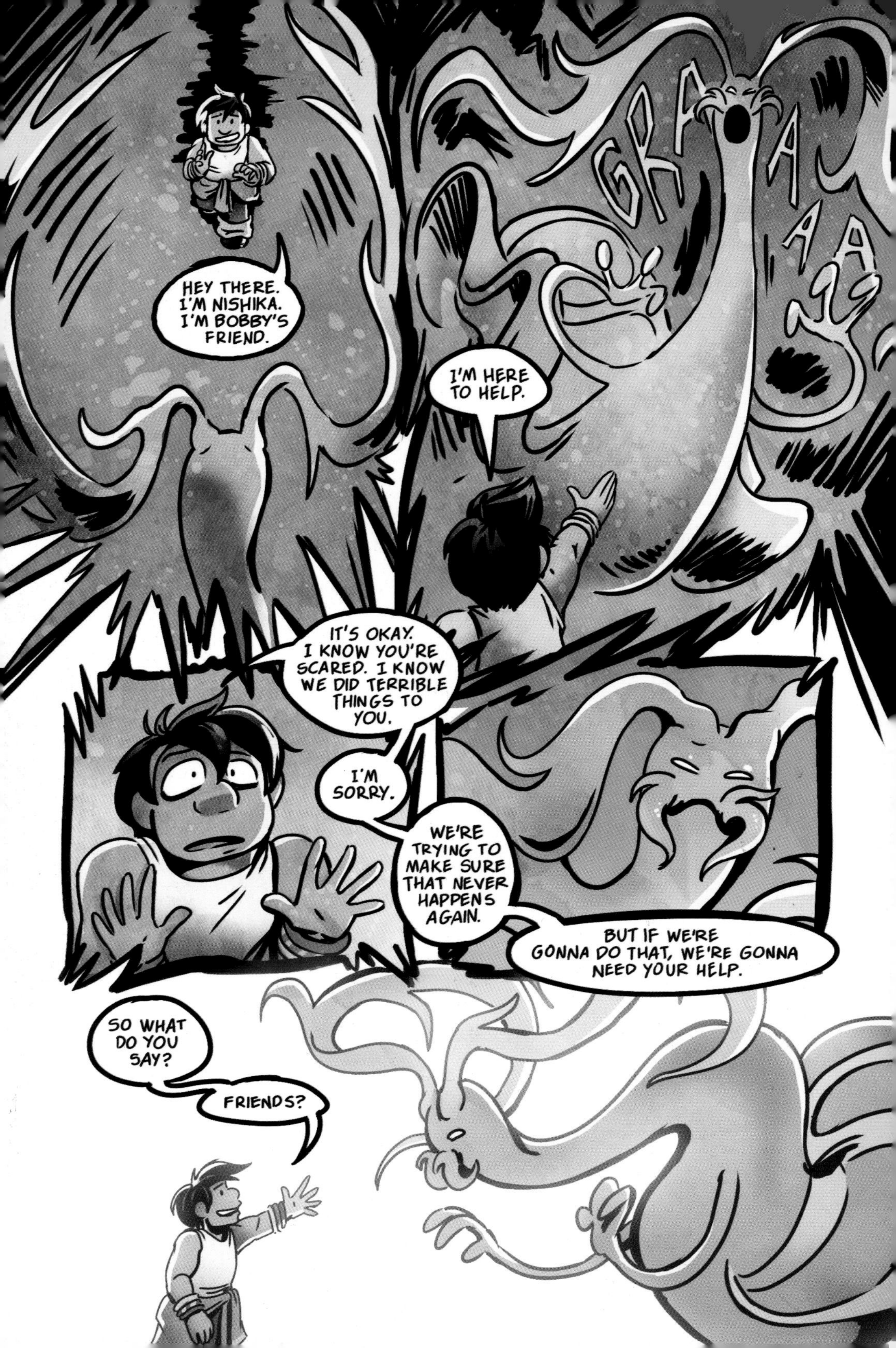
HEY THERE. I'M NISHIKA. I'M BOBBY'S FRIEND.
GRAAAAA
I'M HERE TO HELP.
IT'S OKAY. I KNOW YOU'RE SCARED. I KNOW WE DID TERRIBLE THINGS TO YOU.
I'M SORRY.
WE'RE TRYING TO MAKE SURE THAT NEVER HAPPENS AGAIN.
BUT IF WE'RE GONNA DO THAT, WE'RE GONNA NEED YOUR HELP.
SO WHAT DO YOU SAY?
FRIENDS?

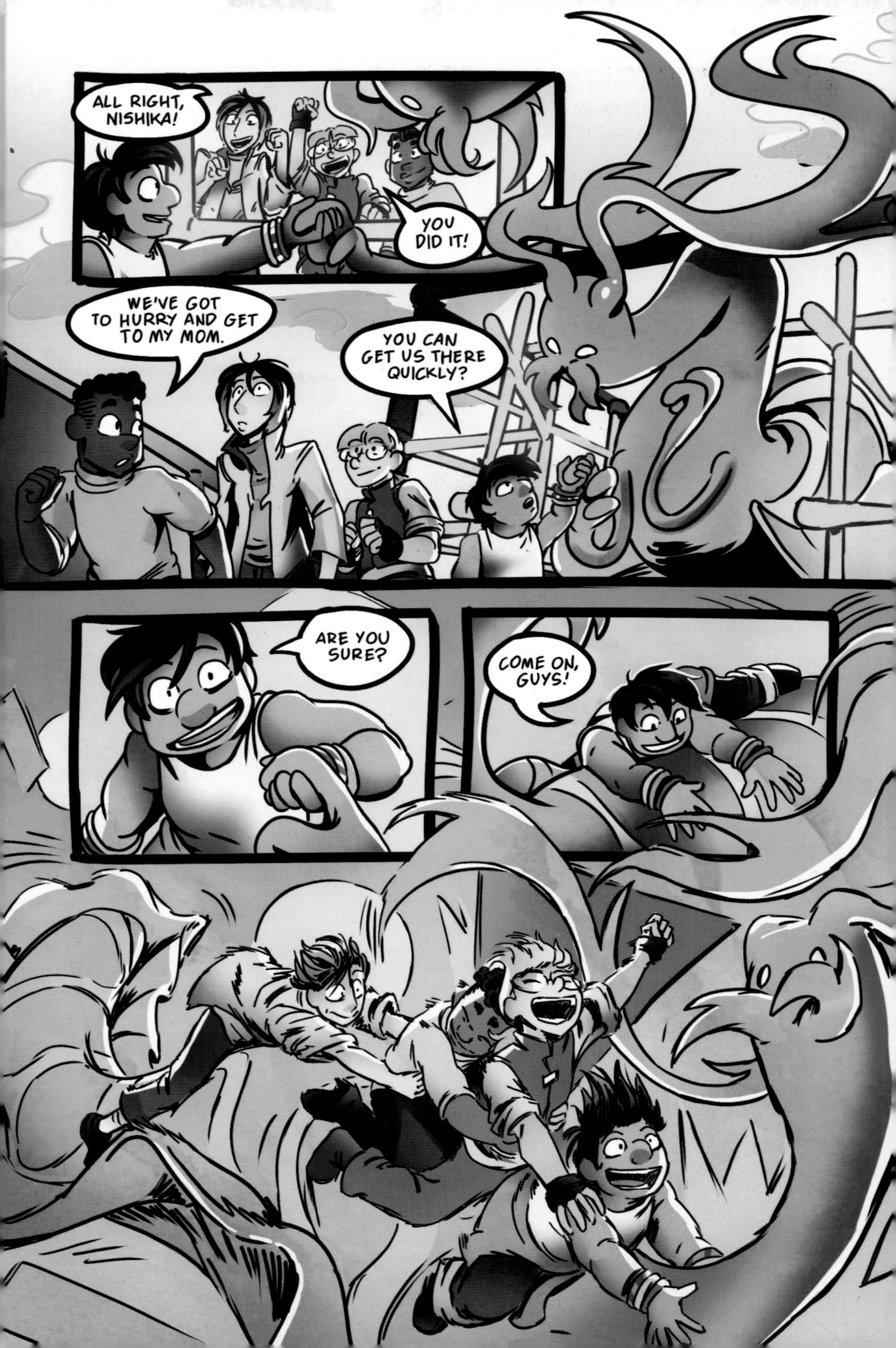
ALL RIGHT, NISHIKA!
YOU DID IT!
WE'VE GOT TO HURRY AND GET TO MY MOM.
YOU CAN GET US THERE QUICKLY?
ARE YOU SURE?
COME ON, GUYS!

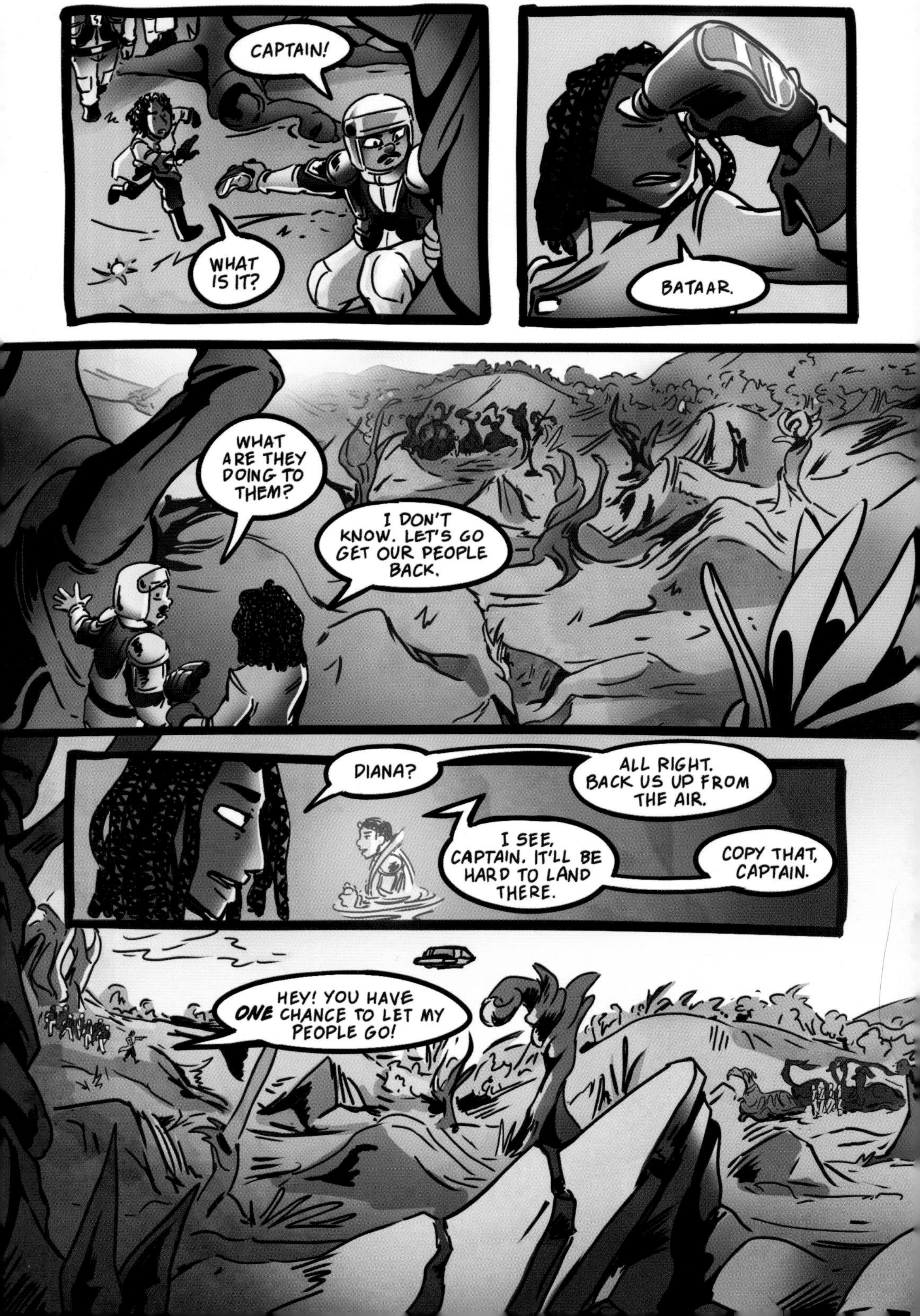
CAPTAIN!
WHAT IS IT?
BATAAR.
WHAT ARE THEY DOING TO THEM?
I DON'T KNOW. LET'S GO GET OUR PEOPLE BACK.
DIANA?
I SEE, CAPTAIN. IT'LL BE HARD TO LAND THERE.
ALL RIGHT. BACK US UP FROM THE AIR.
COPY THAT, CAPTAIN.
HEY! YOU HAVE ONE CHANCE TO LET MY PEOPLE GO!

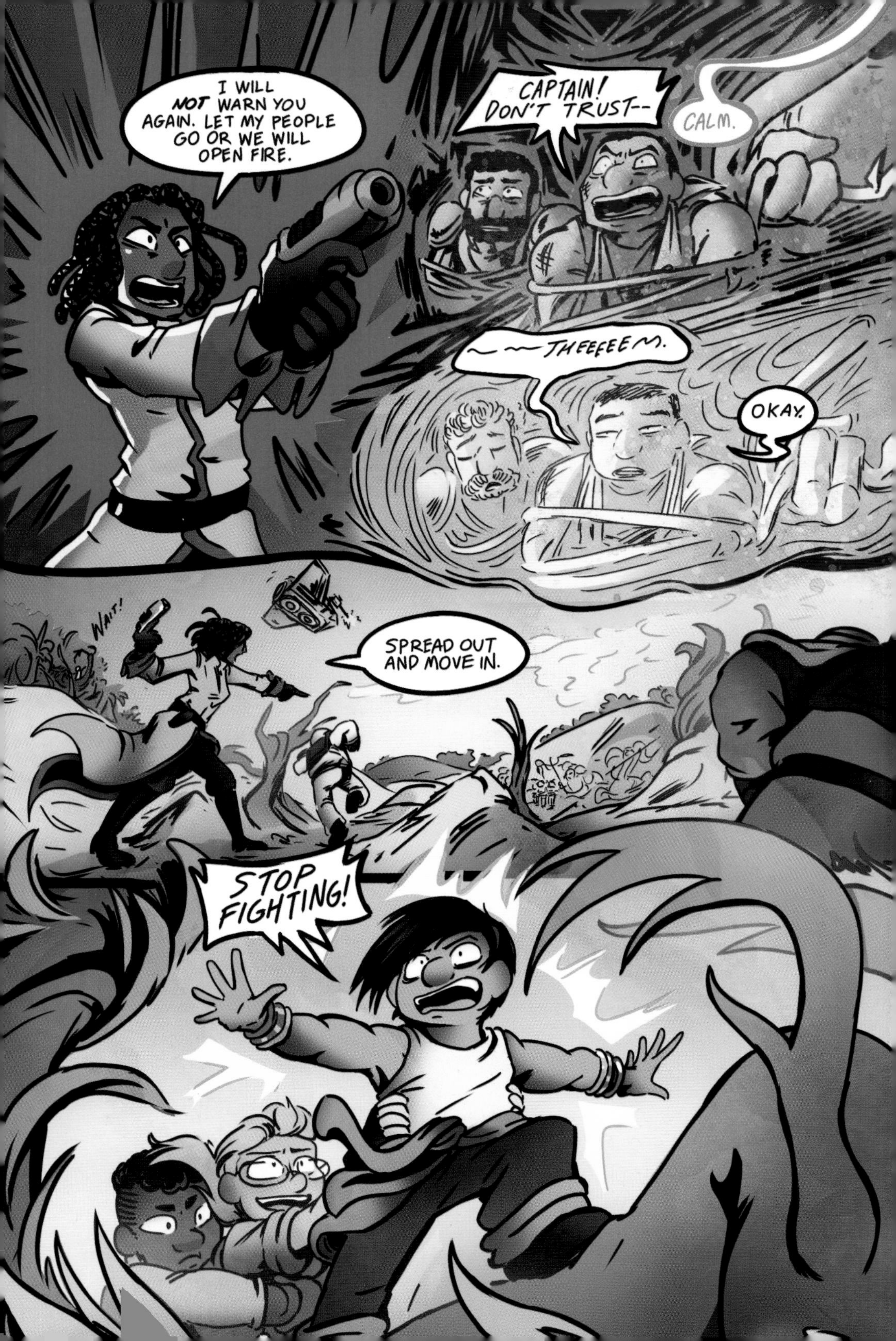
I WILL NOT WARN YOU AGAIN. LET MY PEOPLE GO OR WE WILL OPEN FIRE.
CAPTAIN! DON'T TRUST--
CALM.
~~THEEEEEM.
OKAY.
WAIT!
SPREAD OUT AND MOVE IN.
STOP FIGHTING!

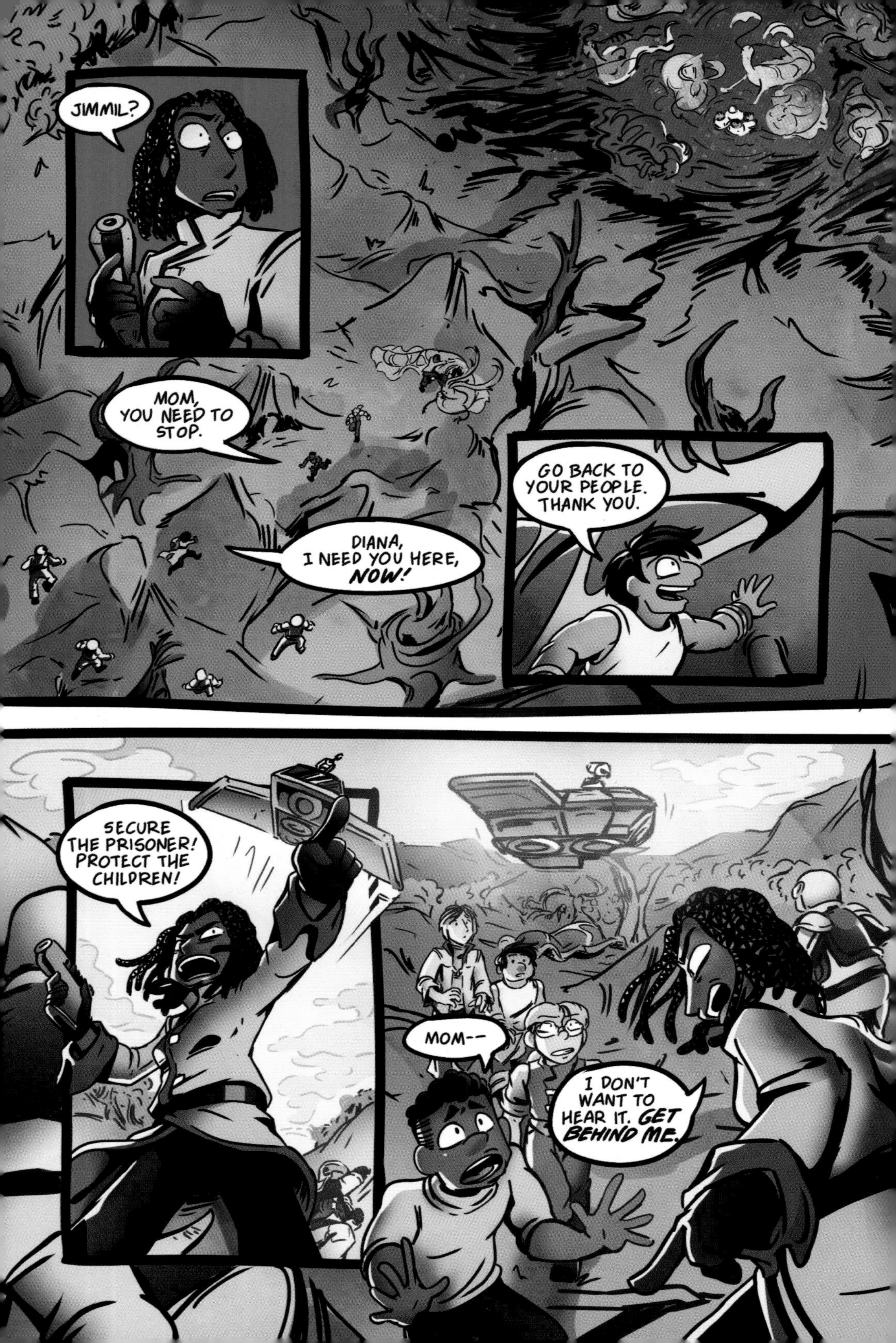
JIMMIL?
MOM, YOU NEED TO STOP.
GO BACK TO YOUR PEOPLE. THANK YOU.
DIANA, I NEED YOU HERE, NOW!
SECURE THE PRISONER! PROTECT THE CHILDREN!
MOM--
I DON'T WANT TO HEAR IT. GET BEHIND ME.

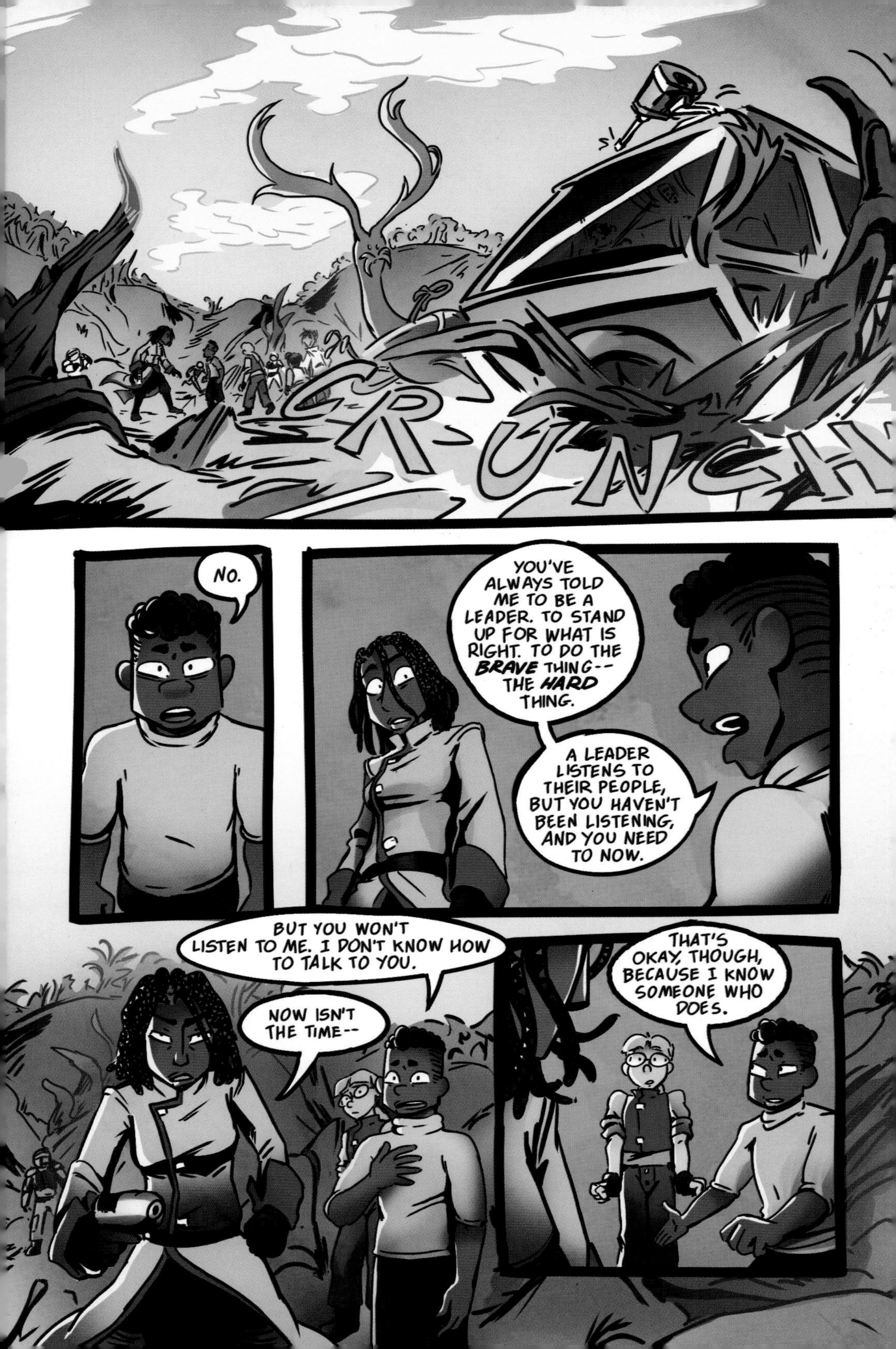
CRUNCH
NO.
YOU'VE ALWAYS TOLD ME TO BE A LEADER. TO STAND UP FOR WHAT IS RIGHT. TO DO THE BRAVE THING-- THE HARD THING.
A LEADER LISTENS TO THEIR PEOPLE, BUT YOU HAVEN'T BEEN LISTENING, AND YOU NEED TO NOW.
BUT YOU WON'T LISTEN TO ME. I DON'T KNOW HOW TO TALK TO YOU.
NOW ISN'T THE TIME--
THAT'S OKAY, THOUGH, BECAUSE I KNOW SOMEONE WHO DOES.

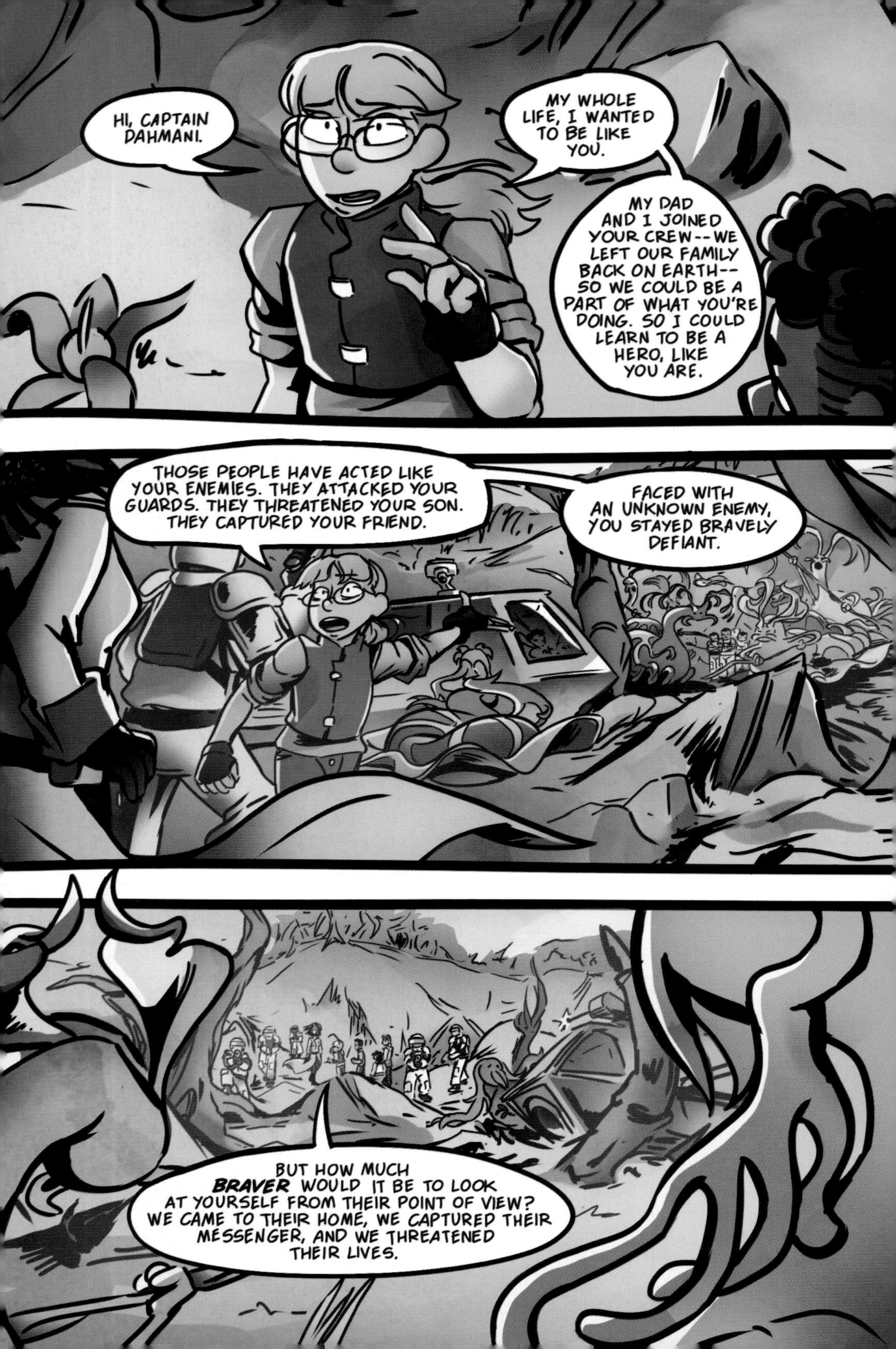
HI, CAPTAIN DAHMANI.
MY WHOLE LIFE, I WANTED TO BE LIKE YOU.
MY DAD AND I JOINED YOUR CREW--WE LEFT OUR FAMILY BACK ON EARTH--SO WE COULD BE A PART OF WHAT YOU'RE DOING. SO I COULD LEARN TO BE A HERO, LIKE YOU ARE.
THOSE PEOPLE HAVE ACTED LIKE YOUR ENEMIES. THEY ATTACKED YOUR GUARDS. THEY THREATENED YOUR SON. THEY CAPTURED YOUR FRIEND.
FACED WITH AN UNKNOWN ENEMY, YOU STAYED BRAVELY DEFIANT.
BUT HOW MUCH **BRAVER** WOULD IT BE TO LOOK AT YOURSELF FROM THEIR POINT OF VIEW? WE CAME TO THEIR HOME, WE CAPTURED THEIR MESSENGER, AND WE THREATENED THEIR LIVES.

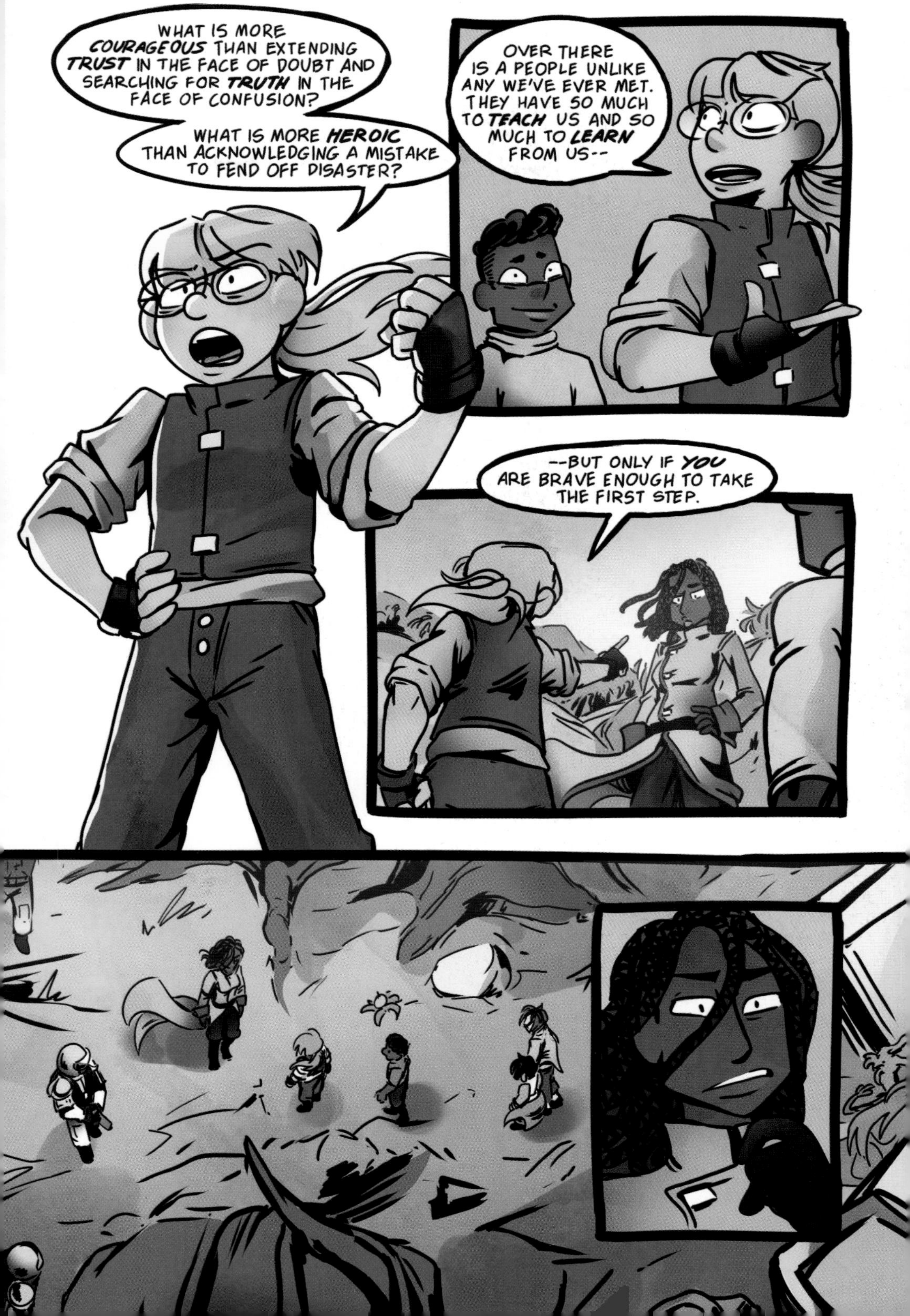
WHAT IS MORE COURAGEOUS THAN EXTENDING TRUST IN THE FACE OF DOUBT AND SEARCHING FOR TRUTH IN THE FACE OF CONFUSION?
WHAT IS MORE HEROIC THAN ACKNOWLEDGING A MISTAKE TO FEND OFF DISASTER?
OVER THERE IS A PEOPLE UNLIKE ANY WE'VE EVER MET. THEY HAVE SO MUCH TO TEACH US AND SO MUCH TO LEARN FROM US--
--BUT ONLY IF YOU ARE BRAVE ENOUGH TO TAKE THE FIRST STEP.

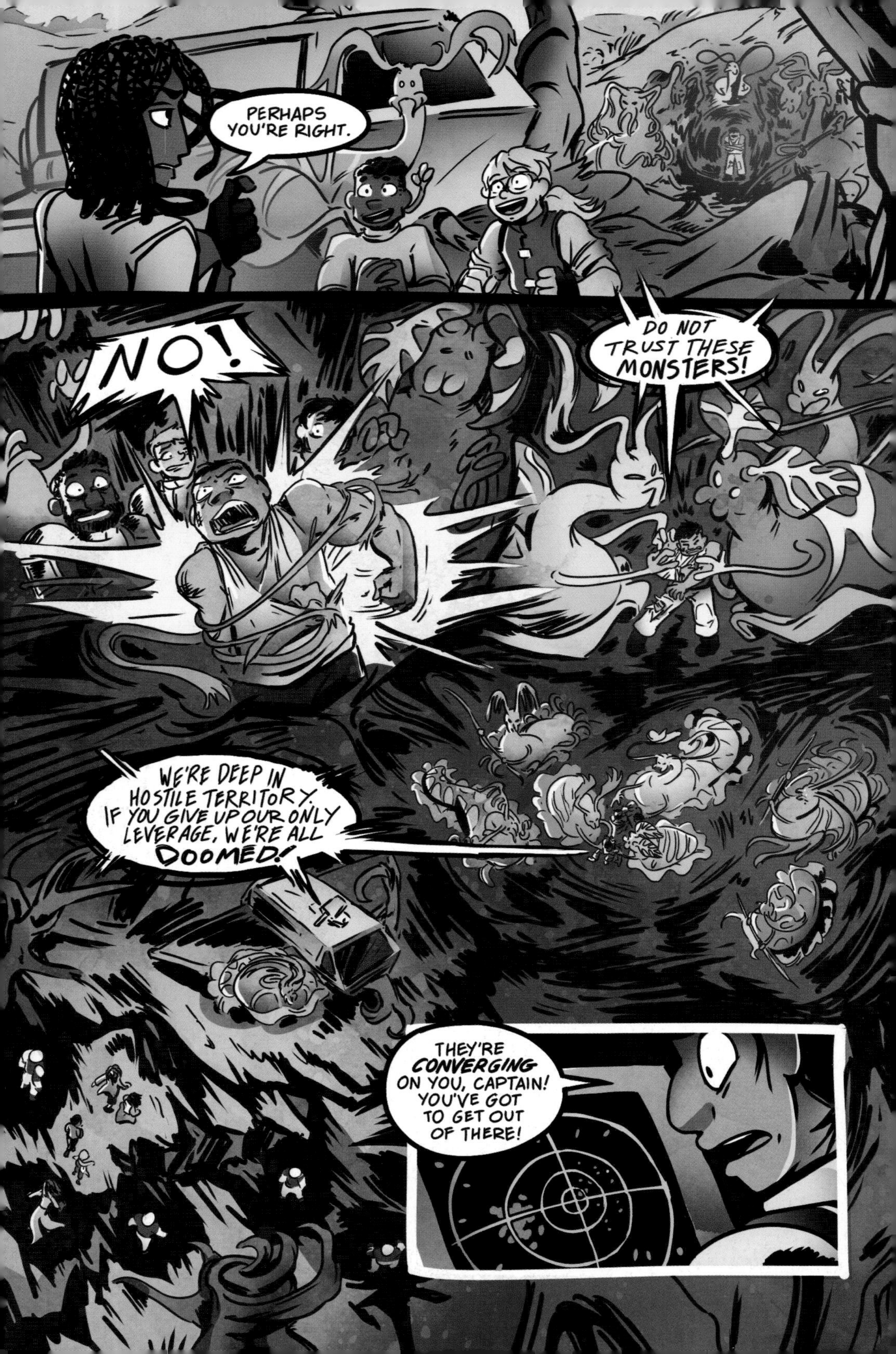
PERHAPS YOU'RE RIGHT.
NO!
DO NOT TRUST THESE MONSTERS!
WE'RE DEEP IN HOSTILE TERRITORY. IF YOU GIVE UP OUR ONLY LEVERAGE, WE'RE ALL DOOMED!
THEY'RE CONVERGING ON YOU, CAPTAIN! YOU'VE GOT TO GET OUT OF THERE!

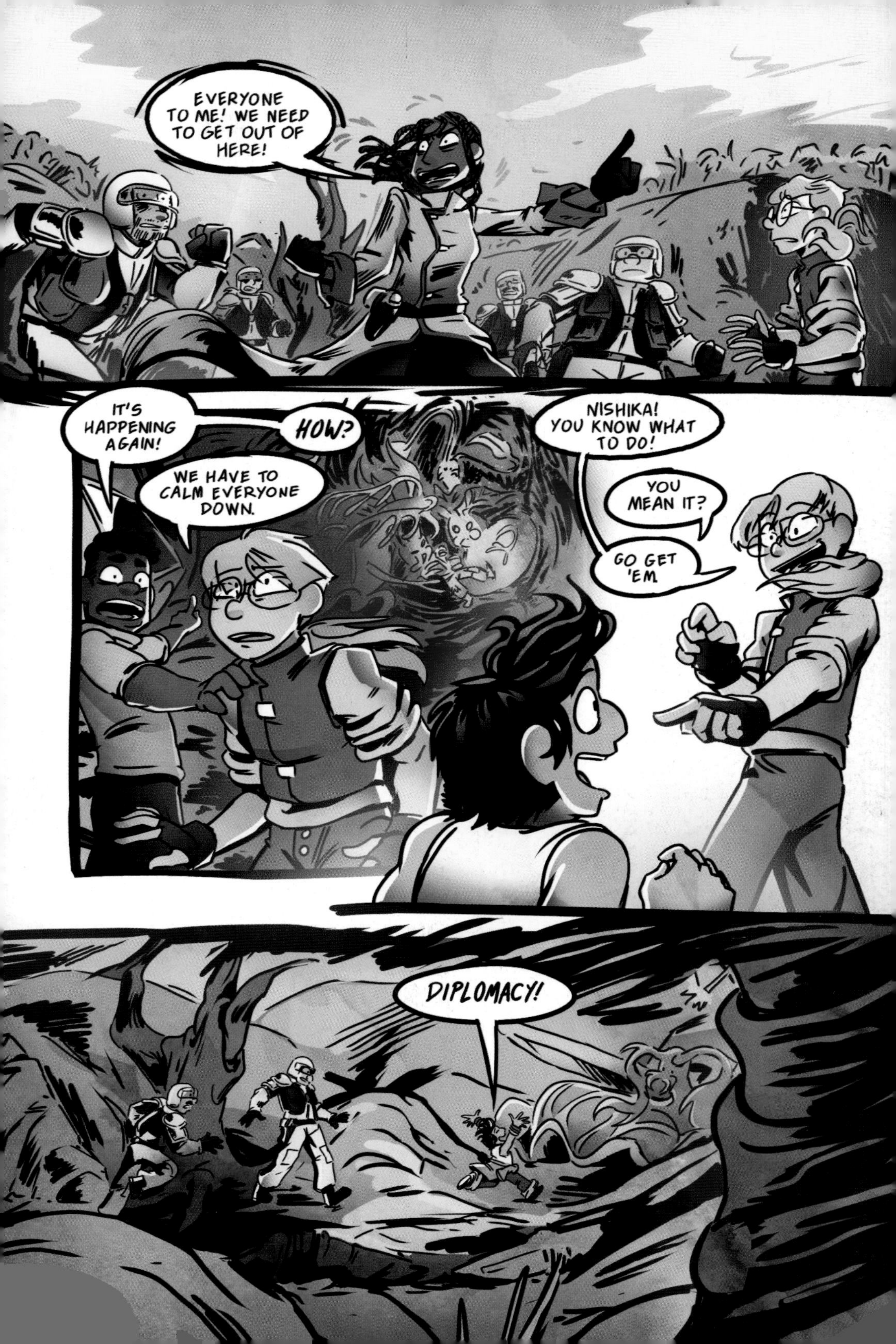
EVERYONE TO ME! WE NEED TO GET OUT OF HERE!
IT'S HAPPENING AGAIN!
HOW?
WE HAVE TO CALM EVERYONE DOWN.
NISHIKA! YOU KNOW WHAT TO DO!
YOU MEAN IT?
GO GET 'EM
DIPLOMACY!

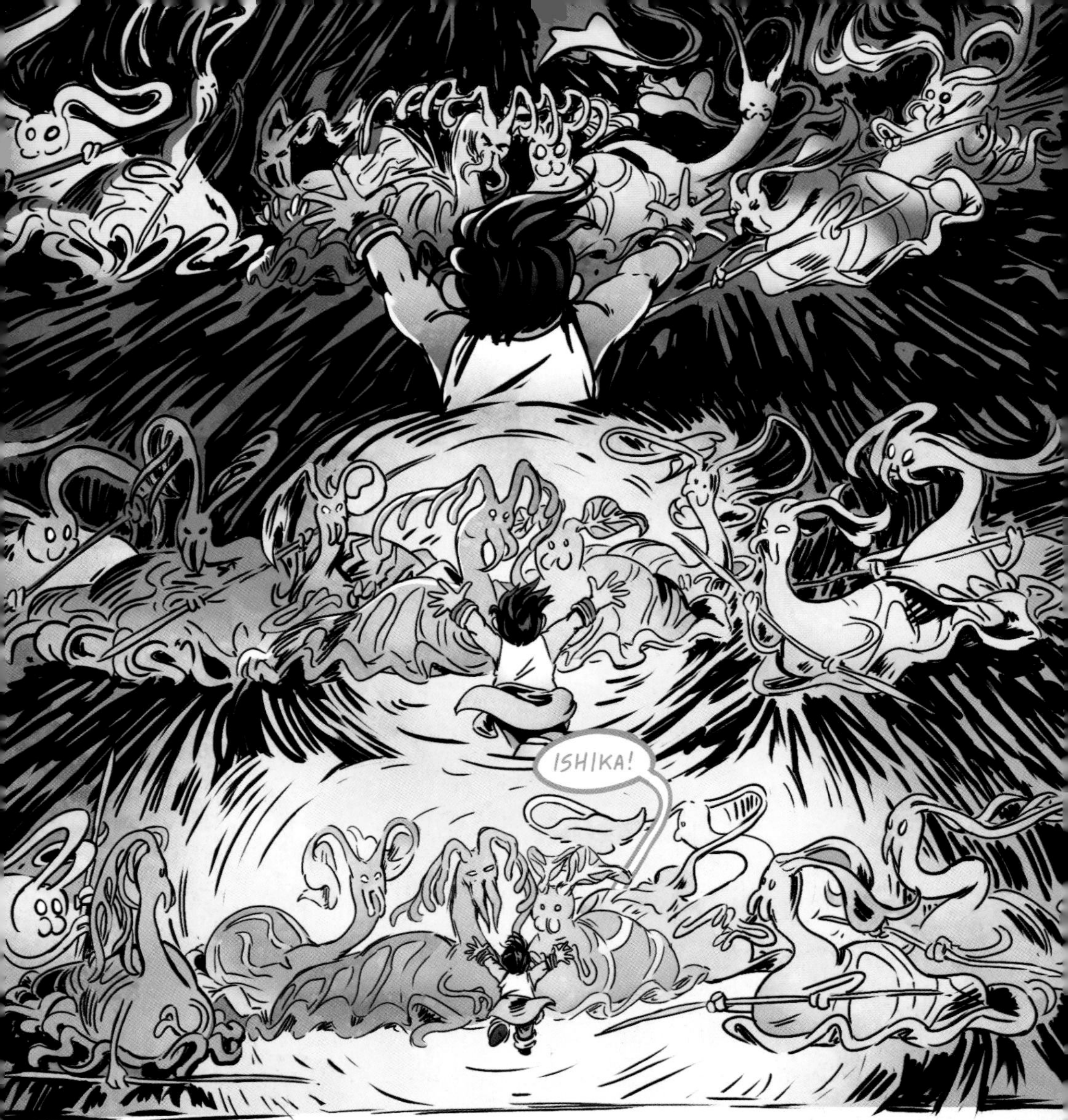
ISHIKA!

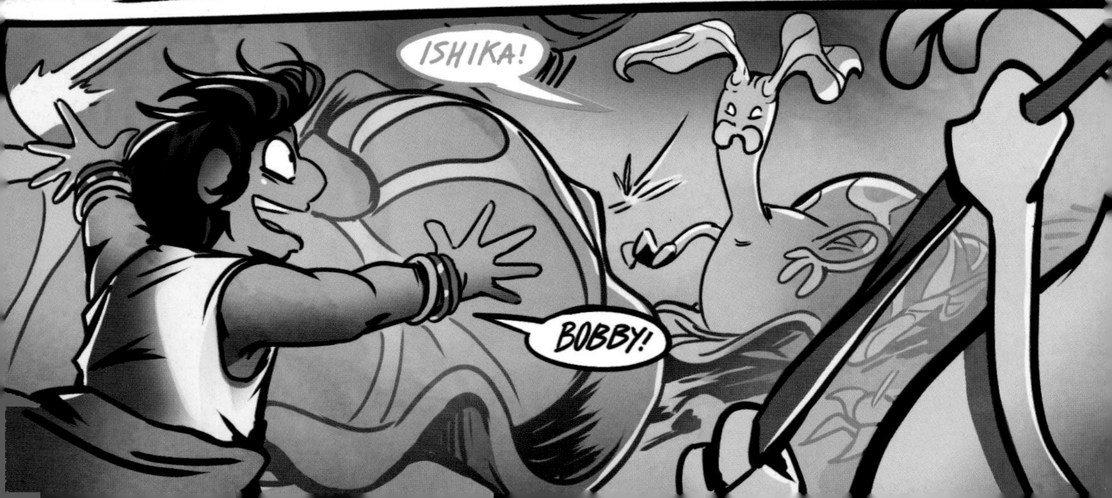
ISHIKA!
BOBBY!

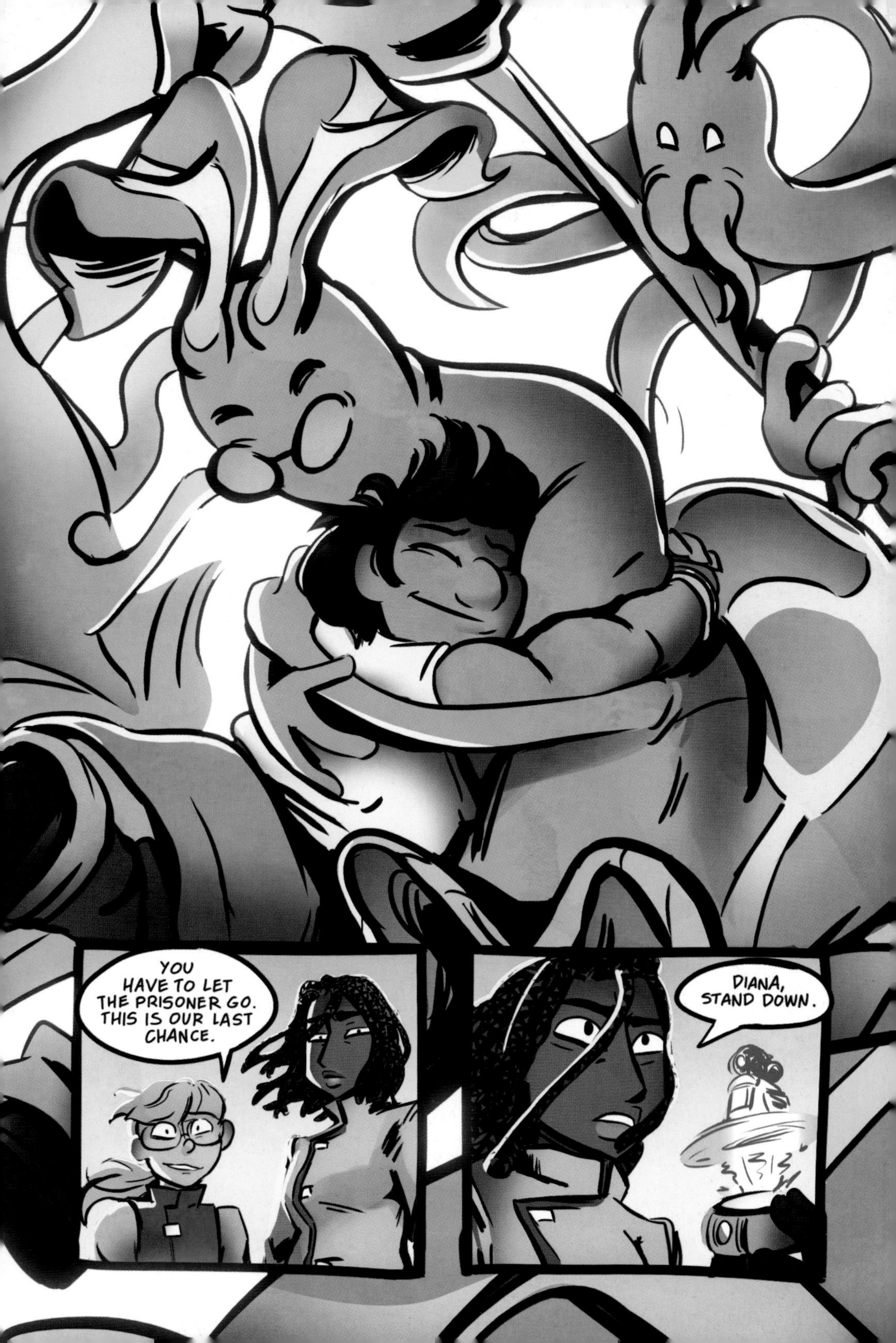
YOU HAVE TO LET THE PRISONER GO. THIS IS OUR LAST CHANCE.
DIANA, STAND DOWN.

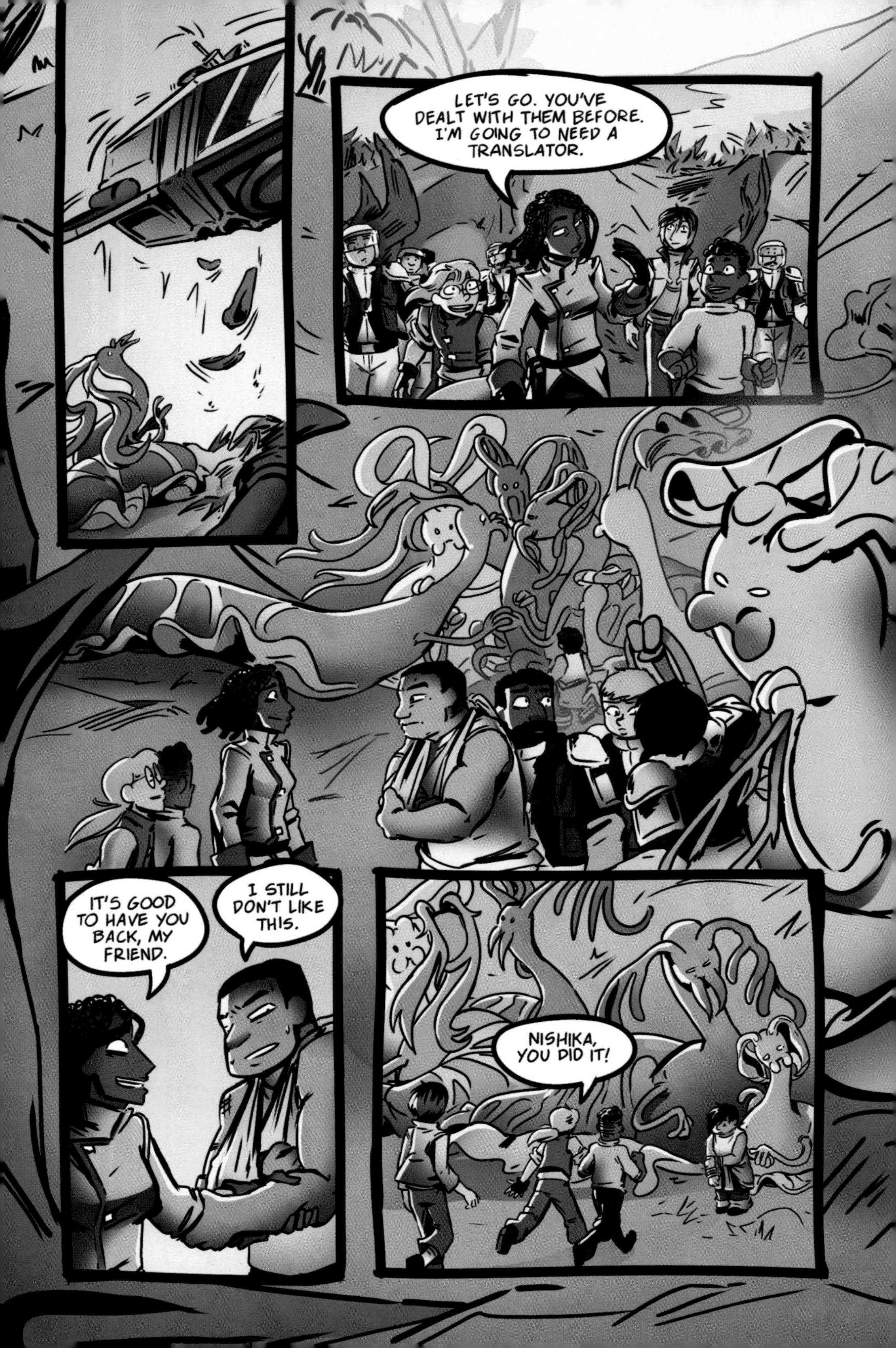
LET'S GO. YOU'VE DEALT WITH THEM BEFORE. I'M GOING TO NEED A TRANSLATOR.
IT'S GOOD TO HAVE YOU BACK, MY FRIEND.
I STILL DON'T LIKE THIS.
NISHIKA, YOU DID IT!

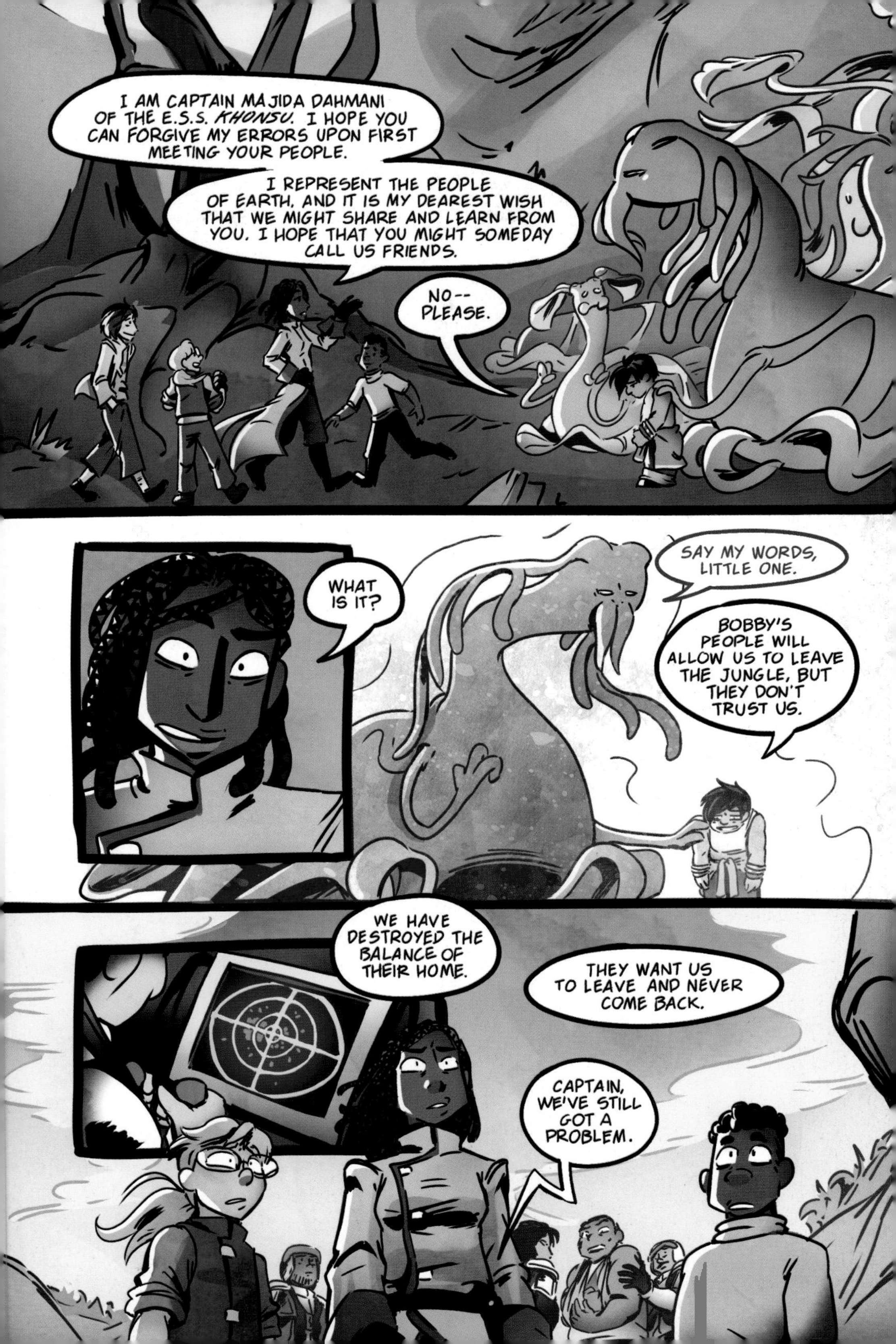
I AM CAPTAIN MAJIDA DAHMANI OF THE E.S.S. *KHONSU*. I HOPE YOU CAN FORGIVE MY ERRORS UPON FIRST MEETING YOUR PEOPLE.
I REPRESENT THE PEOPLE OF EARTH, AND IT IS MY DEAREST WISH THAT WE MIGHT SHARE AND LEARN FROM YOU. I HOPE THAT YOU MIGHT SOMEDAY CALL US FRIENDS.
NO-- PLEASE.
WHAT IS IT?
SAY MY WORDS, LITTLE ONE.
BOBBY'S PEOPLE WILL ALLOW US TO LEAVE THE JUNGLE, BUT THEY DON'T TRUST US.
WE HAVE DESTROYED THE BALANCE OF THEIR HOME.
THEY WANT US TO LEAVE AND NEVER COME BACK.
CAPTAIN, WE'VE STILL GOT A PROBLEM.

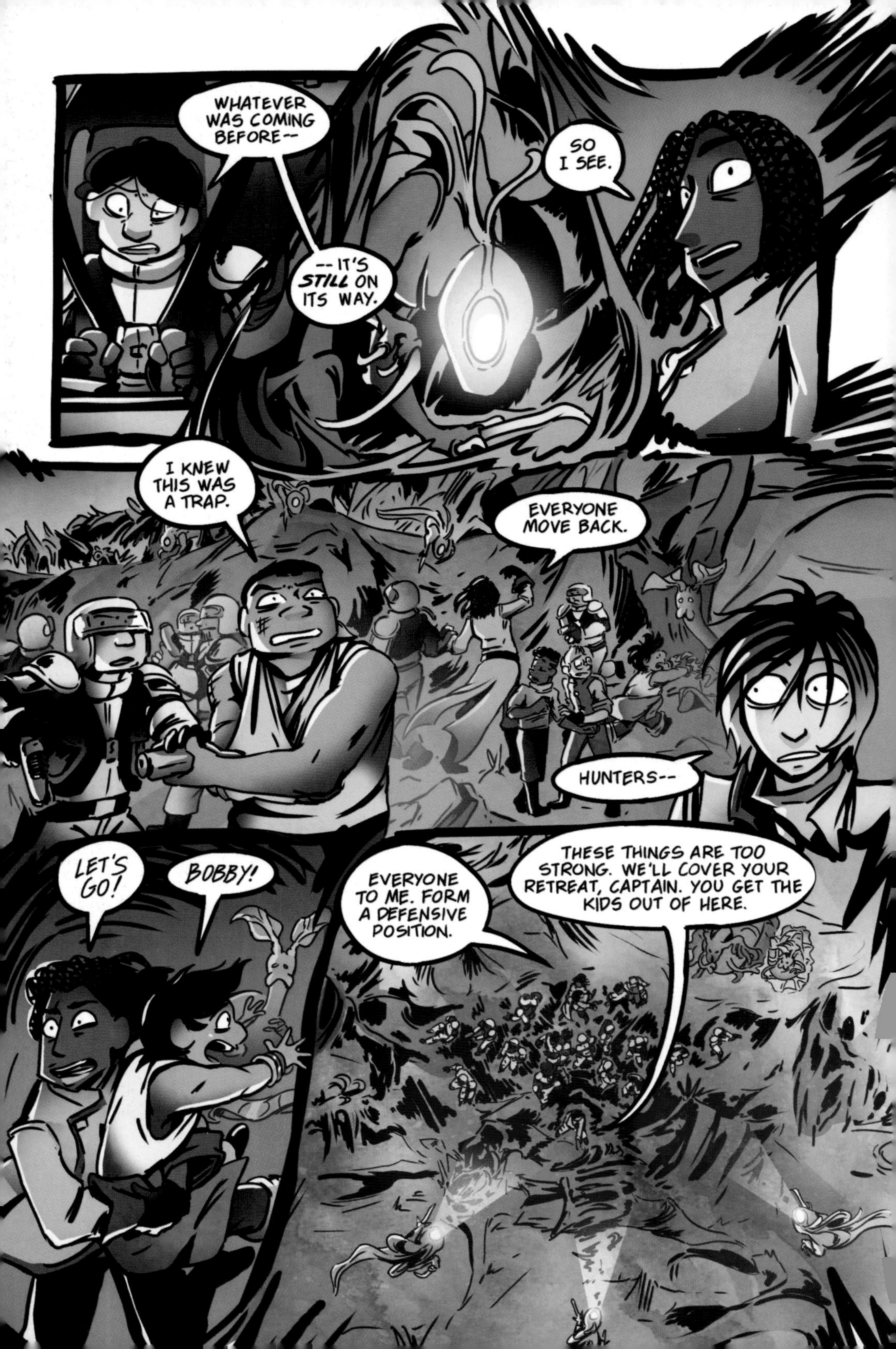
WHATEVER WAS COMING BEFORE--
--IT'S STILL ON ITS WAY.
SO I SEE.
I KNEW THIS WAS A TRAP.
EVERYONE MOVE BACK.
HUNTERS--
LET'S GO!
BOBBY!
EVERYONE TO ME. FORM A DEFENSIVE POSITION.
THESE THINGS ARE TOO STRONG. WE'LL COVER YOUR RETREAT, CAPTAIN. YOU GET THE KIDS OUT OF HERE.

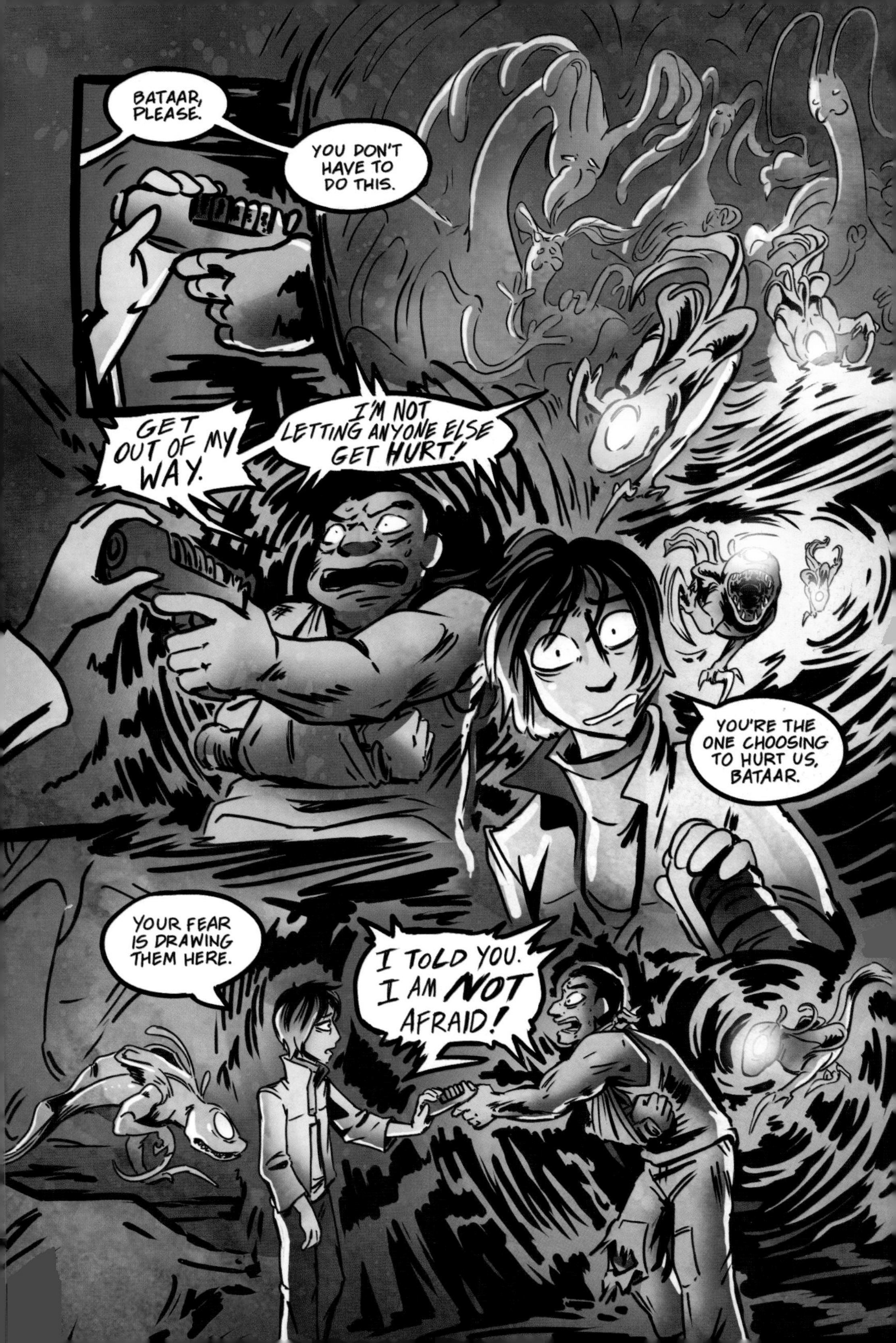
BATAAR, PLEASE.
YOU DON'T HAVE TO DO THIS.
GET OUT OF MY WAY.
I'M NOT LETTING ANYONE ELSE GET HURT!
YOU'RE THE ONE CHOOSING TO HURT US, BATAAR.
YOUR FEAR IS DRAWING THEM HERE.
I TOLD YOU. I AM NOT AFRAID!

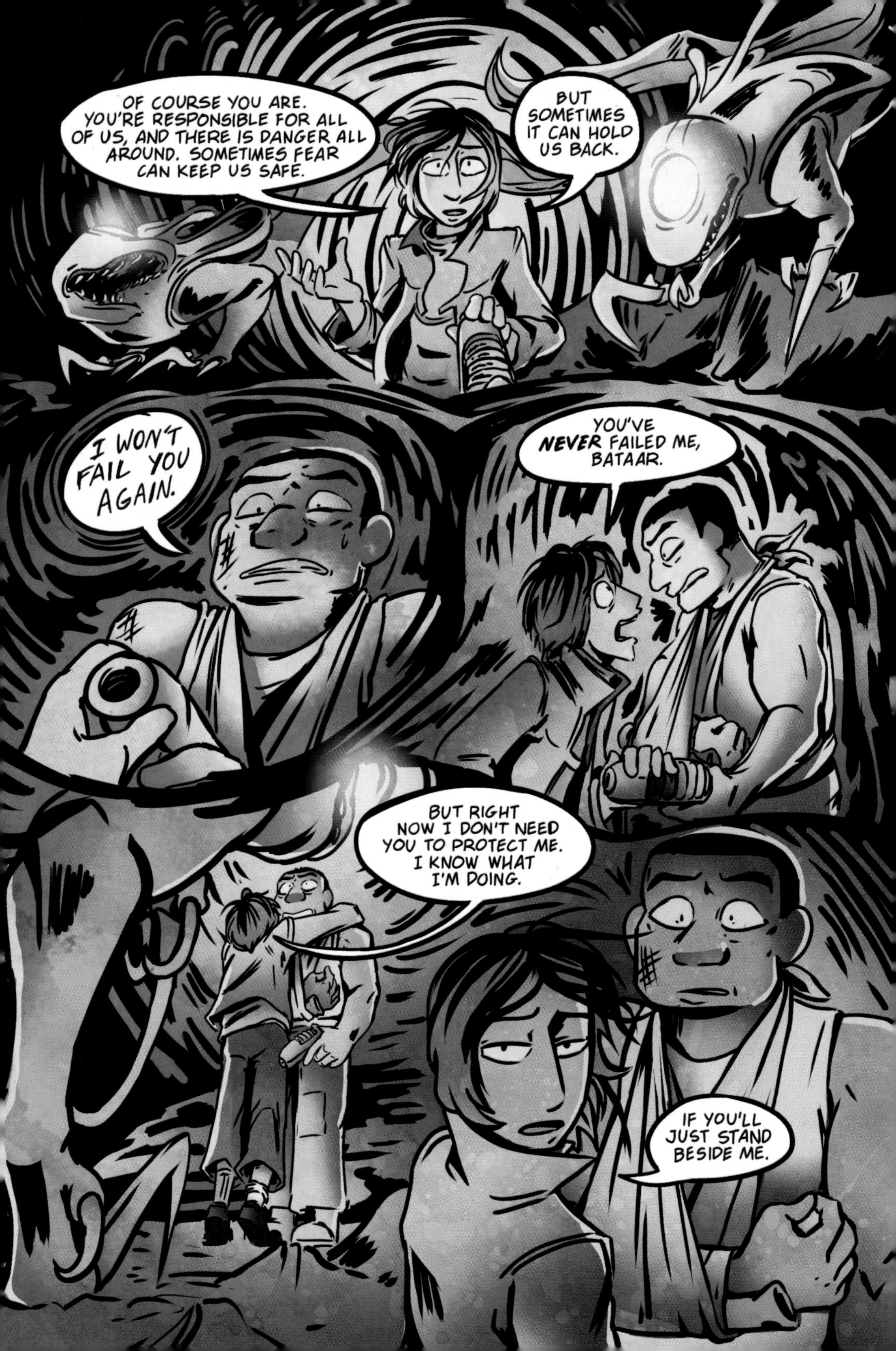
OF COURSE YOU ARE. YOU'RE RESPONSIBLE FOR ALL OF US, AND THERE IS DANGER ALL AROUND. SOMETIMES FEAR CAN KEEP US SAFE.
BUT SOMETIMES IT CAN HOLD US BACK.
I WON'T FAIL YOU AGAIN.
YOU'VE **NEVER** FAILED ME, BATAAR.
BUT RIGHT NOW I DON'T NEED YOU TO PROTECT ME. I KNOW WHAT I'M DOING.
IF YOU'LL JUST STAND BESIDE ME.

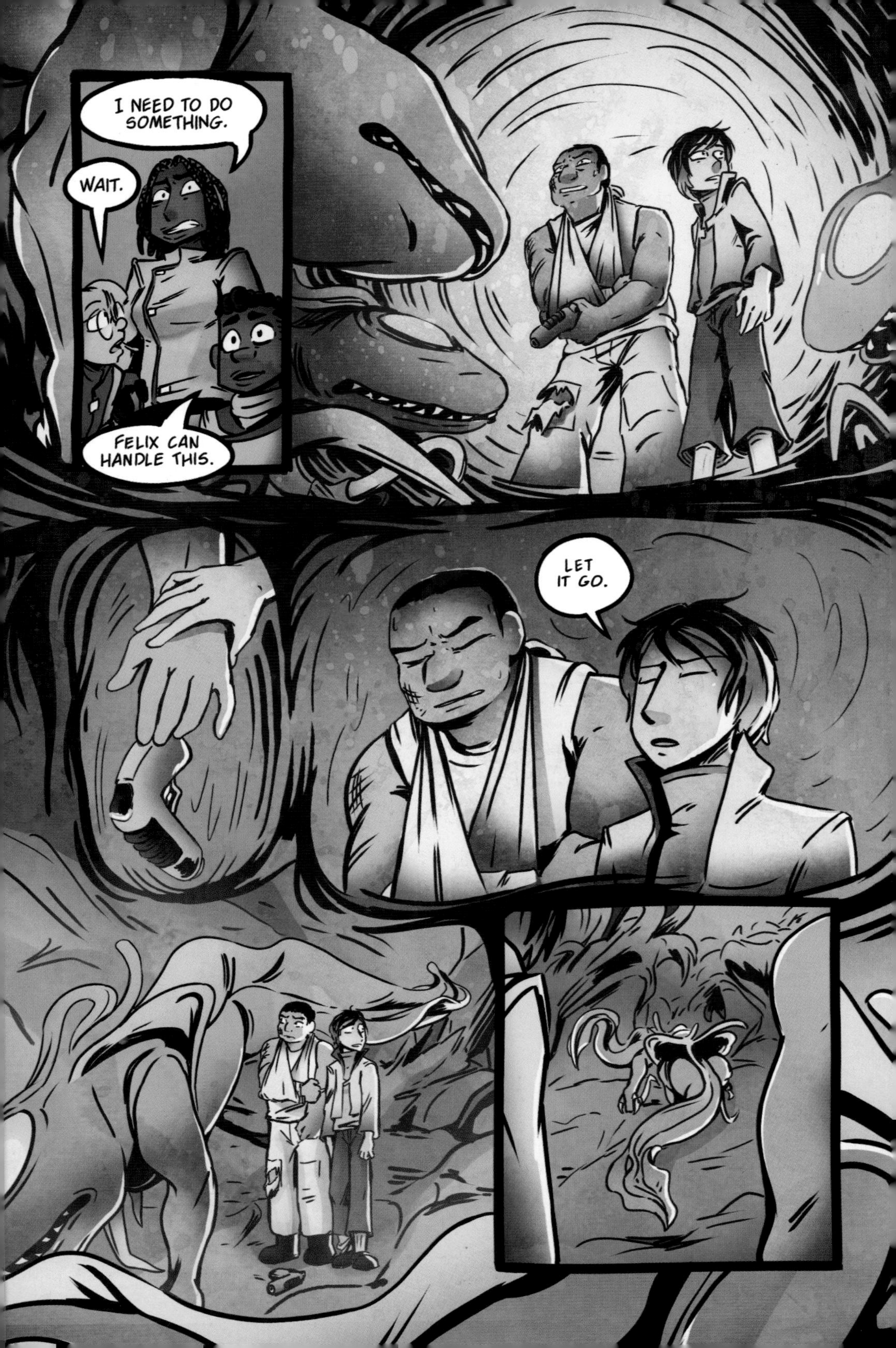
I NEED TO DO SOMETHING.
WAIT.
FELIX CAN HANDLE THIS.
LET IT GO.

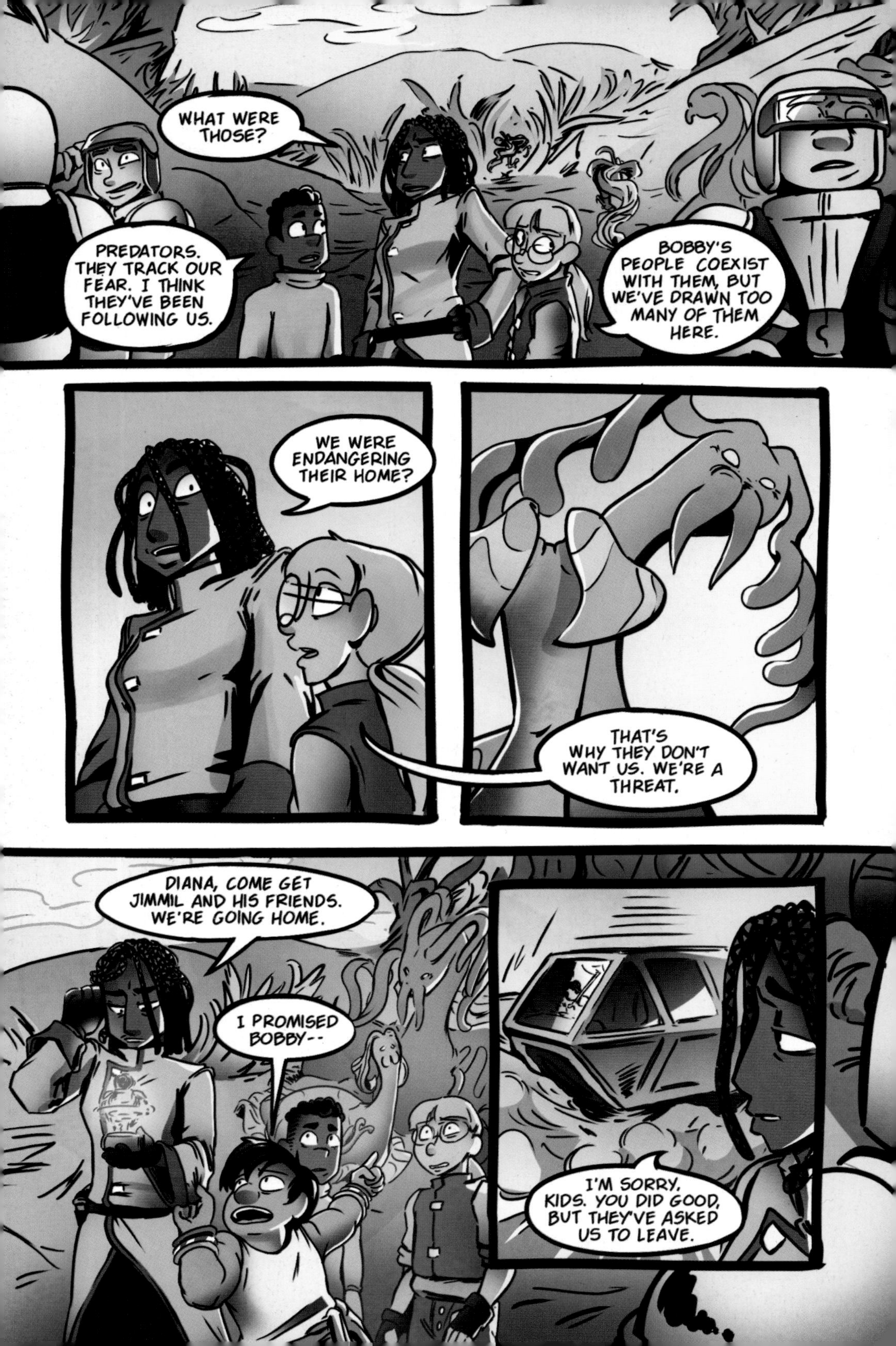
WHAT WERE THOSE?
PREDATORS. THEY TRACK OUR FEAR. I THINK THEY'VE BEEN FOLLOWING US.
BOBBY'S PEOPLE COEXIST WITH THEM, BUT WE'VE DRAWN TOO MANY OF THEM HERE.
WE WERE ENDANGERING THEIR HOME?
THAT'S WHY THEY DON'T WANT US. WE'RE A THREAT.
DIANA, COME GET JIMMIL AND HIS FRIENDS. WE'RE GOING HOME.
I PROMISED BOBBY--
I'M SORRY, KIDS. YOU DID GOOD, BUT THEY'VE ASKED US TO LEAVE.

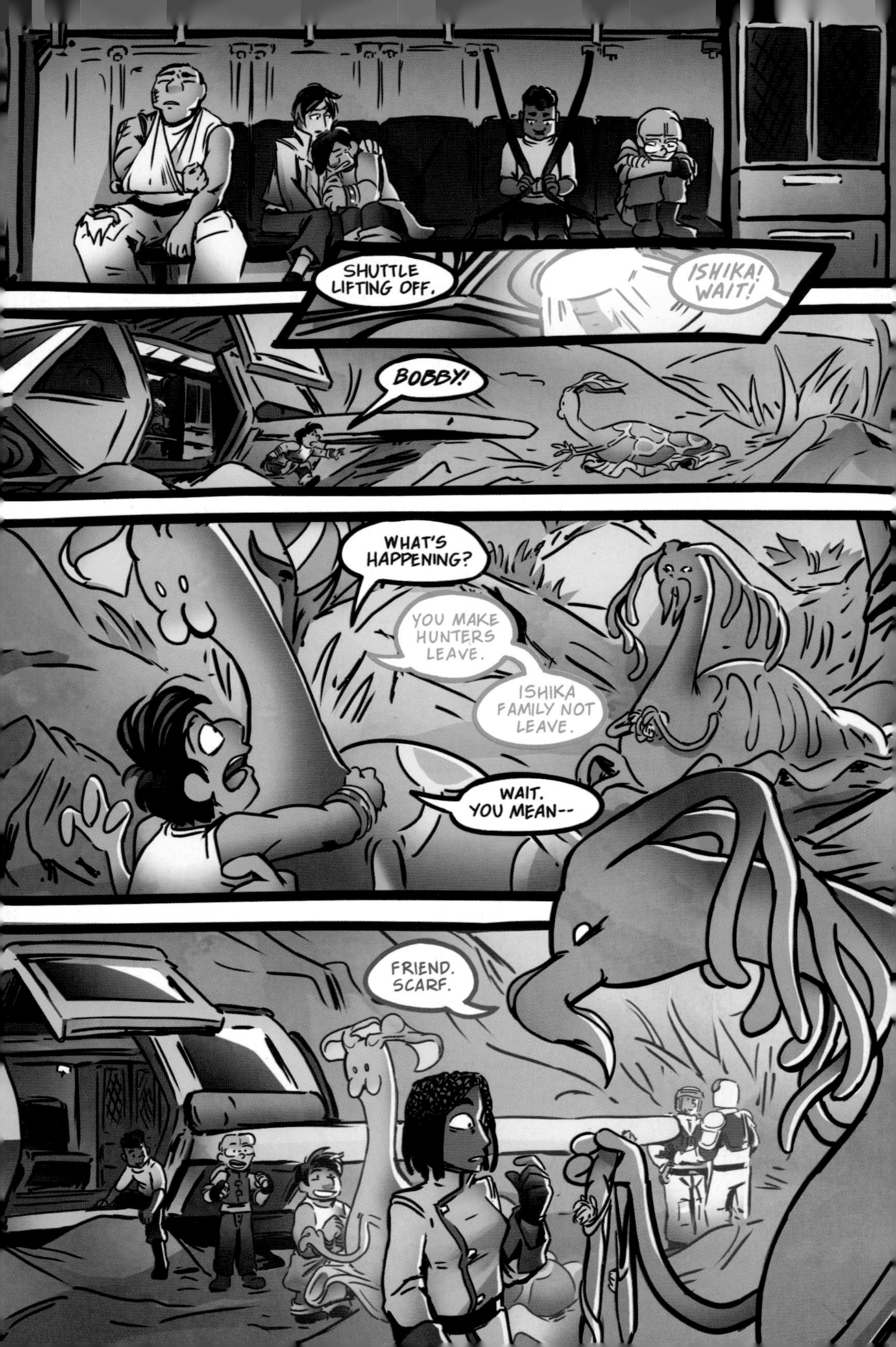
SHUTTLE LIFTING OFF.
ISHIKA! WAIT!
BOBBY!
WHAT'S HAPPENING?
YOU MAKE HUNTERS LEAVE.
ISHIKA FAMILY NOT LEAVE.
WAIT. YOU MEAN--
FRIEND. SCARF.

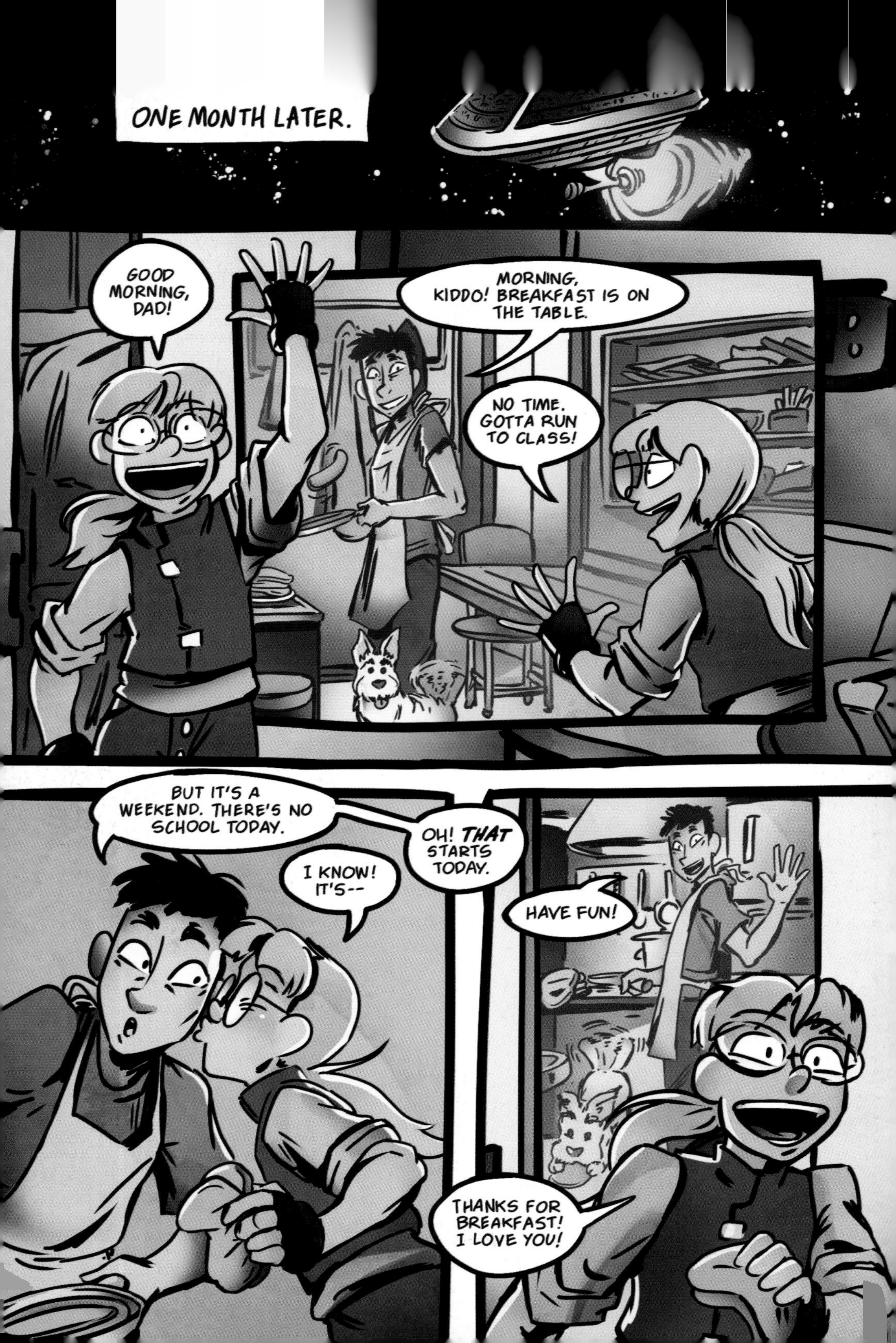
ONE MONTH LATER.
GOOD MORNING, DAD!
MORNING, KIDDO! BREAKFAST IS ON THE TABLE.
NO TIME. GOTTA RUN TO CLASS!
BUT IT'S A WEEKEND. THERE'S NO SCHOOL TODAY.
I KNOW! IT'S--
OH! *THAT* STARTS TODAY.
HAVE FUN!
THANKS FOR BREAKFAST! I LOVE YOU!

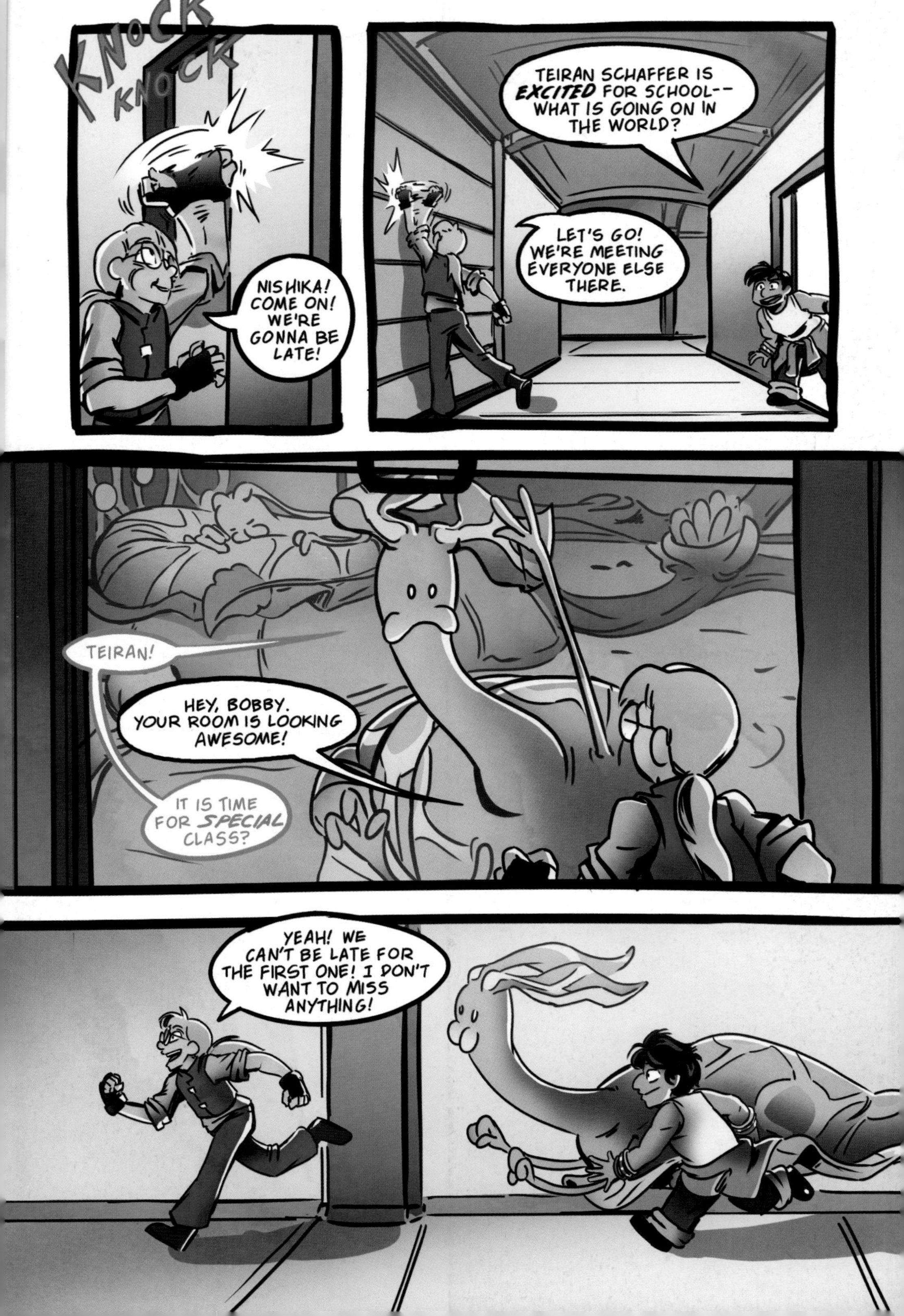
KNOCK KNOCK
NISHIKA! COME ON! WE'RE GONNA BE LATE!
TEIRAN SCHAFFER IS EXCITED FOR SCHOOL-- WHAT IS GOING ON IN THE WORLD?
LET'S GO! WE'RE MEETING EVERYONE ELSE THERE.
TEIRAN!
HEY, BOBBY. YOUR ROOM IS LOOKING AWESOME!
IT IS TIME FOR SPECIAL CLASS?
YEAH! WE CAN'T BE LATE FOR THE FIRST ONE! I DON'T WANT TO MISS ANYTHING!

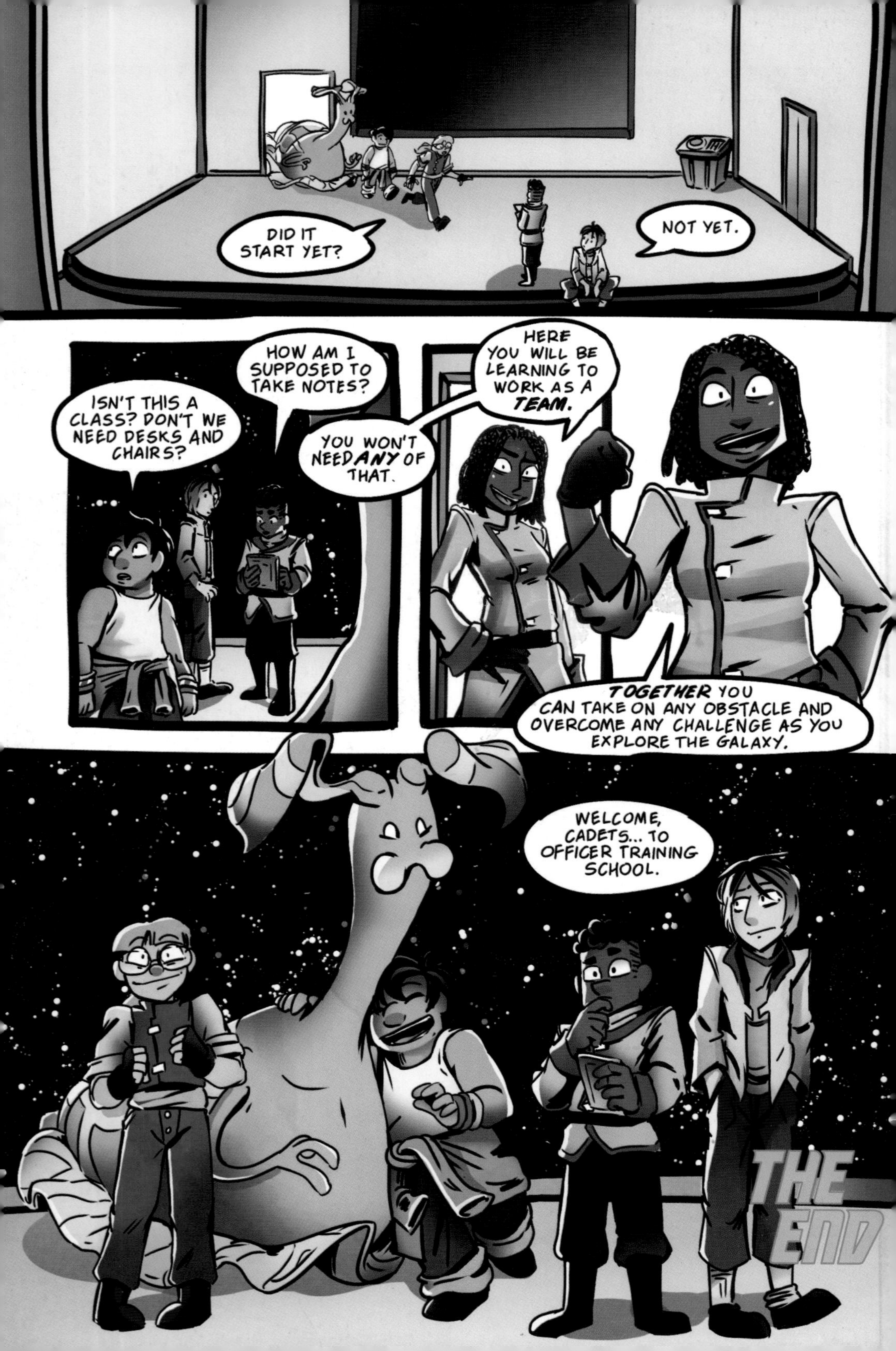
DID IT START YET?
NOT YET.
ISN'T THIS A CLASS? DON'T WE NEED DESKS AND CHAIRS?
HOW AM I SUPPOSED TO TAKE NOTES?
YOU WON'T NEED ANY OF THAT.
HERE YOU WILL BE LEARNING TO WORK AS A TEAM.
TOGETHER YOU CAN TAKE ON ANY OBSTACLE AND OVERCOME ANY CHALLENGE AS YOU EXPLORE THE GALAXY.
WELCOME, CADETS... TO OFFICER TRAINING SCHOOL.
THE END